OF ELVEN BLOOD

Leslie Fish

Published by

The Writers of the Apocalypse

Marion, Illinois

www.apocalypsewriters.com

Of Elven Blood
Fish, Leslie

Second edition
copyright 2016

Published by The Writers of the Apocalypse
117 N Carbon Street, PMB 208
Marion, IL 62959
www.apocalypsewriters.com

Ebook ISBN: 978-1-944322-23-6
ISBN Print: 978-1-944322-18-2

PREFACE

What if Elves truly did walk among us, but had no Elf-Land to retreat to? How would they survive in a world ruled by mortals? And how to tell a new story using old—in fact ancient—material? That, to quote Shakespeare, is the question. Haven't stories about elves been done to death?

No, not by a long shot.

What I did was to go back to the well-mined but still unexhausted source of ancient Greek, Roman, Norse and Celtic mythology, and add a new twist to it. Stories of humans who mate with The Gods and produce bloodlines with a spark of divine powers occur in both Greek and Roman myths; in fact, the great Roman epic *The Aenead* relies for much of its plot on the idea that the hero's father, a prince of Troy, begot Aeneas on no less than the goddess Venus. The myth that elves breed slowly among themselves, but exchange their children for mortal babies as 'changelings', appears often in Celtic folktales. Tales of people—or other creatures—who die and are then raised up immortal occur often in Greek myths; in fact, that's the usual explanation for the names of the constellations. The Celtic myth of the eternal battle between the Seelie and Unseelie courts is mirrored by the Norse legends of the Schwartzelven and the Lichtelven. And of course the idea of killing an enemy and taking his 'mana', by devouring or keeping some part of him, is found in folklore all over the world.

So, how to bring all these elements into a modern-day setting? What I did was pull them away from Fantasy and closer to Science Fiction by giving them sort-of-rational explanations: psychic phenomena and bizarre mutations, instead of "magic". Then I dropped them all on an unsuspecting modern woman with thoroughly modern problems, and let her work through them in a totally contemporary fashion.

All this goes to show that "magic" can happen right here, right now, rather than in some semi-medieval other world. Magic is alive, and well, in the present day. Enjoy!

--Leslie Fish <;)))><

PROLOGUE

NO ONE CALLED HIM ELF-LORD ANYMORE, not in this day and age, but he could never for a waking moment forget what he was.

He woke at dawn, as had been his custom whenever possible for the last thousand years, dressed, and went out the back door into the early light. The yawning stablehands ahead of him went straight to the barn to see to the horses, but he turned down a different path and plodded out beyond the fences into the wild desert land.

Once away from the immediate sight of civilization he paused, reflecting once more on how different this land was from his native northern forests, and drew the crystal pendant out of his shirt. The facets of clear quartz reflected the banners of cloud in the lightening sky, and he fixed his eyes on them as he recited the ancient chant. It never failed to settle his mind into the deeper levels of meditation from which the power could be raised. Though his talent ran to Empathy rather than Prophecy, this exercise always served to clear his mind for the day ahead—and sometimes, on rare occasions, he truly did catch a glimpse of the future. That was reason enough to continue this daily ritual through the years, and the centuries, even if he could no longer entirely believe in the old High Gods.

"Lady of moonlight, Lord of thunders," he dutifully whispered in ancient Gaelic, peering at the crystal and trying once again to see beyond it. "A boon I beg of you, a glimpse of what shall come…"

A spark of deep blue light darted through the crystal, flared for an instant, and was gone.

It had not been a flash of sunlight.

Startled, he stared at the crystal and tried to regain the vision. No, it wouldn't come again; he'd had, just as he'd asked, a glimpse and no more. The best he could do was try to interpret it, and the best interpretation he could make was: *one of us approaches.* Only that, and no more.

He raised his head to frown thoughtfully at the empty desert, wondering who the newcomer was and how soon to appear, and why. The glinting stone gave him no further answers.

…The last time this happened was when that Unseelie bastard came hunting, in… 1976, was it? Another hunter, then?

No, somehow that didn't feel right. *A Seelie elf, then? Or one unknowing?* That felt a little more likely. *Of course Helen and Benjamin are coming…* But no, this had the feel of a newcomer, a stranger.

That was exactly all he could tell, but it was enough to brighten his day. *Third level alert,* he decided, setting the cord back around his neck and tucking the crystal pendant safely under his shirt. *No change in behavior, but watch and be ready.*

He turned back to the house, fighting down the old hope that for once the old high gods had chosen to roll the dice his way, for the good of his kind and against their long and slow extinction.

Just this once, he pleaded silently as he marched toward the back door. *Just this once!*

1.

ROXANNE WAS JUST PASTING DOWN the last illustration on the end-page of the union's monthly newspaper when Jack Palumbo—the General Secretary himself, big and stocky and balding—stepped out of his office and invited her inside. Surprised, she toweled the ink and contact-cement off her hands, shook her black hair out of its temporary knot, grabbed up a pad and pen and trotted into the union's inner sanctum.

The local delegate, Bill Carminski, was there before her, nervously wringing his wiry fingers. So was Wendy Wexler, the reedy editor-in-chief, seated on the worn couch beside him. Palumbo sat in his aging swivel chair behind the desk, big hands fussing idly with dues-report summaries. Only Palumbo wore a suit in the office; everyone else, Roxanne included, dressed in practical slacks and knit shirts which made them look hard-working and casual. Right now, all of them looked grim.

Wondering what this was about, Roxanne settled in the only remaining chair and propped her pad on her lap. She caught herself chewing on the end of the pen, and sternly made herself stop; she'd ruined too many pens that way.

"You won't need that," said Palumbo, waving toward her pad. "This is strictly confidential, Fellow Workers."

"Is the FBI coming after us again?" Wexler snapped. "They held up the paper at the Post Office last month, just so they could get all the members' names and addresses-"

"No, not them." Palumbo gave all of them a quelling look. "Something worse. You remember that little fracas we had back in November, when we helped those Teamster reformers take over those shops in Cleveland?"

"Hell, yes!" Carminski enthused. He'd been involved in that one. "The reformers got a lot more than a foot in the door. Given half a chance, they'll clean up that bloody union and pitch the old gangsters out on their butts. Glad we could help!"

"Trouble is, those old gangsters won't go down without a fight," Palumbo growled. "And the word 'gangsters' counts, here. They've got Mafia connections, and they're using them."

The other two bit their lips. Roxanne felt her jaw drop, and hastily pulled it back up.

"The reformers knew there were going to be reprisals," Palumbo plowed on, "And they were prepared for it. We're not, and we'd better be."

"Us?" Wexler squeaked, her red hair almost standing up.

"Yeah. We're next," Carminski guessed. "They know we helped the reformers..."

"...and this is Chicago," Palumbo finished for him. "We can expect what the reformers got: shot at, houses torched, cars wrecked, that kind of thing. I got word this morning, and I just got off the phone with the rest of the General Executive Board, and they'll spread the word to any of our locals that need to know— just in case they need to call an emergency election to replace us."

"Replace us?!" Wexler and Carminski yelped in unison.

"Uhuh. Truth is, us guys here at HQ are the likeliest targets."

"Wonderful," Roxanne muttered. Just a few minutes ago she'd been putting the paper to bed without a care in the world... Well, no major cares, anyway. And now this.

"How do we go about securing the office?"

Palumbo flicked a brief appreciative smile at her. "No problem after hours," he said. "Once that security-gate's down, nothing's gonna get in here—including firebombs. All the vital stuff is locked in fireproof cabinets that you couldn't break with an axe, and we've got the backup records on disc elsewhere, anyway. All we've got to do here is clean up everything flammable before we lock up at night."

"The paper!" Wexler wailed. "I'll run the flats over to the printer today, tell him to send the finished copies straight to the warehouse, and we'll clean up everything else.

"Roxanne—"

"I'll get on it," said Roxanne, starting to rise.

"Siddown," snapped Palumbo. "We're not finished yet. There's still the problem of security during working hours—"

"I'll get volunteers from the local," Carminski promised. "We've got a couple of guys out of work who'd make great guards."

"—and that's not all." Palumbo glared around at all of them. "We've got to watch our own butts, personally. We all work here, so we're all targets. Me, of course, but all the rest of you, too. Check the street before you step out into it. Check your cars before you so much as stick the key in the ignition. Check out your homes. If you've got kids, take 'em to school yourselves, and bring 'em back yourselves. Don't go anywhere alone. Full wartime drill, people. I'm serious."

"...Shit...." Wexler muttered, drawing raised eyebrows from the others. In the office, profanity was usually reserved for crises on the order of dropping heavy weights on one's toe.

"I'll have to inform the local," Carminski mumbled to himself, running his fingers through his thick dark hair.

"How long will this go on?" Roxanne asked, imagining herself checking for Mafia goons everywhere, taking security procedures, being grateful for once that she had no children, and wondering what she could do about her cats. The little creatures could be kept indoors for a time, but not forever. She couldn't live like that forever.

"Until the next Teamster election, which will be in four months. After the election, either the reformers will take over and the bad guys will lose their clout with the Mafia, or the old bastards will win and feel secure enough to stop spending bucks on goons."

"Four months?!" Wexler groaned. "We've got to play this game for four months?"

It was Carminski's turn to mutter "Shit..."

None of them even brought up the idea of calling the police. This was, after all, Chicago.

***

The last page of the paper was finished in less than an hour. Wexler promptly snatched up the finished flats, scrambled into her coat and sneaked out the back door with Carminski, glancing up and down the wind-scoured alley before running for her car.

Palumbo stayed shut up in his office, though Roxanne could hear him talking on the phone almost constantly. She searched the front office for anything flammable, locked up everything that was needed and threw the rest in the trashcan. When the can was filled, tamped down and filled again, she decided it was time for a break. The washroom had never looked more inviting.

After washing her hands, Roxanne stopped at the old fly-specked mirror and looked at herself. No, she didn't appear as shaken as she felt. Same old face: long straight raven-black hair, dark blue eyes, high cheekbones and clear jaw-line, pale-tan skin...ah, just beginning to roughen, ever so slightly, under the eyes. And were those the first hints of lines between her eyebrows?

I turned 30 last week, she recalled. Time was passing. She had only ten more years, at most, if she wanted to have children. Strange how she hadn't even thought of that since Ronnie had run out on her, two years ago. He'd left exactly enough money in their joint bank account to pay for the abortion. Strange how she hadn't thought of marrying, or even taking another lover, since then.

I'm done with all notions of romance, Roxanne considered, looking at herself.

Very deliberately, she slid her hands under her breasts and lifted them, studied them with a critical eye, monitored herself for the least tingle of sensual feeling—and found none.

It was surprising how sexual feeling changed when one outgrew silly ideas of romantic love. Looking back, she had to admit that Ronnie hadn't been that good a lover; the excitement had come mainly from her own belief that he loved her, that more than their bodies were touching. Delusion: all delusion. She remembered him carefully tying on his fancy new track-shoes that last day. That should have warned her. *Want to see how fast he can run? Tell him you're pregnant.*

That had been the end of it, except for the abortion a week later. Since then, she'd gotten more satisfaction from her own hands and deliberate fantasies than she'd ever had from Ronnie, to be honest—as he'd never really been. Even her sexual fantasies had nothing to do with what everybody called love: just searing images of handsome bodies–usually characters from movies—and honest desire with no pretensions, no lies about caring or forever.

And even that was beginning to lose interest for her. She was beginning to not care about sex, either. Perhaps she was suffering from a gland problem...

I turned 30 last week. What do I have? Roxanne let her hands fall and stepped back to get a longer view in the mirror. *No children, no husband, no lover...and no real desire for any.*

She still had a good body, at least: big breasted, long-legged, lean and athletic—partly due to habitual exercise, partly from hauling heavy cartons about in the office. That body would doubtless upset Momma, could she see it now: too strong—coarse, Momma would say—a perfect match for her rough hands, rougher tongue, defiantly Working-Class job and attitude.

In the years of working for the union office she'd learned to haul weights like a dockworker, swear like a trooper, drink like a sailor, and think like a union organizer—but that hadn't discouraged men from looking at her. She could still win a man's interest, if she wanted it; she'd noticed Carminski giving her hopeful looks, though he hadn't said anything. She simply hadn't wanted it.

She still had friends, mostly from right here in the union office. She knew, without asking, that Palumbo and Carminski and Wexler would risk their necks for her—even against the threat of Mafia goons. So would Bob and Meredith, her nearest neighbors in the local. Solid friends, all of them: people whose honesty and courage and kindness she never had to question. Good friends were better than a bad lover, as she had cause to know.

She still had her painting, even if she could afford to do it only on weekends nowadays, even if years of dragging around from gallery to gallery, making no sales, had convinced her that she'd never make a living as an artist. Her friends liked her paintings anyway; she never lacked for Christmas gifts.

She had her cats: two elegant Siameses, Crimp-Tail and Sable-Foot, who were company enough in the efficiency apartment which was all she could afford on an honest—therefore poor— union's office-salary. Whenever she came home from work she could hear them yowling in greeting, even before she got her key in the front door, and they always wanted petting before food. They'd been known to desert a full food-dish to leap up and curl in her lap, purring like little engines. Their furry uncomplicated love as all she needed, really.

She had a job she loved: serving one of the few honest labor unions in the city, keeping thousands of people from being abused at their jobs, occasionally organizing yet another job-shop and spreading the union's protection. It was vitally needed work; most Americans weren't aware that only one-tenth of the work force had any union at all—good, bad or indifferent. Yet the presence of that one-tenth, and the promise that those numbers could always grow, kept other employers in line and kept governments from writing off The Little Guy—people who would otherwise have, as they said here in Chicago, no clout. Yes, it was work she could believe in, could spend her life doing, and not feel as if she'd wasted her years.

Damned if she'd let a bunch of Mafia thugs take that from her!

Feeling much more resolute, Roxanne marched out of the washroom and back to the front office. She picked up the over-loaded trashcan, wondered if she should put on her bulky down-stuffed jacket, and decided against it; she wouldn't be out in the cold that long. She muscled the can down the short hallway, past the literature-storage room on the right and Palumbo's office on the left, out the back door—with a cautious glance down the al-ley—and over to the dumpster. It seemed to take forever to empty the stupid thing, with all the paper-scraps compacted in it. Roxanne remembered that she hadn't secured the literature-storeroom yet, and heaven knew how much trash she'd find in there.

Best to leave the dumpster open to wait for another load. She tucked the empty can under her arm and went back inside.

Once inside the back door, hearing it whisper closed behind her, Roxanne noted the sound of Palumbo yelling furiously in his office. She guessed he was arguing with one of the out-of-town delegates. Well, no business of hers. She paced the few steps to the storage room and started in.

From right behind her came the boom of a gunshot.

Then a second shot, and the pearled-glass window of the inner-office door shattered.

Entirely on instinct, Roxanne dashed through the storeroom doorway, darted to the end of the freestanding bookshelf and ducked down behind it, setting the metal trashcan beside her.

The storeroom door was still wide open.

Holding her breath, Roxanne peered through the narrow slot between the shelved pamphlets and watched the doorway.

There came the familiar squeak of the inner-office door opening, then the crunch of heavy and hurried footsteps on broken glass.

Then a man came walking, very fast, past the storeroom door. He glanced at the doorway in passing—showing three-quarters of his face, no more—but didn't stop. In another second he was out of sight, and only the sound of his footsteps through the outer office marked his passing.

Roxanne closed her eyes, listening, imprinting the image of him on her brain: medium-brown hair, florid face, small dark eyes, as tall as the top of the poster on the corridor wall—maybe 5'10"—tan trenchcoat, brown gloves, couldn't see the shoes.

He'd been shoving something into his inside coat-pocket, something with a thick black handle, much like the grip of an automatic pistol.

Distantly, she heard the bell on the front door jingle as the door opened, jingle again as it closed.

Gone.

She started to lunge to her feet, wanting to run into that office across the hall, see if Jack Palumbo was still alive—but then she thought again. What if the killer hadn't gone out that front door, but was waiting to see if anyone came out of hiding, if anyone else was in the office. She crouched, frozen with indecision. *Go? Stay?* Jack could be dying. The killer could be waiting. Wasn't there some way to be sure?

The idea came wordlessly, a picture.

Roxanne crept out from behind the bookshelf, crawled on hands and knees to the doorway, lay down on the floor and slowly, carefully, shoved her head—just down to the eyes—past the doorframe, and peered down the hallway into the front office.

All she could see were the feet of a chair, a desk and the breakfront counter: nothing else, nothing moving.

She slid out a little further, getting a wider view of the bottoms of the office furniture. Still nothing, and no one. It occurred to her that if she couldn't see the front door or windows, nobody watching at the windows or door could see her, either.

Jack could be dying.

She crawled across the hallway floor on her hands and knees, pawing through shards of broken glass, as quietly and fast as she could.

The inner-office door was slightly open, enough that a soft push swung it further.

The motion couldn't have been seen from the door or windows, but Roxanne winced as the door creaked. She froze, listening, but there was no other sound: no footsteps coming back. She crawled hurriedly through the doorway.

Jack Palumbo lay on the floor in front of his desk, two glossy red spots lying like flattened poppies on the front of his shirt, a small lake of blood spreading from under his back. His eyes were half-opened, and not moving.

For an instant, a shock of exploding sorrow blinded Roxanne. She bit her lip until the one pain neutralized the other, climbed unsteadily to her feet and tiptoed around the massive body to the desk. The telephone seemed to shine like a beacon.

Don't touch anything! she reminded herself, but then remembered that the killer had worn gloves. No fingerprints. It was safe to touch the phone; no prints would be there but Jack's. She lifted the receiver, then froze again.

Who should she call?

Not the police. Not in Chicago. Not for a Mafia crime.

The FBI, then?

Oh no, not them: not after last month's fun and games with the stolen mail. They couldn't be trusted either.

Who did that leave?

Roxanne took a deep breath, and then dialed the operator.

"Please connect me with the...Criminal Investigations Division of the state police. It's urgent."

The operator, bless her, was fast. The phone rang only once before someone at the state police office picked it up.

Roxanne rattled off the address as clearly and expressionlessly as a robot, then paused to choose her next words carefully. "I have fresh...very fresh evidence of a...an inter-county felony. A murder, in fact. Please come quickly. And please be careful not to disturb the evidence as you come in."

The anonymous trooper, to his credit, asked her only to give her name and repeat the address. He promised that an investigative team would arrive within 20 minutes, cautioned her not to leave the area, and hung up.

Roxanne set the receiver carefully back in its cradle, moved to the ancient swivel-chair, thought again, crouched down and crawled into the knee-hole of the desk, shuddered heavily, and sat down to wait.

***

Good as their word, the state police—two carloads of them—arrived within 20 minutes, almost to the second. Roxanne didn't leave her lair until she heard them announce themselves and call her name. She picked her way back around the desk, and the body, being careful to walk exactly where she'd stepped on the way in. Afterward, she huddled in one of the front-office chairs to answer their questions, not wanting to go back there again. The questions were thorough, precise, to the point, and not repeated.

The forensics teams came and took samples off her clothes and hands and shoes.

Roxanne took care to relate everything she remembered from the earlier conversation in the office, everything she knew about the Teamster-reformers incident—though that was little.

In the midst of the questions, Wexler and Carminski came running in the front door. They looked rumpled, out of breath, and frantic.

Right behind them followed a stereotypically perfect Chicago cop. He wasn't wearing a uniform, only a badly-cut suit, but his mean-dog expression—and the lump under the left armpit of his jacket, and his hand reaching for it—were dead giveaways. Roxanne did the best thing she could think of on short notice; she pointed at him and screamed.

Everybody but Wexler and Carminski—who kept running until they literally ran into the troopers—froze and turned to look.

"Who's that?!" Lorraine yelled, pointing to the cop.

The cop opened and shut his mouth, shifted his grasp under his jacket and came out with a badge-wallet. "Detective Sergeant Oshansky," he bellowed. "And those two—" He pointed to Wexler and Carminski, "—are fleeing a crime-scene!"

The state-cops converged on all three of them, and the next few minutes were a howling chaos of shouted questions and answers. Oshansky kept yelling his accusation and demanding to know what the state troopers were doing in his jurisdiction. Carminski wailed when he learned that Jack Palumbo was dead, but Wexler yelled urgent news above the racket.

"Somebody took a shot at us as we were coming out of the printer's!"

"—scene of the crime," Oshansky added.

"Hell..." was all Roxanne said, momentarily ignored. The gears of her mind were spinning as rapidly as they ever had in her life.

One hit-man here to kill Jack. One at the printer's. How did he know where they'd be? Followed them from the office? How did he know who they were? We don't publish photos of our office staff...

The only conclusion was that someone had done his home-work, visited the office—they did get a few walk-in visitors every week—and therefore knew who worked there.

Including me.

She let the rest of the avid conversation flow past her as she took the next logical step, and the next. Slowly, almost stiffly, she went to her desk and picked up her purse, shrugged into her bulky jacket and pulled out her key ring. She turned to the near-est trooper, who was eyeing her questioningly. "When I leave here," she said, very calmly, very clearly, "Please come with me to my apartment. I think the killers might be lying in wait for me there."

***

There was no sound of the cats calling as Roxanne climbed the stairs. Perhaps they could hear or smell the other two men with her and were shy of the strangers, or perhaps it was some-thing else. Her fingers shook as she unlocked the door, and then stepped back. The first man went in with his gun drawn; the other waited by the door with her, a hand under his coat. The minutes stretched impossibly long before the first investigator came out again.

"Clear," he announced. "But I can't tell if anything's been disturbed. Could you please check, ma'am?"

Roxanne complied, padding into the front room as if she were walking on eggs, scanning for every detail, for anything that wasn't the way she'd left it that morning. There: a newspaper lying on the coffee table, not quite as she'd left it. But could the cats have done that? There: the cats' food and water dishes were slightly further apart than she'd left them. The cats had never done that before, but it was always possible.

There: the toilet-seat was up. The cats couldn't have done that.

And where were the cats?

Roxanne tried calling them. A faint mew sounded from under the bed. She knelt down and looked, and saw Sable-Foot and Crimp-Tail crouching in the shadows against the wall, huge-eyed, whiskers trembling, and very quiet.

"Yes," she sighed, pulling herself back to her feet. "Someone's been here. Nothing's been taken, but somebody was in here. They know who I am."

The investigators looked at each other. "We don't have a Witness Protection Program," the nearer one said. "We'll have to call in the FBI anyway..."

"Shit," Roxanne said quietly, as she slumped onto the bed.

From beneath her, the cats mewed a little louder, almost in sympathy.

***

The Regional Director insisted on a face-to-face meeting with Roxanne, who didn't want to leave her apartment without one of the state police beside her. One of the investigators agreed to come with her, and she could tell he was secretly amused by her distrust for the FBI. They arrived at the FBI office five minutes early, but the Director kept them waiting for another quarter-hour. Roxanne had come prepared; she pulled a paperback mystery novel out of her purse and settled down to read.

The state investigator grinned at her, pulled out his notebook and spent the time reviewing his case-notes. When the secretary said they could enter the office, Roxanne unhurriedly put her book away and the state investigator grinned further.

The inner office was large and austere, and the man behind

the desk was likewise. He had noncommittal brown eyes, brown hair, gray suit concealing a body that looked fairly athletic, and a heavy-jawed face that would have looked surprisingly young if not for his hard expression. The nameplate on his desk simply read: Wilson Harding, Regional Director. He was not, Roxanne guessed, a man who gave anything away—except possibly his garbage.

She sat down in the nearest chair facing the desk, without being asked. Her protector did likewise. Harding only stared at her for long moments, saying nothing.

Roxanne returned the favor.

"So," he finally said, as if conceding points in some obscure game, "You want to enter the Witness Protection Program?"

"No, I don't," Roxanne replied levelly. "The state police have convinced me that I must."

Harding frowned slightly at the investigator, who said nothing, then looked back to Roxanne. "Why didn't you call the local police when you discovered the body?" he asked.

Roxanne was ready for that. "The Chicago police are notoriously unreliable when it comes to dealing with the Mafia." She couldn't resist adding: "Besides, they're no friends of the union; we're too honest and idealistic for their tastes."

Harding didn't so much as blink. He kept staring at her, and Roxanne got the distinct impression that, under his expressionless exterior, he was undressing her with his eyes. "If you thought this crime was Mafia-related," he went on, "Why didn't you call the FBI?"

Roxanne's eyes narrowed. "Same reason," she said.

That got a blink out of him, but nothing more. "Yet you want us to put you in the Witness Protection Program," he repeated, implying that she was an incredible ingrate.

"I've already answered that question," Roxanne reminded him.

"That was our idea," the investigator cut in, almost spelling out the words. "She's an eyewitness, and can identify the Alleged Assailant. Her testimony will be vital, once we catch up to him. We don't have the facilities for keeping her safe until then, and we have good reason to think the perpetrators are hunting her."

Surely Harding knows all this, Roxanne considered. *Why did he have to ask? Why did he want to see me personally?*

"There's always protective custody," said Harding.

"In a Chicago jail?" Roxanne sneered, "Or state prison? I wouldn't last a week, and you know it."

The Director and the investigator looked at each other. They knew it was true. Why had Harding even offered?

Harding leaned back in his chair and folded his hands, as if he'd come to a decision. "If she's vital to your case, we'll proceed," he said, not looking at Roxanne.

"Go to room 147 and fill out the paperwork. One of our agents will contact you within 48 hours. I trust you can keep the witness safe until then?"

"Of course," the investigator frowned.

"That's it, then. Please go to room 147."

With no more ceremony than that, Roxanne and the investigator got up and left the office. The man apparently knew his way around the building, for he led her on down the corridor toward the assigned room. He didn't seem terribly pleased with his success.

"What was all that about?" Roxanne dared to ask. "Why did he want to see me at all?"

"To check you out for himself, probably," the investigator shrugged. "The FBI doesn't think much of us, either. ...And you weren't exactly friendly toward him."

"The feeling was mutual. I don't think he'd have liked me any better if I'd fawned on him like a dog." And she had to wonder about that. Was Harding normally this cold to civilians, or was it dislike for the union itself, or just personal hostility, or what?

She certainly didn't want the Mafia thugs knowing where she was, but she didn't like the thought of the FBI knowing either. When she got to wherever they sent her, she decided, she would do something about that.

***

"I'm Dianne Berringer," the FBI woman smiled, trying to look motherly. "I'll set the paperwork in motion, and I'll be your contact when we get…where you're going."

She sounded kindly as she recited the procedure, and even offered to let Roxanne choose her own new name.

What name? Roxanne considered. She'd always liked her own well enough.

Perhaps she could just translate it from the original Michigan-French. Defarge meant "of the forge"—blacksmith. No, the name Smith would be a real giveaway. *Farrier, then?* That would do. But she'd keep something of her heritage in the first name, too.

Lorraine, as in Cross of Lorraine. "Lorraine Farrier," she said.

Just to be perverse, keep something of the old Indian line, too. "Lorraine Minnehaha Farrier."

Agent Berringer pursed her lips, but typed the name faithfully into the computer.

"'Lorraine M. Farrier it is, then. And I moved up your birthday by three months. You'll have to remember it."

That would be June 21st, Roxanne calculated. *Summer solstice.* According to the old folklore she'd once researched, that was supposed to be a magical date: a time when creatures from other realms could cross the barrier into this world. *I'll believe that when I meet a unicorn, or an elf, or a dragon.*

It occurred to her that she'd already met one kind of legendary monster, and she shivered.

Agent Berringer didn't notice, but kept on typing. "We'll have to get you a new hairdo and photos. We should have everything done in 48 hours. Will you be ready to leave by then?"

"I'll manage," Roxanne said, hearing her voice quiver.

***

The next two days were absolute hell. Roxanne packed as few clothes as she could live on, gave away much to other members of the local, and packed up everything else. Bob and Meredith, who had a comfortably big apartment, volunteered to keep her property safe in their spacious basement-locker. They also agreed to keep Sable-Foot and Crimp-Tail, since they loved cats, and the little animals had returned the feeling every time Bob or Meredith had come to visit.

Giving away the cats, she found, was the hardest part of leaving. The little creatures were delighted to get out of their carrying-cases after the drive, poked about Meredith's kitchen exploring and purred ecstatically when Bob scratched their fuzzy ears, but spent equal time on Roxanne's lap extorting caresses. They had no idea that she would leave them there and not come back for a long time—probably months, possibly years. It was almost impossible to slip away from them and get back to the car where the state investigator patiently waited for her.

Once inside the car, Roxanne caught herself crying—and couldn't stop for long minutes. The investigator waited, not starting the car, and handed her a packet of tissues.

"I know it's rough," he said awkwardly, trying to be kind. "Sort of like abandoning your kids, I guess."

Roxanne cried harder.

He patted her shoulder clumsily. "They'll be all right," he insisted. "They'll be happy and safe, and you'll come back soon..." He stopped there, realizing that there was no guarantee that the case could be brought to trial anywhere near soon. He sighed, reached into a pocket and handed her a card. "Here," he said. "You can always get in touch with me at those numbers."

Roxanne blew her nose, wiped her streaming eyes and looked at the card. The name on it was Gerald Weber, CID, with two phone-numbers and an email address. She felt absurdly grateful. "Thank you," she whispered, tucking the card into her change-purse. Not the wallet: she'd already given that to Bob and Meredith. "I guess we'd better go meet the FBI agent now."

Weber nodded sadly, and started the car.

I'm done crying, Roxanne decided, crumpling the tissue. *That does no good either.*

***

Berringer was waiting, with a thick envelope in her hands. "Here's your new ID—that hairstyle looks very nice, by the way—and the car's right downstairs. Why don't we spend the driving-time reviewing your new identity?"

"Why don't you tell me something about where I'm going," Roxanne asked, bitterly feeling the ends of her shortened hair. It reached barely below her collar now.

"And how I'll live when I get there?"

"Oh, there'll be plenty of time for that on the trip. We'll be driving all the way, you know. Less chance of anyone seeing you."

"A long drive, I take it?"

"All the way to Arizona," Agent Berringer smiled. "That's where my home office is. It's the last place anyone would look for a Chicago girl."

Roxanne blinked, dredging up all she knew about the Grand Canyon state: tall cactus, colorful desert, blistering heat, and artful Indian silver jewelry. "About as different from Chicago as you can get," she had to agree.

***

Two days later Roxanne—no, she must think of herself as Lorraine now—stood at the window of her studio apartment in Tucson, Arizona, and watched Agent Berringer drive away. She wasn't sure what she felt, beyond slightly unreal and slightly insulted. Yes, the FBI had provided the basics: a tiny apartment, sparsely furnished with a second-hand sofa-bed and bureau, a wallet-full of new identity papers including a suitably-dated college transcript, a nondescript 10-year-old gray Ford out in the parking-lot, and enough money to live on frugally for a month.

There was also the agent's card, with contact-numbers, propped on the paid-for-this-month telephone. Berringer had insisted that Rox—no, Lorraine now—phone her at least once a week, give her any letters to be mailed to old friends, inform her of any changes in location, or "call just if you feel like chatting."

Unlikely, thought Rox/Lorraine, mechanically unpacking her duffel bag. She didn't trust the affable FBI agent, simply on general principles. Yes, she'd keep the card and make dutiful calls once a week, but that was all, thank you. Anyone naive might call it paranoia, but she had worked for an honest labor union in Chicago, and she didn't trust the FBI. She certainly wouldn't depend on them. If she wanted to talk to someone, she'd call state-investigator Weber; at least his concern had been genuine.

She absolutely would not be dependent on the FBI for her housing and income.

She'd get a job of her own, a cell-phone, then her own apartment, and eventually a used car of her own—without informing any of them. For that matter, in this state she could buy a gun. When Weber said the case was coming to trial, she'd take herself back to Chicago and put herself under his protection, no one else's.

First step: get a job.

There was a current local newspaper on the chipped plastic kitchen/dining-room table. Rox/Lorraine got up and dragged herself to it, feeling unaccountably tired. *Not exactly jet-lag,* she thought, opening the paper and turning to the help-wanted section. *More like transplanting shock...*

There were the usual ads for telemarketers, clerks, and factory-hands: standard jobs in any city. Then her eye was caught by something she would never have seen in Chicago: an ad for a horse-feed salesman.

Horse-feed...?

With a jolt, she remembered that this was one of the great desert states; its economy depended heavily on mining—and ranching. There were still ranches here.

And cowboys. And Indians.

Rox/Lorraine let her eyes drift away from the paper, swept up in a childhood dream. When she was young she'd loved horses, gone riding whenever possible, spent summers at camps that specialized in horses and riding. She'd even imagined being a cowgirl when she grew up—or, better yet, a horse-rancher. Now a bizarre twist of fate had dropped her into a land where the old dream was remotely possible.

Why not? I have enough money; I can afford to spend time hunting for the job I want.

The paper, she knew, was not the place to look for that kind of work. She searched the meager apartment until she found the phone books hidden in a cupboard, and pulled them out. Yes, there were white-pages and yellow-pages books for the city, but there was another book—much thinner—that covered the rest of the county. She opened the third book and searched the yellow pages under 'ranches'. There was a surprising number of them, but most of them included the word 'cattle' with the names.

Not quite what she wanted. She looked under 'horses'.

There: a much shorter list. Short enough—she glanced at the shabby clock on the wall—that she could probably phone all of them today. *Right now, in fact. Why not?*

Her sense of dislocation changed to a lighter, bubbly feeling—like being slightly drunk on champagne, or hope. Rox/Lorraine caught herself laughing, composed herself, spent five minutes planning what she'd say, and then dialed the first number.

"Hello. I'm...Lorraine Farrier, and I'm looking for work. I'm good with horses. Do you have any use for a groom, exercise-rider, general handyman, or anything like that?"

The first rancher—his wife, actually—sounded surprised, cheerful, regretful that there was no work available, and recommended a name further down the list. Rox/Lorraine thanked her, drew a connecting arrow to the rancher the woman had mentioned, but dialed the next name in order anyway.

A dozen calls later she'd harvested a dozen kindly refusals and half a dozen recommendations, none of which had panned out either. Still, she persevered. Chasing dreams wasn't supposed to be easy, and the hunt itself made her feel young again, which she hadn't felt in a long time. She dialed the next number, the next name: Treemark Arabian Farm. She'd always loved Arabian horses.

This time it was a man who answered, a deep baritone voice, oddly resonant. "Yes?" was all he said.

Rox/Lorraine repeated her set piece, and then waited.

There was silence for a long moment. "Why are you looking for work on a ranch, instead of in the city?" he asked.

It wasn't what she'd expected, but it was a reasonable question. "I love horses," was the only answer she could come up with. It was the truth, after all.

Another long pause. Then: "But do horses love you?"

That was distinctly odd. She abruptly remembered standing on tiptoe to reach the back of a pretty bay mare, and the mare turning to nuzzle her ear. "They like me, anyway," she heard herself saying. "Especially when I brush them. They whuffle softly, and nudge me with their velvet noses..." Now why on Earth had she said something as silly as that? "They're always willing to let me pick up their feet and clean them." Well, this was dream-chasing, wasn't it?

Again, a pause. This time, she thought she heard a brief chuckle. "And can you talk to them?"

Truly bizarre. A dream. Flow with it. "A little. I don't know very much of the language."

"I see." The voice turned decisive. "Come out here tomorrow, and ask for Brian Treemark. Here are the directions..."

Rox/Lorraine scrambled for a blank piece of paper, wound up using the newspaper's margin, and wrote down everything exactly.

"Tomorrow then, Ms. Farrier." The phone clicked off.

But isn't tomorrow Saturday? ...Then again, it's a ranch, not an office...

She set the receiver down very carefully, feeling dizzy. Slowly, precisely, she tore out the page of the newspaper, folded it, got up and walked—feeling as if she were floating—to the half-unpacked duffel bag. She must choose the right clothes to wear tomorrow: something suitable for riding horses, working in stables, showing how well she could work and not how 'businesslike' or pretty-pretty she looked, so very different from what was expected in the city. A good pair of blue jeans would do, a long-sleeved shirt to keep the desert sun off her arms, her boots—a bit fragile and ornamental, perhaps, but they'd do until she could buy others—some kind of sun-hat, practical underwear, belt-purse, no jewelry.

Almost in a daze she put away the rest of her clothes, rummaged through the lightly stocked refrigerator, microwaved a frozen dinner and ate without tasting it. Afterward she showered mechanically, wrapped herself in her bathrobe and unfolded the sofa-bed, and watched forgettable movies on the small television until she felt sleepy enough to lie down. Not once could she shake the feeling that she'd just changed her life irrevocably, simply by chasing a childhood dream.

***

The adult dream, when it came, started just as it had for the past few nights. She was back in the storeroom, crouching behind the bookshelf, listening to the killer's footsteps crunching quickly through the glass on the floor.

This time he didn't hurry past the open door. This time he came running in, pulling his gun back out of the coat-pocket, knowing she was there. "I'm Lorraine now!" she shouted, standing up where he could see her, then dodging to the other side of the standing bookshelf. He fired, missed, and then came after her, running along the side of the bookshelf.

She gripped the edge of one shelf and heaved mightily. The entire bookshelf fell over on the man, crushing him to the floor. "I'm Lorraine!" she cried again, leaping atop the fallen bookshelf and dancing on it, jumping up and down, trying to crush the man buried under the metal and paper.

After awhile she realized that the man was gone, pounded flat, nothing left but his rumpled trenchcoat. A horse's whinny sounded from the doorway. "I'm coming," she called to the animal, and ran out the open door. Beyond it lay the wide sunlit desert, and a black horse stood there, waiting for her.

"I'm Lorraine," she said, going up to the beautiful creature and stroking its satin neck.

"I'm your future," said the horse, not moving its lips.

Lorraine, as she was now, took hold of the horse's mane and wondered how to mount without stirrups. The dream faded.

***

She woke in the morning, remembering everything. Setting her jaw so tightly that her teeth ached, she dressed quickly, took up the paper, went down to the nondescript gray car and drove out toward the highway, following the directions exactly. It had been a long time since she had felt this sense of excitement, of a quest beginning, and she wouldn't waste it now.

She wouldn't sully it by calling to tell the FBI where she was going.

2.

TREEMARK ARABIAN FARM was not what Lorraine had expected in a ranch. The lavish application of money was apparent even in the plain wood sign and fences that flanked the wide gravel driveway. The tall posts and rails had been treated with some chemical—probably creosote—that darkened the wood, then painted and sealed with some sort of clear lacquer that held up well in the searing sunlight. The very gravel in the long driveway was fine-grained and red-toned. The grass in the pastures to left and right was tall and thick enough to suggest deliberate watering, which couldn't have been cheap in desert country.

The house at the end of the driveway reinforced that impression. Huge and rambling, all fieldstone and glass, shadowed by overhanging slate roofs, it was clearly an original design by some architect used to six-figure fees. The long driveway circled in front of the house and then meandered toward a half-visible large white-painted stable, flanked with a tanbark-filled training corral with a seven-foot post-and-rail fence. The driveway was almost completely packed with cars, most of them late model, some of them visibly expensive.

The horses grazing in the pastures were definitely Arabians, quick and elegant and beautiful, obviously purebreds.

Lorraine tried to remember what purebred Arabian horses sold for, and how big the market for such luxury items could be. All the reasonable calculations she could make led to the same conclusion. There was no way that training and breeding and selling horses—even animals as fine as these—could provide the money to pay for a place like this. The money had come from elsewhere. *Inherited?* Possibly.

Investments? That only led to the question of where the original investment money had come from. *Business?* Again, possible—but what kind? An honest, or at least legal, trade?

Drugs? Money-laundering for organized crime? Had she jumped from the frying pan into the fire?

It's too early in the morning to be paranoid, Lorraine decided. *Just be careful, and observe.*

She parked the car in a narrow gap in the shadow of the house, went up the flagstone walk to the door and rang the ornate bell.

Within a few seconds the carved-oak door opened soundlessly, revealing a slim gray man in a dark suit. He could have been a secretary or butler or possibly the owner himself. "Yes?" he asked politely, with a faint British accent, and Lorraine knew that this wasn't the voice she'd heard on the phone.

"I'm Lorraine Farrier," she said, refusing to cringe before this classic representation of wealth. "I have an appointment with Mr. Brian Treemark."

The butler/secretary/whatever didn't turn a hair. "He'll be at the stables at this hour." He pointed. "Simply follow the drive around to the first barn."

As Lorraine turned to look, she noted the door soundlessly closing on her. How efficient. She considered getting back in the car, and then decided to walk. She could do with a bit of exercise, and besides, her aged car had every right to sit in that elegant driveway. She followed the gravel drive around the house toward the stables.

***

Brian Treemark closed the cell-phone and set it back in its holster on his belt. So, the intriguing woman who loved horses was on her way here, and he had less than five minutes to prepare. He took a quiet step closer to the narrow wooden cabinet near the barn door, mentally cataloguing its contents. If his visitor were no more than she seemed, there'd be no need for any of the weapons there. If she were one of his kind, he could put her down quickly and question her at leisure.

Meanwhile, he could observe unseen.

Yes, here she came around the corner of the house. She was medium-tall, wide-shouldered and big-breasted, with a slender athletic build and long legs, suitably dressed for stable-work though her hat and boots looked more ornamental than enduring, moving with the easy and economic strides of someone used to physical work. She had straight black hair and dark eyes of undetermined color, a strong face with a calm but alert expression, and long-fingered hands with practical short nails. Not above 30, he would guess. No weapons visible.

He stretched his empathic sense, trying to read her.

She came closer, to the rail of the training-ring, and his senses relayed a message that made him twitch in astonishment.

The feeling was there: muted, dim, but unmistakable. She was his kind, yes, but Uninitiated. No danger, no—but no doubt she was also totally ignorant of what she was.

Against all odds, the fates or gods had delivered this incredible raw material into his hands. It was unbelievable.

Wait, he reminded himself sternly. He knew nothing of her spirit. She would have to be tested like any other innocent newcomer before he could make any further judgment.

Treemark turned to his nearest groom, a lanky redheaded man, and pointed down the corridor to a particular stall door. "Let him out," was all he said.

***

Lorraine was following the drive beside the training-ring when she heard the ringing whinny, more like a screech of fury, and the heavy drumming of hoofbeats. The sound came from the open stable door leading into the training ring, and a moment later a light-chestnut stallion came bursting out through it. Two men holding ropes came running out after him, but Lorraine had eyes only for the horse.

He was a very young stallion, she saw now: moving with the gawky extravagance of a colt, probably two years old or less. He leaped into the training ring, saw that there was no exit, and ran furiously around the ring, bucking and whinnying. A single circuit didn't satisfy him; he ran three times around the ring, screeching shrilly, tossing his head and tail and kicking a few times for good measure. At one point he laid eyes on Lorraine and made a show of snapping at her, though she stood easily a yard out of reach.

Showing off, she realized, noting that the men had halted beside the door and were watching. In the animal's gestures she saw something she recognized, something she'd seen in plenty of human adolescent boys—and a few men old enough to know better. He was throwing a tantrum, trying to impress the whole world with the fact that his precious feelings had been hurt and his sacred pride insulted—demanding that everyone pay attention to him.

She'd seen that before. She knew how to handle it with a human. Now, how to communicate her response to a horse? No words would matter, and few sounds; gesture would be everything.

Lorraine gave a loud "Huh!" expressing infinite disgust, and turned her back. She switched her hair for good measure, hoping it looked enough like a horse's tail to get her point across.

The young stallion stopped in his tracks and stared at her, ears up and eyes wide, astounded—and of course offended—

that anyone could respond like that to his tirade.

Lorraine kept her back turned, and ignored him.

The stallion reared up, screeching his tale of woe, pawed the air for several seconds, and then came down hard enough to make the ground ring. He added another kick and tail-toss for good measure.

Lorraine, not looking at him, blew through her lips as if driving away flies.

The stallion put on his best performance yet, hopping in a circle, bucking, kicking, rolling his eyes and tossing his head, wailing his complaints to the world.

Lorraine continued to ignore him.

Finally the stallion grew tired and stopped, panting. He turned his head toward Lorraine and gave a long whinnying wail, plainly saying: *"Don't you care about my feelings?!"*

She gave him an owlish look, then turned sideways and worked her jaws as if chewing, clearly replying: *"You're a bore. I'd rather be eating than listen to you."*

The stallion drooped his ears and gave a long piteous wail: *"Oh, I'm so abused and miserable!"*

She gave him another wry look, and snorted: *"What have you got to whine about?"*

Catching her eye, the stallion turned his muzzle toward the far fence and tossed his head at it: *"I want to run free, and that stops me!"*

She looked at him, looked deliberately at the fence, then tossed her head likewise and snorted again: *"Jump over it, then."*

The stallion looked at her, looked at the fence, and wiggled his ears in indecision.

His bluff had been called. He'd have to put up or shut up, and the fence was seven feet high. He stamped, whinnied defiantly and tossed his head: *"I will jump it! I will!"*

Lorraine blew through her lips and turned away. *"Sure you will. Right. Uhuh."*

The stallion pranced in place for a moment, working up his nerve, then whinnied *"Look at me!"* and charged the fence.

Lorraine didn't turn her head.

At the last second, the stallion changed his mind. He dug in his heels and skidded to a stop, just short of banging into the heavy rails. He whipped his head around to see if Lorraine was laughing at him.

Lorraine only snorted and worked her jaws again.

The stallion, ears drooping, plodded away from the fence and glanced around as if looking for something to eat, trying to pretend that the whole embarrassing scene hadn't been important anyway.

At that point one of the men came toward him, carrying a rope and a bucket that sloshed water. The stallion glared at him, but sniffed at the water. The man set down the bucket and waited. The stallion thought for a moment, then wiggled his ears, came to the bucket and shoved his nose in it and began to drink. The man reached forward and stroked the bowed neck, patted, spoke soothingly, and finally slipped the rope around the stallion's neck. He waited until the horse had finished drinking and lifted his head, then slipped another noose deftly around the animal's muzzle to make an effective halter. The stallion let his ears droop, and didn't protest.

The second man, red-haired and lanky, came forward to pick up the bucket. The first man handed him the end of the halter-rope. The redhead took it and turned away, toward the stable door. The stallion followed him without complaint, and both disappeared into the stable's shadows. The first man came over to the near fence, climbed neatly up the rails and down the other side, and strode to where Lorraine waited.

She saw now that he was wearing a good cotton shirt over his tight jeans, that he had wide shoulders and a muscular body but stood little taller than she did. He had black hair and red-toned skin, but with distinctly Celtic features and sea-green eyes. He looked young, but moved with the confidence of long experience.

"What would you have done," he asked without preamble, "If he'd gone over the fence?"

Lorraine recognized his voice from the phonecall. "I would have followed with the bucket of water until he got tired, and hungry, and thirsty. Then I would have lured him with the water, and led him home—just as you did."

"And if he'd refused to come for the water?" His eyes assessed her frankly.

Lorraine shrugged. "Any horse that prefers freedom and thirst in the blazing desert to guaranteed food, water and shelter in the service of man is born to be wild. You could never have kept him, no matter what you did."

The man twitched a brief smile. "And you are?"

"Lorraine Farrier. I'm looking for Mr. Brian Treemark."

"You've found him."

The man held out his hand. Lorraine took it, wondering if he'd turn the clasp into an arm-wrestling contest, but he only gripped briefly and let go.

"Come on up to the house," he said, moving past her. "Let's discuss your possible employment here."

Lorraine followed warily.

Treemark's course led across a stone-flagged patio flanked with deep flowerbeds and fruit-trees, through a wide porch walled with trellises of passion-flower vines, into a large but casually furnished dining-area with a huge and professional-looking kitchen to one side.

Beyond that was a vast livingroom with beamed ceilings and an enormous fireplace at one wall; it was practically upholstered with deep-piled black carpet, Indian-motif wall-hangings, and numerous overstuffed couches that looked as if they were covered in genuine leather. The coffee tables were stripped and polished cedar-boles, looking as if they weighed half a ton apiece, covered with thick glass tops and studded with large brass rings. More brass rings decorated the fronts of the sofa-arms, the window frames and the ceiling-beams. Only one of the beams supported a hanging brass planter, from which trailed a feathery flowering vine. The wide windows—looking out on gardens and trellises and part of the front yard—were flanked by heavy dark-green velveteen curtains drawn back by satin-rope ties set in brass rings. The fireplace-screen and tools were also polished brass. A curving staircase and a few arches and corridors led away to other parts of the house, which Lorraine could barely glimpse in the dim filtered sunlight. The whole room seemed to be a velvet-lined jewel-box, twinkling with gold.

As they walked through, a woman came padding down one of the corridors. She was wearing, Lorraine noticed, a classic 18th Century Spanish costume, complete with a lacy mask. Lorraine tried not to stare, remembered that this was the weekend, and recalled all those cars in the driveway. There must be a costume-party going on. Well, it was none of her business.

Treemark led her through one of the archways, down a hall lined with floor-to-ceiling bookshelves, and into a very different room. This was a cozy office with a wide but mostly-bare desk, soft upholstered chairs with a matching couch in one corner, paintings of landscapes on the walls and a discreet file-cabinet tucked against the back wall beside another door. Treemark sat down behind the desk, waved Lorraine into one of the chairs facing it, took up a blank note-pad and a pen.

"So, Lorraine Farrier..." he said, scribbling. "Date of birth?"

Lorraine remembered to use the new date, June 21st.

"Born where?"

"Detroit, Michigan."

"Social Security number?"

Lorraine hadn't memorized it. She opened her belt-purse, took out the new card and handed it to him. Treemark glanced at it, wrote down the number and handed it back.

"Last employer?"

Lorraine almost went blank, and then came up with the information Berringer had given her. "The WEEKLY TRADER, a little swap-mart newspaper. It went belly-up when the owner died last month. I worked there since I got out of college."

"And where was that?"

"College? Uh, Michigan State University. ...Oh, you mean the paper? Chicago."

Her eyes kept straying to the way the muscles in his shoulders moved under that shirt. Nobody got muscles like that working in a business office. A man as handsome as this could have made a living in Hollywood. What was he doing in a small city in Arizona? Nothing about this place, or its owner, fell into any pattern she could recognize.

Treemark looked up, catching her with his sea-green eyes. "It's said that there's always work in Chicago. Why did you come all the way down here?"

Lorraine held perfectly still, reminding herself to be calm. "I got tired of the ghastly Chicago winters," she said. "I'd grown tired of the whole city, and wanted a change. My Aunt Dianne lives here, and I had some money saved, so..." She shrugged.

"How long have you been in town?"

"Two days now."

Treemark raised an eyebrow. "Quite a career change, from newspapers to horse-farms."

Lord, how could she explain this? "I've always loved horses, but there aren't many stables left in Chicago. I worked for the paper only because I needed a day-job..."

Oh, now she'd really talked herself into a corner. Any explanation she made would sound stupid. Damn!

"Day job?" Treemark prodded.

Lorraine smiled bitterly. "I'm a failed artist," she admitted. "A painter whose work didn't sell. When I came here and saw all the ads for horses… Well, I thought, if I can't make a living at one thing I love, why not try the other?"

"Painting, and horses." Treemark gave her a genuine smile that lit up his whole face and made Lorraine catch her breath. "You might try painting portraits of horses, while you're here. There actually is a market for that."

Lorraine couldn't help laughing at the thought. "That would be too perfect! Horses for my day-job, and selling my art..." She shook her head. Fate wouldn't be that kind.

Treemark must have seen something of that in her look. He turned his eyes back to the note-pad and resumed writing. "Family? Next of kin?" he asked, formal again.

"Mother, back in Detroit. My brother lives there too. Some cousins nearby." Not that she'd seen any of them in years, or wanted to. "Some friends in Chicago." *Remember your story!* "My Aunt Dianne here."

He gave her a thoughtful look, and then went on. "Experience with horses?"

"Lots of riding, and summer riding-camp, when I was in school—right up until I left college." *I didn't have much chance thereafter.*

"Married?" He scribbled on, not looking at her.

"No."

"Any boyfriends, or plans to marry soon?"

"No," Lorraine snapped.

Treemark barely flicked an eyebrow. "Current address?"

Lorraine really did go blank, and had to fumble in her purse for the little notebook where she'd written down the particulars of her new identity. She found the address and phone number, and rattled them off hurriedly. "I just moved in," she explained, wondering why she felt the need to apologize.

Treemark raised his head and gave her a long look. "Could you get out of the lease, if you had to?"

"I...don't know. Why?"

He took a deep breath. "The job here is a live-in position. You'd have to be available at all hours in case of an emergency with the horses. Would that be a problem for you?"

Live here?! "Oh no, not at all." *Not even the FBI will know where I am.*

He gave her that impossibly lovely smile again. "Can you start today?" he asked.

Lorraine felt her heart jump, and then reined it in. "Tomorrow," she said. "I'll have to go home and pick up my things, then try to get out of the lease..." She knew she wouldn't; even the effort would alert Agent Berringer. She'd just walk out. "Buy a few necessities..." *A cell-phone. A toothbrush. A gun.* "I'll be here as soon as I can." *I've got the job! I've got the perfect job!*

It occurred to her that the incident with the young stallion in the training ring had been some sort of a test, and she'd passed. She'd passed well enough that Treemark hadn't even asked to see her ride, or clean a stall, or curry a horse.

"Very good." Treemark set down his pen, shoved back his chair and stood up.

"I'll show you to your room, then."

"Room?" Lorraine echoed, getting to her feet. *Not 'quarters' or 'bunkhouse'?*

"Of course." Treemark opened the door and gestured her to it. "You'll be staying here in the house."

Like a servant— Lorraine caught herself. *Well, what else is an employee?* "Ah, that's nice. It's a lovely house."

"Thank you, " said Treemark, leading her back into the livingroom. "I designed it myself."

Aha! That would explain— "You're an architect?"

"No," he smiled, "I only did the basic designs. Stadler and Associates turned that into blueprints. I'm actually a psychiatrist—a licensed sex-therapist, to be precise."

Lorraine burst out laughing. Yes, that would explain much. "I take it you practiced for awhile in Beverly Hills, or someplace like it." She glanced knowingly around the lush livingroom.

Two more party-guests had joined the costumed woman for drinks and quiet conversation around one of the coffee tables. One was a man in a monk's robe, and plain black mask. The other was a woman in a Victorian nightgown and a white lace mask.

None of them looked up as Lorraine and Treemark passed.

Treemark gave her a brief, calculating look. "Something like that," he said, "But I made my money in investments, besides what I inherited."

Lorraine nodded in comprehension as the observed facts fell into a pattern.

Treemark must be older than he looked, but that could be the result of artful plastic surgery. Inherited money, investments, and a profession where he could command fees of a couple hundred dollars an hour: that was how he afforded this place. It all made sense now.

No drug-money. No Mafia. I'll be safe here.

"This is the staff wing," Treemark said as he led her through an archway and into a carpeted corridor lined with doors, perhaps a dozen of them. The one he led her to opened on a bedroom as big as her whole apartment back in the city, with its own bath-room, already made up with good linens and a satin quilt on a genuine four-poster double bed. There was a large oak-wood bureau with a mirror, a nightstand and bookcase—all empty, except for the clock and telephone on the table.

"That's actually part of an intercom system," Treemark ex-plained, pointing to the phone. "The only outside line is in my office."

Lorraine shrugged, reminding herself to buy a cell-phone on the way home. She noticed that there was no radio. She recalled that she hadn't yet seen a television in the house, either.

"It looks lovely," she said, wondering how many other employ-ees bunked in this wing. She'd seen only two so far, butler and groom, but could guess that there were more: one maid at least, certainly a cook, possibly a gardener. She wondered if all of them had servants' quarters as fine as this. *I haven't seen all of the house, or anything like it.* Suspicion began to nibble at her again.

"It will do, then." Treemark led her back out to the corridor. "Let's go discuss your contract."

Contract. Business. Be practical, Lorraine warned herself as she paced after him.

Yes, he's rich and clever and extraordinarily handsome. If I were a fool for romance, I could easily fall in love and break my heart over him -- and he could easily cheat me on the contract while my head was in the clouds. Read the fine print.

***

The contract Treemark handed her, back in the welcoming lit-tle office, was straightforward enough. It left the job-title blank, but he filled it in with 'general stable-work'. There was a paragraph guaranteeing 'complete medical and dental treatment' which made Lorraine smile at its simplicity; as written, it would take care of her even if she suffered serious injury or disease. Right after that, not surprisingly, was a clause requiring a 'health examination' for employment. There was another paragraph promising 'room and board' that even specified the room and 'fully balanced meals'.

"It looks too good to be true," she commented. *There has to be a catch in it somewhere.*

"The wages aren't," he smiled. "I pay rock-bottom minimum wage. Of course, you don't have to spend any of it on rent, food or utilities."

Lorraine chuckled, seeing what this meant. *Hard work, minimum wage, and company housing—but still, I could do a lot worse.* She couldn't help adding: "Is there a company store, too?"

Treemark looked blank for a moment, then caught the reference and burst out laughing. His laughter was like deep bells ringing. "Oh no," he whooped. "You'll have to go into town for everything else. So, will you be my wage-slave?"

It was Lorraine's turn to laugh as she recognized the old union term. "Yes," she grinned. "It sure beats working for a trade-paper."

He handed her a pen, and she signed.

"That's it, then." He took the contract and stood. "I'll show you out to your car. Please try to get here as soon as possible tomorrow. I'd like to get the medical examination done early."

"You'll do the exam?" *Ah, with a bit of groping on the side, perhaps?*

Treemark shrugged. "Or my colleague will. Up to you. But I don't think it will matter; you're obviously sound of wind and limb."

Horseman's term. 'Colleague'? "You run a clinic out of your house?"

"It saves on rent, and it's useful if there are any accidents at the stable." Treemark pointed to the door in the back wall. "Our examination room is right through there."

Lorraine shrugged. Again, this made sense. "I'll be here bright and early tomorrow," she promised.

With no further word Treemark led her out through the livingroom, into a tiled and paneled entryway, to the front door. Lorraine noted the spy-hole and discreet but impressive locks on the door; the man wasn't a fool about security, either. She stepped out into the blistering heat, hearing the door close softly behind her, and went down the flagstone walk to the driveway.

I've got the job, she marveled again. *I've got the perfect job!*

She couldn't help skipping down the flagstones to her car.

***

Behind the door, Treemark watched through the spy-hole and smiled as he saw Lorraine skipping like a little girl down the flagstone walk. He'd won the first round, drawn her in. Barring some unforeseen catastrophe, she'd be back in the morning. There were still several vital steps to go, and he'd have to persuade her to stay and accept them, but yes, she would return.

He turned around and leaned his back against the door, feeling a vast satisfaction and a monumental fatigue. This first round had been hard-fought, and hard-won. He'd never met any Uninitiated—and very few mortals—who were so wary, so subtly defensive, and yet so fearless. Where had she learned that, and how? He would have to discover it, delicately prise the knowledge from her, lay bare the scars and try to heal them, uncover her true potential and train it to its full glory.

Like taming a wild mare, he thought. She had entered his land like a splendid wild horse come in from the desert, unconsciously showing her natural beauty and the magnificence of her paces, yet watchful and cautious, ready to fly at the slightest sign of danger. He knew nothing of her but what he'd read from her speech, body-language and dim aura, yet that little was a gift from the fates—almost as if the balance of the universe had shifted in his favor, in the direction of his kind, for once in all these centuries.

He would take every precaution, use all of his skill, even call upon the aid of his best allies—but he would not waste the gift.

And for now he had to return to his guests, his patients, and his other work.

***

On the way home Lorraine stopped first at a convenience store and bought a toothbrush and a city map. She also looked at the city's yellow-pages and found the address of the nearest Radio Shack and gun store. It took half an hour at the Radio Shack to buy a simple cell-phone, get the instructions, sign the contract—cheap, no-frills, basic-with-long-distance—and activate the phone.

The visit to the gun store took much longer. To a recent Chicago resident, just walking in the door gave her an almost indecent thrill, like going into a porno-shop. The place was disappointingly clean, spare and businesslike; only the goods displayed in the cases made her shiver. A clerk hovered nearby, waiting politely.

"I'm a total beginner," Lorraine admitted. "I need a beginner's gun, but something I can use for self-defense."

The clerk smiled in complete understanding. "You should start with a revolver, then. A .38, or a .357 if you can afford it."

"I can," said Lorraine, thinking of the thousand FBI-provided dollars in her account.

"We have a shooting-range in the back, and I believe the instructor is on duty right now. Ten dollars range-fee, another five for eye-and-ear-protection rental. May I see your license, please?"

It took a moment to realize that he meant her driver's license. He examined it, made a quick call to a police number, handed back the license and gave her some forms to complete. As simply as that, Lorraine found herself the new owner of a large chrome-plated .357 magnum revolver. Of course the holster cost more, and the 'training ammunition', and the 'serious ammunition', and the paper targets and ear-plugs and goggle-rental fee and range fee, so that by the time she made her way to the shooting-range more than half the money in the account was gone.

It doesn't matter. I have a job, Lorraine reminded herself, as she went to talk to the instructor.

The instructor was gentle and patient and very thorough. By the end of an hour Lorraine had memorized the safety rules, learned how to string up a target and aim, learned the difference between ".38 wad-cutter practice rounds" (bang) and "half-clad hollow-point .357 serious rounds" (BANG), and learned not to flinch when firing either. By the time she'd used up the 50 practice rounds, she managed to hit the target reliably within eight inches of the center—which, the instructor informed her, was very good for a complete beginner.

She also learned that it was perfectly legal in this state to walk around with a pistol in a holster, worn openly on her belt, so long as she didn't go into a post office.

Feeling weary, elated and slightly unreal, Lorraine unlocked the door to her apartment and stepped in, acutely conscious of the weight of the gun on one hip and the holstered cell-phone on the other.

She was three steps into the apartment when she realized that something was wrong.

It might have been something as subtle as a changed scent, or possibly the discarded newspaper wasn't in quite the same position, or perhaps the window-shade was half an inch higher than she'd left it, but Lorraine knew—beyond question or doubt— that someone else had been in the apartment. She knew it as surely as she had known that day in Chicago.

A quick glance showed her that nobody was in the all-in-one main room. Almost without thinking, she drew the pistol and held it down by her waist as she tiptoed to the tiny bathroom. A quick shove opened the door, revealing that no one was there, either.

Whoever it was had come and gone, leaving almost no trace.

Lorraine slumped on the sofa-bed, thoughts whirling. Could the Mafia have found her, already? How? Could it have been the FBI, checking up on her without warning—and, supposedly, without her knowledge? Could it have been something as harmless as a snoopy apartment manager hoping to peek through her underwear? She dragged herself off the sofa, went to the bureau and checked the underwear-drawer.

Nothing seemed to be out of place. Her little store of jewelry was untouched.

Chewing her lip, Lorraine went to the apartment phone and dialed Berringer's number.

The agent answered on the second ring. "Oh, Lorraine!" she cooed eagerly. "Where have you been?"

Caller ID, Lorraine guessed. *She knows this number.* "Why, how did you know I'd been out?"

"I've been trying to phone you all morning. Where were you?"

"Out shopping," Lorraine temporized. *It could be a lie. It could have been her that visited.* "I've bought a cell-phone, so you can reach me when I'm out."

"Oh, you have to be careful with those things, dear. They're radios, you know; somebody could use radio equipment to listen in."

"I'll just be careful what I say, then, Aunt Dianne. Ah, here's the number." She rattled it off. "I'll probably be out tomorrow, too. I, uh, want to look over the local churches."

There was a moment's silence, then: "Just be careful, dear. You know the drill."

"Of course I do." Lorraine had to be careful not to snap.

A few more meaningless pleasantries, and 'Aunt Dianne' consented to hang up and let her go. Lorraine thought for a long moment, then dialed the operator and asked for information.

It took 20 minutes to arrange for calls to the apartment phone to be transferred to her cell-phone. It took another half-hour for Lorraine to pack up everything she'd brought with her, stuff it back in the duffel bag, and drag it down to the car. Last, she looked up the address of the nearest branch of the bank that held her account.

All the way to the bank she drove slowly, watching to see if any vehicle followed hers, finding none that did. She drew all but $50 out of the account, took it in cash, and asked for a phonebook. A few minutes' searching gave her the address of a nearby motel, one with an attached restaurant, which had no objections to cash customers and took reservations over the phone. Lorraine left just as the bank was closing, and drove to the motel by back streets as much as possible, watching for tailing cars all the way. She checked in quickly, got a brief meal at the motel's restaurant, went back to her room and locked herself in.

She spent the rest of the afternoon and evening watching television until she was tired enough to sleep, and tucked the gun under her pillow before she finally dared to lie down.

***

This time, when the nightmare came, she pulled out her own gun and shot the hit-man dead. Then she leaped over his downed body to run out the door into the sunlit desert, where the horse waited. This time it wasn't a black mare, but the light-chestnut stallion. Again, she was trying to climb on his back when the dream faded.

She woke shortly after dawn, paid her bill to the yawning desk clerk, and drove out by the low early light toward Treemark Arabian Farm.

3.

THE DOOR OPENED within five seconds of Lorraine's ringing the bell, revealing the butler and Dr. Treemark, who stared at her silently for an instant, then gave her a discreet smile and waved her in. Lorraine hauled her bags into the entryway and turned to watch as the butler closed the door behind her. She noted, with relief, that the butler also closed the deadbolt lock. He turned to reach for her duffel bag, but Lorraine moved away from him. She'd carry that herself, thank you.

Treemark stepped forward, still wearing that slight but reassuring smile. "Let's get you settled in, first," he said, half-turning back toward the livingroom. Lorraine hefted her bag and followed where he led.

As they passed through the livingroom Lorraine saw that, this time, the guests weren't costumed or masked. A man and a woman sat on two of the nearby couches, facing each other across a coffee table. The man was very tall and slender, looking no older than Dr. Treemark, with short dark-brown hair and hazel eyes set in a long, fine-boned face. He wore a bulky blue sweater over casual dark slacks, and a long coat lay beside him, carelessly draped across the couch. His expression, as he glanced at Lorraine, was polite and thoughtful, mild and somewhat distant.

The woman, by contrast, was a striking blonde. Her corn-yellow hair was pulled up into a loose knot, held with a blue ribbon that matched her keen and watchful eyes. Her profile was almost straight from hairline to nose-tip, and her oval face ended in a delicately pointed chin. She wore a soft white long-skirted dress, whose lines could only be called Classical. She looked, Lorraine considered, like an ancient Greek goddess—and clearly dressed for that effect.

Treemark paused to make introductions. "Ms. Farrier, this is Dr. Benjamin Long and Ms. Helen Wood. Friends, this is Lorraine Farrier, my new employee."

Lorraine managed a quick "How do you do?" The other two replied with overlapping "Pleased to meet you" politeness that seemed sincere but revealed nothing.

"This way," said Treemark, moving on.

He led Lorraine down the familiar corridor and into the assigned room. Lorraine dropped her duffel bag on the bed, wondering if she'd have time to unpack immediately.

Instead, he handed her a key on a simple ring and waved her back toward the door.

"There'll be time to unpack later," he said. "For now, let's get the examination out of the way. Would you prefer myself or Dr. Long?"

Lorraine, pausing to lock the bedroom door, decided she'd rather deal with Dr. Treemark, whom she knew at least a little. "You'll be fine," she said. "How long will this take?"

"Perhaps an hour," Treemark shrugged. "Afterward I'll give you the complete tour of the house and grounds. Walter and Steven can show you through the stables. This way, please."

He led her back through the vast livingroom where Long and Wood, busy in conversation, barely glanced and nodded at her as she passed. Dr. Long, Lorraine guessed, was probably the colleague Treemark had mentioned yesterday. Helen Wood was something of a mystery: just a guest, Treemark's lover, or another colleague? He hadn't called her a doctor… *Plenty of time to learn,* Lorraine thought, as she followed Treemark into his office.

The rear door of the office led into an examination room, with a small bathroom to the side and an X-ray room beyond, and apparently a complete state-of-the-art laboratory beyond that. The physical exam was incredibly thorough, including a pelvic—which Lorraine endured only because it was professional and brief—head to foot X-rays, and samples of practically everything.

"I'd love to do an EEG, an EKG and metabolism test too," Treemark confessed when they were back in his office, "But I mustn't let myself get carried away."

"A man in love with his work," Lorraine guessed.

"True," he smiled. "If you'll indulge me with just one more test..." He handed her a stack of Inkblot cards.

Lorraine sighed, but dutifully looked at the cards and described what they suggested: a lady in extravagant Victorian costume, a dog admiring its reflection in a pool, a flying hawk seen from below, two armored knights jousting, a fruit-bat nipping a pear, two winged fairies quarreling over a flower, an exotic butterfly, an elaborate opera-mask, fighting dragons...

"You," said Treemark, as he took back the cards, "Have the soul of a Romantic."

Lorraine frowned at the word. "Artist, rather. If only my paintings would sell."

"It's always possible," said Treemark, rising smoothly to his feet. "I'll analyze the tests and give you the results after dinner.

For now, let's complete the tour."

***

A tour was what it took. The parts of the house Lorraine saw included a small gym, sauna, small outdoor pool—with Jacuzzi and massage-table on the side—a library with computer, a game-room with large-screen television and entertainment system, a walk-in linen closet, a crafts-room with a huge work-table and countless cabinets, and a tool-room with an impressive array of hardware. There were doors and another elegant corridor that Treemark passed by without comment, and Lorraine guessed that they led to other bedrooms. She also guessed that there was another office than the one in the clinic.

As they passed through the livingroom Lorraine noted other guests, dressed in ordinary clothes and unmasked, quietly leaving. The party was clearly over. Lorraine fleetingly wished she'd seen some of it; it must have been quite a spectacle, with all those costumes: a classic Masked Ball, perhaps.

Working his way outward, Treemark led her through a glass-roofed solarium filled with exotic plants, with two tall thick posts set in the middle whose purpose Lorraine couldn't guess. Outside, he pointed out the tool-shed and feed-barn before leading her to the main stables. There he handed her over to the red-headed groom, whom he introduced as Wally, and left her there.

"I'm Lorraine," she said, extending her hand.

Wally took and shook it, looking bemused. "Well, this is the tack-room over here..." he began.

This proved to be a more interesting tour. There were six brood-mares, all with fuzzy long-legged foals, the young stallion she'd seen earlier, an older stallion—storm-cloud gray, named Overcast, very calm and dignified—and then there was the riding stock: a raven-black mare named Leila whom Wally swore could jump incredible heights, a mahogany-chestnut mare being trained for 5-gaited competition, a tall dark-bay gelding being trained for dressage, a dark-gray mare—Overcast's daughter—who "bid fair to be a competition-class cutting-horse", a sandy-bay gelding that Wally claimed was a first-rate hunter, and two matching red-bay mares that could double as "trail horses or a carriage team". Wally was clearly proud of his charges.

Steven, a wiry middle-aged black man, was in the tack-room absorbed with making meticulous repairs on a hunting-bridle. He barely glanced up and nodded when Wally and Lorraine came by. "He can make a first-rate saddle from scratch," Wally explained, "Nobody knows more about leather and tack than he does."

Wally also detailed the features of the stable from one end to the other, pointing out the fire-extinguishers and the intercom as well. The only thing he didn't mention was the tall cabinet by the front door. Lorraine assumed it held the auxiliary first-aid kit.

Her first task, of course, was leading the horses out to the paddock so she could clean the stalls and haul the sweepings to the compost pit. *That's where every groom starts,* she sighed, getting busy with rake, fork, shovel and cart. *No worse than I expected.* The work was no harder than hauling heavy book-cartons around, and smelled no worse than cleaning-fluid. *I could,* reflected, *do a lot worse.*

***

Treemark returned to the clinic office and sat down to study the tests, grateful for the exquisite machines that could run bio-chemical analyses in an hour. The blood-test first: he already knew what he would find—that subtle variation that no one else would think to look for—but he read it anyway, just to be absolutely certain. Yes, Lorraine was one of his kind, beyond a shadow of a doubt. The rest was interesting too, matching something else that he'd observed, confirming the simple psychological test.

He'd seen, from the moment she entered the door, that she was fleeing something. Not afraid—no, not her—but wary, guarded, quietly suspicious of everyone and everything. The muscle tensions, the body language, were those of a wild creature that knew she wandered in strange territory and predators were somewhere near. Unconsciously she took care not to be trapped, to keep her escape-routes open, to keep out of reach unless absolutely necessary, ready to run at a moment's notice. Yet she displayed no fear.

And no particular desire, either. Nowhere in her thought or action was there any awareness of her own sensuality, nor hint of any other emotion either. She could be an ascetic, a Vulcan, an Ice Queen—yet she had an artist's eye for beauty. The passion was there but it was locked down, tightly controlled or sleeping, never allowed to rise up and swamp her iron self-control.

A wild mare, or a warrior in the field? Which predominated: her bone-deep passion for freedom—remembering that conversation about the chestnut stallion—or her soldier-like watchfulness for enemy action? In either case, the result was the same: she could not trust, could never surrender control to anyone or anything, even to her own depths of feeling.

How had she come to this? More vital, how could he heal her of it? Healed she must be, and quickly, to face what he knew was her destiny. Still Uninitiated, she was aging like any mortal, and no longer very young. She could not afford to wait ten years, or even five, for an easy and gentle approach to her own heart. The treatment must be hard and fast, but he had seen that she had the strength to survive it.

He would have to begin very soon.

***

When the last stall was clean and replenished with sawdust and straw, Wally showed Lorraine the way to the stable wash-room and then to the kitchen for lunch. She noticed that Wally and Steven pulled off their stable-boots before entering the house, which made sense, so she copied them. The polished yellow floor-tiles felt cool under her stockinged feet, and the sturdy wooden chairs around the long kitchen table were shaped gracefully enough to support her tired back.

Lunch was an excellent cream-of-asparagus soup, with classic corned-beef sandwiches on fresh-baked bread, washed down with an equally home-made red fruit punch, and Lorraine was surprised to see that the butler also doubled as the cook. He seemed happier at this work, or at least more lively, and she took care to comment that the food was very good.

"Daniel used to be a chef," Steven spoke up. "Worked for a big hotel. Quit it to come here."

Daniel, the butler/cook, seemed mildly offended. "Dr. Treemark," he said firmly, "Is a far better master than that string of wretched managers."

"Master"? Lorraine wondered. Perhaps that was just a common phrase where the man came from; he did have that ghost of a British accent. "Well, their loss is our gain."

The others chuckled knowingly, trading glances. Lorraine wondered what in-joke she was missing.

After lunch Lorraine found herself promoted to exercise-rider. Wally collected the red-bay mares, took one and gave her the other, leaving her to saddle and bridle her own mount. Next, he gave her a safety-helmet and showed her the way to the exercise-ring. This was a larger circular track furnished with half a dozen adjustable jumping-rails, all set low. Wally led the pattern: around the ring inside the jumps at a walk, then a trot, then a canter, and finally out to the jumps themselves. It had been years since Lorraine had ridden over jumps, but she remembered the basics of position and grip, and the mare seemed positively eager to show her the way. After the second jump, Lorraine was caught up in the exhilaration of riding. She took the willing mare three times around the ring of jumps, and would have done more but that Wally told her to stop.

"She's fit to go back to the pasture," he said, "And there's others need the work."

They returned to the paddock, caught two more horses to saddle and bridle, turned the bay mares loose and repeated the process.

By the time the last horses had been ridden through their exercises, when Steven came to help bring them all back to the barn for supper, Lorraine was exhausted and sweaty and saddlesore, sure she'd have ferocious cramps in the morning, and happier than she could recall feeling in years. She helped with the feeding, noting that each horse had slightly different rations according to a chart on the wall, and headed toward the kitchen door for her stablehand's supper.

"Oh, not that way!" Wally insisted. "Go wash and change first. Dinner's in the real diningroom, at seven."

Not dinner at eight? Lorraine chuckled to herself, nonetheless taking off her boots to carry them away to her room. The house was empty now, she noticed: cars and guests gone, leaving the place as polished and hushed as a museum. She was getting the distinct impression that Treemark was the scion of a very wealthy family, eager to make something of himself, certainly, but with no intention of giving up the family's traditional lifestyle.

So even the stablehands dress for dinner. She had a long violet skirt and a nice white blouse, both soft enough to consider semi-formal, some dark pantyhose and a pair of plain black low-heeled dance-shoes. They'd do, especially with the addition of her simple silver necklace. After all, she hadn't been told to dress *up*, and she was still part of the working class.

When she unlocked the room and stepped in, she saw that her duffel bag was exactly as she'd left it. *No snoops here,* she smiled to herself. Of course this meant she'd have to unpack her own bag, but that was no great chore. First, she'd try out that nice big private bathtub.

***

At five minutes to seven Lorraine strolled out to the livingroom, hoping to find Wally or Steven and get some clues from them on how to proceed. She found them, now wearing light slacks and long-sleeved knitted shirts, draped comfortably on one of the sofas, with Dr. Long and Ms. Wood calmly occupying another. Wood was smoking an aromatic black cigarette that Lorraine recognized as an exotic foreign brand. There was a small assortment of half-finished drinks on the coffee-table, and Treemark stood near a cabinet by the wall mixing another. He saw her approach, and smiled.

"Ah, Lorraine," he asked cheerfully. "What would you like to drink?"

"Er, excuse me?" Lorraine fumbled, caught off-guard.

"We use our first names here. What would you like?"

"Hmm, scotch over ice—Brian." It wasn't her first choice—which would have been a good amber beer—but it was all she could think of that fit the setting.

He smiled and obliged. Lorraine took her glass, padded to the coffee-table and settled quietly on a third couch. If Treemark wanted to pretend that they were all social equals here, she'd oblige. Besides, the Scotch was very good.

Dr. Long turned to give her an almost shy grin. "So how are you getting on with the horses?" he asked.

"I love them," Lorraine admitted. "They're very gentle and eager, wonderfully easy to ride."

"Ah, but you haven't tried Overcast or Gold Eagle yet." Wally laughed. "Eagle barely knows what a bridle is, and the old stud has his own notions about the best way to get anywhere. No one but Brian can really do anything with them."

"Eagle will do well enough once he's trained," said Treemark, approaching with his own drink.

"Overcast's all right," Steven spoke up. "You just have to remember that he wants to run and jump."

"Treats every fence and hedge like a goal-line," Wally added.

Lorraine noticed how similar they all sounded, as if they'd been chatting together for years. *One big happy family. Interesting.*

Then Helen turned to her. "Do you have plans to become a show-rider, Lorraine?" she asked, voice as mellow as the tones of a viola.

"I haven't had much time to think about it," Lorraine answered calmly. "Doc—Brian has suggested I paint portraits of horses, see if I can make a career of it."

"Excellent thought," said Helen, glancing archly at Treemark. "I know several owners who'd pay higher commissions for portraits of their horses than portraits of their wives."

"If you mean whom I think," he replied, "The horses are far handsomer subjects."

Everyone chuckled politely. Lorraine wondered how long it would take for the witty banter to turn into sniping gossip.

Just then a maid—or at least a middle-aged woman in a large cook's apron—came out of the kitchen and announced that dinner was ready.

"Thank you, Madge!" said Treemark, heading for the diningroom. "We were getting seriously hungry."

The others rose and followed, Lorraine trailing last to watch the others.

The table was laid with a plain blue tablecloth and simple settings for eight.

Treemark, as expected, went to the head of the table. Helen settled at his right, Benjamin Long next to her. Wally and Steven took the chairs on the left, and Lorraine seated herself beside them. A moment later Daniel came out of the kitchen, carrying a large bottle of pale-pink wine.

"A good white Zinfandel tonight," he announced, pouring into Treemark's glass first.

"I've never met a bad white Zinfandel," Benjamin noted.

"Then you haven't tried it in Mexico," said Steven, making a face.

Lorraine said nothing, only watched as Daniel made his way around the table, filling every wineglass, even at the two unoccupied places, with a subtle flourish. When he was done, he took the now empty bottle back to the kitchen. Lorraine tried a sip, and found that it was indeed very good.

Next, Daniel and Madge came out together, holding respectively a steaming soup tureen and an enormous bowl full of salad. They set their burdens along the centerline of the table, then sat down at the two empty seats.

"It's a mild white Polish borscht tonight," Daniel announced, raising his glass, a"And I think you'll like our experiment with the salad."

"I always love your salads," said Helen, as she reached for the bowl.

Lorraine puzzled at how Daniel unbent at dinner, stopped being the perfect butler—or cook—and became one of the crowd. Curious. He acted less like a servant here than like an artist giving a gallery showing to a small but exclusive clientele.

Steven, who was closest, likewise reached for the soup tureen. He pulled it close, served himself, then passed it on. Helen, Lorraine saw, was doing the same with the salad.

Nicely egalitarian, Lorraine considered, trying to understand the subtle social relationships. Treemark was the owner, the host, the employer, the undisputed master of the household, but he made some effort to disguise that, and distinctions between the rest were blurred. Was this a standard aristocrat's manor playing at equality, or a truly communal household with Treemark as the public figurehead?

All she could tell for certain was that some game, other than owner-guest-servant, was going on here beneath the surface.

Puzzling over that, Lorraine took her turn with the salad and soup. Since the thick soup was still steaming, she started on the salad first. It was fluffy with endive, romaine and kale, sprinkled thickly with chopped tomatoes, purple salad onions, and a surprising number of almonds. The dressing was an interesting variation on spicy-Italian, and the whole combination was very, very good. She finished in short order and turned her attention to the soup, which was likewise excellent

Scattered conversation flowed past her, mostly concerning the horses, with some asides into the availability of certain groceries. Madge grumbled at the difficulty of finding good kohlrabi at this time of year, and argued with Daniel over where the best suppliers might be found. Steven observed that it was easier to find exotic horse-feeds, and Daniel speculated about rising prices of good timothy-hay. Helen and Treemark worried over a broodmare with a sore ankle. Benjamin and Lorraine concentrated on their food and replied only when questioned, which wasn't often.

When the bowls were empty, Daniel and Madge rose and took the dishes back to the kitchen. A moment later they returned with the main course: a sliced lean pork-roast, cinnamon-spiced applesauce, and a platter of baked acorn squash pooled with a sauce of melted butter and brown sugar. Again, the dishes were set down and then passed.

Lorraine soon lost track of the conversation in pure enjoyment of the food. She couldn't help wondering what idiocy the unknown hotel-manager had committed to lose a chef as good as Daniel.

"Ah, Lorraine?" Madge caught her ear. "Wednesday is laundry-day. You can leave your room open, or just leave the laundry-bag out in the hall for me. You'll have everything back by Friday noon, latest."

"Thank you," said Lorraine, wondering if there was an underlying meaning to that. Was the maid/housekeeper chiding her for leaving her room locked? *Chide away, then.* She wasn't about to leave her room open so that anyone could find her gun, never mind the cell-phone. It occurred to her that she ought to check with Agent Berringer soon, just to allay suspicions.

Dessert was coffee and some sweet apricot tarts, very small and only one apiece, for which Lorraine was grateful; she'd stuffed herself shamelessly at dinner. When Daniel got up to collect the plates, the others rose also and drifted slowly into the livingroom. Treemark caught up to Lorraine, asked her to return to the clinic office to discuss her physical, and paused only to pour drinks for both of them.

Once in the comfortable little office, Lorraine relaxed into her stuffed chair and sipped slowly at her scotch, debating whether to pull off her shoes while she waited. Treemark spread out the papers and x-ray prints on his desk and frowned at them thoughtfully.

"I've noticed a few problems," he commented. "First, you have some small cavities in your teeth that need filling. We can't do that here; you'll have to go into town for it."

Lorraine remembered that 'medical and dental' clause in her contract. "I'm sure you can suggest someone competent," she considered.

"I can. Next problem: you have some ribs and spinal bones slightly out of alignment. They'll need some chiropractic adjustment soon. I can do that tomorrow, if you'd like."

"All right," Lorraine shrugged, considering the numerous small aches that soaking in the tub hadn't erased. She took another sip of the iced Scotch.

"Third..." Treemark gave her a thoughtful look. "How long have you been frigid?"

"Whuh—" Lorraine all but choked on her drink. "Where did you get that idea?!"

"From the test results." He pointed to a string of letters and numbers. "There's nothing physically wrong, but you respond to tactile sensation as if you were wearing body-armor. Your emotional responses are almost nil. For a healthy woman, you have the lowest libido I've ever seen. How long has this been going on?"

Lorraine didn't bother answering that question. "Doctor, I'm your employee—not your patient," she almost snapped. "I don't see how any of this is relevant to my work." *Or any of your business!*

"You're my employee," he agreed, "And I'm responsible for your health-care. If I see a problem, it's my duty to warn you about it."

"But there *is* no problem!"

"Ah, anger." Treemark smiled. "Thank God you can feel that much. How long has it been since you felt anything else?"

Lorraine abruptly remembered that shock of grief when she'd seen Jack Palumbo's body on the floor. *Only five days...* No, she wouldn't tell him about that. But there was something more recent. "Just yesterday, I was delighted to get this job. Just today, I really had fun exercising the horses."

"That's reason for hope. Now, how long since you were last in love?"

Oh, please! Lorraine sighed, remembering that the man was a sex therapist, and doctors tended to see sickness, especially their own specialties, everywhere they looked. "Look, Doctor, I like sex as much as anyone else. It's just that there's no one I'm interested in right now."

"And how long since you were interested in anyone?"

Since Ronnie. It took surprising effort to dredge up the memory. "Two years." *That's not too long, really...* But she remembered thinking about it, about losing interest, only five days ago—just before the murder, in fact.

"Two years?" he repeated, "With nobody, and nothing?"

"Maybe I'm waiting for the real thing," Lorraine growled. "I don't believe in Romance anymore; it's a lie. There's sex and there's friendship, and when the two come together you've got honest love. All the rest is bull."

Treemark stared at her for a long moment. "And how deep does friendship have to go," he asked quietly, "Before you can feel desire?"

Lorraine had to stop and think about that. Bill Carminski, she remembered, was a handsome hunk and a good friend, good enough to trust with her life, and certainly willing if she'd ever shown interest...but she hadn't felt any twinge of passion for him. "I don't know," she admitted. "I just haven't found anybody..."

"In two years?"

"...No."

"Lorraine, what did that to you?"

Oh, hell! "Ronnie," she snapped. "My last lover. Living proof that Romance isn't worth a broken rubber."

"You were pregnant?!" Treemark caught the inference.

"And I told him, and he took off with the bank account. After five years of fine talk and fumbly sex, that's all he was worth."

"I see. And...what became of the child?"

"I had an abortion." Lorraine took a large mouthful of her drink. "Without his paycheck to help, I couldn't make the rent. I wouldn't breed what I couldn't feed—and damned if I'd breed off the likes of him!" There was only a little left of the scotch. She finished it.

"So you learned not to trust," Treemark concluded. "Not men, not Romance...not even your own feelings."

Lorraine shrugged. "Men vary a lot. Romance is crap. Feelings have no sense; they're just reactions. Best to hunt with your common sense first, before you let your feelings run. That is, if I wanted to hunt at all."

"In the natural way of things," Treemark said quietly, "You would want to hunt."

Lorraine had no answer for that. She knew she wasn't too old for it, that the world was full of better men than Ronnie, and that the best revenge she could have on him was to take up with a far better man and be happy. Why hadn't she even tried?

"Lorraine, you must learn to trust again. Life sends us enemies enough, sorrows enough, that we need all the...allies, and all the happiness, we can find. I don't think you want to be a woman of iron all your life. Life can be very long."

Lorraine remembered just what enemies she had. "You have to be very careful with trust."

"And you have to be able to do it, even trust completely, even let your feelings sweep you away at times."

Disaster, she thought, remembering Ronnie, remembering who was after her now. "You can get more than hurt, doing that; you can get killed."

Treemark raised an eyebrow. "Are you living in a war-zone, then?"

"Not here," she answered quickly. "This place is safe." *I think.*

He gave her another long look. "Who's after you?" he asked softly.

Lorraine flinched. *Gave away too much! Think—* "A damned

stalker! I thought I'd left him behind in Chicago, but now I'm not sure. Somebody got into my apartment while I was gone..." Sudden fury seethed in her blood. "If only I knew who it was, or when he's coming! I could set an ambush, put an end to this, instead of having to hide and run."

Treemark watched her intently. "Did you have no allies who could help? No one you could go to? What about your family?"

"Family?" Lorraine snarled, wishing she had a refill for that drink. "My father died nine years ago. My brother's useless, and my mother's worse than useless. My friends— I don't want to put them under siege too." —*any more than they are already.* "And don't even talk to me about the police. I come from Chicago, remember."

Treemark nodded slowly, not taking his eyes off her. "Lorraine, what if I could help? What if I could make you...into a warrior that this stalker couldn't kill? What if you had the power to destroy your enemy? Would you then be able to relax, take off your emotional armor, and trust again?"

Does he mean martial arts? Lorraine wondered, staring at him. *Should I tell him about the gun?* "I don't know," she admitted. "I honestly don't know. I have no idea how I'd feel if I were...Wonder Woman, or anything like it."

Treemark drew a deep breath, as if he'd made a decision. "Come here tomorrow morning, right after breakfast," he said, "And I'll start on turning you into a— a superhero."

"All right," Lorraine smiled. *I need more practice with that gun, and karate lessons wouldn't hurt. He can probably get me a bulletproof vest...* "After breakfast it is."

"Good." He pulled back his chair and stood up. "But breakfast comes early around here. You'd best get to sleep early, too."

Lorraine rose, and picked up her glass. "That won't be difficult," she said. "Another of these and I'll drop like a rock."

"I'll make you one," he promised, "But drink it slowly, while watching TV or reading a boring book."

"TV it is. I can't stand boring books."

Ten minutes later, sitting in the game-room with a drink in her hand and Wally beside her, watching the large-screen television, she wondered if hunting up a book from the library might have been a better idea. There seemed to be nothing on but sitcoms and cop-shows, neither of which held her interest. At least the scotch was good.

*And tomorrow I start martial arts training,*she considered. That was worth putting up with Dr. Treemark, and being psychoana-lyzed at every turn. *If only he didn't have this bee in his bonnet about trust.*

***

Treemark was closing up the liquor-cabinet when he felt Helen slip into the livingroom behind him. "Last chance for a drink," he offered, not turning his head.

"No thank you." Helen slid onto the nearest couch. "How is your little protégé?"

Treemark closed the cabinet doors and turned to face her. "I'll Initiate her tomorrow morning," he said.

"So soon?" Helen raised an elegant eyebrow. "Is this part of your usual obsession, or are you infatuated with her?"

"A little of both, and neither," he said, leaning on the back of the couch. "She has one of the most defensive personalities I've ever seen, and yet no fear. Fury, certainly—and with good rea-son—but no fear. She can become as good a warrior as any of us, good enough to survive those first 12 centuries. I don't need to tell you—"

"No." Helen looked away. "I know how few of us there are."

"And consider this; she's been pregnant once."

Helen whipped her head around to stare at him. "A Conver-gent? Not a Changeling?"

"What else?" Treemark shrugged. "You had no record of her."

"You know there are some I haven't found. God knows what Ishtar was doing all those years, or Legba. There could have been others."

"There's still that pregnancy, proof she's a Convergent."

"If she was telling the truth."

"I'm fairly sure about that. Her anger was genuine."

"And in any case, you want her Initiated as fast as possible." Helen twined her fingers together. "Best lock the doors, then, so she doesn't panic and bolt."

"I don't think she will," said Treemark, letting his eyes rest on the empty fireplace. "She doesn't like running. She has a warrior's heart, if only I can reach it."

"And just how far will you go to reach it?"

"As far as I must."

Helen shook her head and looked toward the darkened win-dows. "I know your methods," she said. "Take care that you don't turn this sword against you while hammering it into shape."

4.

LORRAINE WAS AWAKENED by a loud buzzing nearby, a totally unfamiliar sound. She snapped her eyes open and looked around, recognizing her room in the Treemark house, and finally realized that the noise came from the intercom-phone near the bed. She picked up the receiver and blearily asked: "Wha's happening?"

"Breakfast," replied Daniel's unflappable voice. "We serve breakfast at six in the kitchen, for any who wish to attend." A decisive click revealed that he'd ended the transmission.

"Six in the morning..." Lorraine groaned. Well, this was a farm, after all. The animals would need tending. This was probably a polite way of telling her to get up and go to work. She didn't feel hungry at all, but a cup of coffee would be welcome.

Then she remembered that Treemark had asked to see her after breakfast, to arrange for her martial-arts training. That was a more welcome proposition than raking out stalls. She crawled out of bed and went looking for jeans and a work-shirt.

***

Half an hour later, still holding a half-empty cup of coffee, Lorraine knocked on the clinic's office door. Treemark opened it, waved her in and pointed wordlessly to the nearest chair. The back of it, she saw, was draped with several sheets of newspaper: enough that she had to sit on the first six inches of the seat. *For punching practice?* she wondered.

Treemark, wearing a somber abstracted expression, went to his desk and opened a drawer at its side. "It's a sad commentary on us," he said, "That for the last 2000 years, most Initiations have been even cruder than this."

While Lorraine tried to make sense of that, Treemark pulled his hand up, fast. She barely had time to realize that he was holding a gun before he fired.

Lorraine felt the impact low and left in her chest, knew she'd been struck in the heart, but had no time to think of anything else before the blackness swooped down.

***

She was aware of pulling a deep breath, then a faint echo of pain below her left breast, then an odd feeling in the air—like heat, like pressure, like electric static, like none of these. Somehow it conveyed a sense of presence, as if she weren't alone.

Lorraine pulled her eyes open to see that she was not in bed but in the clinic office, sitting in one of the soft chairs facing the desk. Treemark sat at the desk, hands interlaced, soberly watching her. An ornate knife lay at one side of the desk, weighing down a small stack of papers. Lorraine wondered why she was here, what had happened.

The next second, she remembered.

She flinched, stared at Treemark, and then looked down at her shirt. There was a small ragged hole in it, surrounded by sticky drying blood. Lorraine stared at it for slow-turning seconds before she thought to reach under the shirt and feel her skin. There was more drying blood, but the flesh under it was smooth and unbroken.

"Welcome to the truth behind the legends," said Treemark. "Welcome to Valhalla, or Olympus, or Elfland—your choice."

"This...makes...no sense," was all she could think.

"Look at the back of your shirt," he said. "Look at the papers behind you."

Lorraine twisted about, and pulled her shirt around her until she could reach the back of it. A brief probing with her fingers told her that, yes, there was another hole there—a hole surrounded by drying blood. *In one side and out the other...* She turned further, and looked at the sheaf of newspapers on the chair-back behind her.

Yes, there was a small hole drilled through the layers of paper, its border tinged with familiar red. With almost-numb fingers she riffled the papers, and yes, a flattened bullet-slug fell out of them and onto the chair's seat. Lorraine picked it up and stared at it.

"Yes," Treemark said calmly. "Clean through."

"You shot me," she whispered.

"Yes, and you came back to life. Now you're virtually immortal."

Lorraine struggled to make herself think. The evidence was undeniable. She'd been shot through the heart, and now was whole and alive again.

"Legends", he said... She knew of a legend like that.

She remembered that she'd worn her silver-chain necklace last night, and hadn't taken it off when she went to bed. She raised a hand to the chain and felt that it was still there. It wasn't burning her skin. What did that leave?

"...Sunlight?" she asked.

Treemark blinked, and then caught the reference. "Oh. No,

you're not a vampire. At least, not unless you develop a perverse fascination with blood." He reached into one of the left-side desk drawers and came up with a flask, which he handed to her. "And I think you prefer the taste of whiskey. Try some."

Lorraine managed to get the top off the flask, and gulped the first mouthful fast. It was scotch again. The taste was unchanged, and the burn was enough to make her cough. She ventured another mouthful, and her dizziness faded.

"You shot me!" she accused.

"Would you have preferred a knife, sword or arrow?" he smiled wryly. "A lot of us have been Initiated that way, in ages past."

"You *shot* me!" Indignation was easier to deal with than this madness.

Treemark sighed, pulled the gun out of a desk drawer and offered it to her, butt first. "Would you like to return the favor?" he asked. "At my age, I should revive in five minutes or less."

Lorraine only shook her head and shuddered. She was going to have to face the incredible facts. "What are we, then?" she managed to say, handing back the flask.

"An extremely rare mutation," said Treemark, setting down the gun and putting the flask's cap back on. "From this moment on, you won't age. Sickness, injury, even poisoning, will afflict you only for minutes—and then you'll recover. You will also be extremely hard to kill. Internal injuries, even technically fatal ones, will heal within an hour. If you lose a limb, it will grow back in a few years. You will also find that you have psychic ability, and it will increase with time."

"...How?"

"As near as I can determine the mutation began at least as early as the Late Stone Age, and it's bizarre enough that I could almost believe it was an experiment by visiting aliens. It seems to process large amounts of some obscure form of energy—psychic energy, I suspect—and very quickly, following the genetic patterns of our cells. That's what allows us to regenerate."

He picked up the knife and deliberately cut his arm with it. As the blood flowed, Treemark calmly counted the seconds.

As Lorraine watched, the blood-flow stopped. Tiny sparks of electric-violet light flickered and seethed in the cut, then faded. Treemark brushed away the blood, showing that the wound was gone and the skin was fresh and whole. "Regeneration," he said. "Practical immortality."

"We...can't die?"

"Oh, there are ways: enough heat to completely destroy the body, fast—like a nuclear explosion, or falling into molten steel. Or total dismemberment, or beheading, or complete destruction of the head and upper spine. Avoid those, and you can live...well, forever."

"...What?"

"As near as I can tell, we are the origin of the legend of Elves—and probably the ancient gods, and divine heroes as well. Certainly, some of us posed as gods in ancient times."

Lorraine nodded slowly, trying to take this in. *Proof. Need proof...* She reached out her hand for the knife.

Without a word, Treemark handed it to her.

Despite the pretty carving on its handle, and the quartz set in its pommel, Lorraine saw that it was a perfectly functional knife: slender-bladed and very sharp. She pulled back her sleeve, set the edge against her forearm, and pulled.

The sharp pain made her grunt. An instant later, the blood came welling up. Lorraine dropped the knife on the desk and stared at the bleeding cut. *Real. No trick.*

But she had to watch, see it all. She wiped blood away from the wound, then licked it clean. Yes, there were the raw edges of the cut. It was definitely real.

As she watched, the violet sparks flared in the wound. They tickled. Under them, she could see flesh growing back. It grew as fast as—she struggled for a comparison—wax dripping down the side of a lit candle. In seconds, the cut healed. A ghost of the pain lingered for a few seconds more, then faded. Lorraine stared at the restored skin, tasting her own blood on her tongue, and knew it was real.

"...Elves?" she whispered.

"Elves, gods, immortals—mutants." He shrugged. "There was a colony of us in ancient Britain once; as nearly as I can tell, it was destroyed at least 2000 years ago. The gods of Valhalla and Olympus may have been other colonies. It's difficult to say, since only legends remain. Our psychic ability, variable as it is, would have looked like magic to primitive peoples..."

Lorraine took several deep breaths. Now that the shock was wearing off, she felt amazingly alive—strong, healthy, almost crackling with energy. In fact, she couldn't remember the last time she'd felt this good. And now that her head was clear, she had a thousand questions—one in particular.

"Why did you shoot me?"

"Initiation," said Treemark. "For some reason, the gene can be triggered only by a sudden shock, violent enough to stop the heart—and keep it stopped. That much we've always known. I suspect that in ancient times there was a ritual, a ceremony for it. That would explain myths of human sacrifices, gods who died and revived. Ancient Greek mythology has several tales of semi-divine heroes—and heroines—who died and then rose up immortal. The zodiac is full of them. And there are some similar Welsh myths…" He shook his head angrily. "So much of our history, our knowledge, has been lost—and so many of our kind, too."

"I was born like this, and didn't know?"

"Very few of us know, until Initiation—or even after. We can sense, recognize, the Uninitiated, but they can't sense us. Certainly your own parents didn't know. No one knew, until you ran into me."

That reminder of the here-and-now brought Lorraine back to practicalities. "Is this what you meant when you said you'd...make me into a...an invulnerable warrior?"

"Yes." Treemark smiled. "Your stalker won't know how to kill you. But he can still hurt you, defeat you, unless you learn the martial arts. Yes, you'll still need training—extensive training. I'll provide it."

Lorraine nodded slowly, trying to adjust to the stunning knowledge. "I...need time to take it all in..."

"Take the morning off. Wander around the farm, meditate, and think about what you'd like to do for the next hundred years. Think about how you want to live your life."

"Yes..." Lorraine got up, a little clumsily, and wandered toward the door. *...The next hundred years? Longer? Just as I am?* She probed her teeth with her tongue and found a familiar rough spot. No, the Initiation hadn't filled up her cavities. A glance at her hands, at the faint lines in her wrists, told her that it hadn't made her skin rose-petal smooth, either. She was as she had been, but now she wouldn't change.

As she passed through the door to the living room, she noticed that the feeling of warmth/pressure/static faded. She glanced back toward Treemark, and saw him smile in understanding.

"Yes, that's what happens when our individual energy-fields overlap," he said. "That's how we feel each other's presence. It's also the first of the psychic abilities to develop."

Lorraine nodded, and moved on.

Further into the living room, she felt the warmth/pressure /static sense growing again, but now it had a slightly different... flavor, was all she could think. It came, she saw now, from where Helen sat at one of the coffee tables. The woman caught her eye, and smiled knowingly.

Her too! Lorraine realized. No wonder the woman had re-minded her of a Greek goddess; she had probably been one.

Dazed, Lorraine walked on—out through the dining-area, past the kitchen, where a still different staticky feeling alerted her to Madge's presence even as she saw her.

Another! Are they all...everybody in this house? That, she real-ized, must be the secret they all shared, the underlying hidden relationship of the household. Economic status had very little to do with it. *A colony of Elves. Olympus in the desert.*

She didn't have to ask why these people were so secretive. Even without that tale of the destruction of the ancient British colony, she could imagine what would happen if someone like the FBI, or the Mafia, ever learned the truth, ever got its hands on the...Elves. She shivered. Yes, this was indeed the first day of the rest of her life—and a very different life it would have to be.

Lorraine walked on, not noticing where her feet were going.

Eventually her rambling footsteps took her out into the patio-garden. The sound of voices alerted her to the presence of other people, but this time there was no feel of presence. Intrigued, she walked toward the voices.

At the edge of the garden labored a trio of gardeners, all in work-suits bearing the label of a landscaping company. *Not...Elves,* Lorraine realized, strolling toward them.

Not quite knowing how she did it, she stretched/reached inter-nally, trying to feel their presence. Not until she passed within arm's length of the nearest man did she feel anything, and that was very slight, muted, and vague. *Mortals,* she understood. *Not part of the household.* She wondered if she could learn to feel the presence of all animals too, even plants, in time. Pondering that, she walked on.

As she drifted past the gym she felt that static-tingle again, its tone deeper, more complex. Yet another mutant, another Elf. She peered through the door, and saw Benjamin Long staring back at her. He wore nothing but sweat-pants, and plainly had been working out when he felt the tingle of her presence, for there was a wooden sword in his hand. She saw now what those loose and bulky clothes had disguised; he had a lean build, yes, but the bones were overlaid with muscles like cables, standing stark and visible under the skin. The man was an athlete, and—judging by the wooden sword—a martial artist.

"Are you the martial-arts instructor?" she asked.

Benjamin raised an eyebrow. "So Brian made you one of us?" he countered.

"Just an hour ago. I'm still getting used to the idea." Lorraine stepped into the gym and looked about for a bench to sit on. She still felt a little shaky.

"I thought he might." Benjamin sighed, came over to the bench and sat down beside her. "How much did he tell you?"

Lorraine dutifully recited everything Treemark had said in the office. She noticed that Benjamin was frowning to himself.

"Both too much and too little," he murmured. "Too much of his own theories, and too little of the hard facts. Perhaps he'll get around to the rest eventually. If not..." He shrugged. "You can always talk to Helen."

"Theories?" Lorraine pricked up her ears. "Was he lying to me?"

"Not exactly. Brian has done more research on us than any-one I know, but he trusts too much to legends. He jumps to con-clusions on no more than a few clues."

"Then we're not the Elves, or the ancient gods?"

Benjamin shrugged again. "We could be. Some of us were worshipped as gods in the past... It's not a good idea. His theory about a mutation could be right, though. He developed a blood test that shows subtle differences between our cells and mortals'. It makes more sense than anything else I've heard."

"So how much of all that was true?"

"This history is questionable, but the rest was real enough." He took up her hand and examined it. "What we know for certain is that we're born and grow and age, like ordinary mortals, until a violent death triggers our power—regeneration, immortality and psychic ability."

"I can feel your presence, but I can't read your mind," Lorraine noted.

"That will take awhile to develop. We start by being able to sense each other's presence. In time we attain...empathy, you might call it, first with each other and later with mortals, and even animals. Eventually we reach the point where we can project feelings—emotional and physical states—if not precise thoughts."

"How long does that take?"

"It varies with individual talent, but it's usually a few decades. Much later—" He shrugged. "—Say a few centuries, we get to where we can receive, then project, specific images and thoughts. Again, it varies with talent and training. Some of us have become quite good at casting illusions that way, which is…useful."

"A few centuries!" Lorraine fought down a hysterical laugh. "What comes after that?"

"Telekinesis, the ability to manipulate matter. It usually starts with healing, encouraging the living cells of others to grow and regenerate. I know a few who can do that... including Helen. Training and talent, again. I suspect that next comes the ability to manipulate or move inanimate objects, but I don't know anyone who ever reached that level."

"So, for a few centuries I'll have to make do with nothing but empathy," Lorraine giggled. "I can live with that. How does it work?"

"It doesn't have much range at first, but it expands with time. It's purely receptive for a long time, though." Benjamin's expression grew hard and distant. "With a few exceptions, we can transmit...only when terrified, injured or dying."

Lorraine shivered. "That must be hell."

"Not everyone thinks so." Benjamin looked away, then back. "Being at least minimally psychic, we can pick up the psychic surge of any dying mind—but it's stronger among ourselves. When one of us dies, if another is within his field—close enough to feel his presence—he picks up the surge of the dying man's energy: psychic ability and power, knowledge, some memories...possibly some of his personality. That may have started as a survival characteristic, transferring valuable knowledge to another member of the tribe. Personally, I think that transmitting knowledge while you're alive is ever so much more efficient."

"Agreed," said Lorraine. "So that's how we got the reputation for doing magic?"

"That—and living for centuries, and being hard to kill," Benjamin smiled, "And a few of us have other psychic abilities. Some can 'read' impressions from objects, get glimpses of the future, even teleport. That's enough to set themselves up as kings and queens of Elfland, to use Brian's terms, or even gods among the superstitious."

"Or enough to get themselves burned as witches, during the Middle Ages," Lorraine guessed.

Benjamin shuddered. "Yes. It's really not a good idea."

Lorraine looked down at her hand, thinking that it wouldn't age, wouldn't change, for a hundred years or more. "I should think it's enough to have unending life."

"It should be." Benjamin looked away again. "But there's always someone who's greedy for more, eager to be a little tin god, willing to kill for power."

Lorraine could understand something of that. "Always power-junkies," she agreed. "Always a serpent in Eden."

"And sometimes the snakes take over." Benjamin flinched, then got up quickly. "I should head for the shower. As I said, if you need more information, talk to Helen."

He set his wooden sword on a rack in a corner, picked up a sweatshirt and threw it across his shoulders, waved briefly to Lorraine and walked out.

So there are politics, even among the Elves, Lorraine considered. *Well, nothing's perfect.* Somehow, that made this incredible new life easier to understand. A rumble from her belly reminded her that even elves had to eat, and she'd had nothing but coffee this morning. With a smile, she got up and went looking for the kitchen.

***

It took 20 minutes' fruitless searching before Benjamin thought to look in the stables. Yes, Treemark was there, patiently teaching that empty-headed chestnut stallion to accept a bridle. Benjamin knew better than to interfere, but he waited with increasing impatience until the lesson ended and Steven led the horse away.

"A word with you, Brian." Benjamin crooked a finger, then strolled out of hearing-range from the stables.

Treemark followed, looking a bit wary. "Yes?" he asked. "What's the problem?"

"Lorraine Farrier," Benjamin snapped. "I just had an intriguing talk with her. You triggered her, and you didn't ask her first, did you?"

"I did ask if she wanted to become an invulnerable warrior, and she was willing."

"But you didn't explain any of it!"

"How much explanation do most of us get? I gave her warning beforehand, and explained the rest afterward."

"Not all of it! You didn't tell her what danger she's in, who'll come after her, what she needs to do. You just gave her your pretty theories about elves and ancient gods—"

"—which were very often true!"

"You didn't tell her about the hunters, or their damned blood-sport. When were you going to tell her that?"

"Soon enough. A few days, perhaps. Look, Benjamin, it's a huge pill for anyone to swallow; best take it in small steps—especially with her personality."

"Her personality?" said Benjamin, caught off-balance. "What's the matter with it?"

"She's an Ice Queen: not prickly but defensive as hell, not paranoid but totally untrusting, cold to the point of being emotionless, calmly expecting enemies everywhere, overcontrolled. You've seen that before, haven't you?"

Benjamin said nothing. His face might have been frozen for all it showed.

"She won't believe anything without proof," Treemark went on, "Certainly not a story as vast as this. There are parts of it that very few of us know, for that matter."

Benjamin looked away, then back.

"Let me give it to her in easy stages, Benjamin. I assure you, I won't run any risks with her. She's already agreed to take 'martial arts training', and she'll be safe as long as she stays here."

"You mean to teach her?"

"Teach her, train her, heal those scars in her spirit: all of it."

"Heal her?" Benjamin said coldly, "As your disciple did with me?"

"You needed that, and you know it." Treemark met his eyes without flinching.

Benjamin ground his teeth. "And you think she does?"

"Possibly not. I assure you, I'll give her only what she needs—and I do know my trade."

Benjamin had no reply to that. "Just tell her the truth," he said. "All of it. Too many of us are too damned ignorant..."

"I know, and we both know why." Treemark held his eyes until Benjamin looked away. "How do you convince those who don't want to believe? How much knowledge do you give those who'd make evil use of it? And have you found a better way than mine to end this age-long war?"

Benjamin shook his head in defeat, and walked off.

Treemark watched him go, eyes full of pity. "No one should have to carry the scars you do, old friend," he whispered.

***

In the kitchen, Daniel felt Lorraine's presence approaching. He did a classic double-take when she entered the doorway, and he saw who she was. He gaped for an instant, then smiled.

"Ah, Ms. Lorraine, so you're one of us now?" At work, he was back in his formal butler/cook mode.

"Yes." She dropped into the nearest chair. "Dr. Treemark shot me. Just a few hours ago, in the clinic office. I'm hungry."

Daniel blinked. "Hmm. I was stabbed to death by a gang of robbers, 150 years ago, on the road outside London. Would a roast-beef sandwich suit you?"

"Oh yes. And I think I could use a beer. How did you learn you were a...an Elf?"

Daniel raised an eyebrow, but turned toward the huge refrigerator. "That's Dr. Treemark's favorite term for us. We have only dark beer, I'm afraid; Dr. Long prefers it. I'm exceedingly grateful that I was discovered, taken in and taught by an ally of Dr. Treemark. Otherwise, being neither young nor at all trained at the time, I should have been easy prey."

"Dark beer is fine. Prey to whom, Daniel?"

The man paused to set a chilled brown bottle and a glass mug on the table. "Power-hunters," he sneered. "The Unseelie Court, as Dr. Treemark would have it, or the Schwartzelven of Norse legend, or the Rakhshas of Hindu myth. Would you care for horseradish sauce?"

"Whatever you think best. Who are these...this Unseelie Court?"

Daniel paused to assemble ingredients on a plate. "It's not an organization as such," he said carefully. "One could better say it's a philosophical movement, an error, a pernicious idea, spread from individual to individual among the ignorant. Unfortunately, there are very many ignorant." He set the completed sandwich before Lorraine. "Will that be all?"

Lorraine eyed the bulky sandwich, and wondered if she could even finish it. "Oh yes," she said. *I can always take it with me...* She took an experimental bite, and found it exquisite.

"Then I'll be about my duties elsewhere. Good day." Daniel deftly turned and trotted away through the dining area. Lorraine watched him go, wishing he'd stayed to explain more about Elven politics, but decided it could wait. The beer went perfectly with the sandwich.

***

Benjamin, showered and reclothed in his usual slacks and sweater, followed the tell-tale sense of presence into the livingroom where Helen was waiting. There were two glasses of wine on the table before her, and she handed one to Benjamin without being asked.

"You're displeased with Brian," she said, as he settled on the couch beside her." Is it because of Lorraine?"

"Yes." Benjamin took a sip of the wine, found it acceptable, and set the glass down. "I've seen this before: a teacher making a little army out of his students, propagandizing them toward his personal mission... It makes me uneasy."

"All teachers push their own ethics at their students. It's not always a bad thing."

"No," Benjamin admitted, "And I don't disagree with his mission. God knows, I've been trying to do something similar, in my own small fashion, for centuries. It's just that I worry about his methods."

"I know how obsessive he can be, but look at his results. We're safer here than anywhere outside a temple." Helen smiled and patted her abdomen. "I'm quite content to stay here for the next seven months."

"And how long after that?" Benjamin gave her a tight look. "For the next 25 years? Or whatever age Brian thinks is best for Initiating your child?"

"Why not?" Helen fixed him with a steady gaze. "In Mycenae, I lived for nearly 300 years in the same temple, dutifully churning out babies. It wasn't a bad life, really."

"Mother Hera," Benjamin sighed. "Or was it Rhea, then? I tend to lose track."

"Never mind." She reached forward and clasped his wrist. "Benjamin, why can't you stay? Think of it; the first of us in over 2000 years to be raised by his true parents, to know his destiny from the beginning, to undergo Initiation willingly, knowingly. Imagine one of us with no first-death trauma, no need to run from howling lynch-mobs, no danger of being burned for a witch, no self-horror or self-doubts, no ignorance and no chance of being corrupted by that damned prophecy—"

"All but the last, I'll grant you." Gently, but firmly, Benjamin pulled his hand away. "Any of us can fall prey to that damned greed for power, the lure of becoming a god if you can just kill enough of your relatives."

"You could teach him otherwise."

"So could you, Helen. That's still no guarantee that your sweet baby won't someday chop you into a dozen pieces to consume your ability. That happened to Tiamat, remember: and you have more psychic power than she did."

Helen gave him a long sad gaze. "Are you afraid of your own child, Ben? Do you really think you'll be that terrible a father?"

"I've been a foster-father many times, with very variable results," he sighed. "And I know I have more to fear from total strangers than from someone I might... persuade to love me..."

"Then stay."

"I'll visit often, I promise. I won't be a stranger to the child."

Helen's expression grew knowing. "Ah, there's someone else, then?"

"Several someones, actually," Benjamin smiled. "I've been collecting reliable friends and lovers all over the world, seducing them into loving me and hating the prophecy, hating the whole damned business. I daresay I've collected a slightly larger army than Brian has."

"But have you told any of them the whole story?"

Benjamin looked down at his hands. "I've said that I don't believe in the prophecy, won't play the game, don't want any more psychic power than I already have, and absolutely don't want to become a god."

Helen leaned forward, pinning him with her eyes. "Benjamin, have you told anyone the secret of breeding?"

"No." He gave a sigh that seemed to empty him. "I know that's our last-ditch defense... God, I'm such a hypocrite! Just an hour ago I raved at Brian to tell Lorraine everything, when I don't dare do it myself."

"No, in general terms you did the right thing." Helen took his hand again. "But in her case, there's good reason to tell her. She's not one of our Changelings; she's a Convergent."

"What?" He snapped his head up to stare at her. "How do you know?"

"She was pregnant two years ago."

"You're sure?!"

"Brian is."

Benjamin's face fell. "Brian sometimes believes what he wants to believe."

"He's also very good at research, as you know. If it's true, if she really was born to mortal parents, if she really was pregnant then, he'll find it."

"The child... Miscarried?"

"Aborted. We don't know if she could have carried it to term. But if she could... Oh, think! She might be able to breed much sooner than 1200 years from now."

Benjamin shook his head, refusing to be misled by hope. "How much sooner, Helen? At the age of 1000? 800? 500 years? She'd still have to last that long."

"And she might get pregnant tomorrow. We don't know, Ben. But now do you see why she's so important?"

Benjamin leaned back on the couch and turned his face up to the beamed ceiling. "Breed enough to offset our constant losses, try to prevent the children from falling into that damned blood-sport, and still keep them hidden from the players. I don't see how we can do it. Sometimes I feel so hopeless..."

Helen gripped his hand tighter. "We keep on preaching peace to those who will listen," she soothed. "We keep on looking for newly-Initiated to teach. We keep on creating safe havens wherever we can. But with or without havens, raise our children ourselves or stuff them in mortal parents' cradles—we keep on breeding."

"Easy advice, that last," Benjamin smiled.

Helen chuckled and let go his hand. "In fact, I'd recommend that you bed as many mortal women as possible, spread your genes as far as you can, in hope they'll eventually Converge— and give us more like Lorraine."

***

Lorraine eventually wandered down to the stable, feeling a twinge of guilt for neglecting her work. As she approached the door she felt that familiar static field again, then felt it a second time. *Steven and Wally,* she guessed. *Them too.*

She paused near the doorway, suddenly shy. They'd feel her presence, and they'd know. How would that change her standing with them? Should she walk away for now?

A moment later the choice evaporated as Steven stuck his head out the door to see who was coming. He looked at Lorraine, and then smiled so widely it seemed to split his face.

"Ah, you're one of us now!" he beamed.

"Yes," she said faintly.

Steven sighed in understanding, came over and patted her shoulder. "I know; it's all new, and you're still dazed. Well, just keep remembering the important things, and you'll be all right."

"Important things...?"

"That you're alive, and you're going to keep on being alive, and you'll keep on doing the things you care about. You'll never be stopped by getting sick or injured. You can ride as long as the horse will run."

"Ride... Yes." Lorraine remembered that. "Right. Which of the riding-stock need exercising?"

"That Leila," Steven grinned. "She's feeling frisky, so watch yourself. I'll go saddle her up for you."

A few minutes later Lorraine was in the saddle, guiding Leila toward the exercise-ring. The black mare was indeed frisky, wanting to run, leap and play. She obeyed the reins, but danced all the way to the ring. Lorraine couldn't help smiling.

"Patience, sweet thing," she chuckled to the horse. "Let's get warmed up before you go galloping at the jumps."

Leila hurried through the walking and trotting circuits, took eagerly to the canter, and snorted in delight when Lorraine finally reined her toward the outside of the ring and aimed her at the first jump. The bar was set for three feet, and Leila jumped six.

Lorraine laughed and set her at the next jump. Again, they soared over the puny barrier.

Leila begged for more rein, more speed, and Lorraine gave it to her.

In the middle of a jump Lorraine realized that she was *feeling* the horse: the hot pull of hard breathing, the stretching and pressure of four powerful legs, the delight in her own speed, the joy of soaring victoriously through the air.

This was what Benjamin had meant by "empathy", the first Elven psychic sense.

It's starting early! Lorraine laughed in exultation. *Not in decades, but now!*

Leila galloped and flew, fence after fence, until it seemed to Lorraine that she was riding a solidified wind. Leap after leap, until Lorraine recognized the same jump for the fourth time. Not until they'd finished the circuit did Leila allow herself to be slowed and turned, still prancing and snorting happily, her coat gleaming with sweat. Lorraine slowed her to a trot, then a walk, and finally took her to the pasture. She pulled off the saddle and bridle at the gate, turned Leila loose to play in the field, and walked back to the barn carrying the tack on her shoulder.

Halfway there she caught herself laughing, and understood

why. Steven had been right, and she could ride forever if she wanted to. She would never be too old or crippled to climb on a horse's back and soar over field and fence like a bird with invisible wings, feeling the animal's joy in the running. Life was good, and that was all she needed to reconcile herself to its strangeness.

Lorraine spent the rest of the day at the stables, exercising and currying and raking out stalls, and sang quietly to herself as she worked.

***

Dinner—onion soup, another elaborate salad and an exotic stew—was excellent, but the conversation was subdued. Lorraine noted that Treemark and Benjamin spoke to each other no more than they could help. Helen chatted mostly with Madge and Daniel, Steven and Wally were primarily concerned with the brood-mare whose ankle was less swollen but still sore. Lorraine could feel the aura-fields of all of them, like a soft hum of distant machinery. The sensation had become almost comfortable, and reassurance of their presence. Lorraine felt herself relaxing cautiously, almost as if she were at home.

Home, she remembered. She'd have to write letters to the old bunch in Chicago, arrange a meeting with Berringer to take the letters and mail them. For that matter, could a cell-phone call be traced to location? Could she dare call Weber? Could she trust Berringer? Not Oshansky. Everyone in the city knew about the connections between the Chicago cops and the Mob; what could he have reported, or done?

Lorraine felt suddenly weary of the whole wretched business. No, she'd wait until the next time she went back to town, then drive clean to the other side of the city and call everyone from there. Whoever had gotten into her apartment already knew she was living somewhere in or around Tucson. Let them think she was hopping from motel to motel, and run around the city looking for her while she was safe out here. In any case, she could afford to wait a few days.

She had more important things to think about now.

***

After dinner, Lorraine followed Treemark to the clinic office again. He handed her a scotch-and-soda without comment and waited for her to speak. She took a sip to collect her thoughts, then plunged ahead.

"I want to take the training," she said. "I want to learn everything I can."

Treemark nodded acceptance. "Everything," he agreed. "Understand that this will require unlearning several bad lessons."

"Such as?"

"Tell me: now that you know you can't be killed or injured by any ordinary means, can you allow yourself to trust?"

This again, Lorraine sighed. "I honestly hadn't thought of it, Dr. Treemark."

He looked pained. "Brian," he reminded her.

"Look, if you're going to play my doctor every night, shouldn't I call you one?"

"I'm not playing, Lorraine."

"All right. Look, if a bit of psychoanalysis every evening is the price of my training, I'll pay it. Go ahead and ask your questions."

"Deal," Treemark grinned. "In fact, I'll let you ask the first question. Go on; the ball's in your court."

Caught off-balance, all Lorraine could think of was the way the muscles in his shoulders showed under his knit turtleneck shirt. She remembered Benjamin working out in the gym. "Martial arts," she murmured. "I know why I want the training, but why are you so eager to give it to me?"

Treemark pulled a deep breath, and then let it out slowly. "Because you'll need it," he said. "First, against this stalker of yours. Afterward, against any other stalker who may appear in the future—including others of our kind. Not all of us are good people, any more than all mortals are. And finally, because you need to be certain you can keep yourself safe, so that you can afford to relax your guard." He smiled fleetingly. "Tell me: if you could have kicked your worthless lover's butt around the block, beaten the crap out of him as he deserved, discharged your fury directly back at him who caused it—would you still distrust love so much?"

Lorraine caught her breath as his words conjured up the image. Yes, she could see herself punching Ronnie right in his cute little self-pitying nose, feel the satisfying impact as the cartilage broke, hear him howl instead of whine for once. She was shaken by the rage and joy she felt. "Jesus," she whispered, "I would have loved that!"

"And with good reason. Don't be ashamed or afraid of your anger; you had every right to feel it."

"But if I let it run... If I really had beaten the crap out of Ronnie, the police would have grabbed me for assault." *Or would they?* Now that she thought of it, the last thing police wanted to deal with was 'domestic disturbance'. Chicago police were no different.

Imagine Ronnie wailing to the police that his girlfriend broke his nose because he'd gotten her pregnant and didn't want to marry her or support the baby. She imagined their reaction, and laughed. "No, they probably wouldn't have."

"And how would you have felt the next morning?" Treemark smiled again.

She imagined pitching Ronnie's possessions out after him, putting up the chain-lock, having a stiff drink and a good cry, then picking up the paper and looking for a cheaper apartment, as she'd had to do anyway. She could have gotten up early next morning, run to the bank and emptied out the account herself. She still would have been scrambling for money, still would have had to get the abortion, but it wouldn't have been nearly so bad. "Better," she admitted. "It still would have hurt, but...not so much."

"Enough less that you could still have trusted in love?"

"I don't know..." Lorraine frowned. *The 'T' word again.* He'd manipulated her back to that. "My turn. Another question."

"Ask," Treemark agreed.

Lorraine remembered earlier bits of conversation. "Elven politics," she said. "Just what is the 'pernicious idea' of the Unseelie Court, and how bad is it?"

Treemark flinched as if he'd been struck. A deep pain flashed in his eyes, then faded. "It's greed," he said. "Greed for each other's 'magic'—energy and knowledge and psychic ability. Simple, ruthless greed dressed up in a pious excuse."

He reached to a display shelf behind him, came back with an object that looked like a wrinkled brown baseball, and set it on the desk. With a start, Lorraine realized that it was a shrunken head. *Real?* She poked cautiously at its tiny cheek, and found it… fuzzy. Nobody could have faked that hair. She shuddered and pulled her finger away.

"Yes, that's a genuine Ecuadorian shrunken head, about a century old," Treemark grinned sourly. "Very handy when someone calls me a headshrinker. Do you recall why the Jivaro Indians made such things?"

"…To gain an enemy's magic," Lorraine remembered.

"The Jivaros, and others, took heads. The Plains Indians took scalps. Various peoples in Africa drank the enemy's blood or ate his heart. It's all to the same purpose: to get the 'magic', by which we can infer psychic ability. A common idea among primitive people all over the world: kill an enemy and take his magic." Treemark grimaced. "I have to wonder if they inspired us, or we inspired them."

"Psychic ability... Benjamin told me that if one Elf dies within the...psychic field of another, the survivor gets..."

"Yes." Treemark's eyes wandered to the ceiling. "It's a form of vampirism."

"So we're the root of that legend too?"

"Not the blood-drinking part. But the power... It's the quick way to increase one's skill and psychic ability, a short-cut to what honest people gain by survival and practice." He shook his head angrily. "Power-lust... Long ago, some of us were worshipped as gods. Some of us grew to like that too well. Someone, somewhere, got the idea that if he could steal energy from enough of his kind, he'd have truly god-like powers. Do you see where this led?"

"Serial killers," Lorraine guessed. "Bloodthirsty gods."

"Worse." Treemark sighed. "They spread the idea that this was their destiny, that it was fitting and proper that the stronger gods should devour the weaker. I have to wonder how much the coming of monotheistic religions added to it. Soon enough, it became a prophecy that all too many believed. It started a long genocidal war that destroyed any social unity our ancestors had. That's where so much of our history was lost."

"And...how did the war end?"

"It didn't." Treemark gave her a long look full of sorrow. "It still goes on. Even those who know nothing of our past have heard of that unholy prophecy. Some like the idea of becoming gods, and hunt for others of our kind to kill. Some don't like the idea, and fight the hunters. Some simply run and hide."

"Gang-fights in the park!" Lorraine remembered cases of that, back in the city.

"Not that, at least." Treemark smiled briefly. "The one advantage our side has is that we're willing to form lasting alliances with each other. The hunters tend to let greed overcome them, and turn on their own allies. As a result, the battles are almost always duels: one on one. What little we have of custom and tradition encourages that, so we fight a long slow war of attrition."

"So, outside of this place..."

"Any of us you meet could as easily be an enemy as a friend."

"That's why...the martial-arts training."

"You must learn to fight—and very well—with every personal weapon known to man."

Lorraine drew a long breath, thinking that over. Training like that would take years, and yet she must learn very fast. "When do I start?" she whispered.

"Tomorrow." Treemark picked up a paper from the desk and held it where Lorraine could see it. "You'll have a rigid schedule, and must keep to it absolutely. Yes, the nightly analysis will be part of it, and so will other exercises; you must train your spirit as well as your body, and the training will be hard. Do you understand this?"

"Yes," said Lorraine, looking at the paper. It was a schedule, and it ran from six in the morning to ten at night.

"More: you will have to trust someone—myself, or Benjamin, or even Helen—enough to put yourself in their hands. There is no other way to learn what you need. Do you accept this?"

The 'T' word, thought Lorraine, bridling. Was all this just an elaborate psychological manipulation, a scam to put her in Treemark's power for his own obscure reasons?

But then she remembered Benjamin practicing with the wooden sword. That too, and all he'd said to her, and what she'd heard from Daniel, could all be part of some carefully-crafted plot—but those lean fighter's muscles, meant for use instead of show, those had been real.

Danger was always real. Whether or not the tale of the Unseelie Court was true, she really would need the training.

And there was always the gun under her pillow.

"Yes," she said, and reached for the paper.

5.

LORRAINE WAS AWAKENED at 6 AM by the buzzing of the intercom. As she looked toward the annoying machine on the night-table, her eye fell on the schedule—and she remembered everything. A dozen conflicting emotions ran through her in ten seconds flat, and finally settled on determination. She crawled out of bed and dressed. When she came out to the kitchen she was wearing the pistol holstered on her right hip and the cell-phone on her left.

The presence Lorraine felt this time belonged to Madge, who raised an eyebrow at the holsters, but said nothing. She set a plate and glass on the table in front of Lorraine—orange juice, a hard-boiled egg, fruit salad—and explained: "Dr. Treemark has put you on the training diet."

Lorraine shrugged, and reached for the salt and pepper.

Steven, Wally, Helen and Benjamin came to the table as she was eating. They spoke little, still slow with waking, and they got breakfasts of sausages, toast, coffee and multiple eggs. If any of them noticed the gear on Lorraine's belt, they said nothing about it.

Lorraine waited for Wally and Steven to finish so they could precede her to the stables. Once there, she busied herself cleaning stalls while Steven led out and curried the horses. She worked quickly, remembering the schedule. At 11 AM she headed for the gym, wondering what exercises she was supposed to perform for the next hour, and found Treemark waiting for her.

"Come to the clinic first," he said. "We need to discuss your physical conditioning."

They didn't stop at the office, but went through to the examining room, where Treemark handed her another paper gown. "Strip," he said, pointing to the small bathroom.

She went into the bathroom and changed into the paper gown, but rolled her clothes into a bundle with the jeans on top and the holsters within easy reach.

When she returned to the examination room, she saw something puzzling: four strips of blue plastic-webbing straps, two inches wide and perhaps seven inches long, lying on the examination table. There were also four large brass D-rings. Treemark was holding a glue-gun.

"The immediate problem," he said, "Is not just that you can't trust me, or anyone else, but that you can't trust large parts of yourself. That will require a hard cure, and this is the first part of it."

"I thought we didn't do the psychoanalysis until after dinner." Nonetheless, Lorraine set her clothes on the nearest chair and moved toward the table.

"It must begin now." Treemark lifted one strap, and Lorraine saw that it was threaded through one of the D-rings. "Hold out your arm."

In a sudden flare of insight, Lorraine understood that the straps were meant to be cuffs—one for each wrist and ankle.

"Goodbye," she said, turning back toward her clothes. "I don't do kinky sex."

"This isn't for fun, and you won't leave," Treemark said calmly.

"No?" Lorraine stopped, hand close to the gun-holster. "Why won't I?"

"Not just because you're safe here, but because I have knowledge you want and training you need. This is part of it."

Lorraine paused for a long moment, while Treemark waited wordlessly, then resolutely turned back and thrust out her left arm.

Treemark wrapped the plastic strip around her forearm, just above the wrist, taking care to pull it snug, but not tight. He used the glue-gun to seal the cuff closed, and held the strip together until the glue set. Without a word, he reached for another strip.

Likewise silent, Lorraine held out her other arm. She had to rest each foot on the desk in turn as he applied the ankle-straps.

When the cuffs were solidly applied, Lorraine examined her left wrist-strap and tugged the D-ring experimentally. It didn't pinch, didn't rub, and didn't give. The cuff would stay in place until it was cut away. "How am I supposed to wash with these on?" she asked, concentrating on practicalities.

"They're loose enough that you can slide a thin washcloth under them, and water will pass through the mesh. The rings will fold flat under your sleeves, so they won't interfere with work."

"You thought of everything."

"There's more. There will be no sex while you're in training, unless I give permission."

I won't ask, Lorraine thought, half-angry. "No problem."

"That includes masturbation, and I'll have to trust you about that." He handed her another piece of paper, with another list on it. "These are the exercises you'll need. For maximum effect, perform them naked."

"I'll need a brassiere," said Lorraine, taking the paper. *'Athletic supporter'…*

"If you like, you can also wear an elastic belt over it to hold the breasts out of the way. Now return to the gym and resume the schedule. Benjamin will come fetch you after lunch."

There seemed to be no point in going to the bathroom to dress. Lorraine simply turned her back and reached for her clothes. Behind her, she heard Treemark walk out of the room.

The D-rings did indeed fold flat under her sleeves and socks, just as he'd said.

***

In the house's control-center, which others rarely visited, Treemark watched the screen for the security-camera that covered the gym. Lorraine had chosen the soft foam mat to exercise on. She hadn't put her clothes in a locker but kept them rolled up, with those holsters exposed, close to hand. She was doing the sit-ups—in groups of ten, interspersed with ten leg-lifts forward, side and back—ten repetitions of each set. The arm and shoulder exercises would follow, 100 repetitions of each. He could hear her panting, and her skin gleamed with sweat, but she hadn't slowed her pace.

Her ferocious determination was magnificent.

He could almost see her relentless will, wrapped like a coiled steel spring around her spine. Yes, this wild mare had the heart of a battle-charger. She could be warrior enough to turn the course of this long genocidal war, bring victory at last to the side of life—if only she would consent to be trained, and healed.

And treating her was like picking his way through a minefield. Treemark felt limp with relief that he'd managed to bring her this far, and he knew that the lessons ahead would be harder still. He must not break that iron will; he must lead her to break it herself, consent to surrender, or she might be bound forever by the scars on her spirit.

He didn't know, as yet, just what and where all of them were.

He didn't even know her real name.

'Lorraine Farrier' had records so sparse that anyone would suspect them. An intense Internet search had revealed only a GED certificate and therefore no high school listings, a college degree with no transcript of grades, no driver's license until a few days ago, no employment but a defunct trade-paper in another state, no credit-history whatever, a valid social-security number but nothing else. It stank to high heaven of false identity, probably done with legal cooperation. It made sense, if she was hiding from a stalker.

It also meant that he hadn't been able to confirm her story, and he had to know if she truly had been pregnant or not. His instincts insisted that she'd told him the truth about that—her bitter fury over her lover's abandonment was rooted in more than just being dumped without money—but his instincts weren't enough to convince Helen.

Treemark sighed and turned back to his computer. If the past couldn't yield him evidence, the future would. He must plan the next several steps with infinite care.

***

The wall-clock chimed softly just as Lorraine finished the last arm-circle, and she drooped on the mat, panting. All she wanted was a few minutes' rest, but her shower and lunch were planned for this next hour. She crawled back into her jeans and shirt, not bothering with underwear and boots, and plodded to her bedroom. The tub enticed, but there was only an hour: a quick shower it must be.

As Treemark had promised, the plastic webbing allowed water and soap to pass through. The washcloth was more of a problem and Lorraine soon gave up on it, seeing that soaping and tugging on the cuffs scrubbed her skin well enough.

Once dry, Lorraine pulled out fresh clothes and stuffed the sticky ones in the hamper. She was wondering whether to drag the laundry-bag out into the hallway just yet when her cell-phone beeped. The number on the screen was unaccompanied by a name, but she knew it was Agent Berringer's. With a sigh, Lorraine clicked the 'talk' button.

"Roxanne, where have you been?" The woman was addled enough to use her real name.

"Hi, Aunt Dianne," Lorraine answered, implying that she wasn't alone in the room.

To her credit, Berringer reined herself in. "Where are you, dear?" she asked, sounding calmer. "We haven't talked in days."

Lorraine unconsciously plastered a false smile on her face. "I've been out job-hunting. There are quite a few small papers in this town, you know. One of them has to have an opening, sooner or later."

"Do you think it's wise to go into the same old business?" Berringer hinted.

"What other skills do I have, besides editing?" Lorraine countered. "Newspapers, magazines, book-publishers—I'll try them all if I must. Have you heard anything from home?"

"No news. Sorry." The agent managed to sound contrite. "Do you have any letters to send? I can swing by and pick them up this evening, if you like."

"No, I've been keeping too busy." *How to keep her from going to the old apartment?* "Tell you what, when I've got something to send, I'll meet you for lunch. There are some excellent Mexican restaurants in this town..."

"That would be nice, dear." Berringer sounded a bit relieved.

Lorraine glanced at her clock; she really didn't want to prolong this conversation.

"Oh, here comes the secretary. I'll call later. 'Bye." She hit the 'off' button before the agent could say anything more, then glowered at the silent phone. She'd have to leave the damned thing turned off during her training-sessions. She'd have to get into the city soon to make her calls.

She really didn't want to leave the ranch. Not with this fearsome new knowledge in her head. Not with these cuffs on her wrists and ankles, unseen or not. No, the calls could wait.

Lorraine hurried into the fresh jeans and shirt, checked her holsters again and went off to the kitchen.

Only Steven, Wally and Daniel were present at lunch, and they were too busy with the food and work for much talking. Lorraine's lunch was also specialized: milk, cold sliced chicken, and salad. She ate quickly and dutifully, though the food was marvelously flavored as always.

Benjamin came in just as she was clearing her plate, plainly looking for her. "If you'll follow me," he smiled almost apologetically, "I'll take you to the *salle d'armes*."

Lorraine got up and followed, wondering if meant the gym or something else.

It proved to be something else. Benjamin led her to another door off the livingroom, down a short corridor, and into a wide storage-closet, of all things. Without pause, he marched to the back wall. At a nearby corner sat what appeared to be a circuit-breaker box, and he pulled open the small door and poked two of the circuit-switches.

With a soft grinding sound, the back wall pulled away, revealing a long flight of stairs. *A hidden door and basement too!* Lorraine marveled. *More secrets to this house.*

At the bottom of the stairs lay another corridor, with doors to left and right.

Benjamin led her through the nearest rightward door, into what proved to be a small shooting-range. He glanced at her holster, went to a wall-cabinet and rummaged inside for a moment, and came back holding a plastic bag filled with .38 target-rounds. "We'll start with your regular sidearm," he said, handing her the bag, "Then move on to long-guns. Load up while I fetch the targets and protectors."

Lorraine wondered how he'd known, at a glance, what caliber gun she carried.

She also wondered about those other doors off the corridor. The more she saw of it, the more the house resembled a castle, complete with training facility and prepared to withstand sieges: an odd home for a man who'd asked her to learn trust.

Then again, he'd asked her if—once she was armed and trained—she could afford to trust. Perhaps, armored as he was, he could.

She spent the next hour focusing on targets and gun-sights, with Benjamin making suggestions here and adjusting her stance there. His touch on her arms was light, efficient and professional. By the time the bag of target-rounds was emptied, her shots were hitting reliably within the #8 ring of the target.

"Very good," said Benjamin. "That's enough for now; your arms are tiring. Rest for a bit, and we'll go on to blade-work."

'Blade-work' took place across the hall, in a wide empty room whose only furnishings were some upright padded posts, wall-mirrors, and wall-racks full of medieval weapons: an amazing variety of axes, swords, bludgeons and spears. Benjamin took her to the rack lined with swords, pulled down one of them and felt it for weight and balance.

"Why swords?" Lorraine wondered. "He said I'd learn every kind of personal weapon, but aren't swords a little unlikely?"

"Not really." Benjamin smiled briefly. "If you run into an... Unseelie Elf, he'll most likely be carrying one. Bullets may put us down for awhile, but to do real damage you'll need an axe or a sword. Swords are easier to conceal and carry than axes. Try this one, and see how it feels."

Lorraine took the proffered sword, noting that it had no edge. She swung it in front of her a few times, tried jabbing with it, felt how its weight pulled at her arms. "It feels a little clumsy," she admitted, "Too heavy toward the point."

Benjamin took it away, and offered her a slender sword that suggested Three Musketeers movies. She tried it, and found it too light. "It seems...all handle," Lorraine commented. "It doesn't pull right."

"Try this."

They went through half a dozen swords before they found one that felt comfortable. It was a smaller version of a medieval knight's sword, with plain cross-guards and a long grip.

"Good choice," Benjamin grinned. "That hand-and-a-half Bastarde is wonderfully versatile."

"I think I can use both hands on this son of a bitch," she said— and then wondered why Benjamin laughed.

"No, it's from the French," he explained. "'Batarde'—a 'stick'. Technically though, it's a half-breed: just between one-handed and two-handed length and weight. This means you can use either technique with it: ideally, both. A versatile blade, and I'm delighted that it fits you."

He sounded, Lorraine considered, like one of the eager young teaching assistants she'd known back in college: in love with his subject and delighted to share his love with the rest of the world. She wondered if he made his living as a teacher.

Benjamin chose a similar sword for himself and spent the next two hours teaching her the basic stances and moves for defense-and-riposte, then making her practice them until her initial clumsiness wore off. He didn't cross swords with her himself, but stood beside her and demonstrated the steps, like a dancing-master, until she could move with him.

"Back up," he told her for the third time. "You're not backing far enough."

"I forgot again. Sorry."

"Lorraine," he sighed, "It's one thing not to know the meaning of fear. It's another thing not to know when to make a strategic withdrawal. Now concentrate—and back up."

Lorraine went through the move again, taking an exaggerated step back, which Benjamin pronounced "Better". She repeated, and repeated, until he found something else to criticize.

At 3 PM Benjamin declared the lesson finished, put away the swords and led her back upstairs. "My class is over," he said, dropping into the nearest couch. "You go on out to the pool. And don't worry about a bathing-suit; we all skinny-dip here."

But what will people think of these cuffs? Lorraine, proceeding out to the pool area. *Maybe I can pass them off as high-fashion accessories... Then again, will anyone ask?*

As she came out to the pool-deck Lorraine saw, and felt, that she wasn't alone; Treemark was sitting in the bubbling Jacuzzi, holding a heavy plastic wine-cup filled with dark-red juice, obviously nude, wearing nothing but a crystal pendant on a cord around his neck. On the poolside lawn-table stood a tall pitcher, another wine-cup, a pile of folded white terrycloth and a capped opaque bottle. Lorraine slowed in confusion.

He glanced at her, and merely pointed to one corner of the pool-deck. Lorraine looked closer, and saw a short row of lockers there, half hidden by flowering bushes. She went toward it slowly, not unwilling to shed her clothes so much as her weapon. It took deliberate effort to hang her clothes and gun-belt in the locker and return to the pool. She was painfully aware of the cuffs.

"There," said Treemark, pointing to the pitcher and remaining cup. "It's Daniel's home-made sports drink, much tastier than the commercial brand. I expect you'll need it after all the exercise."

Yes, it was as delicious as all of Daniel's concoctions. Feeling a little reckless, she chugged down the entire cupful. "Now what?" she asked, twirling the cup.

"Now set it down and get into the pool," said Treemark calmly, pointing to the side of the Jacuzzi opposite where he sat. "Settle in front of the jet. I also imagine you're rather stiff after the swordwork."

Cautiously as a deer approaching a water-hole, Lorraine stepped into the small hot pool and arranged herself on the underwater concrete bench so that the water-jet played directly against her back. It was admittedly soothing; Lorraine felt it loosening small cramps that she hadn't known she had. She noted more of those brass rings, hanging from brass lion-heads, set at wide intervals around the little pool, twinkling in the sunlight; they almost gave the illusion that her cuffs and D-rings were matching jewelry.

Treemark leaned back against the pool's curb, eyes closed, saying nothing. The foaming water did little to conceal his body, Lorraine noted. If he had been strikingly handsome in clothing, he was stunningly beautiful without it: more heavily muscular than Benjamin, looking sculpted even through the distortion of the water, like a heroic bronze statue of an idealized athlete—and very nearly as hairless, at least above the waist.

Lorraine resolutely turned her eyes away from him, wondering if he was trying to seduce her, and if so, why. Was her coldness a challenge to him, or did he try to make a conquest of every young-enough female who walked in the door?

No, that was too simple. Even a bored rich man—or Elf, or ancient god—would scarcely spend so much time and elaborate effort on a roll in the hay with a common stablehand. Lorraine knew she was handsome enough, but not such a spectacular beauty — like Helen, for example—to inspire a man to such efforts. No, something else was happening here, and she had no idea what it was.

Treemark sighed and stirred in the water, drawing Lorraine's gaze unwillingly back to him. "Did you find a sword that suited you?" he asked, opening his eyes.

"Ah, yes..." Lorraine floundered. "Ben said it was called a bastard."

"What matters is that you can use it. The sooner you're competent with it, the sooner we can give you an edged blade. Are you thoroughly relaxed, or do you need more time?"

Lorraine considered that, and looked at the water-wrinkles on her fingertips.

According to the schedule, these next three hours were given over to 'physical therapy'—which made excellent sense after all these hours of work and exercise. "As relaxed as I can be without falling asleep," she admitted.

"Come out, then." Treemark pulled himself up from the bench and waded out of the Jacuzzi.

Lorraine followed, eyes downcast to avoid looking at him, and thereby missed seeing where he touched the switch that turned off the water-jets. He went to the lawn-table, unfolded the pile of terrycloth, tossed her an enormous beach-towel and took another for himself. As Lorraine dried herself, she saw that there was a hemmed hole in the middle of the towel so that it could double as a simple robe. She was about to put it on when Treemark, wearing his towel around his waist, waved her to the massage-table.

"Time to straighten out those misaligned bones," he said. "That's one thing your mutant healing-power won't do for you."

Lorraine sighed, and lay face down on the table. She'd visited chiropractors before, and had some idea what would follow. There was no surprise as Treemark felt his way down her back, pausing to lean hard at particular spots, which clicked in response. She let him move her body into various positions, pushing and pulling until bones clunked into place, troubled only a little at the feel of his bare skin against hers, for his touch was firm, sure, impersonal and professional. When he finished she was back in her original position, but with her shoulders feeling much improved.

Treemark went to the lawn-table and returned with the opaque bottle. As Lorraine watched he uncapped it and poured some of the contents into his hand. A scent of almonds and cedar reached her. *Massage oil,* she guessed, turning her face away. *A logical next step.*

Then she remembered the ride with Leila, and what Benjamin had told her about empathy, the ability to read emotions. What she'd done with a horse, she could do with Treemark. As soon as he set his hands on her, if he was planning seduction or more, she would know.

Treemark brushed her hair away from her neck with one hand, and dripped the oil down her back with the other. His next touch spread the oil across her shoulders, with both hands, and that was contact enough. Lorraine called up the sensation of communing with Leila, and *reached* for him.

The connection was surprisingly easy, a deepening and elaboration of the sense of presence—and what she felt through it was Treemark's intense concentration. He was tightly absorbed with doing this right, absolutely right, leaving no muscle untouched. His mind was almost entirely in his fingers. Stroke after stroke, as he spread the oil and probed at the flesh beneath the skin, his emotional tone didn't change, and there was no erotic feeling in it at all.

Lorraine pulled back to herself, puzzled. Treemark was fiercely concerned for her, but not in any way she'd expected. She still didn't know his motivations, but it was just possible that he'd been telling the truth all along: that he wanted her trained, strong and healthy, and no more. At the moment, he reminded her of nothing so much as a sports coach absorbed with a star player.

Or a trainer with a purebred horse.

Convinced that she'd found the key to his interest in her, Lorraine closed her eyes and let herself drift on the sensations of the thorough massage. Yes, she could feel muscles relaxing that she hadn't known were tense. Yes, she'd probably fall asleep if this lasted much longer. Then again, that wasn't a problem; she was safe here, and it had been a long hard day...

She barely twitched as his hands proceeded across her buttocks and down the backs of her thighs. This was no threat, and meant nothing. Let it happen. Drift.

***

Treemark bit back his surge of relief and joy as he heard Lorraine's breathing deepen, felt the last tension fade out of her body and emotional tone. It was possible that she'd gained some use of her empathic ability already, and she mustn't sense him exulting over his victory. But victory it was, and a great milestone passed: a wild mare consenting to take food from a human hand. Beside willingness to learn, she was now willing to be rewarded. She agreed to accept this much of pleasure, expose this much vulnerability—like an armed knight removing one piece of armor, over a non-vital organ. He must give her as much reward for that as she would accept. He would be thorough with the massage, and then let her rest for a time.

But the next stage must follow soon, while she was receptive to it, and that would be a much harder learning. Just how hard, he had no way to predict. He must proceed with as much skill and caution as he'd ever used in his life, lest all her potential be lost—and much of his breed's hope with it.

***

A voice quietly calling her name awakened Lorraine. She raised her head and saw Treemark, now wearing dark sweatpants, standing nearby. She also felt someone else's presence only a little further away. A quick glance showed that it was Madge, collecting the cups from the lawn-table, not looking at them.

Did she see— Lorraine flinched.

No, the long bath-towel/robe was draped over her, so that she was covered from neck to ankles. Treemark must have done that. She felt a flash of gratitude.

"Come with me," he said, "And we'll proceed to the next stage."

Holding the towel/robe around her, Lorraine slid off the massage-table. She remembered the neck-hole in the towel, and quickly slipped it over her head. The terrycloth folds fell around her, draping her body from neck to wrists and ankles, open only at the sides and bottom; if she simply clasped her arms in front of her, the robe stayed completely closed.

Treemark was already moving, walking determinedly back to the house. Lorraine hesitated a moment, thinking of her clothes—and gun—in the locker, then followed.

He led her into the solarium, to the center where the two wooden columns stood, and stopped there. "Stand between them," he said, pointing.

Stretching exercise? Gymnastics? Lorraine wondered, stepping between the columns. They were easily eight feet tall, just under four feet apart, carved with a simple vine-and-flowers design, looking much like the support-posts of some vast door, and their facing surfaces were set with large iron rings at every three inches from top to bottom.

"Put your feet as close to the posts as you can," said Treemark.

Lorraine did, stretching until her ankles touched the wood. She noted that the open sides of the robe had fallen back to her shoulders, and now exposed her legs to mid-thigh.

"With both hands, grip the highest rings you can reach. Then close your eyes and take slow, deep breaths."

Lorraine dutifully reached for the rings. The highest she could grip were just above the level of her head to either side. She grasped them firmly, intrigued by the cool smoothness of the metal, and closed her eyes. She could feel Treemark drawing close behind her, but concentrated on inhaling slowly.

Two metallic clicks sounded nearby, close to her feet. Then two more, closer, and she felt a quick tugging at her wrists. Lorraine snapped her eyes open, looked, and saw that four small padlocks now joined the D-rings on her cuffs to the iron rings of the posts.

She was shackled, spread-eagle, between the columns.

"I told you, I don't do kinky sex!" she shouted, furious. *So it was a seduction after all—*

"In fact, you don't do any sex," Treemark said sternly. "You accept almost no sensory pleasure at all. You are at war with your own nature. You know that war must end, but you take no steps to end it. Instead, you distract yourself with work—preferably hard physical labor—to keep yourself from feeling anything but safe, reliable anger. This stops now."

Lorraine tugged hard at the rings holding her right arm. They didn't give. Neither did the cuff. A quick pull revealed that the ankle-cuffs were likewise immovable.

"Now you'll have no labor and no distractions. You'll have time to think, and feel, and *do nothing else*. You will stand here for the next hour, just as you are, completely alone—and absolutely nothing will happen to you."

Nothing? "What if I have to piss, or worse?" Lorraine tried.

For answer, Treemark shoved an empty gardening bucket between her feet. "Go right ahead," he answered. "The bougainvillea can always use more fertilizer."

Lorraine tried frantically to think of something else to say, then heard Treemark's footsteps fading away behind her. The aura of his presence faded after him. A moment later, she heard the door close.

I'm alone? Was he telling the truth? Was this really just part of Treemark's obscure psychology project, and no more? She sensed no other presence, heard no sound, saw nothing but the glass wall and ceiling and the riot of cultivated flowers.

She was alone. There was no one here to see her or harm her, but also no one who could free her.

An hour, she thought, tugging at her cuffs again. *An hour like this.*

The links held firm.

Time passed, ticking slowly.

Lorraine tried counting seconds, adding up the minutes, as she'd done when she worked as a model for art classes in college. She'd learned to hold absolutely still for up to 20 minutes at a time. At least now she could move a little.

Just an hour... The position itself wasn't uncomfortable. There was enough play in the bonds that she could shift her weight, work her muscles, keep her circulation going.

The worst she had to fear was boredom.

Or an annoying itch...

Well, she could put up with an itchy nose, or whatever, for an hour. She had put up with worse in the past: the time she'd broken her ankle and had to wait three hours in the emergency room before anyone could see her (and Ronnie had left her there, and gone home to bed), that godawful case of food-poisoning that kept her heaving her guts out all night (and brother Georgie whined because she was making so much disgusting noise in the bathroom), having to wear that "cute" little play-suit for hours at Momma's garden-party even though it was too small and cut excruciatingly into her crotch (and Momma snapped "Don't touch yourself there! You're embarrassing me.")—oh yes, there were far worse things than simply standing still!

Lorraine ground her teeth and pulled at the cuffs again. No, they didn't hurt: only annoyed. She could put up with annoyance. She'd felt more impatience with fools who whaffled about their emotional sufferings. Emotional pain was nothing compared to physical pain, as she had good cause to know...

—frostbitten toes from standing in line at the soup-kitchen in a freezing Chicago blizzard because there was no money for food because Ronnie took everything except the price of the abortion and payday was a week away—

...not that emotional pain was pleasant, of course...

—Momma's hysterical phone call saying Pop had dropped dead of a heart attack and come home right away so I made excuses to my professors and got Suzanne to drive me all the way back to Detroit and then Momma met me at the door with a basketful of laundry to wash because the maid had quit last week and she turned to Suzanne who was a total stranger to her and whined "Isn't my daughter awful to keep me waiting like this?" and Suzanne gave me this look of horrified pity and hurried away—

...but when you got both of them at once, injury topped off with insult, oh that was the perfection of misery.

—Georgie Dear threw the decanter at me because I wouldn't give him my pretty new plastic jump-rope and I ducked but it shattered and a piece of flying glass cut my arm and he ran and Momma came in and saw and screeched and at first I thought it was because of the blood but no she grabbed the jump-rope and yanked my skirt up and lashed my thighs with it yowling about how much that decanter cost and the hard plastic raised welts at every blow and Pop heard the noise and bellowed "Shut up that racket" without even coming to look and Georgie peeked around the door smirking and it took days to get that piece of glass out of my arm—

Lorraine snarled wordlessly and yanked at the cuffs, again, and again. A sudden blind rage swelled up like a flood and she fought against the bonds holding her, thrashing hard enough to lift her feet off the ground, not caring that the cuffs were unbreakable, only shaken with a tornado of fury that felt old as the hills: rage against everyone and anyone who loved money and class and bits of property and social standing and their own convenience and power more than living creatures, more than their own lovers or children, more than the future of their own species. Rage as vast as the sea, and fed by just as many sources: fury that had never before had a chance to run totally free.

***

Treemark unconsciously held his breath as he watched the screen with the view of the solarium, scarcely believing what he saw. Lorraine fought like a tiger, struggling so hard and fast that her image blurred. The fury she spent on her own body was incredible. Now she was snapping her teeth like a wolf, sinking them into her own shoulders for lack of a better target. There was a serious chance she would wrench her hips or shoulders out of joint with the sheer force of her rage. He'd rarely seen mad savagery like this, and he could only pray that an hour would be enough to exhaust it.

Helen, peering over his shoulder, chewed her lip. "Berserker?" she whispered.

"Possibly." He didn't take his eyes off the screen. "Imagine that let loose, running in channels of trained skill, with a sword or axe in her hands."

Helen shivered. "The Battle-Madness of Sekhmet. She might be one Sekhmet's descendants, and what then?"

"Then everything will depend on her healing and training." Treemark shivered also, thinking of what that would involve. How well could that wildness be controlled?

How often must that reservoir of fury be drained, and what would be found lying at the bottom of it? He had caught glimpses of gems in those depths. "Somewhere, sometime, she had the capacity to love deeply. Nothing but betrayed love could have caused rage like this."

"Then pray that it still exists, and that you can find it."

6.

LORRAINE SAGGED between the columns, stunned almost oblivious with exhaustion, hearing nothing but the rasp of her hoarse breathing. Her arms were numb, but her left shoulder ached persistently; other than that, she felt nothing but monumental fatigue.

Time passed, featureless.

She felt the approaching aura just before she heard the soft footsteps, and recognized the characteristic tone. Treemark had returned.

Hour...over? she thought sluggishly.

He came close enough that she could hear the whisper of his sweat-pants as he moved, then the louder sound of a pail being set down nearby.

She gasped as she felt his arms encircle her waist, pull tight, and lift her up. He raised her until her legs were straight and her knees remembered to lock, taking her weight off her arms. Then he pulled her body to the left, stretching her right arm tight, giving the left more room to sag. He pressed tight against her, holding her in position, took hold of her left arm near the shoulder and gave it a sudden inward pull. Lorraine grunted in brief shock as the bone clicked heavily into place, followed by the eerie buzzing tickle of her shoulder healing in its restored position.

"Broken or dislocated bones must be properly set," he said, stepping back from her, "Or they'll heal wrong, no matter how fast they heal."

Lorraine said nothing, concentrating on keeping her knees straight.

There was a sound of water, then the feel of a wet sponge stroking her shoulder.

Lorraine glanced sideways, and saw that Treemark had lifted a corner of her robe and was washing something red off her shoulder. *Blood,* she guessed, remembering that she'd bitten herself in her frenzy. *No matter. The wounds heal fast.*

"This is not permitted," Treemark said sternly, moving the sponge to her other shoulder. "This house is a haven of peace for our kind. You are not allowed to harm any person in it, including yourself."

Nice theory, Lorraine thought sluggishly, as the sponge finished its work and went away. She felt Treemark drape something around her neck, looked down and glimpsed what looked like a thick plastic necklace with an odd Y-shaped pendant.

Treemark wrapped one hand firmly in her hair, then suddenly pulled her head back. Lorraine felt her jaw drop in surprise—and then something wide and thick pressed quickly into her mouth, something smooth and Y-shaped that slid between her upper and lower teeth. Lorraine shouted wordlessly and tried to pull away, but his hand held the gag firmly in place. His other hand pulled the straps tight against her lips and cheeks, then pressed them together behind her head with a crisp sound of Velcro sealing. His hands released her, leaving the gag in place. Lorraine shook her head frantically, but the straps held firm.

"You may not harm anyone here," Treemark repeated, "Including yourself."

Lorraine subsided, panting, and explored the gag with her tongue. It fitted neatly between her jaws, holding her teeth apart, but leaving room for her tongue to move. It was joined by a metal shank between her lips to the wide padded strap that covered her mouth, stretched along her cheeks and finally closed behind her head. It was snug, but not painfully tight. She could swallow freely, just not bite, or speak. Lorraine held perfectly still, wondering if this was all Treemark wanted.

Quickly, deftly, Treemark pulled off the robe over her head.

No sex, he said, she remembered.

Too late, Lorraine realized that she'd missed her chance to use her empathic ability, read his emotions and see what he intended. She sagged in the cuffs, panting, wondering how he would touch her next.

There were small unidentifiable sounds, and then she saw Treemark hold the bottle of massage-oil near her left wrist. She flinched as she felt him drip the oil along her arm, across her shoulders, then up the other arm. He reached around her to sprinkle the oil over her breasts, then pulled back and spilled more of it down the length of her spine. Lorraine trembled as the oil trickled slowly over her skin, tickling subtly as it passed.

Treemark gripped her arms just behind the cuffs, held for an instant, then began spreading the oil smoothly across her skin: up her arms, around her shoulders, up her neck and throat to the edge of the gag. His hands were gentle and thorough, and no other part of his body touched her.

Lorraine struggled to set herself into the right frame of mind, summon her empathic ability and *reach* for him.

There: the feel of his presence deepened, became more detailed, clearer. He felt...

Unbelievably, there was no emotion but that same intense, almost scholarly, determination to do the right thing. Yes, there was a sensual appreciation for the feel of her smooth warm skin, but that was minor, irrelevant, shoved off into a distant corner.

He was dedicated to his purpose, and there was no clear image of what that purpose was.

If not sex, what does he want?

She lost her concentration when his hands spread the oil over her stretched armpits and then came around her to slide under her breasts. She shivered as the intimate warmth of his touch rubbed upward, his broad palms pressing over her nipples, and tried to lunge backward, away from his hands, only to press herself against his hard-muscled chest. She pulled forward, away from him, which thrust her breasts back into his hands.

Lorraine ground her teeth into the gag, not wanting to feel this, unable to ignore the sensation of his spread fingers cupping her sensitized flesh. She could see and feel her nipples tightening, rising like rose-stone towers on white hills, castles almost encircled by an invading army; if he moved his thumbs an inch, he'd feel them too.

Instead, Treemark slipped his hands downward and rubbed slow circles over her ribs, working sideways from her upper belly to her back. Lorraine stood motionless, panting in relief. Her nipples still stood erect and taut, and where his hands had passed the oil made her skin even more sensitive; she could feel the faint surge of his breath on her shoulders as his hands stroked steadily down to her waist. She tried again to read him psychically, but got only a quick glimpse—again, nothing but determined purpose—before the feel of his hands dissolved her concentration.

His touch moved lower, skimming over her belly, one finger circling briefly in her navel, then backward across her hips. Lorraine felt her knees tremble and struggled to lock them again, suddenly aware of the mingled scent of the flowers and the damp warmth of the air. She could actually hear the soft whisper of skin on oiled skin as Treemark's thumbs rubbed over the flat bone of her lower back. Then his hands slid lower, and cupped her buttocks.

Lorraine lunged furiously against the cuffs, leaping for escape and finding none.

The implacable hands followed: rubbing, circling, slicking the oil over her buttocks and down to her thighs. She writhed helplessly in the bonds, swept by a sudden hot dizziness so fierce it threatened to make her faint. Dammit, no, this couldn't be arousal; she certainly didn't want Treemark, in fact hadn't wanted anybody in years… But what else could it be?

His hands didn't stop, didn't press deeper, only spread the oil and moved on.

Lorraine sagged in the cuffs as she felt his fingers converge on the top of her left thigh, stroke and circle down. She bit back a sigh as he rubbed the oil into her knee, the tender skin at the back of her leg, down her calf and shin all the way to her foot. She struggled to her feet as his hands closed on the crease of her right thigh and began working downward. The last of her untouched flesh was disappearing under his steady onslaught, leaving her whole body frantically sensitized and warmed until it felt boneless. She shivered as his fingers slid and circled, down and down, until he reached the other foot and finally pulled away.

What now? What now? Lorraine wondered dizzily, waiting. She could feel her pulse beating, slow and heavy, in all her flesh. She couldn't remember being so aware of her body, every muscle and bone and nerve. The tiny hairs on her arms prickled softly, and random muscles twitched, waiting.

From behind her came the unmistakable sound of fingers running across a brush.

Lorraine looked over her shoulders and saw Treemark indeed holding a wide flat brush, like a currying brush except with finer bristles. As she watched he pressed the bristles—soft, soft as a baby's hairbrush—against her left wrist, and then stroked slowly down her arm.

Currying, she thought dizzily. She held utterly still, scarcely breathing, as soft bristles stroked and stroked, down one arm and then the other. A hot shivering seized her, and she quivered from head to foot; the eerie, soft almost-tickling was stirring her nerves in ways she couldn't understand. This couldn't be arousal, could it? Just from these soft, light, implacable touches?

It could be nothing else.

The brush moved on, whispering over her neck and shoulders, throat and collarbones, and Lorraine could no longer keep still. She flinched and twisted as far as she could move, trying to escape those delicately maddening strokes, feeling her pulse surge through all her flesh, beat heavily in her nipples and clitoris, making them itch and burn until they seemed to glow like little red coals.

By the time the brushing ended and Treemark stepped back from her, she was writhing in slow half-delirious waves against the cuffs and groaning softly on every breath. She could still feel the brushstrokes, as if the bristles had dug furrows in the oil and the skin beneath, and her whole body throbbed like the beating of deep drums. She couldn't remember ever feeling this aroused without a man's hands, lips, or body pressing hers.

"You will remain here for the rest of the hour," Treemark said quietly, "And nothing—nothing outside yourself—will happen to you."

Then he picked up the pail, turned, and walked away. She felt his aura fading, then heard the door close.

Lorraine clamped her teeth on the gag, and thrashed helplessly in her shackles.

What was she supposed to do, feeling like this? All her senses were overloaded; the colors of the plants glowed bright as flames, the scents of the flowers and the oil on her skin were subtly intoxicating, she could hear the blood humming in her ears, feel her pulse pounding in every fiber, sensations drowning her mind in hyper-awareness—but with no conclusion, no relief, no end. No one would touch her, and she couldn't even touch herself. She was caught up in a featureless desire, a vast impersonal force that swept her away like a leaf in a hurricane.

It has to fade! she managed to think. Fade, in time: time she couldn't measure, when every second in this maddening-sweet throbbing stretched to eternity. *The rest of an hour, like this...* She groaned and writhed slowly, feeling even the dappled sunlight on her skin as a teasing caress.

***

Helen was waiting in the control-center when Treemark entered, still rubbing the last of the oil off his hands. She looked pointedly at the security-screen, then back to him, as if daring him to watch. Treemark gave the screen only a quick glance, just enough to confirm what he'd expected. "Progress," was all he said.

"You've called up her buried memories, you've summoned her rage and sensuality," countered Helen, "But can you call up the subtler emotions? For that matter, how will you deal with the guilt and rage she'll no doubt feel for losing control so badly?"

"To answer your last question first," said Treemark, dropping into the chair behind the main desk, "From what I've seen of her, she's not terribly prone to guilt—and if I can reach her while she's receptive, I don't think anger at me will be a problem. On that score, I could use your assistance. Help me pick out fitting dress for her."

"Dress?" Helen gave him a sidelong look.

"Goddess of Mycenae, you know more about the psychology of clothes than anyone on this continent, and I think you know what's needed here."

Helen smiled knowingly. "I'll help you this time," she said, "But don't assume I'll be your willing assistant on the rest of this project."

"Helen?" Treemark raised an eyebrow. "Are you jealous?"

"Not of her." Helen fixed him with an unreadable look. "I honestly feel affection for that poor fierce child. It's your own obsession that worries me."

"We've spoken of this before—"

"And will again, be sure." Helen turned and went to the door. "While you tinker with your test-tubes, Dr. Frankenstein, I'll go fetch some clothes."

He watched her go, sighed, and turned back to the monitor. As he studied the screen he reminded himself to be careful; there was always a chance that Helen might be right.

***

The long slow fading of the intense feeling left Lorraine near unconsciousness. She was struggling to stay on her feet when the warning aura came again, and she was too exhausted to think of what this might mean. *Schedule...* she remembered. What came next on the schedule?

She felt Treemark draw near, then a rustle of cloth, and then the terrycloth towel/robe slipped over her head, its folds falling softly to her feet. Treemark spread its sides out to form sleeves, enfolding her in its warmth and armor, and she was dimly grateful. Then came the rip of Velcro parting, and the straps by her cheeks slackened.

The gag pulled away, leaving her mouth empty and oddly bereft. The sudden air tasted of flowers and almonds. Locks clicked near her feet, and the slight tension on her ankles vanished. Another lock clicked, and her left arm fell free to her side. She sagged forward and would have fallen but that Treemark wrapped an arm around her and pulled her close against him. The last lock opened and her right arm dropped free, leaving her supported only by Treemark's body, limp as seaweed washed up on a sun-warmed beach. She could feel the solidity of him through the cloth, but in the wake of exhausted desire the contact was only comforting.

Treemark held her a moment longer, making it clear without words that he wouldn't let her fall, then lowered her gently to the floor. She wondered if he meant for her to lie down, but then he slid an arm under her knees and lifted her again. He moved then, carrying her in his arms, which surprised her slightly, for she knew she wasn't that light.

Lorraine let her head sag against his shoulder and feebly stretched her empathic sense. All she could read was a glimpse of that same determination, underlain with an almost completely chaste concern for her. It was not the kind of concern she would have expected of a lover; it was something still obscure, and she had no strength to probe further. Too weary to think, she withdrew and let herself be carried.

The door to the greenhouse/solarium was open, and beyond it rang the presence of another Elf/mutant: Madge this time. Lorraine briefly wondered what the woman must think of this sight, then decided it didn't matter. Madge had cast herself in the role of housekeeper, and wouldn't question. A single glance showed that the woman was holding a bundle of clothing—Lorraine's folded jeans and gun-belt visible at the top—and the recognizable key to her bedroom.

She let herself drift through the long passage through the house, scarcely rousing when Treemark set her gently into her own bed and pulled up the soft covers.

She dimly noted Madge in the shadows of the curtained room: setting the clothes on a chair, then spreading something at the foot of the bed, then leaving. Treemark stayed only a moment longer.

"Rest for an hour," he said, "Then come to dinner."

He brushed a hand lightly over her forehead, then turned and moved away. The door shut with a decisive click, and then he was gone.

Lorraine gave a long sigh, marveling at her solitude. She moved a sluggish hand against the sheets, intrigued by their smoothness as if she'd never noticed that before.

With effort, she slid her hand up to her belly, then her groin. *No sex, he said.* She pulled her hand away and let it drop, hoping to sink into sleep.

No, she couldn't sleep, but her body lay utterly still and her mind drifted. Her flesh felt softened and strange, as if her sense of touch had expanded; she was quietly aware of her toes and elbows and the skin between her shoulderblades. She could also hear the tiny tick of the electric clock changing numbers, the faint hum of air circulating from the vent above the door. The space around her was scented with the cedar-and-almond of the oil on her skin. If she opened her eyes, she guessed, she would see perfectly well in the curtained dimness.

Was this, she wondered, what Treemark had intended with that ordeal? Was he trying to extend her senses? Why had he chosen that means to do it?

Trust... She remembered his endless talk of trust: trusting others, trusting her feelings... Trusting her own senses, then? Enough to expand them?

Or was this also a means of expanding her psychic ability? Others of her kind prized that power enough to kill for it, steal it from the dying, destroy a civilization in their greed for it. What if Treemark knew a way to increase it by training? Quicker than waiting for age to provide it: better than killing. Yes, that would be consistent with all he'd told her.

Trainer...and I'm a raw colt. That was the only pattern that fit. She wondered drowsily what he was training her for: racing, show, or dressage? *Not for hunting, anyway.*

She let her mind drift further, and considered that it had been a long time since she'd thought of a future any further than the next year. Now she had to wonder what she would do in the next twenty years, or hundred. It seemed inconceivable.

Then she remembered that she could paint.

***

Benjamin came in from the stables, intending to go straight to a shower, when Helen caught him in the corridor.

"Ben," she said, planting herself squarely in front of him, "I get the impression you're avoiding me. You need not be guilty over it, but just tell me why."

He shifted from foot to foot, glanced around for escape and found none.

"I'm...trying to disentangle myself," he admitted. "I promised I'd bring you here safely, and I did, but I never intended to stay. I meant to hang around for only a week, and then go back to Seattle."

"Or Vancouver, or Paris, or the Bahamas," she smiled. "You're always running away."

"It's a good survival trait. Most hunters work at random, you know: hunt through a city, then move on. If I move faster..." he shrugged.

"In that case, why haven't you moved on already?"

"You know the answer! Brian pressured me into training the girl, and now I'm stuck here for a few more weeks, at least—possibly months. Dammit, Helen, did you talk him into that?"

"I wish I'd thought of it, but I truly didn't." Helen tapped her chin thoughtfully. "Brian's at least as devious as you are. Have you considered that he might have another motive, besides Lorraine, or me, for keeping you here?"

"Research." Benjamin's shoulders slumped. "He's been after me to give him names and contact information on everyone I know. Beyond that, he wants my help in finding others—especially new ones, youngsters whom he might persuade."

"And you have objections to that?"

Benjamin glanced up the corridor to where the discreet security-camera watched, then took Helen's arm and led her through the nearest door—which happened to open on the laundry-room. A load of laundry was sloshing in the washer, but Madge wasn't there.

He leaned against the machine, obliging Helen to step closer to hear him.

"You know this isn't the only enclave of— of peacemakers," he almost whispered.

"I know of a few monasteries, temples, similar places…"

"Breeding enclaves, Helen."

"Oh." She blinked. "At nodes on the Ley-Lines?"

"Of course. Protected, all of them." He glanced toward the door. "And of course their keepers search primarily for older ones, old enough to breed, but even they want amenable youngsters—for guards, if nothing else."

"Ah, and you think they'd see Brian as competition?"

"Unless I can persuade them otherwise. That's hard to manage at a distance."

Helen thumped her fist angrily against the dryer. "Are even the sensible ones so paranoid? How will we ever climb out of the Dark Ages if every decent social unit we create squabbles with all the others?"

"You might do something to quell that, yourself," Benjamin

smiled cautiously. "You know, thanks to the wonders of modern technology, you need not tell someone where you are to show them your face. There are some elders who remember you, and would listen seriously to what you told them."

Helen narrowed her eyes in thought. "The Internet," she considered. "Brian's cameras..."

"Real-time transmission," he suggested.

"Oh, I'm such a dolt with electronic things! I wouldn't know how to do it."

"Brian could arrange it, and would, if you asked. The only person who could ever wrap him around their finger is you, oh Oracle of Delphi."

"He's not that bendable..." Her look turned inward, calculating. "But I'll see what I can do about getting your obligations shortened."

***

The buzzing of the intercom pulled Lorraine back from her drifting. She found it easier than she'd expected to pick up the handset. "Yes?" she murmured, tongue a little thick.

"Dinner will be served in 15 minutes, Ms. Lorraine," Daniel's voice chirped back at her. "Please do attend. I've concocted a Chicken Parmigiana with mushrooms and an Artichoke Hollandaise that I'm particularly proud of."

"And an artist needs an appreciative audience," Lorraine smiled, feeling her mouth watering. "I'll be there."

"Excellent." The intercom clicked off.

Only the thought of Daniel's cooking, she reflected, could drag her out of bed right now. She pushed back the covers and slid her feet to the floor, trying to decide how to dress for dinner.

Then the gown laid out on the foot of the bed caught her eye. It was long-skirted and long-sleeved, in a deep wine-red heavy crepe, caught up under the breasts with a wide elastic cunningly disguised by a deep-blue satin ribbon. She wouldn't need to wear a brassiere under it. A pair of matching dark-red sandals on the floor nearby suggested that she wouldn't need hose, either.

Beside it lay a wide blue-and-silver embroidered belt, bearing a blue velvet drawstring purse and a small dagger, with a crystal on the pommel, in an ornamented sheath.

Lorraine stared at the dagger for a long moment, one corner of her mind noting that the ensemble would look wonderfully medieval, another telling her that Treemark was trying to reassure her; if she wanted to wear weapons in the house, he'd be happy to provide her with more. *Still more training?* she wondered, reaching for the dress.

She came to dinner wearing the dagger-belt.

Daniel and Madge were already serving the soup and salad—a spiced beef bouillon and a shrimp cocktail with sweet onion rings—and everyone fell to the food with little conversation. In the brief break between courses Wally and Steven reported on the improvement of the sore-footed mare, Benjamin urged Lorraine to try more of the wine—a most unusual Riesling, he claimed—and Helen pestered a reluctant Treemark for information about someone named Mirosaki.

The main course arrived in short order, and after that the only comments were heartfelt praises for Daniel's art. Madge smirked and murmured something about pre-marinating that made Daniel chuckle—and made Lorraine wonder about the relationship between those two. Gray-haired or not, they were full-fledged Elves and could easily be lovers. She could spare little thought for speculation, though, with the exquisite food absorbing her attention. Whether Daniel had outdone himself tonight or whether her senses were still stretched, the taste of the art-pieces owned her for the duration.

After dessert—a wicked little chocolate-brandy cake—Treemark waved her toward the clinic office. Lorraine shivered for a moment, then strode resolutely toward the door. Treemark followed a few minutes later, bearing a martini for himself and a scotch-on-the-rocks for her. Lorraine took a ritual sip and sank into the comfortable padded chair.

"Are you trying to expand my psychic ability?" she beat him to the first question. She wanted to ask about that peculiar session in the solarium, but not directly, not yet.

Treemark looked surprised. "I certainly hope to," he said. "Why do you ask?"

"That seems to be the coin of the Elven realm," Lorraine replied, thinking of the ancient war.

Treemark winced and took a mouthful of his own drink.

"More to the point, Doctor," she plunged on. "Just what are you training me for?"

"First, to survive." He gave her a long, somber look. "Some of the hunters out there are very old, and very experienced. Second, for... call it missionary work; I shamelessly admit that I want to spread the word far and wide that the prophecy is wrong, the hunt is evil, and that we can live together in peace. Third—eventually—I hope to see you bear and raise a lot of... little Elves. We're an endangered species, Lorraine."

I'll have time for that now, she thought. *Not just five years, or ten, to decide... But I have so much to learn!* "How eventually?" she asked.

Treemark sighed. "A long time. We don't usually become fertile until about the age of 1200. It might happen earlier for you."

"But—but I was pregnant!" Lorraine floundered.

"And if you hadn't aborted, you would probably have miscarried. Pre-Initiation fertility is very rare, and the pregnancies usually end in miscarriage, and it only happens among Convergents."

"...'Convergents'?"

"You weren't born to mutant parents," Treemark said carefully, "But to mortals who were both carrying the gene. It's recessive, and you were lucky enough to get it from both sides. The genes converged. Convergent."

"Then..." Lorraine pressed a hand to her forehead. "Once we're... twelve centuries old, we can... also breed with non-mutants?"

"Yes, though it isn't recommended for women. Unless the man is also carrying the gene, again, you're likely to miscarry.

Lorraine suddenly remembered an ancient myth from one of her Art History classes. It had seemed only grotesque then, but now it made the hair lift on the back of her neck. "Ishtar," she whispered. "Tammuz... Her son was also her lover!"

Treemark frowned. "That's one way to guarantee getting the gene, but it's... not recommended. At least Ishtar had the sense to send his children far away, to distant countries, where they'd breed with total outcrosses."

"And Zeus, screwing around all over Greece..."

"Spreading his genes far and wide. His wife wasn't too happy about it..." Treemark rattled his fingers on his martini glass. "By the time you're of an age to breed, you'll probably also have enough psychic ability that you could pass yourself off as a goddess—or, nowadays, an angel or a saint or a witch. It's—"

"Not recommended," Lorraine finished for him. Another thought occurred to her. "I have a brother..."

Then she remembered Georgie Dear, beer-bellied and already balding the last time she saw him, and crying about it. He'd gone through one marriage already, and his second wife was talking about divorce, and it was easy to tell why; still whining and self-pitying, still demanding coddling and cosseting, going through jobs three times as fast as wives, he was an aging baby who'd never really grown up. The idea of him as an immortal Elf/mutant was ludicrous. Still, an endangered species couldn't afford to be choosy.

"Give me his full name and address," Treemark echoed her thought, "And I'll keep watch on him. If he's a pre-Initiate, we'll know."

His name... That would reveal her real name, and she was still a witness hiding from the Mafia. No, it would have to wait. A few months, a year at most, wouldn't matter; men stayed fertile longer than women. "I don't know where he is," she invented. "I won't know until he writes to me again. He'll do it sooner or later..." *Probably to whine and nag about why I don't come see Momma more often and divert her smothering attention away from him for awhile.*

"Your mother would probably know. Can you give me her address?"

"No!" Lorraine snapped, and then realized she'd have to explain that.

Treemark nodded thoughtfully. "You couldn't go to her when you were in trouble. Why did you say she'd be worse than useless?"

Lorraine seized her glass and gulped another mouthful. *All right, play Dr. Freud with this,* she decided, feeling an unexpected surge of old bitterness. "My mother worships Class the way other people worship their gods. She spent her life nagging Pop to make more money so she could buy her way into Grosse Pointe, and hobnob with the rich and richer, but she kept frittering away money on status symbols. She had to have at least one live-in maid, preferably one who could cook, to do all the housework for her — and when she was between maids, I was drafted. I remember trying to push a vacuum cleaner bigger than I was, and damned near as heavy..."

Lorraine paused for another bite of the scotch.

"...And the house had to be a showpiece, 24 hours a day, seven days a week. Don't dare go near the diningroom, or the livingroom, or anyplace else that visitors were likely to see. If we'd had back stairs, she would have made me use them. Don't touch anything: you might break it. Especially don't embarrass Momma in front of the neighbors. Ultimate sin. The few beatings I remember getting were for breaking things or embarrassing Momma—

that is, if she told me the reason at all."

"Beatings without even explanations?"

"A couple times I heard her come screaming up the stairs and knew she was coming for me, but had no idea why. One time I scrambled out the window onto the roof, but she caught my foot and dragged me back in—and then, of course, her reason was that I'd tried to run away. I never did learn what the original reason was."

"Ah. And the other times?"

"Just one that I remember. I was small enough to crawl under the bed, far enough that she couldn't reach me, though her claws came close. Finally she went running back down the stairs to get a broom and pry me out, but as soon as she was gone I crawled out fast and got through the window. I spent an hour hiding on the roof behind the chimney, until Pop came home and Momma forgot whatever she was going to smack me about. I was lucky it was summer."

Treemark nodded slowly, not taking his eyes off her. "What did she beat you with? Do you remember?"

"Anything handy. Her hands, an eggbeater, a jump-rope once..." Lorraine rubbed her thigh, remembering the welts. "She threw away my jump-rope afterwards, and I never forgave her. Brand new, shiny red plastic: prettiest jump-rope I ever saw. That hurt worse than the welts."

"She raised welts?"

"As I said, it was plastic—plastic sheathing anyway, over a thin steel cable. Welts… I don't think she expected that, but then, Momma never thought ahead about such things."

Treemark rubbed his forehead. "And she threw it away..."

"I think that was the worst," Lorraine considered. "Seeing proof that I had no property—and no rights—that Momma couldn't take away at will. Seeing that for all her fine Liberal talk, she really didn't respect anyone else's rights… especially not mine."

Lorraine reached for the glass again and found it empty. That drew her back to awareness of present time. "No, Momma was not the sort of person I could go to in a crisis. Hell, if the...stalker had worn a fancy suit and talked a good line, Momma would have welcomed him into the house and glibly told me that I had to be mistaken about such a *nice* man."

Treemark twitched a slight smile. "She loved nothing but Class? Nothing else at all?"

"She had a taste for elegance. She knew quality goods when

she saw them, but I think that was just an outgrowth of her Class-worship. If it came to a choice between good taste and fashiona-ble trash, she'd choose fashion. She pretended to love art, too, and for the longest time I believed her..." Lorraine fixed her eyes on the empty glass, letting her voice run down, recalling the pain of an old betrayal.

"How was the truth revealed?" Treemark asked gently.

"My last semester in college," Lorraine murmured, seeing the pictures take form in the glass. "I'd graduated, but stayed on for the summer taking more art classes. I knew my painting tech-nique was clumsy, contrasts too strong, cartoonish. I'd signed up for the tools-and-techniques class, but there was a waiting list. While I waited to get in, I took more life-drawing and model-painting classes. Then Momma showed up…"

She could still remember the fashionable mauve suit Momma wore on arrival; it had looked hideous with Momma's coloring, but it was the height of fashion.

"Momma was impatient; she wanted me to come home so she could run me through the eligible bachelors. She sashayed through the school, made a point of talking to all my teachers, then took me out to dinner... God, she could make a two-hour production out of a simple meal! ...And over dessert she sweetly told me that my paintings were crap, my teachers were only hu-moring me because I paid to be there, and I should give up this nonsense and come home, come home, where I could get a real life."

"But you didn't go?" Treemark's voice came to her past the glass.

"I knew it was a lie. My painting wasn't great, it needed work, but half the students in class were worse than I was. I saw that she would lie about art, lie about anything, just to manipulate Daughter Dearest into doing what she wanted: get a high-class husband and do Momma proud. My mother was a hypocrite, a Class-worshipper and a power-junkie, and I was ashamed to have her blood in my veins."

"Shame?"

"More like total revulsion, but I managed not to vomit where she could see. Instead, I lied right back to her. Smiled sweetly and said I had to finish up the semester, since I'd paid for it, but I'd pack up and come-home-come-home when it was finished. She believed, and went home. As soon as she was gone, I packed everything I could carry and ran away to Chicago. Got a day-job and painted in my spare time. I never did get that tools-and-techniques course, had to pick up bits and pieces from books or other artists... And I never could sell my paintings."

"There will be time, now," Treemark said quietly, "To take the courses you need."

"Yes, there will," Lorraine considered. "There's no time in my schedule now, but later..."

"There's always later. But are you sure she never loved you? There must have been a time when she did, at least a little, or you wouldn't have survived."

"Oh, there was. I remember she was good to me, back when I was too young to talk—or at least to say anything much. I couldn't express an opinion, or complain, or show that I had a mind of my own. Just old enough for Mama to toddle around, dress up in pretty clothes and show off without fear that I'd embarrass her. I'm sure she loved me then."

"You had a sharp mind even then," said Treemark. "I begin to see where you developed that iron will."

Lorraine lifted her glass. "Could I have another scotch without breaking training?"

"I'll mix you a double," said Treemark, rising. "Take it with a long hot bath, and get to sleep early."

"Headshrinking done for the night?"

"For tonight." Treemark smiled. "Get some rest, Lorraine. You've earned it."

***

No one was in the living room when they emerged, and Lorraine couldn't feel any interest in watching the television. Treemark's suggestion sounded better every minute.

She gratefully took the double scotch and padded back to her room, thinking idly of where she could get canvases or a new easel, and a new paint-kit. She would need to borrow a camera to take pictures of the horses; Leila, certainly, wouldn't stand still long enough to be a good artist's model.

But after she'd finished the bath and the drink and slid in between the smooth sheets, her last thoughts were images of the lush flowers in the solarium.

7.

LORRAINE WOKE TO the insistent buzzing of the intercom, briefly acknowledged Daniel's cheery summons to breakfast, crawled out of bed and into her working clothes.

After a moment's thought, she included the holstered gun, dagger and cell-phone.

Again, breakfast was simple: fruit, juice and lean bacon. Lorraine finished quickly, wanting to spend as much time as possible with the horses. To her surprise, Benjamin showed up for breakfast, dressed in boots and hat and blue jeans, and accompanied her out to the stables.

"Let's finish the stalls fast, and get on to the exercising," he said quietly. "There's something I need to show you."

Lorraine nodded quick acknowledgment, and went to fetch the tools.

Between the four of them, the stalls were finished in two hours. Benjamin selected, saddled and bridled the two red-bay mares, mounted one and handed the other's reins to Lorraine. She mounted without comment, one part of her mind reviewing the characters and conditions of the mares, the rest warily observing Benjamin; he seemed preoccupied and thoughtful as he led the way out of the barn, out of the paddock and into the open lands beyond.

Once into the desert, Benjamin heeled his mare to a trot. Lorraine followed, noting that her mare was responding a little sluggishly in the heat. When not scanning the ground ahead for treacherous spots, Benjamin kept his eyes on a rock outcropping ahead. Lorraine noted that the ground there was peppered closely with spindly Palo-Verde trees and shrubby mesquite; that might mean there was water close by—always a good thing to know in the desert.

As they approached the outcropping, Lorraine noticed something strange: an odd feeling of tingling pressure in the air, somewhat like the feel of another elf's aura but lacking the sense of personality, and increasing with their every step. The impression grew stronger as they crossed a circular border of widely spaced rocks until it built into a silent roar, like an invisible waterfall of power. Benjamin led the way between a pair of Palo-Verdes to a small open space at the foot of the mound of boulders. From beneath the rocks trickled a tiny stream that filled a small shaded pool, and on the boulder above the spring was carved the image of the Thunderbird.

"Indian sacred ground?" Lorraine guessed.

"That and more," said Benjamin, sliding smoothly off his mare. "The water's good; let the horses drink."

Lorraine likewise dismounted and led her mare to the pool. The water was crystal-clear, revealing a layer of polished pebbles below, and the horses eagerly thrust their muzzles into the pool. Lorraine sampled the water herself, and found it marvelously cool and sweet.

"Why does the place feel like this?" she asked. "Is it because of the spring?"

"No," said Benjamin, wiping his mouth dry, "That's just an accident of geology—although the phenomena may be related. What do you know about Ley-Lines?"

Lorraine had to think for a long moment. "I read a book years ago... They're supposed to be lines of force that criss-cross the earth."

"No ordinary force," said Benjamin. "It's related to the energy that powers our bodies, I'm not sure how. Various scholars claim it's psychic energy. Others, of course, insist that it's all hogwash because they can't feel it. In any case, it's quite real and very powerful."

Lorraine tried to imagine lines of raw psychic energy stretching around the world like invisible rivers. "Can we...tap into that force somehow, with our psychic ability?"

"I don't know. Certainly I don't know how to do it." He shook his head impatiently. "The point is, where two such lines cross you find what's called a 'node'. This is one of them. You can feel how strong the power is here."

"I'd noticed."

"It's strong enough that even mortals can sometimes feel it." He pointed to the carving. "They often build churches, shrines, temples and so on at such places."

"Understandable." Lorraine dipped up a handful of the delightfully cool water and rubbed it on her face and throat. The steady torrent of the power around her felt equally refreshing.

"Understand this, also. If you were to kill or even wound one of us within reach of a node, the resulting power-surge would burn you to ashes. Nodes are, necessarily, places of peace.

"Ah. Do the Unseelie elves know that?

"Partly." Benjamin frowned at the carved rock. "Because

nodes are so often marked as holy places, the ignorant among us assume that all sacred sites are taboo—whether they can actually feel power there or not. It's a myth that we've encouraged."

"I can see why. But hasn't anyone else discovered that some holy places have power, and others don't?"

"I'm sure some of us have noticed," Benjamin smiled, "But very, very few of us want to take the risk of...experimenting with the taboo.

"No doubt." Lorraine studied the carving, wondering when it had been cut into the rock, and by whom. "So, it would be a good idea to put up some manner of shrine over every node you can find."

Benjamin smiled wider, but didn't answer.

"But aside from that, nobody has ever found a way to tap into the power of the nodes?

He chewed his lip and fixed his eyes on the pool. "A few nodes have reputations for miraculous healings," he murmured. "That's all I'm sure of."

"There are myths, legends..."

"—and fairy-tales. No solid evidence of anything else."

Lorraine ran her fingers through the cool clear water, feeling euphoric and slightly dizzy from the constant stream of invisible power. "There must be a way..." she murmured, thinking of all that untapped power and how it might be used to stop a long, slow genocide.

"If ever you find one, tell me," said Benjamin, gathering up his mare's reins. "Until then, if you're ever pursued by a hunter, run to the nearest node—or, failing that, any sacred place. You might do well to map all such sites anywhere near where you happen to be. Shall we go?"

Lorraine could think of nothing to do but mount up and follow Benjamin back to the ranch, idly noting that her mare felt much more lively and alert than on the ride up here. Apparently animals had enough psychic sensitivity to feel the node's power, enjoy it, and possibly absorb it in some fashion. *If a horse could do it, why not a human being?* She thought about that during the ride home, while exercising the other horses all morning, and during her own exercises afterward.

She was still pondering the problem when she met Benjamin again at the door to the basement armory.

"Do you know of anyone who's studying the nodes, and their

power?" she asked as they proceeded to the shooting-range.

"I know that Brian's trying to locate and map them all," he replied, taking an automatic pistol from a wall-rack. "And you might ask Helen what she knows. Here: hold this like so..."

For the rest of the first hour he made her concentrate on shooting, and the hour after that was devoted to sword-practice. Lorraine dutifully set aside her questions and let the weapons training absorb her attention.

At the beginning of the third hour they were interrupted by the feel of an approaching presence. Helen strolled into the practice-room, looking cool and elegant as always, wearing another version of a classical gown. Benjamin looked surprised and faintly worried

"Enough of the rattling sabers for today," Helen smiled, though her tone brooked no argument. "We'll spend the next hour on different training. Do come along with me, Lorraine."

Lorraine cast a questioning glance at Benjamin, who shrugged, then hung her sword on the rack and duly followed Helen. The Elven woman took Lorraine's hand and led her out of the basement, through the house and out into the back garden-patio. There was a rug and two large cushions set out on the flagstones, and Helen settled gracefully on the nearer pillow. Lorraine sat cautiously on the other before asking just what this was about.

"Psychic practice," Helen said bluntly. "You're very recently Initiated, and therefore have only a little ability yet, but there's no reason why we can't test and train what you have. We'll begin with basic relaxation techniques."

Lorraine got the impression that this was entirely Helen's idea, and Treemark knew nothing about it. She wondered how upset he'd be when he learned of it, and why.

So there were little intrigues, even here in this supposed haven.

"Assume a comfortable position," Helen began. "Close your eyes and concentrate on your breathing..."

The basic techniques, Lorraine soon discovered, weren't much different from the Yoga exercises she'd studied back in college: relaxation, meditation, centering, and grounding. It was surprisingly easy to fall back into those patterns. Helen smiled and moved on to the next stage.

"Can you feel anything more than my presence?" she asked, taking Lorraine's hands.

"Yes..." Lorraine closed her eyes in concentration, wondering how to explain this. She could feel Helen's intent concern, very much like Treemark's, but the general feel—'background tone' was the only term she could think of—was very different. It was like comparing trumpets with cellos, apples with steak, or the Bayeux Tapestry with an Impressionist painting. It was a signature feeling, and its only similarity with Treemark's was the sense of vast intricacy and massive experience. "I feel your…well, character."

"Tell me when you stop feeling it," Helen almost whispered, slowly pulling her hands away.

Lorraine felt the sensation dimming, and reached for it. There: she caught it again, held it steady. She heard Helen moving on the cushion but ignored the sound, struggling to maintain her invisible grip. The feeling grew harder to hold, not slipping away so much as thinning, like ice melting to water that trickled away between her fingers and then evaporated, faded to nothing.

"Now," Lorraine sighed, defeated.

"Open your eyes." Helen's voice quivered.

Lorraine opened her eyes, and saw that Helen—looking astonished—was standing nearly 30 feet away.

"Is this unusual?" Lorraine asked.

Helen nodded slowly. "In one so young...newly Initiated... Oh, yes. I think you'll do very well." She smoothly regained her composure and paced back to her pillow.

"Now, see if you can feel anything else besides me."

Lorraine duly closed her eyes and dropped deliberately into the meditative state of mind. Once there, she sat quietly and let herself *feel* the air around her, then a little further away, further...

Slowly she became aware of the cool mindless life of the plants, spreading their leaves to the sun as unconsciously as sleepwalkers. And there: the darting bright hunger of a bird flying past. And there, approaching, the warm intent awareness of a small animal... a cat, she realized. The little creature stalked through the jungle of ornamental plants looking for something to hunt, not because she was hungry but because that was her purpose in life. Her belly swayed annoyingly but the cat only purred to herself, feeling that she guarded a soft treasure in her bulging abdomen.

Pregnant, Lorraine realized. *Kittens soon...*

She let her awareness move on, around the garden, up to the walls. She couldn't be sure of feeling anything beyond that, as if her range were limited to no more than a dozen yards. Disappointed, Lorraine made another psychic circuit of the garden. There were no other living things in it, only the plants and the passing cat, and Helen of course…

Lorraine stopped there, attention caught on something familiar. Something about Helen was like the cat: that sense of hoarding a treasure in the belly...

"Helen," she blurted without thinking, "Are you pregnant?"

Helen gasped, then laughed aloud. "Very good!" she said. "Oh yes, definitely, you have a talent for this! You'll be more than just a warrior, my dear."

"Who—" Lorraine barely stopped herself in time. *Absolutely none of my business!*

Helen caught the thought anyway. "It's not Brian's," she smiled. "Don't concern yourself over that..." Her smile faded. "Our kind rarely marries. With so few of us old enough to breed, so few of us even knowing that we can, there isn't much point to it."

Helen rubbed her hands across her belly. "For many reasons, not the least being the safety of the children, for a long time we...have acted like cuckoos, giving our children anonymously to mortals to raise."

"Changelings," Lorraine remembered the old legend. "Elf children left in the cradles, while the mortal babies were spirited away… But what became of the mortal children?"

"Sometimes we would raise them as our own. More often, we secretly exchanged our children for those who had died in the cradle. That was once much more common."

Helen shook her golden head, looking bitter. "Nowadays we often leave them on the doorsteps of orphanages, or churches, or go openly to maternity hospitals under false names, claiming to be unwed mothers willing to give up the children for adoption. There are always ways."

"But why?" Lorraine couldn't help asking. "Why can't you raise your own children?"

Helen's expression turned grim. "For one thing, our knowledge of breeding is one advantage we have over the Unseelie—and we must keep that secret at all costs. Second..." She sighed heavily. "Children are such easy hostages. Do you understand?

Lorraine nodded slowly, feeling a chill pass over her.

"Third..." Helen's face went absolutely expressionless. "Should any of our children be seduced into Unseelie ways, we must be capable of...defending ourselves, even to the death. This would be extremely difficult with a child one had raised oneself."

Lorraine understood, and thought she'd be sick. "This has to stop..." she whispered.

Helen smiled gamely, like an armored knight about to charge into battle. "To be honest, I intend to break with two thousand years of tradition and take the risk of raising this child myself. I believe I can do it safely, here at Brian's enclave. If I can keep the child out of sight of the Unseelie for just twenty years..." She broke off there, and the silence stretched long.

"Can't the father help?" Lorraine ventured, sourly remembering that men often disliked caring for their children.

Helen's smile softened. "Actually, Brian's in a much better position to do that, and he's as eager to take the risk as I am. I don't need a husband, really." Her gaze wandered outward, beyond the garden. "When I was young, women never married. We took consorts—for a season, a year, a lifetime—but it wasn't at all the same thing. Life was very different then. Villages, towns, such cities as we had—they were the protected enclaves where the women lived and raised children, and where the sick and injured and old could come and be safe. Healthy men and childless women would go out to hunt and farm and fish, but children were always brought to the enclaves, where everyone cared for them. In those days no one would be so insane as to harm a child, or so cruel as to refuse food to one. If a mother died, there was always someone to take on the care of the child. If nothing else, there were always the temples and their priestesses, and priests..."

"If it's not a rude question," Lorraine couldn't help asking, "...How old are you?"

Helen chuckled. "It's certainly not rude among friends, those we can trust not to be greedy for our life-force. I've lived for 3926 years. My birthday is in early October, as they call it now."

Lorraine realized that her mouth was hanging open, and hastily pulled it shut. She floundered mentally, searching for something else to say, and found it. "The Ley-Lines. The nodes. Is there anyone who knows how to tap and use their power?"

"He told you—" Helen looked startled, then thoughtful. "Well, I know of a woman—one of us, quite old—who has a cabin in Scotland built directly over a node. She's very psychic, reputed to be a witch, in fact. Surely she didn't choose that site by accident, though what she does with it is anyone's guess, she being quite secretive. I heard of another, a man in China, who lived in a cave that was said to be magical—and he had a great reputation as a sorcerer. Unfortunately, he was killed some four centuries ago. That's all I can tell you—at this point."

"I see I have my work cut out for me," Lorraine murmured. *Life's work,* came the unbidden thought. Following that came a vision of what this could mean in the ancient Elven war of attrition. Unseelie elves killed each other for power, and the Seelie elves had less power because they didn't cannibalize each other, but if one could draw power from the nodes—let alone use it—then that would tip the balance. She couldn't yet see how it might be done, but she knew it was possible. *I could end the war.*

She was still thinking of that when the silent ringing of another Elven presence announced Treemark's approach. He strolled into the garden, glanced once at Helen, then turned to Lorraine.

"Sorry to end the lesson," he said, "But it's time for your physical therapy session."

Lorraine shivered, remembering what that meant, but she pulled herself to her feet. "Tomorrow then, Helen?" she asked, almost fearing that the answer would be no.

"Tomorrow," Helen promised, smiling.

Lorraine turned away and duly followed Treemark out to the pool.

***

Even as she hung her clothes in the locker, Lorraine felt an expectant sensuality creep up on her. She took care not to look at Treemark as he stripped unselfconsciously and walked into the Jacuzzi; it was more difficult to follow him without looking. The hot water and the soft pressure of the water-jets were relaxing, comforting, subtly seductive, and Treemark's easy silence left her too aware of the feeling. Struggling to keep her mind clear, Lorraine almost defiantly tossed him a question.

"How long have you known about the node out behind the house?"

Treemark snapped his eyes open, looking surprised, then thought a moment and smiled. "So Ben's shown you that, has he?"

"Why didn't you tell me yourself? About the nodes, safety on sacred ground, all of it?" Lorraine realized she was looking for an excuse to be angry with him.

"How much did you expect to learn all at once?" he replied calmly. "There's an enormous amount of information, and you've been here less than a week."

So I have! Lorraine was jolted to remember. It seemed she'd been part of this household much longer than that.

"But to answer your question, I didn't discover it until after I'd bought the ranch and started building the house. If I'd known, I would have built the house around it. As it is, there's a chapel in the house—properly blessed, consecrated, everything—which can hold up to 50 of us, if needed. I'll show it to you tonight, after dinner, if you'd like."

"The Elven version of a bomb-shelter?" Lorraine smiled. "Just tell me how to reach it. I'm really not religious."

Treemark didn't answer, but only closed his eyes and leaned against the edge of the pool.

That, Lorraine considered, was odd. Usually psychiatrists tried to keep you talking. In fact, she wanted to keep talking. The near-silence of the pool area felt almost oppressive.

"Do you know," she tried again, "Of anyone who's been able to tap the power of the nodes—for anything but preventing fights, I mean."

"No." Treemark didn't open his eyes. "Lorraine, stop talking, close your eyes and relax. This too is part of your training."

He'd guessed what she was doing, Lorraine realized. Inwardly fuming, she dutifully closed her eyes and leaned against the wa-ter-jet. The comforting warmth reached for her again, and she silently fought it off. Even if she couldn't talk, she could still keep her mind engaged.

Think: think about the nodes and how their power could be used. It was raw psychic energy, the same kind that Elven bodies processed; it could be absorbed, much like drinking the water from that spring. How could it be channeled, focused, dis-charged? The only way she'd seen the energy discharged was in the rapid-healing process. That might be a clue...

"Just how does the healing work?" she asked. "What's the mechanism?"

She heard Treemark sigh, then a heavier surging in the water. Then she felt his hand clamp on her neck, and a sudden hard pressure near the skull. It went through her like an electric shock, leaving her body numb. Lorraine gasped and opened her eyes in time to see Treemark stretch out her left arm, holding the wrist near one of the ornamental brass rings. Something flashed in his hand, under the water, and then clicked.

Even as she realized that he'd just fastened her wrist to the brass ring, he took hold of her other wrist and pulled her arm out sideways. Another link clicked. As feeling prickled back into her body, Lorraine saw that she was shackled to one of the rings in the pool, and Treemark was holding her other wrist—with another link attached to the cuff—next to another of those not-so-ornamental brass rings. That and his stern expression were clear warning. Still more shocking was the fact that he'd numbed her whole body, even for just a few seconds, with that simple grip on her neck. How had he known that? What else could he do? Lorraine kicked at him under the water, reaching nowhere near him.

"Enough of this," said Treemark. "You can't afford to break training, not this early at least. Now, will you stop this pointless resistance or must I shackle your other wrist?"

Lorraine stopped kicking and glared at him. Yes, he could do that. Then he could simply leave her there, for as long as he wished, where anyone could come out and see her like that. Lorraine shuddered, and kept still.

Treemark released her wrist. "Enough," he repeated. "You've used physical exertion, even self-inflicted pain, to ward off feeling—and now you're using intellectual concentration. This is not allowed. You must continue your treatment, with no obstruction from your defense mechanisms."

"Oh, it's all for my own good, is it?" Lorraine snarled. "I've heard that before!"

"I'm not your mother," Treemark answered, then slipped to her other side and released her left wrist from the brass ring. It had been fastened, she saw, not with a lock but with a simple snap-link. With one hand free, she could easily have opened the link herself.

Treemark unfastened both links from her cuffs, pulled out of the pool, stood up and walked away.

Lorraine thought that over while he went off to the garden-table, rummaged about on its surface, and came back. He touched her neck again, but only to lift up her hair.

She trembled as she felt a brush whisper across her scalp. "What are you doing?" she hissed.

"Braiding up your hair, simply to get it out of the way."

Lorraine could think of no answer to that, nor of anything to do but sit still and let him proceed. She was intensely aware of the feel of the brush, his hands pulling up her hair on top of her head, clasping it with an elastic tie and then braiding down the length of the rest. *What game is he playing?* she wondered again—and then recalled her psychic ability.

Remembering Helen's lessons of not an hour past, Lorraine made herself relax, drop into meditative state, ground herself, center, extend her awareness and *reach*. Yes, There was the heightened sense of him, and the same intent professional concern of a trainer for a raw colt. And underneath that...

He was afraid for her.

Startled, Lorraine almost lost the thread of contact. She recovered fast and reached deeper.

Yes: he feared that she might be somehow ruined, lost in some obscure cul-de-sac from which she would never emerge, snared in some weakness that would limit her, harm her... might even lead to her death. He had seen others of their kind lost like that.

Lorraine pondered that as he put the last tie on the end of her hair, got up, put away the brush and came back into the pool. "Just sit still," he said calmly, settling on the ledge opposite her. "Think of nothing. Just relax and let the water do its work."

Lorraine closed her eyes, let her head rest on the edge of the pool and her body hang limp in the water. She thought she might stretch out her legs and float, but it seemed to be too much trouble to move. The seductive warmth was creeping up on her again, but she could see no point in resisting it. Lorraine let herself drift She didn't rouse until she heard Treemark climb out of the pool again. "This way, please," she heard him say, as if from a distance. It was difficult to pull herself up from the water and follow him sluggishly to the massage-table. Again, the towel-robe was waiting; she let him drape it over her, wrap her in it and rub her dry. Let him do it, since he was willing to make the effort.

Lorraine lay down on the table, felt him pull the rear half of the robe up over her head, then fold it into a small pillow and tuck it under her turned cheek. She smelled the almond-and-cedar oil before she felt his hands spreading it on her back, and smiled slightly. No danger in this. His touch was, as always, chastely professional. Lorraine *reached* drowsily with her psychic power and felt no change in his mood. He spread the oil smoothly from her wrists to her toes, not neglecting her neck, then began rubbing meticulously at her feet. Lorraine let herself drift again, noting distantly that his thumbs pressed into precise spots along the roots of her toes, her arches, and her heels. No part of her went numb this time, but the pressure seemed to echo deeply. She felt a muscle in her thigh twitch, then relax, and a vague tickling stirred within the bowl of her pelvis.

Blood pulsed lazily in her flattened breasts, and her shoulders seemed to melt. Only when his hands began working up her ankles did Lorraine remember the term "pressure points": places on the body where pressure could trigger muscles to relax, blood-vessels to expand, nerves to flare or shut down. Treemark clearly knew more about such things than her Yoga instructor had ever dreamed: knowledge that could be used to heal, or as a weapon. Lorraine recalled that swift grasp on her neck that had paralyzed her for long seconds. What did he intend now? All she felt were her muscles melting into warm puddles, joints here and there clicking into place, a drowsy dreaminess that filled her complete-ly, and a soft hypersensitivity that made his every touch echo mysteriously down her nerves...

A sensitivity that was growing, slowly and implacably, into a vast and quiet desire. She could feel the blood pulsing, slowly but heavily, in her nipples and clitoris—and more, as his knowing hands pressed their way across her buttocks—in her anus and vulva, and deeper, arousing a tiny spark of itching need in her vagina. Lorraine clenched her teeth, knowing she should be out-raged at what he was making her feel, but unable to summon her fury. This was no clever seduction but an involved treatment; he'd called it therapy and meant it as such. Her new abilities told her that he wasn't lying. He had some deeper purpose, and she still didn't know what it was.

In time his hands left her and gently pulled the folded cloth out from under her face, but she floated onward in the sea of sensu-ality where he had brought her. She dimly felt the terrycloth slid-ing over her head, settling softly on her back, and knew that he would let her rest, untouched, for long minutes more. *Just a frigid-ity-cure?* she wondered, drifting. *Sense-expansion? What?* She could find no answers, but there was no urgency to the question.

Eventually Treemark came and tapped her foot, drawing her back to the present.

"It's time," he said. "Come to the solarium."

Lorraine shivered slowly, knowing what that meant. Almost dreamily she slid off the massage-table, letting the robe fall shut around her, and followed Treemark away from the pool, through the rosebush-flanked door, into the great glass-roofed room.

Again he guided her through the sun-dappled forest of flowers to the two columns. He said the same words, and Lorraine moved like a sleepwalker into the same place, the same position.

She scarcely noticed as he clicked the locks shut on the D-rings of her cuffs, and acquiesced without a second thought as he applied the gag. The perfume of the mingled scents seemed overpowering, making her dizzy, and she was almost grateful for the support of the columns. Was this physical surrender what he wanted of her? Just willing passivity, and no more?

No: a quick psychic contact, through his touch, told her that there was something else. His hands pulled away and left her waiting, wondering.

The answer wasn't long in coming. Again Treemark pulled the robe away over her head, and again his hands spread the oil. He was taking up exactly where he'd left off yesterday. Lorraine, knowing what was coming and how it would feel, groaned softly.

Yes, the same slow and deep massage melted her muscles and left her skin tingling. And then the brushing followed. By the time he was finished, she was writhing slowly and wailing quietly on every breath.

Treemark stepped away from her, repeating the same promise as yesterday, then turned and walked off. Lorraine struggled aimlessly against the unyielding cuffs, knowing that his ritual words were true; nothing would happen to her, absolutely nothing: no harm, and no relief either. Nothing would touch her. She could do nothing now but wait, and inevitably think, and feel: think about the uglier aspects of her past, or yield to the sensuous enticements of the garden and feel…

Lorraine howled to the silent flowers in more than frustration: something closer to despair. She had to admit now that she truly hadn't wanted to be cold-blooded. She had always had capacity for overwhelming desire, but had never let it free by her own will: hadn't used it when she could have, when she could have satisfied it. She had never let herself go completely, not even with Ronnie when she'd thought he loved her, never let anyone see her this abandoned, this vulnerable.

To what? she managed to form a thought. What was the worst that a man could do to her now? *Fuck rough?* She could match him, eagerly. *Bite, scratch, punch?* She would heal. *Throw cruel insults?* She would laugh. *Give me a disease?* She couldn't be diseased now. *Get me pregnant?* Not for centuries yet. *Abandon me?* She'd find another. *Turn psycho and try to kill me?* Unless he knew the mutants' secret, she would revive. The only way a man could truly hurt her now would be… to refuse her.

Even before she'd been Initiated, she realized, there hadn't been that much harm a man could do—nothing she couldn't counteract. There were plenty of medicines to prevent disease and pregnancy. A weapon under the pillow would settle a psycho, or any lesser abuser. Anything else was entirely dependent on her own feelings, her own willingness to be hurt...

...Her own willingness to let someone else's words or opinions matter to her.

Sex—or frigidity—wasn't the problem. It never really had been.

Panting, quivering in the cuffs, Lorraine deliberately conjured up her old sex-fantasies: images of brawny handsome heroes from book-covers or movies, hotly embracing her. What had been the appeal of those imaginary lovers? Nothing but pure, raw, passionate sex—with maybe a little playful affection—and no more.

Lorraine let herself sag, inwardly seeing a veil of illusion torn away. Treemark, she realized, had been right about one thing.

It wasn't herself she didn't trust, nor her own desires, nor even men in general.

It was love.

And for good reason!

The memories came welling up, too many of them, and Lorraine could find no way to stop them. She thrashed uselessly in the cuffs, remembering all too many bitter lessons.

***

Helen glanced at the digital camera, peered at the computer-screen, took a deep breath and rattled her fingertips on the keyboard.

"Erda, greetings," she wrote, jabbed the Send key, and waited.

"Who is this?" promptly appeared on the screen, just below her message.

Helen smiled. Yes, the use of the old name had worked. "Helen of Mycenae," she typed back, "And I can prove it. Can your computer receive real-time graphics?"

"Yes," came the quick reply, "All major formats."

Helen sighed in relief. If the woman had asked for some particular computer-gobbledygook program title, she didn't know what she would have done. "Stand by to receive," she typed, and sent, then carefully pressed another key. A tiny icon blinked on the screen, and Helen smiled up at the tiny camera mounted on top of the computer. "Do you recognize me?" she added.

This pause was longer, but finally, words came: "Yes. It's been a long time, Helen."

"You're hard to find," Helen couldn't resist sending.

"For good reason," came the quick reply. "What do you want?"

Well, if Erda wanted to cut straight to the chase, Helen could oblige. "Truce. Alliance," she typed. "You have a breeding haven. So do I. Common interest."

Another long pause, then: "Yes. What do you intend?"

Helen smiled grimly as she typed. "Trade males. Trade information. Arrange common defense. Interested?"

"Trade information, yes," Erda replied cautiously. "Maybe others later."

"Deal," Helen wrote. "What other communications besides this?"

The answer came up on the screen: a short list of email addresses. Not trusting her computer-skills, Helen quickly wrote them down on a pad.

"Got it," she typed. "Any phone numbers?"

"Not yet," Erda replied quickly. "Maybe later."

"Very well," Helen agreed, understanding the woman's caution. "I'll send genealogies, known locations, contact numbers for known breeders." Yes, that should bait the hook well. "Will send secure e-mail," Helen typed, smiling. "Half an hour or less."

"Good enough," Erda replied. "I'll sign off here and wait."

Helen gave a sigh of satisfaction as the connection closed. She was willing to bet her nearest hoard of diamonds that Erda's next message would include willingness to trade phone-numbers. "Off to a good start," she murmured, reaching for a small notebook on the desk.

***

Lorraine was mind-wandering when she felt and heard Treemark returning. She pulled herself back to her feet, watchful and wary. He settled his hands on her shoulders and began massaging them gently, not probing for pressure-points now, only rubbing away small cramps and tensions, comforting and no more.

"From this time forward," he said quietly, "When I'm present, you can halt the proceedings at any time—simply by consenting to trust yourself to a lover, in the usual fashion. You can signal your willingness by nodding your head three times."

Lorraine held perfectly still, guessing what he meant. She could consent to take him. It was not, as she might have thought a few days ago, simply a seduction attempt; this too, as he'd said, was more treatment and training. She didn't doubt that he'd be an accomplished lover who could satisfy her as thoroughly as he'd aroused her. He could be every bit as good as the heroes of her fantasies, and offering exactly the same appeal: passionate sex, and nothing deeper than light affection.

The problem was that his words and opinions did matter to her. That—not sex—would make her vulnerable.

Yes, I could trust him, thought, *Up to a point at least...*

But I won't.

Resolute, she shook her head and held it high.

Treemark only sighed. His hands massaged her shoulders for a few moments longer, then dropped away—and returned with the brushes. Again he stroked her with the soft bristles from scalp to feet, then said the ritual words and walked away, his aura fading.

Yes, he was leaving her like this for another hour. Lorraine yanked futilely on the cuffs, knowing what would happen now. Either she would slip into erotic daydreaming, intensely aware of her senses, or else her mind would wander into more dreary memories of old mistreatments and betrayals that would conjure up her lifelong fury. *Enforced meditation,* she understood. *He knows he's making me remember, and feel…*

She could think of no way to prevent it, and wasn't even sure that she should.

***

Treemark came into the control-center and was not terribly surprised to see Helen still there. "Any luck with your friend?" he asked, careful not to mention names.

"A good beginning, anyway." Helen gave him one of her enigmatic smiles that he found so intriguing, and irritating. "But I meant to tell you something else. Did you know that Lorraine can identify auras?"

"Identify…?" That got a classic double-take out of him. "Tell them apart? Tell who— So soon?!"

"And more," Helen smirked. "Within close range, she can pick up sensations—and emotions. She's an empath, and yes, this soon."

Treemark dropped into the nearest chair. "Then she knew…"

"Just so. And she still trusts you." Helen glanced pointedly at the monitor-screen. "That's a considerable recommendation, considering what you're doing with her."

Treemark gave her a hurt look. "What did you think I intended, Helen?"

"Let's just say I was worried about your ambitions getting the best of you."

"That's why you didn't tell me about Lorraine's ability?"

"I only learned it this afternoon." Helen shrugged. "You were busy with her until just now; I didn't have a chance before this."

Treemark heaved a deep sigh. "Well, it's good to know I put every foot right while wandering around in the dark."

"I never doubted your skills, Brian," Helen murmured, looking at the screen again, "Just your tendency to…over-enthusiasm. You're pushing her very fast, you know."

"I know." Treemark followed her gaze. "But it can't be helped."

***

Measureless time later, Lorraine pulled up from daydreaming to feel and hear Treemark returning. She kept still as he replaced her robe, released her from the columns and carried her off to rest. This time she sank into sleep as soon as she felt the blanket cover her.

***

Benjamin leaned on the fence and tapped the bucket, hoping to get Overcast's attention. The gray stallion flicked an eye and twitched an ear at him, but kept on chewing at the grass. He wasn't that hungry for molasses-meal right now, but he'd keep the offer in mind. Ben sighed, and reminded himself to be patient.

At that moment he felt another aura approaching, looked up quickly and saw that it was Brian coming toward him. He frowned, as unwilling as the stallion to be interrupted.

Brian strolled up and leaned on the fence beside him, looked at the bucket and then at the horse. "He'll come when he's good and ready," he said. "Very lordly about his prerogatives, is Overcast."

Benjamin set down the bucket and stretched his back. "The sun will be down in another half hour," he noted. "If he won't come in by then, he can stay out all night."

"It's not likely to rain." Brian studied his friend thoughtfully, noticing the subtle tensions and drawing the inevitable conclusions. "You're getting irritable again."

"I am *not!*" Ben snapped, then realized what an ass he'd just made of himself, and scrambled to cover his lapse. "I'm worried because I've stayed too long. I should have been back in Seattle yesterday."

"You told me you had no pressing engagements," Treemark gently reminded him.

"Maybe I lied." Ben wouldn't look at him.

"Why should you?" Treemark asked innocently.

Benjamin glowered at the stallion, and didn't answer.

"Ben, you're restless enough that you're not even lying well." Treemark carefully turned his gaze away, as if more interested in studying the horse. "Is it that time again?"

Benjamin only hissed between his teeth, picked up the bucket and shook it. "Come on, you great lout," he grumbled at Overcast. "Come now, or I'll take it back to the barn."

The stallion rolled an eye at him, and deliberately cropped more grass. Benjamin glared at him.

"I know exactly how you feel," said Treemark.

Benjamin set the bucket hard on the ground. "That's it," he snapped, carefully addressing himself to the horse. "Come or stay, it's all the same to me."

With that he turned on his heel and strode off toward the house. Overcast raised his head, stared at the retreating human, then turned a bewildered look at Treemark.

"No," Treemark smiled, picking up the bucket, "It was nothing you did."

***

The intercom buzzed like an annoying fly. Lorraine swam up toward consciousness, just far enough to recognize the sound and understand what it meant.

Dinner. Was she really hungry? *No,* she decided rebelliously. For once she'd skip formal dinner with the household and catch up on sleep. She could always raid the icebox after hours. Lorraine turned her back on the pesky noise, pulled a pillow over her head and sank gratefully back into darkness.

Perhaps 40 minutes later, the intercom buzzed again. This time Lorraine came awake enough to roll over and answer it. To her surprise, this time the voice on the other end was Helen's.

"Lorraine," she coaxed, "Since you skipped dinner, I thought I'd bring you a little something. Can you come to the door, or shall I go fetch the master-key?"

"So there is one," Lorraine frowned. So, Treemark could come in anytime he wanted.

"Only one, kept locked in the office. Shall I get it?"

"No, I'll open the door." Lorraine set down the handset a little harder than necessary, slid out of bed and stumbled her way to the door. Her body still felt boneless, like a skinfull of warm water. She turned the lock, then went straight back to the bed.

There was, she noticed, another dress—likewise semi-medieval in cut, this one dark blue laid out at the bed's foot, along with the elaborate belt and its sheathed dagger. It would, she guessed, probably look wonderful on her. *Why bother?* she thought crossly. She wasn't going anywhere. It wasn't worth the effort.

A moment later Helen came in, carrying a tray that bore a wineglass, a teacup, and a covered bowl. She glanced around the room, smiled fleetingly, turned up the lights and came over to the bed.

Lorraine, realizing that she must look either sick or sulky, pulled up her knees to make room. Helen sat down on the bed, set the tray between them and pulled the lid off the bowl with a flourish, revealing a salad of cold chicken slices on a bed of oriental vegetables.

"Daniel's excellent Thai salad," Helen smiled. "Perfect for light appetites. The wine is a mild Bordeaux, I believe, and of course there's green tea."

Lorraine sighed, picked up the fork—no chopsticks, she noted—and duly took a bite of the chicken. Whatever the dressing was, it had a marvelous exotic flavor that drew her back for another bite, and another. "My compliments to Daniel," she said between bites. "I wasn't slighting his cooking."

"Ah. Just tired?"

"Yes. Really."

"There's still the evening therapy session." Helen smiled gently. "You can go back to sleep afterward, but you really shouldn't miss it."

Lorraine glared at her, gulped the wine faster than it deserved, then realized she was being childish. "Just why," she asked coolly, "Is Dr. Treemark so interested in my development?"

Helen raised a dark-blonde eyebrow. "Can't you believe the obvious?" she said. "You're a fledgling, newly Initiated and quite vulnerable, of an endangered species. Of course he's protective of you; any honorable one of us would be. Of course he's subjecting you to intense training. So am I, for that matter."

"Not quite the same." Lorraine took another bite of the salad and chewed it thoroughly, thinking of just how to phrase this. "For all the psychic training you've given me, you haven't tried to get into my mind the way he does. Precisely why is he doing that, Helen?"

The ancient blonde woman gave her a long unfathomable look. "Precisely because he's a healer," she said. "He's devoted to his art, and to our survival. He can't see an injury without trying to heal it."

Or a good horse without wanting to ride it? Lorraine considered. "So he sees me as... What? A horse with a sprained leg?"

"A little more than that." Helen's eyes bored into hers. "You must know that you're damaged goods, Lorraine. You may hide it well from mortals, but to anyone who's had a few centuries' experience it's rather obvious."

Lorraine grabbed the teacup and hid her face behind it, desperately hoping that she wasn't blushing. The bitter taste of the tea was a startling contrast to the wine.

"'Scars slow the sword-arm'," Helen went on. "There's a war going on, and we want you to survive. It's as simple as that."

"All right." Lorraine set down her cup, no longer hungry, and no longer sleepy either. *So I've gone from one war to another, and I have to be in top condition to face this one. All right.* "Back to Boot Camp."

She slid off the bed, feeling the towel-robe trail behind her. No, no point putting on more clothes, but she did pick up and strap on the dagger-belt. She marched out the door without looking back at Helen. The carpet pressed softly against her bare feet as she paced steadily down the corridor, across the empty livingroom, through the offside door and into Treemark's clinic.

He was there, behind the desk, with two glasses of scotch and ice, waiting for her.

Lorraine dropped into the padded chair and reached for the nearer glass. The cool, smoky taste was comfortingly familiar, and she let herself relax a little. Now that she thought of it, there was something else she remembered. "I have to go into town tomorrow, phone my Aunt Dianne..." *And Detective Weber.* "...and maybe have lunch with her. I don't want to phone from here." *Phones can be traced. The FBI does a lot of that.* She wondered if he would protest, or ask why.

Treemark only nodded. "Ben's going to fetch some supplies from the city," he said. "You can go with him, late in the morning. By all means, take your weapons." He leaned forward and gave her an intense look. "Don't go far from him. Remember: you're now prey for the Unseelie, there's likely to be at least one in a town that size, and you're not yet fit for combat."

"I know," Lorraine agreed. She took another sip of the scotch, suddenly weary. "I feel like a damned draftee."

Treemark took a sip from his own glass, and then set it down. "I can tell that you're angry," he said, "And not just about that. What else is there?"

Angry? Yes, now that she thought of it, she'd been angry since this afternoon—and she remembered why: the memories that the enforced meditation had dredged up.

"Because I've been cheated," she snapped. "Cheated all my life. Nobody ever said they loved me, but to use me by it. Dear Momma: 'If you really loved me, you'd wash the dishes without being told.' Dear Papa: 'Of course I love you. Now sit up straight and act like a lady.' And of course, good old Ronnie: 'If you loved me as much as I love you, you'd care about my feelings'—and that always meant babying him, giving him whatever he wanted, never complaining, never daring to put my own needs first. Right! The horny boys back in school were at least honest enough to say 'Let's have some fun' when that was exactly all they wanted. No one ever said 'love' honestly, not to me. It was always just a manipulating tool."

And that hurt. Lorraine felt her eyes stinging, and drowned the sensation in another sip of scotch.

Treemark nodded perfect understanding. "So you had honest one-night stands, but no honest lover. Did you at least have an honest friend? Ever?"

"Yes," Lorraine admitted, remembering. "Buddies in high school, in college—good for rapping all night about life, the universe and everything—fellow-workers in the union... people I could trust with my life, if I had to..." Tears stung again as she remembered Crimp-Tail and Sable-Foot. "I had to leave my cats with Bob and Meredith. I know they'll be good to them, make them members of the family..."

"I take it you loved your cats."

"Yes, and they loved me, in their honest little furry fashion." Lorraine took another sip, then set the glass down. "True friends, but no true lover. Funny how you can trust someone with your life, trust them with your cats, but can't trust them with your heart."

"Why is that, do you think?" Treemark asked, very softly.

Lorraine stared at the glass as if it were a crystal ball, half-hypnotized by the intricate way the light reflected off the ice, and tried to clarify her thoughts. "Because... it's an imposition. Unless someone already feels that way about you, then dumping your own feelings on them is... giving them a burden, an obligation they didn't ask for, no matter how generously they bear up under it. ...And of course, if they turn out to be the wrong sort, then you've only given them an opening to use you."

"But how..." Treemark spread his hands, almost helplessly. "How do you know if someone feels...that way...about you, if you don't give them a chance to show it?"

"Show it?" Lorraine thought long and carefully about that. "I think...that's what classic courtship is about. An honest friend whose feelings began turning that way could always send you a valentine, or some flowers, or invite you on a picnic—just the two of you, with nothing else to do or talk about... Little things like that."

"And no honest friend ever tried those little things with you?"

"No. Only the dishonest ones did."

Treemark shook his head. "Lorraine, either you've had incredibly rotten luck, or else you put out signals that said 'don't even try'."

"Or I just had a narrow circle of friends," Lorraine considered. *While I was with Ronnie, everyone kept a respectful distance. Afterward... Bob and Meredith were unquestionably an item. Jack— oh God, Jack! —had a wife and grown children. That left only Bill, who honestly would have liked to bed me, but never...courted, never made a pass at my heart. And those were all the close friends I had.* "...And I didn't go looking for more."

"Didn't go hunting," Treemark murmured. "Not for sex, not for love, not for any more friends. Why, Lorraine?"

Lorraine gave a deep sigh, and sagged back in the chair. "I suppose I'd given up. Got tired of looking for diamonds in dungheaps, tired of risking slavery or burdening a friend every time I tried... Hell, I had a few good friends and my little cats, a vibrator and a good stock of sex-fantasies, and that was enough to live on."

"You got used to living on starvation wages!"

Lorraine grinned tiredly at the old union slogan. "So how do I organize and strike for a better love-life?" she tossed back at him.

"'Organize' is the word." Treemark rubbed his forehead. "You have to summon the strength, and the will, to go out and hunt for new friends—test and observe until you're sure of their honesty, then make the first move, give the opening, let your friends know that you can be loved. Make the effort. Can't you believe that it's worth it?"

Effort? It took enormous effort just to reach out and pick up her glass. "The problem is," she said, "That in the last two years I never met anyone I cared enough for to make that effort, take that risk. And in my current situation I'm not likely to meet anyone soon."

That truth hung in growing silence between them. They both knew she dared not leave the ranch for any length of time, not for a long while yet, and that among the ranch's inhabitants the candidates for anything more than friend were very few. *I'm not about to throw myself at the stablehands, or the guests, or you, just because I'm needy,* Lorraine smiled as she drained her glass. *Impasse.*

"There are always ways," Treemark sighed. "Go on to bed, Lorraine. You'll have a lot to do tomorrow."

Lorraine left the glass, pulled herself to her feet, and plodded out of the office, back across the livingroom and down the corridor. She found her bedroom door closed but unlocked, Helen and the tray gone, and the blue dress removed to a nearby chair.

Lorraine took off the belt and tossed it on top of the dress, then slid under the covers. The smooth sheet pulled at her like a magnet, and she was asleep almost before she'd drawn up the quilt around her.

8.

In the morning Lorraine dressed with more than usual care, knowing she wouldn't have time to change between raking out stalls and going into town. She settled on a sturdy but trim pair of jeans, her second-best boots and a good blue knit shirt; she could scrub those off quickly, if she had to. Finally she stuffed her wallet in her hip pocket and added her cell-phone, gun-belt and hat, smiling as she thought of what a perfect cowgirl she would look. The townsfolk were probably used to seeing such.

At the door she found a waiting laundry-bag filled with clean clothes and linens, just as Madge had promised. Lorraine shoved it into her room, closed and locked the door behind her.

Breakfast was fruit, ham and juices again, and Daniel seemed not at all put out that she'd missed dinner the night before.

"I really liked your oriental salad," she felt obliged to say.

"Excellent," Daniel beamed. "Then I do hope you'll attend dinner tonight; I'm attempting some variations on a theme of sushi."

At that point Benjamin, Steven and Wally came in, and Daniel busied himself with fetching their breakfasts. Ben glanced at Lorraine's shirt, and smiled.

"Brian says you'll be coming into town with me," he said, "We'll have to finish the stalls early."

"Can do," said Lorraine, determined to pull her share, not give Treemark any excuse to change his mind and keep her at the ranch.

She ate quickly, and got out to the barn before the others. Leila welcomed her with a loud nicker, and Lorraine decided to start on the black mare's stall first. Leila nudged Lorraine's ear with her soft nose as she was led out to the hitching-rail, and Lorraine took care to pet her well.

She met the others coming in, spared them barely a nod, fetched the tools and got busy on the stall. She could feel their auras as they worked, not too far away—unless her practice with Helen had stretched her sensing range.

The barn was silent except for the sound of her rake and the faint whickerings of the horses in the other stalls. Lorraine filled her cart quickly, rolled it out to the compost-heap and dumped it, then brought it around to the near wing of the feed-barn to fetch straw. The straw-room was nearly full, and it took only a moment to fork half a bale into the cart.

As she was about to roll the cart away she noticed an odd sound nearby—a soft animal noise, in the hay-room next door, where none of the animals were supposed to be.

Puzzled, Lorraine moved quietly out into the aisle and peered around the partition into the hay-room.

She saw Wally lying on his back across two bales, his neck arched, his shirt open to the waist, and his legs spread wide. Steven knelt between those spread thighs, resting his weight on one arm while his other hand unfastened Wally's belt-buckle. He was bent over Wally, hungrily licking the man's arched throat, working his way downward. As his cat-quick tongue reached the hollow between the collarbones, Wally groaned softly and dug his fingers into the hay. Steven chuckled, and pulled open the fly of Wally's jeans.

Lorraine turned away quickly, holding her breath, and hurried back to the straw room and her cart, trying hard to ignore the blush heating her cheeks—and the embarrassing excitement that she had no business feeling. She pulled the cart back to the stall as quietly as she could, her thoughts whirling; she could have sworn, from the way they both acted toward her, that they preferred women...

But I don't know how old they are, she realized. They could, either or both, have been centuries old—and still too young to breed. What was 'perversion' to a creature that could not breed, nor be diseased, nor be permanently injured? How would it be to have sex with no consequence but pleasure, for centuries? Would there be any good reason not to experiment, explore, and learn what sensations were possible?

As she spread out the straw in Leila's stall, Lorraine considered that with her desires unleashed, anything was possible. She had uncounted centuries to do her own exploring, and it was anyone's guess how the rest of the world's standards would change in that time. For that matter, could mortal standards even apply to Elven-kind? The very concept of 'kinky' was becoming irrelevant.

Lorraine shook her head crossly, went to bring Leila back, and moved on to another stall.

Not until three stalls later did she realize that she'd sensed Steven and Wally from nearly 40 yards away.

***

Benjamin came to fetch her just as Lorraine was dumping the

fifth load into the compost-heap. "It's nearly ten o'clock," he said. "Just leave the cart by the door; we've got to get moving."

Lorraine nodded quick agreement, stopped to brush off her boots and inspect her jeans, and then trotted after him to where the dark-green pickup truck waited behind the barn. Ben steered the truck down to the driveway by the front of the house, and there Lorraine noted a strange car parked in the circle and a middle-aged couple—ordinary mortals—walking toward the door. She wondered, as the truck rumbled down the drive to the front gate, if those were horse-people come to ask about training, or clients at Treemark's clinic. He did, she remembered, have a working life outside of Elven politics.

The black highway stretched before them, with the outline of the city in the distance, and Lorraine leaned back on the seat. "So where are we going," she asked, "And what do we do when we get there?"

"Feed-store first," Benjamin said, not taking his eyes off the road, "Veterinary supply store next, then lunch at a chili-house next door. One thing Daniel doesn't do is authentic chili."

Lorraine smiled and watched the street-signs go by, memorizing their route, just in case she ever needed it.

At the feed-store she helped Ben load several barrels of molasses-meal and rolled red oats. At the veterinary-supply store, less than two blocks away, he handed a list to a clerk and stood waiting patiently.

The ideal time to call, Lorraine thought, moving quietly toward the door. Yes, there was a pay phone just outside. She pulled out her wallet, opened the change-purse and took out Agent Berringer's card.

Berringer picked up on the first ring.

"Hello, Aunt Dianne," Lorraine said quickly, implying nearby ears. "I thought I'd give you a call to say hi."

"Lorraine, where are you now?" Berringer sounded rattled.

"At a job interview." Lorraine gripped the receiver tightly and smiled, smiled. "This time next week, I hope to rejoin the ranks of the gainfully employed."

"I mean, where are you staying?" Berringer snapped. "You're not at your apartment."

"Oh? What makes you say that?" Lorraine managed to keep her voice light.

"You haven't answered your phone."

"Right. I accidentally turned it off. Sorry."

"All your clothes and effects are gone, and there's dust on the table. Lorraine, you haven't been there in days—"

"And just how did you learn that?" Lorraine growled, dropping all pretenses. "Did you pick the lock and walk in?"

There was a long moment's silence.

"You weren't there when I called or dropped by," Berringer took up the flow, admitting nothing, "So I got the manager to let me in. Just where are you, Lorraine? If you don't cooperate with the terms of the Witness Protection Program—"

"I'm skipping from cheap motel to cheap motel," Lorraine lied glibly. "I have been, ever since I came home on my second day in town, and found that somebody had gotten into my apartment while I was out."

There was another silence. Lorraine grinned humorlessly. "I believe I'm exercising a little more security-consciousness than your office is, Aunt Dianne. Tell me, who broke into my apartment—and stole absolutely nothing? Who even knew that I was there?"

"It could have been someone from our office, checking for bugs." Berringer didn't sound terribly convinced herself. "A memo could have been misplaced. It happens..."

"I think I'll just keep on motel-hopping, then. It's expensive, but I expect to have a job soon."

"Lorraine, we have to meet." Berringer sounded a little desperate now.

Lorraine flinched, wondering if she could avoid this, or if there was any safe place. Her eye fell on the restaurant's sign nearby. "All right," she said quickly. "I'll be at Alberto's Chili House on 14th, near Main, for lunch. It's...really authentic chili."

"Alberto's...14th, near Main..." Berringer was either writing it down or repeating it for someone else's benefit. "Ah, I know where that is. Shall we say, noon?"

Lorraine remembered she wasn't wearing a watch. Still, it couldn't be too much after 11AM right now. Time enough to prepare. "Noon's fine," she said. "See you then."

She hung up the phone quickly, before Berringer could say anything else.

And now what, besides explaining things to Benjamin? Lorraine rattled her fingers on her belt, brushed her left-hand holster, and remembered the cell-phone. Yes, there was someone else she wanted to talk to.

She stepped away from the pay phone, leaned against the

front window of the veterinary-supply store so that Ben could see her easily, and pulled another card out of her wallet. Dialing took a little longer than she'd expected, but the call went through.

"Detective Weber," said the familiar voice.

"Hello, this is..." It was frightening how she had to pause to remember her real name. "Roxanne Defarge. I hope you remember me."

"Hell, yes!" Weber sounded honestly pleased. "How are you doing? They treating you okay? —Hey, is this line secure?"

Lorraine thought of all the rerouting that a cell-phone system would have to go through on a long-distance call, and smiled. "Secure enough. I just wanted to know how my case is going."

Weber took a deep breath. "We've found a man who fits your sketch perfectly. Actually, it was the New York City cops who spotted him, while they were watching... somebody else. Mafia, all right. Good thing we'd faxed them the sheet and sketch... Anyway, I can't tell you exactly what's going down, you understand—"

"I understand."

"—or if they're going to send him back here to be ID'd, or if you'll have to go to New York, or when. The FBI isn't telling us anything..." He paused, as if embarrassed that he'd said too much. "Look, is there a safe number where I can call you, tell you when we'll need you to ID the guy?"

Lorraine thought hard and quickly about that. "I'll see about getting one," she offered. "Meanwhile, I'll call you." *See what he says now.*

"Is that safe?" he asked, immediately.

Lorraine sighed in relief. "Oh, yes." *Cell-phone long-distance, satellite-bounce. No way anyone in Chicago could trace me.* "I'll talk to you tomorrow, then."

"All right. Keep safe, Roxanne."

"Goodbye, then." She clicked off the phone, and shivered in the heat. Had she guessed right? Would Mafia goons have the technology to trace a long-distance cell-phone call? Would anybody, even the Feds? What about the phone-company itself? *At worst,* she considered, *They'd trace me to a street in Tucson... today, anyway. What about tomorrow?*

"Lorraine?" Benjamin's voice startled her. "Are you all right?" He'd come out of the store holding two loaded bags, and she hadn't heard him approach.

I have to trust him, at least a little. Lorraine gnawed her lip.

"We've got a problem," she admitted. "Aunt Dianne insists on having lunch with me. I told her noon, right here..." She jerked her thumb toward the chili-house. "That'll give us time to scope the place out, get separate tables, and see who comes in."

Benjamin only stared at her, one eyebrow rising.

"My aunt's not terribly careful," Lorraine tried to explain. "And I suppose you heard about the stalker who's after me."

Ben pulled his eyebrow back down. "All right. You go in first, and get a table where you can see the door. Take your time looking over the menu."

***

The chili-house was small but clean, though the smell of peppers permeated the air. The menu was printed on a lighted board stretched behind the counter, and the prices were cheap. The seats were half filled, mostly by Latino men who looked like laborers. A few of them, she noted, also carried pistols in discreet holsters on their belts. Everyone seemed calm, quiet and polite. The two counter-clerks were efficient and cheerful.

There was a smoking-section, under an array of ceiling-fans, and the background music came from a Mexican radio station.

Pop-music, thank God, not mariachi. I hate mariachi. Lorraine nursed her lemonade slowly, running covert glances between the front door and the table halfway across the room where Benjamin sat, working his way slowly through tacos and coffee, pretending to read a paper. The clock on the wall read ten of noon.

Then she felt a tingle, light at first, then steady and unmistakable: the aura of another mutant. *Not Ben.* Lorraine almost choked on her lemonade, recovered quickly, glanced at Benjamin and at the doorway. No one had come in, no one was near the front door, and Ben—aside from a slight tension in his shoulders— didn't seem to have noticed.

Someone from the ranch? Who? Why? And why not show themselves? No, someone else... And that someone else could easily be one of the Unseelie, a hunter.

Lorraine slid her hand down to wrap around the grip of her revolver. *Don't look nervous,* she reminded herself. *Whoever it is, they can't tell which of us in this crowd is the mutant...*

Quickly as it had come, the sensation faded. The unknown mutant had moved out of range, possibly fleeing, possibly lying in wait. She saw Benjamin flick a glance to the door, then shrug slightly, and then turn back to his paper. *Be calm,* Lorraine considered. *They can't just come in and start killing, not in a town where maybe half the people carry guns. If it's a hunter he'll wait outside, try to catch us alone... But while we're in here, we're safe.*

She was still pondering that when she saw Agent Berringer come up to the door and push it open. The woman seemed a little flustered as she looked around the crowd.

Lorraine remembered that Ben was watching. *Act as if she's my aunt. Wave to her.*

Berringer saw the signal, recognized Lorraine and came trotting over to her table.

"Hi, Aunt Dianne," Lorraine smiled prettily. "Now that you're here, let's get some chili."

"It looks authentic, all right," Agent Berringer retorted with a smile just as wide.

Lorraine pulled out her wallet and held out three singles. "Just a cup of green chili for me," she said. "I'll have to get back to the grind soon."

"My treat," said Berringer, waving the bills away. She hurried off to the counter to make the order. Lorraine noticed Benjamin watching her. They traded glances briefly, and Ben rolled his eyes and went back to his paper. A few moments later, Berringer returned with two cups of chili, three spoons and a coffee. She set them down on the table with exaggerated care.

"Thank you!" Lorraine gushed, then dug quickly into the chili to forestall conversation. The chili was, in fact, surprisingly good: mild on the pepper, containing a whole complex of subtle flavors. Berringer nibbled at her cupful of red chili as if expecting it to explode, seeming almost disappointed when it didn't. Lorraine took her time finishing, waiting for Berringer to do the same.

Finally Berringer gave up, and set down her spoon. "Lorraine," she said quietly, "I understand your worry, but you must keep in better contact."

"I'll leave my phone on, promise," Lorraine smiled again. "Isn't this great chili?"

"It's fine. Lorraine, that isn't enough. Where are you staying, right now?"

"I was at a Motel Six until this morning." Lorraine wasn't going to give an inch. "Right now, all my stuff is in the car. I'll pick another cheap motel at random after work-hours today."

"We have to be able to reach you when necessary." Berringer leaned closer, looking terribly sincere and concerned. "And not just through your phone."

"Why?" Lorraine dared. "Is something happening with the case? Have you caught him?"

Berringer blinked. "I haven't heard any new information," she said. "But when it comes, we may have to pick you up and send you back to Chicago very quickly."

Weber knows more! Lorraine felt her alarm-bells going off. *He said it was the FBI that wasn't talking to him...* This meant three possibilities: Weber was lying, or Berringer was, or Berringer's boss hadn't told her anything. Given Weber's reactions, she'd guess he'd been telling the truth. "What's wrong with simply phoning me and arranging a pickup?"

"Lorraine!" Berringer rolled her eyes in exasperation. "A cell-phone is a radio. Anyone with the right radio equipment could listen in."

"But they'd have to know just the right frequency, wouldn't they?" Lorraine countered. "Who's going to tell them?"

Berringer blinked, and evaded. "It can be found with the right equipment. You can't give information about where you are over a cell-phone, dear."

"Then call me and say only that I should go to a pay-phone." Lorraine shrugged. "That should prevent eavesdroppers—unless, of course, *your* phone is tapped."

Berringer looked offended, then frustrated, then calculating. "Well, at least tell me where you'll be working," she tried.

"I'm not sure yet. It depends on who hires me, you know."

Berringer sighed, and then looked Lorraine up and down. "You said you had a job-interview today? In those clothes?"

Lorraine was ready for it. "You told me not to go into my old business, so I'm trying for warehouse-work. You couldn't get further from office-work than that."

"…Warehouse?" Berringer unconsciously rattled her fingertips on the table. "Well, do you have any letters you want mailed to your friends back home?"

"Not yet. No news 'til I have good news. But tell me, Aunt Dianne, is it possible to trace a long-distance cell-phone call?"

Berringer gave her a startled look, then frowned. "You're not planning to call your friends in Chicago, are you?"

"Of course not." *Just a cop.* "But please answer my question."

"It's possible," Berringer admitted, "But difficult. You'd have to go into the phone-company computer... But of course, anyone with the right equipment could find you at this end, as I said."

"But no one in Chicago could?"

"Oh, no. Not without going through the phone company."

"So all I really have to worry about is someone hunting me right here in Tucson." Lorraine leaned back, smiling grimly. "And that comes back to my original problem. Who's hunting me right here in Tucson, and how did they learn where I was?"

Berringer looked startled, then quietly furious. "We have no reason to think that anyone is hunting you here."

"My apartment—"

"We're checking on that right now. It's possible that it was someone, something, totally unrelated—perhaps just a snoopy landlord, or building-manager."

"Then why are you so concerned about my using a cell-phone here in town?"

Berringer opened her mouth, and then shut it again. "Standard procedure," was the best she could do. "General precautions. Cell-phones aren't secure."

"Then I'd best keep on flitting from motel to motel, saying nothing of where I am on the phone—not where I'll be staying, or working either."

"Lorraine," Berringer tried one last time, "We can't protect you if we don't know where you are."

It sounded sensible, except for one obvious flaw. "You never promised me round-the-clock guards. I daresay you couldn't afford to provide them." Lorraine found she was growing tired of the whole silly argument. "Look, Dianne, my only safety lies in hiding out where nobody knows me. If even you don't know where I am, nobody else can find out either."

Berringer gave up, and pulled back her chair. "Leave your phone on, then," she sighed. "Call me only from pay phones. Don't call out to anyone else."

"No problem." *Nobody but Weber.* "Are you sure you wouldn't like more of this chili?"

"I have to get back to work." Berringer got to her feet, turned and walked away with no further words.

Lorraine waited until the woman had gone out of sight, then got up and strolled over to Benjamin's table. "How fast can we get out of here?" she asked him quietly.

Ben frowned, and set down his paper. "Right now," he said. "Straight into the truck." He pulled out the truck's keyring, picked up the tiny black box dangling from it, and pressed a button. "Right now," he repeated, sliding to his feet.

The walk from the table to the front door took less than ten seconds. The quicker walk into the truck, whose doors were now unlocked, took less than five. Slamming the doors, starting the engine, clutching into gear and pulling out of the parking space took another twenty.

As they slowed to turn at the intersection, Lorraine felt the stranger's aura again. It was definitely unfamiliar.

"He's back!" she whispered. "Who is he?"

"I don't know," Benjamin muttered. "Keep an eye on the rear-view mirror."

Lorraine duly watched the mirror, memorizing the shapes and colors of the cars behind them, as Ben turned to the left and picked up speed. She had played this game before, in Chicago, against police and Teamster goons, and knew what to look for. The aura-sensation faded as they approached the end of the block, and Benjamin quickly turned left again.

"Trying to get behind him?" Lorraine guessed.

"Or just go the way he doesn't expect." Ben frowned at the road ahead. "He'll expect us to run for the highway, or head for the nearest safe ground. If he knows the city well, or has a map…"

He passed the next intersection and kept going. Now they were headed in the opposite direction from the way to the ranch. Lorraine kept watching the mirror, and saw no recognizable cars. Another intersection drew near, and again Benjamin turned left.

There was still no feel of an Elven aura. Ben drove another two blocks before turning left again.

"Spiraling outward?" Lorraine asked, still watching.

"Two wrongs don't make a right," Ben chuckled, "But three lefts do."

It took her a few seconds to catch on, and laugh. Benjamin continued for another six blocks, until the road ended in a T-intersection. He muttered what sounded like an obscenity in a foreign language, and turned left again. The road to the ranch lay that way.

"Do you think he just stumbled on us by accident?" Lorraine asked.

"Probably. No one outside the ranch knows that you're Initiated, and I've taken great care to insure that nobody else knows I'm in town." Ben frowned. "But then, the truck belongs to Steven. It might be somebody who recognized it, someone after him."

"We'll have to tell Steven that." Lorraine gnawed her lip. "If I weren't here, would you still avoid whoever it is?"

"Yes." Benjamin glanced at the mirror, and then turned left at the next light. "I don't care for surprises; I'd much rather learn who's in town from a safe distance."

"How do you expect to find out?"

"Tell Brian. This is his turf, and I'm sure he has his sources."

Lorraine studied the mirror, made certain that no familiar cars were anywhere near, and risked a long look at Benjamin. There was nothing of fear in his expression: just a grim and narrow-eyed calculation.

At last he pulled back onto the long road leading out of town, and city buildings gave way to suburban houses, then empty tracts of desert. Ben picked up the speed, keeping scrupulously to the posted limit. There was no feel of another Elven aura anywhere. Whoever the stranger was, they'd lost him.

And was it only coincidence, Lorraine wondered, that the unknown mutant had shown up just before Berringer had?

***

The paddock-flanked driveway seemed to welcome them home like a lover's arms, and Lorraine found herself relaxing as soon as they pulled onto the graveled road.

She was unspeakably happy to hop out of the truck, summon Wally for help and start unloading the barrels while Ben trotted off to report to Treemark. Lorraine was a little vexed to remember that she'd missed her exercise-hour, but perhaps the effort of unloading the truck would make up for it; the simple, necessary, physical effort was oddly soothing.

Afterward she went into the house to find Benjamin. He was in the livingroom, talking quietly with Treemark.

"–could have been a purely random encounter." The doctor glanced up at Lorraine. "I'll deal with it, Ben. Now get on with lessons."

Benjamin frowned, but rose smoothly to his feet and strode toward Lorraine.

"We'll work on shotgun today," he said, leading her toward the basement door.

Lorraine followed, saying nothing but thinking much. It was good to know that Treemark was taking the incident seriously.

In the gun-room Benjamin, good as his word, handed her a 12-gauge pump-action shotgun and set her to work at the 25-yard range. Only the first two shots were wasted on Lorraine's surprise at the noise and recoil; after that she settled down to fixing her attention on bead-sight and target, and her shots reliably blew out the center-rings.

"Very good," Benjamin noted. "You've fallen naturally into the Zen of shooting. Tomorrow, I think, we should go outside and practice on clay pigeons. Now it's time for blade-practice."

Startled, Lorraine glanced at the clock above the door and saw that indeed a whole hour had passed. "I didn't think it was more than twenty minutes!" she marveled.

"As I said," Benjamin smiled, taking the shotgun from her hands, "The Zen of shooting: everything disappears but the gun and the target. Now try to apply that same concentration to the sword."

Lorraine followed him into the *salle d'armes* and took up her usual blade, which she was beginning to think of as The Bastard. After only a few days, it already felt comfortable and familiar in her hands. Benjamin led her through the stretching and warm-up exercises, then the basic blocks and ripostes, then the simple attacks and withdrawals, then combinations. Lorraine threw herself into practice with a tight concentration whose source she didn't question, seeing only the blade and the space of air beyond it that defined her invisible target. She no longer watched herself making the moves, but felt them: particular cues of muscle-tension and pressure.

"Good, good," Benjamin purred at her shoulder. "I think we can start sparring in another few days. I'll have to choose the right weights for the wooden swords."

Lorraine only nodded once, not taking her eyes off the blade and target. Now that she had the forms fairly well memorized, she wanted to pick up her speed. It was important to combine the attack-withdrawals with blocks..

The feel of Helen's approaching presence came as a surprise. Again, an hour had slipped away unnoticed.

"Go on," said Benjamin, gently taking the sword from Lorraine's hands. "I'll finish up here. You're coming along very well."

"Indeed," murmured Helen, leading the way back upstairs. "Your concentration is admirable...and perhaps a little intense."

"That's a problem?" Lorraine puzzled

"Not in your training, no." Helen gave her a sidelong look as they paced down the corridor. "But I'm curious as to the reason."

Lorraine guessed what she meant. "Someone's after me. Isn't that reason enough?"

"I heard about what happened in town today." Helen pushed open the door to the garden. "It's reasonable to be wary and prepared. It's not reasonable to let fear dominate your life."

"But I'm not—" Right there, Lorraine had to stop and think about that. It wasn't fear she had felt that morning but tension, fierce alertness, and...anger. She'd felt anger at that intruding unknown mutant, and anger at Agent Berringer. Now that she thought of it, she couldn't remember the last time she'd felt real fear. *The gunshot in the office—*

No, that had dropped her into the same tension, alertness—with an underlying current of stubborn rage. She hadn't felt fear itself, at least since Ronnie had left her. *And how long before that?* "Not afraid: angry!" she realized. "I haven't been afraid in years."

Helen gave her an odd look. "You mean, you translate fear into fury? Automatically?"

"I don't know," Lorraine admitted. "Maybe I've...simply worn out fear, worn it to exhaustion long ago, so that now..." She dropped onto the nearest cushion, struggling to clarify her thought. "Something threatens me and I promptly think of what harm it will do, how much that will hurt...and it makes me angry. I've been hurt enough that the threat of more..." There: she saw it. "No more Ms. Nice-Guy! I want revenge. I want to hit back—and if I can hit first, all the better. If I can hit faster, harder, surer..." The total picture was awesome—and, yes, a little frightening. It was almost a relief to know that she still could be frightened. "I would...like it. Enjoy it." Now she had to ask. "Helen, am I in any danger of becoming a...bloodthirsty..."

"Thrill-killer?" Helen finished for her. "Not if you can worry about it. Not if your enjoyment comes from defeating a threat. I think that's more a case of ecstatic relief than perverse pleasure."

How can I tell the difference? Lorraine pondered.

"Meanwhile, let's sharpen your skills further," Helen went on. "Let's see if you can tell the direction of an approaching aura. Now, close your eyes and start the breathing exercises."

Lorraine closed her eyes and duly went through the steps into light trance-state, then tried to feel Helen's position as the woman got up and moved quietly around the garden. It was difficult, like trying to locate the direction of a scent. She found that she could do it only at a limited distance; too close, within about five yards, and the sense of presence surrounded her.

Nonetheless, Helen seemed pleased with the results. "That's

quite good enough," she said, "To tell you which way to run while there's still time. An excellent survival characteristic."

Indeed, thought Lorraine, as she felt another approaching aura. It took little effort to identify it as Treemark's, and she could guess as well as feel his location.

It was, after all, time to go to the pool again.

9.

LORRAINE FELT the familiar sensual lassitude steal over her before she finished hanging her clothes in the locker. The feeling grew stronger as she stepped into the pool where Treemark was waiting, and she knew that if she wanted an answer to her question any time before dinner, she must speak quickly.

"Is there any defense against that neck-grip you showed me?" she asked as she settled into the water.

"Only to duck," Treemark smiled, "Or armor your neck. Now relax, Lorraine."

Lorraine dutifully settled back against the side of the pool, positioning her back against the bubble-jet, and let her muscles go limp. Yes, it did feel very good to unwind, let the day's tensions seep away into the blood-warm water, drowse in anticipation of what would come without thinking about it. She couldn't remember when she'd last been able to relax like this, feel this safe...even protected. In fact, she couldn't remember when she'd last felt protected at all. For all its weirdness, Treemark's ranch had become her haven—in more ways than one.

***

Treemark silently watched as Lorraine rested her head on the edge of the pool and almost visibly unwound herself. His wild mare had come to accept his care and training, was no longer ready to gallop back into the wilderness at the slightest hint of captivity.

She was coming to see possibilities in herself, and accept them with a will.

He almost shivered in relief, then sternly reminded himself that the danger was far from past. Today's incidents had thrown her back into combat-mode, and he must not allow that to continue. He must persuade her not to leave the ranch again, to remain in his protection, allow herself to accept her own vulnerabilities— and the need for them. She would not simply submit to his judgment on this; he must give her reasons to convince herself.

And it must be done soon. Her potential was too vast to waste.

***

Again, Lorraine roused when Treemark called her out of the pool, and her body obeyed slowly. The massage-table beckoned, and she spread out her towel-robe and lay down on it without waiting for Treemark's assistance. She closed her eyes, noting the familiar scent of the oil, and sighed quietly as he spread it on her shoulders. He stroked the oil smoothly down her body, and began massaging from her feet upward again, and Lorraine let herself sink into the sensation.

It occurred to her that rich women spent ridiculous money on health spas to get such treatment as this, while all she had to spend was half a day's labor as a stablehand.

And, of course, submit to being Treemark's protégé—with all that involved. But that certainly beat being shot by a Mafia thug, or killed by some Unseelie mutant.

No, she decided, *The price isn't too high.*

Treemark's fingers pressed gently into hidden nerves on either side of her neck.

"Here," he said, "Is where to apply the paralyzing grip." The pressure lightened, and his fingers slid down to another place on her back. "Here, to paralyze from the waist down."

His hands moved up to her shoulders, pressed at specific spots. "Here, to completely relax the muscles of the arms."

Lorraine memorized every touch, wondering how to apply them to another body, understanding that this was another lesson.

"There are also particular points," he went on, sliding his hands down to her feet, "Where the right pressure can cause either severe pain or extreme pleasure. It will take time to learn them all. I'll give you a chart later."

Lorraine didn't answer, guessing that he would eventually demonstrate that chart on her own body. She could imagine several uses for that knowledge, but wondered why he was giving it to her. Was it simply because she had asked? Was this another way of trying to win her trust?

As his hands worked on her, Lorraine felt her mind and body drift apart. Her softened flesh accepted the slow-building pleasure, dissolved into it, enjoying even the soft beat of her pulse, while her mind chewed over her questions like a determined puppy on a bone. How much trust did Treemark want, or expect? She had to trust him with her safety, had trusted him with her body—up to a point—and with some seriously ugly parts of her past, and her feelings about them. What more did he want?

He couldn't possibly be in love with her. Her psychic gift would have warned her of that.

And I, she smiled to herself, *Am in no danger of falling in love with him.* For that matter, she was in no danger of falling in love with anybody.

Thought stopped there, concluded, with nowhere else to go. Lorraine sighed and let the last corner of her mind sink into the sweet lassitude that had taken her body.

Measureless time later, Treemark tapped her foot to waken her. Lorraine drew a deep breath and pulled herself off the massage-table, already feeling a prickle of anticipation tingle through her veins. The tingling increased as she followed Treemark to the solarium and rose to a fierce dizziness as she took her place between the columns. The scent of the flowers seemed overpowering. She closed her eyes and breathed deeply, listening to the metallic click of the locks—and then noticed a difference in the sound.

A quick glance showed that this time he hadn't used locks but snap-links. She could probably unfasten them herself if she wanted to, if she really worked at it, if it was truly worth the effort. She dismissed the thought as the gag settled between her teeth.

"Remember," she heard Treemark say, as if from an echoing distance, "You can stop the proceedings at any time, simply by consenting..."

Lorraine shook her head impatiently. No, she would not trust him that far—not with that intimacy. She would accept him as her employer, trainer, therapist—no matter how intense the therapy became—but not as a sex partner, not as anything approaching a lover. No.

"So be it," Treemark sighed.

Again he massaged her until her muscles slackened, then stroked her all over with the teasing soft brush, and Lorraine didn't even try to resist. When he was finished she hung motionless in the cuffs, barely hearing Treemark walk away.

This time, for some reason, the first image that flickered through her passively waiting mind was of horses: Overcast, standing quiet and dignified in his pasture, and Leila scampering playfully around the paddock. It occurred to her that she would like to paint them, in fact wanted to paint again. Why hadn't she thought to bring her old paint kit with her? Now she'd have to assemble a new one, and probably get an easel too, when she drew her first pay…

***

Treemark came out of the security-center and into the

livingroom, he saw Helen and Ben sitting at one of the tables. Their heads were close together, and their posture spoke of tension. They started guiltily as they felt his aura, and pulled away from each other. Knowing what day it was, he could make some guesses about the nature of their plotting.

Best to tackle it head-on. He came up to the couch, positioned himself between the two of them and leaned on the headrest.

"So, Helen," he said mildly, "Do you mean to attend the weekend session this time?"

Helen shook her head firmly. "Not my cup of tea, Brian," she said, not looking at him.

Treemark smiled. "Then can I ask you to stay in the security office and monitor the cameras? The rest of us will be busy, I'm afraid."

Helen pursed her lips, and the faintest hint of color pinked her cheeks, but she nodded her head.

"And you, Ben? Would you be so good as to attend?"

Benjamin tensed—just a little; his control was excellent—just enough that only an acute observer would catch it. "Yes," he said quietly, then cast a look of almost desperate appeal at Helen. "I still have a few demons to exorcise."

Helen bit her lip, nodded again, and looked away.

As if he couldn't bear even that much sympathy, Benjamin pulled himself to his feet. "Now I'd like to go exercise Overcast, if you don't mind."

"By all means," Treemark agreed, knowing what Ben truly needed. "He needs more work."

Benjamin didn't run, but his strides lengthened as he strode away.

Treemark sighed and took a step away, toward the solarium.

"One moment, Brian," Helen stopped him. "I've discovered something interesting about your little protégé."

"Yes?" Treemark halted.

"I've learned something remarkable about that ever-ready rage of hers, and I think she may be descended from Sekhmet after all. She just might be the warrior you're looking for."

***

Lorraine hung in the cuffs, drowsing, half-dreaming, only the pressure on her shoulders and feet keeping her awake. She felt Treemark's aura approaching before she heard his soft footsteps and she tensed slightly, remembering that only the first hour was past.

Treemark came up behind her, settled his hands lightly on her shoulders and began massaging again: gently at first, then deeper. Lorraine leaned into the touch, enjoying the release of the small tensions. She could almost have purred. His hands worked slowly up her arms, then down, then forward, and she was amused to find that he spent more time on her chest-muscles than on her breasts, though that touch made her shiver slightly.

She remembered to extend a psychic probe, and found only the same concern, the same touch of apprehension, the same not-at-all-sexual purpose behind every touch. She still couldn't be certain if that purpose was only what he'd said, what Helen had said, but it was no threat to her. She let herself drift, enjoying the feel of his hands on her, and then the brushing.

Eventually he brought his touch back to her shoulders, and there held still. Again he asked his ritual question about consent.

This time she had to stop and think about it. Would it really be so dangerous to accept him as...well, not a lover but a sex-partner? Certainly he'd be good at it. Certainly she would enjoy it. She need not give it any emotional weight; one thing she'd learned these past few days was that she could enjoy impersonal sex. There was a clear division between sex and love, and letting a man into her body didn't mean letting him into her heart. Surely he would see that, and not presume that her consenting to sex would mean consenting to anything else.

But is that really what I want?

No, it wasn't. Fantasies aside, she did want more than impersonal sex, and that desire could betray her. There was the danger that she might begin to feel too much for him—yes, trust too much, risk falling in love with him. No: he was her employer, her trainer, her therapist; she would not make him her lover. No.

Lorraine raised her chin high, and shook her head.

Treemark rested a gentle hand on her shoulder. "Are you afraid?" he asked gently.

Of you? Get real! Lorraine shook her head indignantly.

Treemark sighed, patted her shoulders, and then moved away.

Lorraine felt a tremor take her as she felt his presence move away, and that surprised her. *Am I afraid?* she wondered. *If so, what am I afraid of?*

After awhile an answer suggested itself. *Change...*

Yes, she had changed profoundly since coming here, and not

just by being Initiated into immortality and psychic power. Treemark had led her, step by step, into accepting feeling—even into accepting helplessness before it. That, she realized—helplessness, loss of freedom, loss of self-control—that was one thing she truly did fear.

Yet here she stood, accepting it. Treemark had led her to accept it. Knowingly or not, he had made her face what she feared and had showed her something beyond it..

How much further down this path would he lead her? How much further before she changed beyond all recognition?

Two visions danced before her: a doomed hero howling in despair as the light of the full moon changed his body into that of a wolf—and a butterfly drying its new wings in the sun, looking back at its broken chrysalis and marveling that it had ever been just a caterpillar.

***

In the security office Treemark watched the monitor screen viewing the solarium, wondering where the forced meditation was taking Lorraine this time. He desperately needed to know, but could not ask directly; this was a question too deep for words. He could only proceed and observe, and pray that her own responses would give him the answer.

A glance at the clock showed him that there was another half-hour to go.

Lorraine hung limp in the cuffs, her weight suspended from her shoulders—promising pain of eventual cramps from the strain—yet he dared not let her down yet, dared not interfere, break the schedule. Predictability was exquisitely important just now: stability and security, which Lorraine sorely needed but would never ask for. She needed so much, and would not ask. It was not pride, he knew, but something worse: the deep-seated belief that her prayers would never be answered, that she must fight for whatever she wanted because it would never be freely given.

It was pure hell trying to fight against a conviction like that.

***

Lorraine slowly grew aware of Treemark's returned presence, and passively let her body be taken down from the columns and returned to her room, but she didn't ascend to full consciousness until she was alone in her own bed. She lay still for long moments, drowsily feeling out her body and wondering what had changed.

…I know I could enjoy sex again…

But sex, she knew, was only part of the story. So was friend-ship. Between the two there was a gap that she'd never been able to fill.

I thought I had it with Ronnie, but that was all one-sided. I was a fool not to see it sooner.

She hadn't seen it, she realized, because she'd had no stand-ard of comparison.

Ronnie's easy lies had slipped past her guard because she didn't know what to look for.

Because…

I've never been truly loved.

It was bitter knowledge, but looking back now she saw that it was true.

Momma's endless manipulations, Pop's indifference, Georgie's self-centered whining—all of it labeled 'love'—they'd set her up to be taken in by the first clever liar who wanted her, just as abusive parents set up women to be taken in by abusive husbands. She'd been set up, tricked, scammed, and only her own stubborn will had pulled her out of it with any of her self-respect intact.

Lorraine turned and pressed her face into the pillows, blotting angry tears.

Tricked and robbed! No one had ever shown her real love, so now she didn't know how to look for it, and probably wouldn't recognize it if it stood before her. She'd been robbed of that un-derstanding, and of her chances for happiness.

No… She punched the pillow. *I can still learn. I have time.* She had centuries in fact, possibly thousands of years. It wasn't too late for her.

But she had no idea how to begin.

She was still pondering that when Daniel buzzed her intercom with the fifteen-minute warning for dinner.

At his words Lorraine realized that she really was hungry, and the thought of Daniel's cooking literally made her mouth water. She slid out of bed and glanced toward the chair. Yes, there lay the blue semi-medieval dress, complete with low slippers and knife-belt, waiting patiently for her. She pulled off the towel-robe and reached for the clothes.

***

Dinner that evening was, as promised, variations on a theme

of sushi—complete with three different kinds of exquisite dipping-sauce—accompanied by green tea and sake, finishing with sweet almond cakes and plum wine.

Lorraine ate ravenously, barely noticing the conversation around her, which flickered back and forth over the topic of some sort of party planned for the weekend. Lorraine dismissed the subject as no concern of hers; as a stablehand she'd be expected to keep out of the way. In any case, she had more important things to think about. She waited in the livingroom until Treemark came in and poured two drinks, then followed him into the clinic office.

As soon as he'd closed the door Lorraine dropped into the nearest chair and reached for the nearer glass of scotch. Treemark took the other, raised it in a brief toast, then set it down and waited for her to begin. All she could think of was his last question to her earlier that day.

"I'm not afraid; I'm angry," she said. "And I damn-well have good reason."

"Which is?" he asked, raising an eyebrow.

"That my own family set me up to be a mark, a chump, a victim." Lorraine took a quick gulp of her drink, then set it down. "They never really loved me, never showed me what love was, only fed me a lot of lies so that I'd fall for anybody who talked a good show. They thought I'd be their good little chump, but I saw my way through that. Instead I became Ronnie's chump, and it took me five years to see my way through him. Well, I'm nobody's victim now. But…"

"But you're alone."

"Yes." Lorraine fixed her eyes on the glass, watching the light play through the amber fluid. "You asked why I never went hunting again. Maybe it's because I don't know how. I wonder if I'd ever recognize love if I saw it. I'm sure I wouldn't know how to ask for it."

Treemark drew a deep breath and let it out slowly. "Would you know how to give it, then?"

"I gave it to Ronnie, for all the good that did me." She suddenly remembered Crimp-Tail and Sable-Foot. "And my cats. God, the only honest love I ever got in my life came from animals!"

"Only the cats?"

"And a dog. I had a dog when I was growing up: a big gentle collie, named Laddie. He was killed by a car when I was twelve. And there were horses, though I never had one of my own."

"But never a human being?"

"No. Not one." Lorraine picked up her glass and took another sip.

Treemark gave her a long, penetrating look. "Then how did you survive?" he asked. "Where did you get the strength, the will, to fight your way out of all that and make a life for yourself?"

"Animals," Lorraine shrugged, remembering. "Reading lots of animal stories when I was little, sympathizing with the creatures. Nature. Walking through the woods, seeing how all life linked together, and that I was part of it—with as much right to live as any other beast. Art, beauty: I fell in love with the pictures in the storybooks, and it grew from there. I wanted to paint animals like that, and then I wanted to paint everything. Mama encouraged it, until... Well, I told you that story."

"Yes." Treemark hitched his shoulders higher. "You're an ironwood tree."

"I beg your pardon?"

"The ironwood grows here in the desert, in the thinnest soil, with the scantiest water. It grows slowly, but it's extraordinarily tough. Its wood is so hard that it can't be cut with an axe, and so dense that it won't float. It survives on crumbs of nourishment, and it's almost impossible to kill."

Lorraine smiled at the image. "Flattery will get you somewhere..."

"The question is..." Treemark leaned forward and rested his chin on his interlaced fingers. "Could you bear to get more water, better soil, sweeter weather?"

She paused for a long moment, understanding the metaphor perfectly. "I'd...like to. I just don't know how."

There was another long pause as Treemark thought that over. "You can start with little things, small harmless feelings," he finally offered. "Helen makes a good confidant; you could cry on her shoulder about trivial annoyances, and she'd sympathize."

The thought of burdening Helen with trivia was laughable. "Not little things with her," Lorraine admitted. "She's... Wasn't she an ancient goddess, once?"

"Indeed she was," Treemark smiled. "Countless women confided in her, and she comforted them all. She's used to sharing women's sorrows, Lorraine. There's nothing you could say that would shock or offend her. She would never..." His eyes narrowed. "...Scold you, or laugh at your emotions, or belittle your feelings."

Lorraine flinched, stung by a sudden image, a very old memory.

"What is it?" Treemark asked quietly.

"Laugh at feelings…" Lorraine realized she was grinding her teeth, and made herself stop. "It must have been food-poisoning that dragged me out of bed with that godawful gut-pain. I managed to crawl as far as the bathroom, and was trying to haul myself up to the toilet when Momma came in to repair her makeup. She wanted to know what on earth I was doing crawling around on the floor, tearing the knees of my pajamas, and didn't I know how much clothes cost? I had to think about how to put it delicately, how to explain that the pain in my gut was so bad I thought it would kill me, without using nasty no-no words like 'pain' or 'dead'. I tried 'bellyache'. Momma was busy putting on her lipstick, and she said 'take a seltzer-pill' without looking at me. I couldn't think how to say that seltzer would be far too little and too late. All I could come up with was 'I feel like this is the end'. Momma laughed, and said 'Ooh, that's so cute!', and trotted off to tell Pop that I'd said something cute. Thank God she shut the door behind her and left me alone. I managed to get on the toilet and stayed there for the next couple hours, crying, while my guts emptied out."

"Gods," Treemark muttered. "How old were you then?"

"No more than six." Lorraine smiled grimly, seeing a pattern form. "I was seven when I had the earache, and Pop wanted to give me a lecture on Proper Behavior. His voice was so loud it hurt, so I finally yelped 'Be quiet! You're hurting my ear!', but that only made him bellow louder about how You Don't Talk To Me Like That. He saw I was holding my ear and grinning with pain, so he took his belt to my butt for being 'sassy'."

Treemark snapped something in what might have been Latin.

"I really didn't mind that much; the pain in my backside took my attention off the pain in my ear. As soon as he let me go, I ran off to the bathroom and poured peroxide in my ear, and that helped. I got an eyedropper and kept pumping peroxide in my ear, and the pain stopped within a day or two."

"Had to do it all yourself..." Treemark frowned. "By the way, what did your father do for a living?"

"He was a doctor. Why?"

"Gods! ...And I suppose he took it as a personal offense if his own children were sick?"

"Only if we did it in public. If we were sick in private, he'd give us a dozen treatments at once and set Momma to fuss over us. Georgie liked that attention. I didn't. Momma didn't like giving it, either."

"And of course your brother was no help."

Lorraine took care not to grind her teeth. "When I was nine, I sprained my ankle. I made the mistake of letting Georgie see me hobbling around in the bandage. He made a point of kicking me right there to make me howl."

"No more than nine..."

"Oh yes, I learned at an early age. Never show weakness; it's a burden to your friends and an opening for your enemies."

Treemark nodded thoughtfully. "But at least you had friends."

"A few, from school or the neighborhood. When I had the sprained ankle I had to walk slowly. My girlfriends would walk home with me from school, stepping slowly to match me, but I could see that they were impatient. One by one they'd speed up and move on, until I made the last block by myself."

"Didn't any of them want to come home with you?"

"Oh, no." Lorraine tapped her chin, remembering. "I understood why none of them wanted to come into the house with me. One or two experiences with Momma or Georgie were enough to make them stay away. I could go to their houses happily enough, but when I came home Momma would shrill at me for not telling in advance where I'd gone."

"Did you try telling her in advance?"

"A few times. Either Momma would exercise her power by forbidding me to go, or she'd interrogate the other children until they wanted to run away. I tried going to my friends' houses first, then phoning to tell Momma where I was, but she'd always call back and natter at the children's mothers. I couldn't stand the expressions on those women's faces as they listened to her, or the pitying looks they gave me when she'd finally hang up." Lorraine pulled a deep breath. "I really didn't want to burden my friends with my troubles. It was just too humiliating."

"Hell," Treemark whispered.

"Self-sufficiency at an early age," said Lorraine, seeing the pattern clearly. "Who else did I have to rely on?"

"Just animals, storybooks and art," murmured Treemark. "And there were no adults you could trust? Not at school, or church, or anywhere?"

"There were several teachers I liked... Ah, but I knew that any adults I talked to would sooner or later talk to Momma. I had to be careful what I said to them."

"Gods, the loneliness..." Treemark rubbed his forehead. "You became used to being lonely, and in time it no longer hurt."

"I wasn't totally alone; I've always had pets."

"But never a human being you could completely trust."

"I tried it with Ronnie." Lorraine shrugged. "You know how that ended."

Treemark sighed and leaned back in his chair. "You have to start somewhere. I swear to you, Helen can be trusted."

"Probably," Lorraine admitted. *Up to a point, anyway... But where is that point? Where is it with anyone? When will I meet someone whose trust-limit is too far away to find?* She drained the last of her drink, and yawned hugely.

"Time you went to bed," Treemark smiled. "Pleasant dreams, I hope."

"I don't think I've dreamed since I've been here," Lorraine considered, pulling herself out of the seductively comfortable chair. "At least, nothing that I remember."

Treemark was silent behind her as she walked out of the clinic. She caught herself yawning again as she plodded down the corridor to her room. It seemed to take forever to peel off her clothes and slide between the welcoming sheets, and sleep reached for her gently but swiftly.

***

This time she was aware of dreaming, and knew she'd remember it in the morning even though all she dreamed of was the empty solarium with an easel standing in it, and on the easel sat a canvas, perfectly blank, expectant, waiting for the first brush-stroke.

10.

NEXT MORNING dawned softly, almost cool, with a thin banner of high clouds near the horizon. Lorraine was halfway through currying Leila when she noticed Steven carrying some feed into the stall and remembered all that had happened yesterday—including Berringer.

"Steven," she stopped him, "What address did you have for that truck registration?"

"Hmm, I'll show you in a minute." He stuffed the fresh hay into the manger. "Why do you ask?"

"I'm going to have to give Aunt Dianne an address." Lorraine sighed in resignation. "I don't want it to be the ranch. Let her think I'm working as a delivery-woman for some feed company."

"Or a loader for a delivery-company," Steven smiled in understanding. "I actually had some cards made up. Take one." He pulled out his wallet, riffled through it, came up with a card and handed it to her. It read 'Johnson Hauling & Delivery', with an address in town and a phone number.

Lorraine memorized the information, stuck the card in her back pocket and thoughtfully turned on her cell-phone before she went back to currying the black mare.

Two hours later, while Lorraine was leading the bay gelding out to pasture, the phone beeped for her attention. She took care to let the gelding through the gate before she picked up the phone and answered. "Yes?" was all she said.

It was Agent Berringer, sure enough. "Lorraine, how are you?" she crooned prettily. "And where are you staying now?"

"Well..." Lorraine pulled the card out of her pocket and studied it. "It looks like I've got a job—and I'll get a free room with it, if I don't mind sleeping above the shop. It's certainly a place where no one would think to look for me."

"Lorraine, you must give me the address." Berringer was all business now.

"All right, all right." Lorraine dutifully read off the address, then added the phone number for good measure. "But I won't be there during the day," she finished. "This farm-delivery business gets me up early."

"But you'll be there evenings?"

"Unless I'm out at a movie, or something. Mr. Johnson's really a nice guy, and he knows all the good cheap restaurants in town." *Go on, take the next step.*

"That's your new employer?" Berringer nudged.

"Yes. Really a very decent sort. The pay's not much, but the benefits are good."

"What sort of...benefits?"

"Medical and dental insurance with a low co-pay," Lorraine rattled off glibly. *Go on. Ask if I got the job by agreeing to screw the boss.*

She could almost feel Berringer mentally searching for the right question.

"You seem to be on good terms with your employer," was the best she could manage.

"Oh yes," Lorraine smiled toothily. "As I said, he's a very nice man. Also much older than I am. Downright ancient, in fact." *Chew on that.*

"And...what is the business, exactly?"

"As I said, farm deliveries. We drive to the stores, I help load, and then we drive to the farms, then I help unload. Not very challenging, but I get to see lots of pretty countryside. Right now I'm looking at about a dozen cows." *Go on. Ask what else I'm doing.*

All Berringer said was: "That sounds harmless enough. Let me know when you have letters you want sent, and do keep in touch, dear."

"Will do," Lorraine temporized. "Ah, it's time to unload again. Goodbye, Aunt Dianne."

She clicked off the connection, wondering. Did Berringer, and the invaded safe- house, have anything at all to do with that unknown mutant? Or with a Mafia stalker?

And why hadn't the woman mentioned the suspect caught in New York? Could it be that she still didn't know?

Lorraine chewed her lip thoughtfully as she went back to the barn. She found Steven raking out the last stall, with Overcast tied out in the corridor patiently waiting to be curried. She took up the brushes and groomed the grateful stallion while she considered just what she wanted to ask.

"Steven, is there anyone answering that number you gave me?" she tried.

"Just a voice-mail service," he replied, not slowing his rake. "I check it once a day."

"And...is that address real?" she asked as she worked the curry-comb down Overcast's back.

"Oh yes." Steven smiled. "Most of us keep apartments or

rooms here and there, just in case we ever have to leave quickly. It helps to keep up other IDs, too."

"I see." Lorraine thought that over as she circled the comb on the stallion's flank. "That must be expensive."

"Save your pay and invest it," Steven chuckled. "Bonds are best. What's ten years, or twenty, after all?"

"I hadn't thought about it," Lorraine realized. "I haven't started thinking in long terms."

"I could suggest some good investments," Steven smiled, pulling the loaded cart out of the stall, "And all sorts of ways to keep them from being traced."

"I'll ask you about that sometime," Lorraine promised, thinking that there was also the ancient trick of buying jewelry, or plain gold, and keeping it handy. *Or burying a cache of gold out by the sacred spring...*

There was indeed much about immortality that she hadn't thought of, and needed to learn.

Just before lunchtime, she made her way to the back of the barn and phoned Detective Weber.

"Ms. Defarge, glad to hear from you!" His words sounded genuine. "Yes, I've got some news. They're going to send our suspect back here to Chicago in another few days. We'll need you then for the lineup. How fast can you get here?"

Berringer said nothing about that! Which of them is lying? "Ah, give me a day's warning," Lorraine said, thinking hard. "Here's my phone number..." She read off the numbers of the cell-phone, hoping that Berringer had told her the truth about the difficulty of tracing long-distance cell-phone calls. From the area-code he might learn that she was somewhere in Arizona, but no more. "Please don't pass that on to the local cops."

"Not to anybody!" he snapped. "I'm not stupid, ma'am."

"All right," she smiled, and clicked off.

She stuffed the phone back in its holster and strolled toward the kitchen, thinking long and hard. Even lunch—an exquisitely spiced ham salad—couldn't distract her. She caught Steven on his way back to the stables and drew him aside.

"Is there any way," she asked him quietly, "That you can check on that other address of yours? See if anyone's been in there while you're away?"

He gave her a thoughtful look, and nodded. "It's got burglar-alarms that link to the phone here. If anyone gets in, I'll hear about it. What are you expecting?"

"That our unknown friend might be after you, might find that address, and might come looking."

Steven nodded, understanding. "Maybe I should go check my voice-mail, and other things." He turned away from the barn and headed back into the house. Lorraine sighed, and went off to her training exercises.

***

Down in the shooting gallery, Ben handed her a rifle this time. "We'll have to go outdoors to practice with its full range," he explained, "But you can learn the basics here. Pull it tightly to your shoulder, just like the shotgun..."

It was more difficult than the shotgun, but Lorraine managed to place her shots within the 6-ring by the end of the hour.

In the *salle d'armes* they went quickly through the previously-learned blocks and attacks, and Ben led her smoothly into a new, more complicated routine. Lorraine worked at it slowly, then faster, pleased to see him smile in approval. Ben, she knew, had no hidden agenda concerning her; he was her trainer and nothing more, and his smile meant simply that she was learning well.

"How many years do you think it will be," she asked impulsively, "Before I'm fit to face one of the Unseelie elves in combat?"

Ben raised an elegant eyebrow. "With any luck, just one year of intense training should make you competent to hold your own against the average opponent. Of course, there are older ones who are far more skilled. You'll have to keep learning, and practicing, all your life."

"I expected that."

"And not all combats will be honorable." He frowned. "In fact, those who insist on coming after you, when you make it clear that you don't want to fight, are precisely the sort who won't fight honorably. I'd recommend a fast draw, a shot to the heart, and then a speedy retreat."

Lorraine couldn't help laughing. "No different from dealing with street-thugs, then."

"Not really. Once you're practiced with a pistol, I'll teach you fast-draw. You'll also need some training in small-combat-unit strategy and tactics."

"How large is a 'small' combat-unit?"

Ben chewed his lip for a moment. "I've heard of a couple fellows who had combat-squads of half a dozen or so, and another who hunted his prey with large dogs... All dead now, thankfully.

There are always a few who get themselves into positions of authority—police, military commanders, and so on—and use mortals to round up their prey for them. Still, they have to identify their prey personally before they can take any action, which will give you time to escape."

"Like Mafia bosses." Lorraine shivered, then wondered if she'd said too much.

"Precisely. It will be some time yet before you have the expertise to deal with that sort. For the next couple centuries or so, I'd recommend running."

"Couple centuries..." There it was again: the suddenly vast element of time. Lorraine shivered, then twitched as she felt an approaching Elven presence. She could identify the signature feel of the aura. "Helen," she said, a moment before the woman came into sight. Ben glanced at her, surprised.

"My turn," Helen smiled as she glided into the room. "How are the lessons in mayhem going?"

"Quite well," Ben admitted, taking Lorraine's sword from her hand. "I think she'll be ready for, ah, advanced lessons soon."

Helen gave him a dubious look, then turned to Lorraine. "Come along," she smiled. "Time for practicing other skills."

As she followed Helen out into the corridor, Lorraine dared to ask just what Ben had meant by 'advanced' lessons.

"General sneakiness," Helen sniffed. "Ninja tricks adapted for the modern day. Not my field of expertise, I'm afraid; my arts run more to subtle politicking and, to be blunt, seduction."

After a moment's surprise, Lorraine realized that Helen meant the word in the more general sense: as a social or psychological tactic. She sighed. "That's unlikely to become *my* field of expertise."

"Don't sell yourself short, child." Helen led them into the garden, where the rug and cushions waited. "Now, we'll briefly run through what you've already learned, then try energy-drawing."

"Drawing?" Lorraine puzzled as she settled on the near cushion.

"It's possible to pull energy from natural sources around you." Helen sank gracefully onto the other cushion, took Lorraine's hands in her own and squeezed. "That's the one form of 'magic' that I know how to use well. Let's see if you can master the technique. Now, relax and sink into trance-state."

Lorraine closed her eyes, measured her breathing, and sank into the now-familiar feeling of receptivity. Once there, she took care to feel out her own body, then the earth beneath her. Finally she *felt* her way around the garden, searching for other living things.

This time no bird or cat ventured near; there were only the plants and Helen. "Ready," Lorraine murmured, wondering what the next lesson would entail.

"First, try to feel the core of life-energy in yourself." Helen's voice seemed to come from a distance. "Feel it in your body, in your breath and heartbeat..."

That was easy enough to imagine; it was easy to feel her breathing, and a little more thought revealed the soft surge of her pulse. It was easy to picture the energy circulating there, more of it glowing in her spine and rising up to her head. Lorraine remembered the violet sparks that had healed the cut in her arm, and pictured the energy in her body as being that color. She saw herself as an intricate knotted net of glowing violet threads, and wondered if the light could show through her skin.

"Now imagine that energy as…sort of magnetic, drawing not metal but other energy to itself," Helen's voice guided her. "Feel for energy outside yourself, and draw it to you."

Lorraine dutifully *felt* for an energy-source nearby, and found one: a softly glowing swirl of heat/light/pressure that seemed to be the same color as her own. *Come to me...* She imagined pulling at it, like a magnet. Yes, it was coming; the warm light flowed toward her, making her own net-of-light glow brighter, warmer, flaring softly with every pulse, strangely sweet and invigorating. She felt that energy filling her, tickling-electric and delightful, and felt as if she could laugh exuberantly or jump up and dance...

"Lorraine, stop!" Helen's voice shocked her with its sudden fright. "Stop!" Hands yanked hard away from hers.

Shocked up from the depth of her concentration, Lorraine snapped her eyes open. She saw Helen sprawled on the pillow, wide-eyed, panting and pale.

"What happened?" Lorraine asked.

"Hap..." Helen gulped. "It worked. You drew...from me! Gods, so hard...fast…"

Lorraine stared at her, jaw dropping. Helen looked as if she were close to fainting. *I did that?!*

Horrified, Lorraine pressed her hands to either side of Helen's face and—without thinking of how she did it—pushed the energy back. She could feel, almost see, the violet light flowing...

"Enough," Helen gulped, gently pulling her hands away. "I

think this means that you definitely have the ability." She muttered something Lorraine couldn't catch, about Convergents and hybrid vigor.

Lorraine sat back on her heels, feeling slightly dizzy. *I can draw or send psychic energy...* She remembered that sacred site out in the desert. "Got to get back there and try..." she murmured.

"I'd recommend practicing with inanimate sources for awhile," Helen smiled, patting her hair back in place.

"The sacred site..." Lorraine managed.

Helen stared at her for a long moment. "Yes," she agreed quietly. "We should go out there, perhaps late Sunday. We'll be rather busy tomorrow, I'm afraid."

Yes, there was that party which Helen must doubtless attend. At least that would allow the stable hands more time to exercise the horses. Perhaps, Lorraine considered, she could risk riding out to the spring alone—or possibly she could ask Steven or Wally to come with her.

"You do understand, don't you," Helen's quiet voice dragged Lorraine's attention back to the here and now, "That you can use this ability as a weapon?"

Lorraine shivered. "I think I'll need a lot more practice... Helen, I'm sorry! I didn't mean to harm you; I just didn't realize what I was doing."

"I know," Helen smiled. "You don't strike me as the sort who hurts people just to see if they can do it."

How do I strike you? Lorraine suddenly wondered. How did the other Elves here see her? She must appear cold, grim and standoffish...possibly dangerous. That wasn't what she wanted.

Was this tied to what Treemark kept saying about trust? Did she have to trust others in order to be trusted herself?

"Helen, it's not easy for me to trust people..." She had to use the T-word again.

"It's not easy for any of us, given our age-old war," Helen admitted.

"I still need to."

"We all do. We're social animals, and really can't live solitary. That's the dilemma that all of us face; you're not alone in it." Helen squeezed her hand gently. "The progress you've made with Brian shows great courage."

Lorraine looked up, startled. She realized that, as one of her trainers, Helen would necessarily know something of what Treemark had been doing—but Helen's view of it amazed her. "It was just a bargain. There was nothing of courage in it."

"No?" Helen raised her eyebrows. "Not brave, allowing your-self to be totally helpless, when you know how… cannibalistic our kind can be?"

"If he'd wanted to kill me and consume my ability, he could have done it the first day, when he Initiated me."

"Quite logical, as a certain Star Trek character would say," Helen smiled. "What's remarkable is that you could be so logical in such an emotionally upsetting situation."

Lorraine frowned, remembering. "If I let my emotions rule me, I'd never have survived that winter when Ronnie took the money and ran. Hell, I'd never have survived my own childhood."

"Yet you came out of it with a better heart than most."

"All right, I'm a pretty good survivor of the mean streets," Lorraine smiled. "So I'm a…street urchin that you're training to be a...knight? Is that how everyone sees me?"

"A little more than that." Helen leaned closer. "We like you, Lorraine. What's not to like? You're brave, intelligent, beautiful, determined, and good-hearted. Of course we want you to survive and we want you trained to your fullest potential, but we also want you for a friend—not just an ally."

"I see." Lorraine chewed her lip for a long moment. "Is Brian in love with me?" she asked, even though she knew she hadn't felt that in him.

"He's in love with his ideal of you." Helen seemed sure of herself on this. "He sees your potential, and he's impatient for you to fulfill it. If he's pushing you too hard, too fast—"

"No," Lorraine smiled grimly, "Not really. I can take it."

"Is that pride or machismo talking? Lorraine, you have nothing to prove—not to me or to him."

"Just to myself..." But Lorraine wondered if that answer was too easy, too pat. Could it be that she was willing to suffer almost anything Treemark did to her, just to stay here? She knew how poor her survival chances were anywhere else. She thought of trusting her fate to Berringer, or Weber, or trying to strike out on her own with that other mutant lurking about, and shivered. "I suppose I'll have to..." *That word again.* "...trust that you know what you're doing."

"And we have to trust you." Helen squeezed her hand once more. "You have knowledge that could destroy all of us, if you were to give it to the Unseelie—or to mortals. You know the se-cret of our breeding, which no one outside the enclaves knows.

You know where we are: seven of us, some quite old, a real feast for the hunters. And never mind what would happen if knowledge of our very existence were to reach mortals, and persuade them."

"Witch-hunt," Lorraine snapped, remembering the old union's history. "You needn't worry about that from me."

"Just so," Helen smiled. "Go on. Take the next step. Ask."

"All right. Why did you—and Brian—trust me, right from the start?"

"Partly because all the tests Brian ran on you showed that you were the sort of person he wanted. Partly because you already knew the secret of our breeding. You're a Convergent; you knew your true parents, and you'd been pregnant."

"So..." Lorraine saw the rest of it. "The only choices were to kill me or take me in."

"And we took you in." Helen smiled gently. "I don't think we chose ill."

Lorraine looked around the garden, thinking hard. "What happens if I...fail the course? What if I can't be the warrior Brian wants?"

"Then you can be a good foot-soldier, with the rest of us," Helen chuckled. "It would be enough if you simply survived long enough to have children."

"I'll have to train hard just to do that," Lorraine considered. "She who shoots and runs away may live to breed another day."

Helen whooped over that. She was still laughing when they felt the wave-front of Treemark's approaching presence.

***

As she stepped into the pool Lorraine felt the sweet lazy sensation steal over her again and realized, quite calmly, that Treemark had conditioned her to this—and to acceptance of the rituals of the solarium, too. It was astonishing to think that he'd done all that in a single week; she could have sworn she'd been here much longer, as if time moved more slowly within these walls. Had he been anyone else, had she not been able to read his emotions at will, she would easily have believed that all this was some perverse sex-and-dominance game, intended to make her his slave—in mind, if not in fact. But if that was all he'd wanted, she knew, it would never have worked; she would never have yielded this far. So she was left with the same nagging question, and Helen's answer hadn't been enough.

If she wanted an answer now she'd best ask it fast, before the well-imprinted lassitude set in.

"Just one question, Dr. Treemark," she said as she settled onto the underwater bench. "What do you want from me, really? Why… all this?"

He didn't smile, but gave her a long thoughtful look. "I want you healed, trained, and on our team—as quickly as possible," he replied. "It's a dangerous world for our kind, and we need all the help we can get."

"So how does the bondage and the conditioning come into it?" she dared.

"Crash-course," he replied calmly. "Cleaning out old wounds, resetting badly-healed spiritual bones, as fast as I can. If you were weaker, more fearful, more fragile, I'd use different techniques and take much longer. That would be dangerous, all things considered."

Lorraine puzzled over that, dismayed that it made such good sense. This was indeed a dangerous world, particularly for her, and Treemark didn't even know most of it. *Berringer or Weber: which one was lying? And where does the unknown mutant come into it?*

"And that's two questions," Treemark smiled. "Enough, now. Relax."

Lorraine dutifully leaned back against the pool's wall and the bubbling jet, and let her mind go blank. There was, after all, no point in chewing over those unanswerable questions right now.

Only later, during the massage-session, did Treemark speak to her again. "There will be a gathering at the house, tonight and tomorrow," he said as his hands worked over the muscles in her shoulders, "Of certain friends and clients of mine. These are people with specialized needs, some very like yours. The main feature will be psychodrama, for which the participants require considerable privacy, so everyone but myself will be masked. "

Lorraine said nothing, but listened carefully. She remembered the costume party of the weekend before; so, that had been something more than an ordinary Masked Ball.

"It will begin at dinnertime. To preserve the guests' privacy, and the necessary mood, I'll ask you to stay out of sight—in your room, or outdoors—until Sunday afternoon. Daniel will send meals to you there. I may call on you to assist in the clean-up, in which case I'll provide a mask for you also. Can you manage this?"

Lorraine made a faint sound of agreement, and then chuckled.

"What, it's an orgy?" she murmured, even as she extended her empathic sense to reach him.

"Not exactly." She could *feel* Treemark smiling. "But certainly acting-out. I learned long ago that simply talking out one's psychological quirks truly isn't enough. Eventually one has to act them out, involve the body, the whole being. That is, in part, what I've been doing with you."

So you have! Lorraine realized. Those strange sessions in the solarium had raised feelings and thoughts that she would never have imagined otherwise. For that matter, the combat-training with Benjamin had given her a calm, a perspective and confidence, that she hadn't found anywhere else; that certainty had worked into her brain from the nerves and muscles upward, instead of the other way around. *Physical conditioning! Reaching the mind through the body...* Yes, she was beginning to understand Treemark's methods, and she wasn't afraid of them.

She said nothing further, but relaxed into the pressure of his hands. Soon enough the massage and the rest afterward were finished, and Treemark led her to the solarium, and the columns.

***

"'On life, on death, cast a cold eye. Horseman, pass by'," Treemark quoted, watching the monitor. The screen showed Lorraine, immobile as a statue between the columns. Helen peered over his shoulder, and shook her head. "Pride, or something else?" she asked.

"Something else," Treemark considered. "Her self-control, her iron will—they're her most precious possessions, as she sees it. If only I can show her that her integrity is more than those."

"Death before surrender," Helen sighed. "Where have we seen that before?"

"For that matter, where have we seen the opposite?" Treemark smiled. "He learned, she can learn, and she seriously wants to learn. She'll survive. I'm not pushing her too hard, Helen; it takes heavy measures to even bend that ferocious will." Treemark cast a last look at the screen, then turned to face Helen. "Now I have to go help with the preparations. Please watch the monitors, and tell me if anything changes."

"I will," Helen agreed, not too reluctantly.

Treemark gave her an exaggerated bow, and padded out of the security office.

Helen waited until the door whispered shut behind him,

glanced again at the screen and its motionless subject, then reached for the telephone. Dialing the overseas number took interminably long.

"Yes?" a guarded female voice answered.

"Sandra, may you live long," said Helen, in ancient Attic Greek. "It's Helen."

"I could guess," said the other woman, in the same language. "No, I won't tell you the location of my haven. Don't ask me again."

"Sandra, please: we're not at war. We have the same goals—"

"And different tactics. Is that the only reason you called me?"

"No," Helen sighed. "I called to tell you that I've found another fledgling—and she has powers as great as yours."

There was a moment's tense silence, and then Sandra's voice came back. "What abilities, specifically?"

"Empathy, at considerable distance. Directionality, between 10 and 40 yards or so. And…she can draw or transmit power." Helen thought for an instant, then added: "I don't know her range on that, besides direct contact; we just discovered it today."

The woman on the other end of the line drew a deep breath. "And you want me to train her?"

"Someone must; I'm out of my depth here."

"When can you send her to me?"

"Not for several months yet. She was Initiated less than a week ago, and she's not even minimally competent with weapons. I wouldn't risk her outside the house, let alone on a journey that long."

"I can come to you." The woman's voice betrayed her eagerness.

"What?" Helen chuckled, "You expect me to give you the location of *my* haven?"

There was a frustrated silence on the line.

"Besides," Helen added, "Benjamin's staying here for awhile, and I don't imagine you want to see him again."

"Dammit, Helen!" the other voice snapped. "Just what do you want?"

"I want your advice and assistance while I'm training her here. Once it's safe for her to travel, I'll send her to you. Are you willing to do that much?"

"Yes," Sandra accepted grudgingly. "I'll leave this line active. Call me whenever you can."

"Agreed." Helen smiled fiercely. "Tomorrow, then."

"A little earlier, please. It's the middle of the night here."

"All right; six hours earlier."

"Tomorrow, then." The line clicked off.

"Yesss!" Helen hissed in triumph. "Yes, keep talking to me! I'll win you over yet!" She glanced again at the monitor screen, and saw that nothing had changed. "There's a stronger will than yours, Sandra. To deal with her, you'll have to ask for help and I'll be there."

***

Lorraine was staring at the calla-lilies when she felt/heard Treemark approach.

He stripped off her robe, without a word, and began massaging her again. Lorraine relaxed into his touch, feeling her muscles yield gratefully as they released dozens of small cramps. It was wonderful to give her consciousness over to the feel of those hands, not to have to concentrate any longer, let someone else take up the burden of holding her attention. She sighed in relief as his hands worked over her, sinking into the sensation.

"Yes, it's good to let go," Treemark said quietly. "Yes, you can defy the flesh and its needs—for a time, at least—but sooner or later you must release that control, and that release can be very good."

Lorraine frowned, thinking about that, even as she felt him working around to her chest, and necessarily to her breasts. All right, she could see the need to relax, release herself on occasion. *To everything there is a season"…but how long a season?* There was a concept here, too vast and vague to see clearly, something about time spent in combat and time spent at peace…

"A spring can't remain under tension forever, or it will break," Treemark was saying as he worked his way downward. "The same is true of the spirit. You've kept the spring compressed, under tight control, for entirely too long. Release or break, Lorraine and I will not see you broken."

She shook her head in confusion, not quite understanding this; what tension did he mean? There was a sense of another vague idea, looming like a boulder in the mist, that she couldn't quite grasp.

"You've been living in an emotional combat-zone for so long, I think you've forgotten what peace is like. Do you even know how to release yourself completely? Give up all control? Or do you stay guarded even in sleep? I suspect that you don't know the answers yourself."

That last, Lorraine had to admit, was probably true; she certainly didn't understand what he meant, couldn't imagine how to be except as she was. What did he mean by giving up all control? Go limp? Stop thinking? What? "If you have no experience of it, I can't explain; it has to be shown."

She could guess that he meant something beyond falling into the meditative state of mind she'd become accustomed to, here in the solarium. She still couldn't imagine what that could be.

Treemark finished with her right leg, and began on her left. "The bow must unbend," he went on. "The control must be released. If you can't let it go yourself, it must be released for you. This is a knowledge you desperately need, whether you know it or not."

Lorraine stopped listening, seeing that there was no point to it. He might as well have been discussing Chinese poetry for all she understood.

Treemark finished at her ankle, withdrew for a moment, and returned with the brushes. "If you consent, if you can consent," he said, almost sadly, "Then we can end this process and use gentler means. If not, then we must go on as we've begun."

Lorraine barely caught the drift of that, the same old polite request for surrender that she would never give. As always, she shook her head.

Treemark sighed. "So be it. You will remain here for one hour…"

Same old, same old. Lorraine didn't listen.

Treemark sighed again, and plied the brushes. Lorraine was quivering by the time he walked away.

She was left alone with nothing to choose but three directions of thought; she could sink into that dreamy erotic feeling again, or let more ugly old memories come bubbling up out of the past, or think about painting.

And she could think about painting for only so long.

***

This time it was Helen who sat at the desk before the monitor-screen, and Treemark who watched over her shoulder. They waited silently, noting how long the solitary battle lasted and how fiercely it was fought, making their own guesses about the nature of the defeated warrior.

"I've never seen fear of intimacy like that," Helen murmured, shaking her head.

"It's a little more than that, I think," Treemark noted.

Helen sighed in resignation. "And with all your skills, you can find no better method?"

Treemark shook his head. "None so fast, nor so sure."

"You must know by now…" Helen gave him a calculating look. "That whoever she chooses, it won't be you."

"I know." Treemark's look was grim. "But her choices are few."

"I've been trying to expand them," Helen admitted, "But so far I haven't been able to lure anyone here. No one safe, anyway."

"Paranoia, the inevitable weakness of our kind," he muttered. "And I don't dare wait any longer with her."

"Why not, Brian? Why the desperate hurry?"

"Partly because of you, my dear." Treemark smiled at Helen's indignant look. "It was you who insisted on developing her abilities as fast as possible, and now she has them in abundance. Now she's a rare prize to the hunters, and a potential danger to the rest of us."

"The rest of us? How so?"

"Think of all that power—in the hands of a warrior, who has no one to love."

11.

FOR ONCE, sleep eluded Lorraine; eventually she gave up trying for it and turned to the more practical question of dinner, for one feeling she was certain of now was hunger.

Her appetite surprised her; she knew she'd be ravenous in another hour.

The party… She'd have to stay hidden in the staff's quarters, but that wouldn't be a problem. Daniel would send dinner to her room, and she'd spend the evening here.

But doing what? Boredom hadn't been a problem before, but now… It wasn't likely that she'd be able to use the entertainment center, and if she wanted to get a book out of the shelves in the hallway, she'd have to put on some sort of mask.

Lorraine sat up, briefly surprised at how supple and energetic she felt, and reached for the lamp on her bedside cabinet. As she clicked it on, she saw two new items on the cabinet top: a feathered mask and a slender notebook with no title on the cover.

Yes, Treemark had thought of everything, even her entertainment. She picked up the book and thumbed through the first few pages.

There were illustrations, anatomy charts of the human nervous system, marked with little arrows leading to numbers. A few pages further were short chapters devoted to each of the numbers, describing the effects of various pressures on particular nerve-centers. This was the chart he'd promised her, a detailed course in everything from sensual stimulation to the Vulcan Nerve Pinch. It was fascinating, and she felt an urge to try out the listed touches on herself.

For that matter, she'd like to try them on someone else.

Her imagination, so well trained by those sessions in the solarium, began weaving together a picture of the Ideal Lover. Physical features first, of course: a nice lean body, well-conditioned as everyone here seemed to be, thick dark hair but pale eyes, good clean features…

She laughed aloud as she realized that she'd just conjured up a picture of Benjamin. Talk about impossible dreams: her teacher, of all people. Ridiculous.

But I need someone…

She set down the notebook, pulled up her knees and rested her chin on them.

Was Treemark trying to prove that he'd told her the truth, that he had no hidden motives, that he could be trusted? Was this really all about trust, as he'd said from the beginning?

Did she dare let him lead her further down unknown paths to a promised freedom? His bizarre methods had worked so far, shown her truths and capacities she would never have imagined by herself; where else could they take her?

She was still pondering that when Daniel rang to let her know that dinner would be arriving soon.

***

In the security office, Helen watched the screens with an almost hypnotized fascination. Yes, the proceedings were as formalized as an ancient king's state dinner; there sat Treemark in solemn black, across from the fireplace, holding his heavy silver cup like a scepter. Wally and Steven, in unobtrusive black shirts and trousers and masks, waited near the drawn heavy curtains. Now came the guests, all masked in various forms, all in costumes that ranged from scanty loincloths to fantastic creations, waiting to bow in turn over Treemark's proffered hand before taking their seats on the couches. Ah, there was a couple in fantasy-barbarian fur bikinis; no trouble telling what their fantasy was. The classic cowboy and the man in the monk's robe were a little harder to guess.

And here came Madge and Daniel, likewise in subdued black and likewise masked, bringing the food and drink. The theatrics would doubtless begin soon.

Helen sighed, remembering far-off times and places when this was done in temples, with priestesses guiding the ceremonies. Now it was done in a private clinic, in secret, with a doctor in charge. A pity, really. Modern humans had paid a heavy price for progress: burdens of unnecessary guilt and shame, losses of freedom and imagination. Once they had accepted that godlings and magicians and elves walked among them; now, the best they could do was imagine space-aliens, and be scorned when they did. What would they do if they ever learned that Elves still walked among them?

***

Dinner was luscious, as always: slices of duck with orange sauce over wild rice, another unusual and delicious salad, simple steamed asparagus with spiced butter, and a good white wine that Lorraine couldn't identify. She took her time enjoying the meal, and set the empty dishes on the dresser when she was done. A quick call through the intercom got no reply; Daniel was out of the kitchen. Well, she could always bring the dishes back in the morning.

Now what?

Well, there was still that mysterious book of neuro-anatomy. It should take her at least an hour to finish, longer than that to memorize the information. She grinned as she reached for the book, thinking of how she could apply the knowledge... Eventually, anyway. Lorraine was down to the last page in the notebook when the intercom-phone rang again. *Good timing,*she thought, picking up the handset. A quick glance at the clock showed that it was surprisingly late. "Lorraine here," she said.

"Lorraine," Daniel's voice replied, "Please come discreetly to the solarium. Dr. Treemark has need of your assistance."

"Yes," Lorraine murmured, hearing the phone click off. *The solarium?!* She was surprised at how annoyed she felt, and sternly reminded herself that of course that meditation-garden served other needs than just hers. Those ring-studded columns had been there a long time...

She remembered to drape the towel-robe back over her, and put on the mask. A glance at the mirror startled her; she looked like a depiction of some ancient Egyptian goddess, hawk-headed, draped in that timelessly-simple robe. Feeling a little unreal, Lorraine made her way out the door and down the corridor.

The archway to the livingroom was closed off with thick sound-muffling curtains, the lights had been dimmed, and she saw no one else in the hallways. She pushed open the door to the solarium, feeling the familiar silent ringing of an Elven aura, recalling that she'd never seen this place at night and it would probably look very different in the dark.

Different it was: all in darkness except for a solitary overhead light that shone down on the columns—and the man stretched between them. He was tall and slender, she saw—and naked, except for the wrist and ankle cuffs, the familiar gag, and a head-covering mask that suggested an owl or a cat. He hung limp in the restraints, and after the first instant's shock Lorraine was shaken by a sense of familiarity.

So, she wasn't the only person who needed to stand here in the enclosed garden, alone with her personal demons.

No, not alone: she saw Daniel—in a plain domino mask—

standing in front of the man, gently wiping him down with a soft damp cloth. Beyond them, she could make out the figure of Treemark, putting something into a large box and taking out a folded quilt.

As Lorraine stepped closer, feeling the confusion of multiple auras, Treemark draped the quilt carefully around the naked man's shoulders. He glanced up at her and signaled her closer, then pulled away the man's gag and bent to unfasten his ankle-cuffs. Daniel set down the washcloth, pulled the quilt closer around the man's body, and wrapped supporting arms around his waist. Treemark unfastened the wrist-cuffs, and the man sagged bonelessly against Daniel. Treemark took hold of his shoulders, and together they lowered him to lie on the floor. He breathed deeply, but didn't move. Treemark held the man for a moment, patted his covered shoulder, then got up and came to Lorraine.

"I must see to the other guests," he whispered, "And he's too heavy for Daniel to carry alone. Please help take him back to his room, and stay with him until Helen comes."

"Yes," Lorraine murmured, remembering her own sessions and the need to rest afterward. What cruel memories had this man faced? Had he fought blindly in the cuffs, to the point of wrenching his shoulders out of place? Had he needed the gag to keep from sinking his teeth into himself, for lack of a better target? Or had he suffered even worse?

"One more thing," Treemark added. "Tomorrow, keep to your schedule as best you can—only be sure to wear a mask in the house and avoid the guests if possible. I won't be able to meet you at the pool, but come here as usual."

Lorraine only nodded, shivering with a feeling she couldn't name. Treemark smiled and moved on, past her and out the door. Lorraine almost tiptoed over to where Daniel crouched beside the quilt-wrapped man, lifting him gently by the shoulders.

Seeing what was needed, she laced her arms around the man's knees and lifted them—

—and even through the layers of cloth, she could *feel* what and who he was.

Benjamin!

Lorraine could think of nothing to do but wrap him in her arms and hold tight, wondering what other comfort she could give. His body felt lean and solid and almost feverishly hot, even through the thick quilt. *Oh Ben,* she wailed silently, *What brought you to this?* Her gentle, witty, patient teacher: she couldn't imagine why he needed such ferocious treatment, what he could have suffered to bring him here. *Poor Ben!* What demons drove him, that he too needed to stand in forced helplessness, or more? She couldn't begin to understand it, couldn't think clearly about this, only hold tight and try to comfort him, rocked with an aching sympathy that wrung tears from her eyes. *Ben, Ben, what can I do?*

Daniel nodded to her, hefted Benjamin in his arms and lifted him carefully.

Lorraine matched him, and found that the weight was considerable but not more than she could handle. Benjamin sagged in the quilt, and didn't move. Daniel leading, they carried him carefully to the door, out into the hallway and down the guest-wing. It occurred to Lorraine that she'd never been down this corridor, and didn't know which room was Ben's. Fortunately, Daniel knew the way; he led them to the last door on the left, managed to open it, and took them inside.

The room was as comfortably furnished as Lorraine's, with a single lamp lit and the heat turned up. They lowered Benjamin carefully onto the wide bed, on his side, and Daniel tucked the quilt a little closer about him. Lorraine noted that Ben was still marginally conscious, for his hands had clenched on the quilt as if he feared to let go. No, she wouldn't leave him like this—not alone, as she had always been.

"Please stay with him," Daniel whispered. "I'm needed elsewhere."

Lorraine nodded quickly, and settled onto the bed beside Ben. Daniel padded out, and quietly closed the door behind him. Lorraine stared at her silent teacher, knowing well—so well—that he needed comforting, reassurance that he wasn't alone.

Impulsively, she lay down at his back and wrapped her arms as far around him as she could reach. *No, not enough.* She pressed her knees to the backs of his knees, touching as much as she could through the thick cloth, and gently stroked his arm through the fold of the quilt, sharing warmth with him. It was contact enough for her to reach and *feel* for him.

All she could read from him was a vast shuddering relief and exhaustion.

Relief from what? she wondered. Did he too need to dredge up ugly memories, relive them and wring them dry of feeling? Did he battle silently with old enemies, casual or deliberate torturers, perhaps long dead in real life? Or was it himself, elements of himself, that he fought? Surely he couldn't need his sexuality reawakened, not like her.

Then it occurred to her that she had no idea how old he was. He might have lived through centuries of hard history, and suffered unspeakable miseries. He might have been a galley-slave, or tortured by the Inquisition, for all she knew. Her own hardships might be nothing compared to his. A wave of aching sympathy swept her and she hugged him tighter, wishing she could use her empathic powers to send as well as receive. As it was, she had only touch to tell him he wasn't alone, that he was safe, that a friend was near. All she could do was squeeze gently, stroke his arm, and try to comfort him as simply as a cat would, by curling close around him

Eventually she noticed that his hands had relaxed their death-grip on the quilt, and his breathing had softened. He was, at last, truly asleep.

A few moments later another familiar Elven aura approached, and Helen slipped noiselessly into the room. She took in the scene at a glance, held a finger to her lips and slid onto the bed.

"It's all right now, Lorraine," she whispered. "I'll stay with him until he wakes. You can rest."

Almost reluctantly, Lorraine loosened her grip and carefully rolled away. Ben didn't move or wake, and she was grateful for that. "What could he have suffered—" she began, and then caught herself. It wasn't her place to ask.

"He was once a mighty warlord," Helen answered, sadly trailing her fingers over Benjamin's forehead, "Fierce and cruel, demanding tribute from a wide domain, slaughtering any who defied him, a terrifying legend in all the lands around. In time he learned better, and became as secretive as the rest of us… No, more so: eternally watchful, rarely letting his guard down, so rarely letting anyone draw close."

Overcontrolled, Lorraine realized. *Like me.*

"Poor Ben," she sighed, winning an understanding look from Helen. She got up and tiptoed out the door, taking care to close it quietly behind her, and paced back down the hallway to the staff wing and her own room.

Once there, she locked the door as usual. The notebook was lying where she'd left it, and she put it back on the cabinet, then took off her mask and dropped it beside the book. *I'm not alone,* she thought, as she pulled off the robe and slipped under the covers. *Not even with the knots in my own soul. Not even among Elven-kind. Not even in this house.* There was something both humbling and wonderfully comforting in that. A sudden image of herself between the columns sent a wave of nameless heat through her, and it grew dizzying as she thought of Benjamin in her place.

She felt incredibly tired, but it was a long time before she could sleep.

12.

LORRAINE AWOKE well after dawn, and remembered everything. For long moments she lay still, listening to the early-morning near silence of the house, images of last night replaying before her eyes. The one that kept recurring was the memory of Ben between the columns, as she'd seen him last night. She couldn't understand that, and she couldn't stop thinking about it.

Neither could she deny that she was aroused.

Lorraine pressed her hands to her thighs and seriously wondered how to deal with sexual frustration. This hadn't been a problem in a very long time, and she had no idea what to do about it. Unless she went ahead and used her hands—and thereby, she knew, broke her contract with Dr. Treemark—she would literally have to go and ask his permission. *Doctor, may I please have some sex?* The idea was ludicrous.

She pulled up her knees and rested her chin on them, and faced the inescapable conclusion.

Congratulations, Dr. Treemark; you've taught me that I need sex and I need other people.

I need an honest lover.

Now tell me how I go about getting one.

Well, nothing would be served by sitting around here. Lorraine sighed, crawled out of bed and went looking for the day's clothing. Something fit for stable-work: hat, knit shirt, bluejeans and boots, with belt and usual accoutrements. If the arousal hadn't passed by the time she finished breakfast, she could always come back here and take a cold shower.

***

Daniel wasn't in the kitchen, but Madge was. She smiled a somewhat sleepy greeting at Lorraine, and set out the usual training breakfast: fruit, milk, hard-boiled egg, and some slices of Canadian bacon—much protein, little sugar, less oil, no starch. Lorraine noted that the hour was late for her—almost eight o'clock—and finished fast

Out in the barn, Steven and Wally were already at work. Nodding a swift apology to them, Lorraine grabbed a rake and pitchfork and hurried to catch up on cleaning. The work went quickly, and by lunchtime all the stalls had been cleaned and all the horses curried and fed. Wally and Steven opted for a leisurely lunch, but Lorraine only grabbed a quick sandwich and headed back to the barn.

The arousal had passed, but she still felt a persistent itching of nervous energy. She wanted a good long ride, and the horses could use the exercise. Now, which one?

Leila nickered a greeting, and Lorraine decided. It took less than ten minutes to saddle the black mare, despite Leila's eager dancing, and they were soon trotting out of the stable-yard toward the exercise ring.

Feeling the mare's eagerness, and remembering her earlier concern, Lorraine steered instead toward the open land. She could see the tumble of rocks on the horizon that marked the sacred spring, and there was no fear of getting lost. For a moment she felt a qualm about riding out alone, but then remembered the gun on her hip.

The land ahead stretched straight and flat, with good clear spaces between the brush and cactus, no sign of treacherous prairie-dog holes, and there was no reason not to let the eager little mare run. Lorraine smiled, leaned forward and touched her heels to Leila's flanks.

Leila whickered gratitude and started off at an easy canter. Feeling no objection, she speeded her pace to a joyful hand-gallop. Lorraine bent slightly over the mare's neck, laughing softly at the fast-flowing smoothness of Leila's gait, and used only the slightest touch of the reins to aim her up the clear path toward the distant outcropping. The wind of their own making flowed around them like water in a stream, and Leila's long stride ate up the ground before them. Lorraine laughed aloud into the sun, wishing only that the dainty mare really could be a legendary Elven-steed who could run on forever.

The thickening brush near the spring made Lorraine regretfully rein the mare down to an easy trot, and she searched for the pathway to the pool. Unless she'd come at it from the wrong angle, the ring of bordering stones should be visible soon...

A motion off to her left caught her eye. Lorraine looked, and saw another rider: a tall man on a gray stallion, trotting from shadow to shadow among the tall saguaro cactus. She recognized the horse as Overcast, and the man—*Benjamin.*

He was out of aura-range, and didn't seem to have seen her; he looked thoughtful, preoccupied, letting Overcast pick the route.

Lorraine turned Leila aside quickly, guiding the bewildered but willing mare behind a thick Palo-Verde tree, then stopped and waited until she was certain Benjamin had ridden past.

...Being ridiculous, Lorraine chided herself as she waited. *Nobody knows I've guessed his secret. Act normally, and he'll never know. Just think of him as my teacher. Forget the scene in the solarium. Think about something else. The border-stones...*

She resolutely turned her attention to seeking a way through the thickening brush, steering Leila back around the tree to more open ground, moving toward the spring. She felt the first faint tingle of the site's power just before she saw the low rocks, and yes, there was a pathway; it was marked by flanking spindly trees, by two stones set wider apart than the rest, and by old hoofprints. Leila either felt the power too or smelled the water, for she picked up her pace. In a few more steps, the pool and the spring and the carved rock above it opened out before her.

With a sigh of relief, Lorraine slid off Leila's back and led the mare to the pool. The water was wonderfully cool and sweet, as before, and they both drank their fill.

Almost reluctantly, Lorraine tied the mare in the shade of a mesquite and set out exploring.

The power centered at the point where the spring bubbled out from under the boulder, and spread out from there in a smooth circle. The brush crowded too thickly for Lorraine to make her way around the outcropping, but the power radiated evenly wherever she could reach. It felt sweet, energizing, and blank—like a mutant's aura, but with no mind under it.

What is its relationship to the healing-power?

She could think of only one way to learn it. Biting her lip, she pulled a thorn off a low cat-claw bush and scratched it across her arm.

Droplets of blood had no sooner beaded up in the scratch than the violet sparks came—fast and thick—and healed the cut. The tingling seemed stronger than from earlier cuts she remembered, and there was a distinct sense of heat.

Frowning thoughtfully, Lorraine dropped the thorn and pulled the knife from her belt. As the blade touched her skin, she noticed that feeling of heat again.

Is the power drawn to metal?

She went to where the mare was nibbling at a clump of grass, and felt the bridle's bit and buckles. They seemed warm, but she couldn't be certain if that was from the node's power or the heat of the sun-drenched air. Holding the knife by the blade, Lorraine carefully paced away from the spring and then back toward it.

Yes, the heat increased as she drew closer.

She remembered Ben saying that killing or wounding another elf near the node would cause a power-surge that could burn an Elven body away. That implied more than just the presence of metal.

Clenching her teeth, she drew the edge of the knife across her arm.

The pain of cutting was enough to make her grunt, but it was forgotten in what came next: the fast and fierce sizzling of the healing-sparks and a sudden flare of heat in the knife—hot enough that she could feel it through the wood of the grip. The sparks in the cut seethed into a brief and tiny bolt of lightning, and more sparks played over the blood on the knife. More: she could feel noticeable heat in her belt-buckle, in the clasps of her brassiere, the copper rivets of her jeans and the ornamental buckles on her boots.

It took long seconds for the light to fade, longer still for the heat to dissipate.

Metal, blood, my own power-net... Lorraine tumbled the images over and over in her mind, trying to see the relationship between them. The node's power and the Elven healing-power had to be one and the same, but was it transmitted by the metal? Why was it drawn to the fresh blood as well as to the cut itself? Did the simple kinetic energy of the cutting motion add to it?

Long moments of thought gave her no answer, but suggested another experiment.

I could draw from Helen, or transmit...

Just to be cautious, Lorraine moved to the outer rim of the circle of power. There she sat down, closed her eyes, ran through her usual meditation exercises, then concentrated on feeling and visualizing the web of Elven-power in her own body.

It was surprisingly easy this time: the steady power of the node could be readily felt, seemed to illuminate her own network, even at this distance. Lorraine drew a deep breath and cautiously *pulled.*

The surge of power was astonishing. She felt a blast of heat like the wind from a furnace, not at any one point but all through her flesh. If she hadn't already been sitting, it would have knocked her down. The bits of metal in her clothing were hot enough to sting.

She stopped pulling, shut off the flow fast, and sat panting, sweating furiously, until her temperature returned to normal. The desert air on her wet skin felt cool by comparison.

Why the heat? she wondered dizzily, trying to remember details from her long ago high school Physics class. *Energy dissipated? Blocked? ...Because it had nowhere else to go?* She recalled something about electrical flows, and ground-wires. Another experiment suggested itself.

Lorraine picked up the knife, noting that her blood still stained the blade, and pushed its point into the ground near one of the border-stones. Very carefully, she touched one hand to the knife's hilt, closed her eyes, summoned the vision/feel of her energy-web, felt for the steady stream from the node, and gently *pulled.*

The power-surge came slower this time, and lighter. Lorraine remembered how she had sent the power back to Helen, and tried to copy that feeling in her outstretched arm while the rest of her network maintained the light pull on the node. It was difficult to hold the image, the feel, but after a long moment she got the distinct impression of energy flowing, of something not-quite-heat soaking into her from the direction of the spring and rolling down her arm to the grip of the knife. This time no heat dissipated into her clothes. Yes, she was sure she felt it: smooth, steady, not dangerous so long as she was careful how much she drew and how clearly she directed it...

Heat began stinging her hand.

Damn! Disappointed, Lorraine stopped pulling at the power-source, let the image in her mind fade, and opened her eyes.

Steam was rising from the ground close to the knife, and the wood on its grip bore streaks of char-marks.

It worked. Lorraine stared for measureless time at the knife and the undeniable evidence. *Was it the metal, or my blood, or both?*

There was a way to find out.

Lorraine pulled the knife out of the ground, went to the pool and cleaned it thoroughly, then returned to the border-stones and sat down again. She would have to cut deeply, she realized, in order to spill enough blood before the accelerated healing-power closed the wound. Again she set the blade against her arm and drew it hard across the skin. The pain was almost, but not quite, enough to distract her from reaching out and turning her arm so that the blood fell onto the ground. Quickly, even as the violet lightning sizzled in the cut, she dropped the knife and stretched out her hand over the spot of blood glimmering in the dirt. She closed her eyes, called up the vision/feel again, and pulled, and transmitted.

At first she thought nothing was happening, but she didn't dare increase the amount of power she drew; it was better to tighten her concentration, fix on the feel of power flowing... Ah, and there it was: that distinct sense of energy rippling in and through and out. Despite the distance—only a little space—between her hand and the blood-spot, the power was definitely streaming there. *Grounding,* she thought. *Metal transmits it, but blood alone will do.*

Then she noticed a growing smell of burning meat.

Enough! Again she broke off the flow and opened her eyes.

The blood-spot was now only a smear of soot, and the ground—again—was steaming. *I must tell Helen about this,* was all she could think. But then, where could she find Helen today, with her schedule suspended by the weekend gathering? She didn't know which room the Elven woman was using. She wasn't even sure how the intercom system worked. *Fool,* she sighed to herself. *Just have to wait until Monday, when lessons resume...*

At that point she felt the unmistakable aura of an approaching mutant. Lorraine froze, remembering that unknown mutant in the city, remembering that any stranger of her kind that she met could easily be an Unseelie hunter—and then noted that the tone of the aura was familiar. She also noticed that her hand had found the butt of her revolver without conscious thought, and guiltily pulled her fingers away. Slow hoofbeats drew closer, and a horse and rider appeared through the brush.

It was Benjamin, still riding Overcast. He must have seen her after all.

All Lorraine could think to do was stand up, plaster a faint smile on her face, and say nothing.

"Should you be out here alone?" reining to a halt beside her. "You're really not trained, you know."

Lorraine let out a breath she hadn't realized she'd been holding. "Well, I'm not unarmed," she admitted, grabbing up the knife and stuffing it quickly in the sheath. "And you did say this was a safe place."

"Safe to be in, not necessarily safe to travel to or from." Benjamin smiled as he swung easily off the gray stallion and led him toward the water. "I'd be happy to escort you home, or wherever you're going," he tossed over his shoulder.

"Home, if that's all right with you," said Lorraine, following him. "I think I've learned everything here that I can, at least today."

"Learned?" Benjamin looked back toward her, reminding her of a hound with pricked-up ears, as Overcast bent his head to drink. "What have you been studying here?"

"The power-flows..." Lorraine searched for the right words. "I think it truly is the same kind of power that our bodies use. Close to the source, a thorn-scratch heals in seconds."

"You're certain?" Without waiting for an answer, Benjamin went to the nearest thorn-bush and deliberately scratched his hand on it. They both peered at the tiny cut, counting seconds.

"…Three, four— There!" Benjamin marveled. "You're right. If it isn't the same energy, at least it transforms readily into it. Fascinating! It would explain the reputation for healing..."

Lorraine smiled, unaccountably relieved to see him back in his usual mood: happy being the teacher, the scholar, eager in the hunt after knowledge. "I think," she offered, "I understand—at least a little—how it can also destroy, why our kind can't kill or wound here."

"How? Why?" Now he looked like a hound hot on the scent, almost quivering with eagerness.

Lorraine was happy to tell him, if only because it made him so delighted, so normal again. She explained her experiments, having to backtrack a few times to describe her training-session with Helen, and finally pointed to the sooty spot on the ground as evidence. Benjamin stared at it with all the rapt attention of a zoologist discovering a new species of butterfly.

"Wonderful," he murmured. "We've got to tell Helen; she knows more about such things. The implications... Gods, I can't even imagine them." He turned to look at the stallion, who was still drinking. "Can you speed it up, old fellow?" he said, precisely as if talking to a human. "We really need to get home soon."

Overcast rolled an eye at him, and finished drinking almost deliberately slowly.

They rode back to the ranch at an easy pace chuckling at how Leila flirted shamelessly with Overcast, and the stallion pretended not to notice.

"Hussy," Lorraine laughed, reining the mare away to a safe distance. "She's not even in heat yet."

"You'll know when she is," Benjamin promised. "Overcast will start paying attention."

"Very practical of him." Lorraine glanced ahead to where the ranch came into view, thinking how good it was to have Benjamin back to his usual self. Then she remembered what Helen had hinted about the man's real age, and history. No, she couldn't imagine him as a cruel barbarian warlord. That, she realized, was her own failing. Again she felt that nagging suspicion that, for all her experience in the normal human world, she was woefully naive. "Benjamin," she ventured, "Can I ask you something? About my training, I mean."

"Certainly," he shrugged, "Although I must say you're coming along quite well."

"It's a subtle problem. I can barely see it myself..." Lorraine chewed her lip, hunting for the right words. "I feel that I'm lacking something: curiosity perhaps, or forethought."

"I doubt that, seeing what research you've done."

"Wrong sort of subject." Lorraine fiddled with the reins. "I mean... I just realized that I don't know the last names of anybody else on staff, or where their rooms are, or what they do when they're not working, or how the intercom works, or...even the layout of much of the house."

"So you're not snoopy." Benjamin smiled. "At the risk of sounding hopelessly outdated and sexist, I'd say that's a charming trait in a woman."

"It's not just a lack of snoopiness, it's that I never even thought of it. I never bothered to ask about the intercom, or where all the fire-exits are—things like that. Treemark offered to show me the house chapel, and I didn't take him up on it."

"Hmmm. Those are bits of information important to your safety," Benjamin considered. "Why do you think you weren't curious about them?"

"I don't know." Lorraine struggled to see the pattern clearly. "It's as if I'm… cut off from part of the world, or have blinkers on, or...live in a fortress dug into a mountain, with just one entrance. I watch that entrance for approaching enemies, but I never seem to look anywhere else...or for anything else...so I miss a lot. Damn, is this making any sense?"

"Actually, yes." Benjamin's gaze turned distant and abstracted. "Like wearing a 15th-century jousting helmet: excellent armor, superb for defense, but it narrows your field of vision so that you can see only straight forward. You miss everything that happens off to the side."

"Exactly. I think I ignored everything...off to the side, because I thought it was irrelevant: neither threat nor help. Now I'm beginning to wonder what I've missed, how important it really is." Lorraine saw a glimmer of sense emerging. "In fact, I don't know what I'm missing—and that worries me."

"I know that feeling." Benjamin's voice was almost too soft to hear. "I think it's...learning that there's a part of yourself that never had a chance to grow, but wants to grow now. All you can do is let it run, follow where it leads, learn what it needs...for good or ill."

"For good or ill..." Lorraine vividly remembered him limp between the columns—and fiercely thrust the thought away. "How do I let it run? I don't even know how to do that."

Benjamin heaved a deep sigh. "Follow your impulses, with your eyes wide open. Trot around exploring, if only to discover what your impulses like. It's risky, but... Well, I don't know any other way."

"I see." *I think I do. But what impulses do I have? ...Aside from the obvious, of course.*

Lorraine pondered that as they came down the trail to the barn, saying nothing further. Benjamin too seemed lost in thought, but his silence was oddly comfortable, companionable. Together they rode to the barn, dismounted, unsaddled the horses and let them into the pasture. At the sight of the lush grass Overcast abandoned his dignity and Leila forgot to flirt, and they both fell to cropping hungrily. Lorraine remembered to gather both the saddles and bridles and carry them away to the tackroom. By the time she came out again Benjamin had disappeared, but she didn't feel his absence as abandonment; as engrossed in his thoughts as any classic absent-minded professor, he'd no doubt gone looking for Helen. Lorraine felt surprisingly relieved that somebody else would tell Helen about today's experiments. She felt a pressing need to be alone right now.

Remembering Treemark's warning about the guests, Lorraine went around the outside of the house, down the meandering flagstone walk, until she found the door at the end of the staff wing. Nobody was in the hallway, and she made it to her room unseen.

Now what? It was past time for weapons-practice, or for psychic training, not that Helen or Ben were keeping to the schedule either. The next item on her list was soaking in the spa, but Treemark wouldn't be there, and other guests might. The idea of wearing her mask into the water was laughable.

She could perhaps go fill in those blanks in her information, look for the chapel, and learn about the intercom system...

But that would mean wandering through the house while the guests were about.

No.

There was the notebook, which she could read again and try memorizing…

She tried, truly she did, but her concentration kept skittering away. She kept remembering Benjamin between the columns, and then herself. *Similar needs, similar treatment, similar reactions…?* Ben wasn't just a colleague or friend of Treemark's, but a client too; he'd needed whatever he'd gotten in the solarium last night. *As much as I do…*

A glance at the clock showed that it was nearly time to go there herself. Her eye caught the feathered mask, carelessly dropped, near the notebook. Her robe was also waiting, at the foot of the bed.

Lorraine stripped off her stable-clothes and tossed them in the laundry hamper, then glanced at the ample bathtub, and decided that putting on her robe could wait. Good hot water was a fine treatment for fatigued muscles, and somebody would notice if she strolled the hallways still smelling of horses. Yes, the water came up hot and plentiful, and there was a little jar in the corner of the tub that she hadn't paid attention to before but clearly contained bath-salts. Lorraine poured in a small handful of the turquoise crystals, which released plentiful foam and a strong herbal scent. *Lap of luxury,* she chuckled to herself as she stepped into the rising water.

For the first time in days, washing under the webbing-straps was an annoyance. In fact, Lorraine couldn't help being aware of them, and of the twinkling brass D-rings.

The image of Benjamin between the columns rose again, contrasted with a flickering montage of other scenes: Benjamin riding Overcast, teaching her swordplay, dropping little nuggets of history here and there, eagerly studying the charred spot at the sacred spring. His inexplicable need, and its satisfaction, was as much a part of him as all the rest.

The memory of his naked body kept flickering before her eyes, and she couldn't avoid the obvious conclusion any longer. He was beautiful, he was what she'd imagined as an ideal lover, and the thought of him was arousing.

He's my friend, dammit! Lorraine scrubbed furiously, trying and failing to push the image away. She had no right to think of him like that, wasn't supposed to know his secret. *But I'm supposed to understand...*

She rubbed slower, slower still, as her thoughts circled repeatedly and found no resolution, finally dwindling away to nothing. She still thought of nothing as she dried off, went back to her bedroom and slowly put on the robe and mask. Lorraine thought to look at herself in the bathroom-door mirror. The reflection that stared back was every bit as exotic as yesterday; she looked like an Egyptian goddess, or the priestess of some obscure cult, or the oracle of some long-forgotten shrine. Feeling a little unreal, she made her way out the door and into the corridor.

She met no one in the hallways, though she could faintly hear people talking behind the curtains. Lorraine paused at the door to the solarium, then determinedly shoved open the door and walked in. She paused among the banks of flowers and wondered why she was doing this, why she hadn't waited at the door for Treemark to arrive. *Following an impulse, as Benjamin said,* she realized. She hadn't been impulsive since she was a child.

...Laddie wanted to play, so I kept tossing him the Frisbee and he chased it and brought it back and it was such simple innocent fun that I lost track of time until I noticed the shadows growing long so I put him back on the leash and hurried home and sneaked in the back door so I could feed him before Mama could find me and give me some other task to do but she walked into the kitchen just as I was setting the dish down and she shrilled at me for being out so late and kept on yattering all the way through dinner while Georgie smirked and Pop ignored her and ate and I realized that she loved to hear herself talk and loved to make herself feel superior by belittling others and that was the moment when I stopped even trying to love her or love any of them anymore but I knew I'd be stuck with them for another six years— God, six years!—before I could escape to college and I'd have to plot and maneuver and manipulate them just to survive and I didn't know how I could stand living like that down the long bleak tunnel of the future...

She felt Treemark's aura before he opened the door, and turned to face him as he came in. For an instant she thought of telling him what she'd learned about Benjamin, begging to learn what he needed and how she could help, but caught herself in time. She wasn't supposed to know, and it wasn't her place to ask.

Treemark smiled briefly as he saw her waiting, and led her to the columns as usual. Again, he fastened her cuffs to the rings – and again, she noticed, he used simple snap-links instead of the usual locks. He pulled her robe away, over her head, but left the mask in place: reassurance, perhaps, since there were strangers to her in the house. It was ironic that she could stand here, nearly naked and bound, yet safe and anonymous.

Lorraine flinched as she felt him spread the oil on her shoulders, feeling unusually sensitive. It was no doing of his, as a quick empathic probe told her; Treemark was concerned and absorbed as always, with no change of feeling. It was her own reactions, her needs, that had changed. She could feel the waiting desire that had plagued her all day rising steadily, even as her body relaxed under his hands.

Trust, she remembered. It was all about trust: of herself, desire, emotions, and other people. In some way she had indeed learned trust. Now she was willing to take risks, and her body knew it.

Lorraine pondered that as Treemark finished, and asked the usual question. Again she shook her head, heard him give the usual reply and walk away, but that didn't matter; she had something important to think about, a mystery to unravel, and she had all but the last clue.

It had something to do with Benjamin, with discovering that he had needs much like hers, that she wasn't alone in this.

And perhaps there were others. Those people who came to attend the weekend party, for the 'psychodrama' as Treemark called it… What did that mean? Acting out, yes, but what? Old miseries? …Or their solutions?

How would I have solved…?

Her imagination willingly unraveled a possibility, an image, a stark daydream.

Back at the old house…and there's Pop in the big chair, reading his newspaper and not noticing me. Go upstairs. I'm here to pack up what I need, the last I'll ever take from this house. Certain clothes, books, my old toys—everything that Mama didn't sell or give away while I was in school. It will all fit in the big suitcase. There. Start packing.

And of course Mama comes and natters about how my clothes are terrible and my makeup is worse, and why don't I ever do anything nice with my hair. Ignore her until I've closed the suitcase. Now… Yes. Turn and look at her, and say it. "I'm going to another city, to work on a newspaper and become a painter in my spare time, and you won't hear from me again—no more than a card a Christmastime, if that."

Ah, and she starts the shrilling, the questions, blocking my way…

Use the suitcase. Knock her on her ass! …And walk past her. God, I've been wanting to do that for years, and it feels so damned good!

Oh, of course she follows, screeching, down the hallway. She can't let her prey escape that easily. …But all I have to do is set down the suitcase, turn and…raise my fist! Mama always was a physical coward; I saw proof enough times. She never threatened anyone or anything that wasn't much smaller than she was—and now I'm bigger. Yes, I'm a good three inches taller than she is, and much stronger from all those years working for the union. Mama claimed that muscularity was 'coarse' and 'unladylike'—because I could use it to threaten her! Oh, of course! "Vi-o-lence is evil" because she was no good at it!

Yes, she backs off—quickly—and falls back on her ultimate trick, the hoo-boo-booing. "Ooh, you're wicked to make your Mama cry! Ungrateful daughter! You don't care anything for my feelings! You have no compassion!" …That used to work on me, back when I was still trying to love her, trying to make her at least respect me… But it doesn't work now. "Give up, you stupid woman. No, I don't care about your feelings anymore."

And oh, the lovely look of shock. How dare I, how dare anybody, not care about Mama-Dear's precious feelings! I can't help laughing as I pick up the suitcase and head on down the stairs; it feels so damned good to be free—free of Mama's last chain.

Hmmm, Pop harrumphing at the foot of the stairs: he must have heard it all.

Bellow, bellow, threaten, threaten. He raises his hands…and I raise the suitcase, ready to throw it at him and follow with a fast punch and kick, tricks I learned on picket-lines…

Damn, but there really are advantages to learning all about 'vi-o-lence'! All that supposedly-pacifist crap comes down to nothing but: 'Don't learn to fight, so you can't fight ME.' But I did learn to fight, and I can, and I'm not afraid or ashamed to.

And he sees it! Sees it in my eyes—maybe in my full-grown size, possibly in my position on the stairs above him—and he backs away. God, yes, he's a coward too!

Isn't it a cliché that bullies always are cowards? Why did I never see it before? …Or did I guess, when he always left the beatings to Mama? "Goodbye, Pop. I'm off to seek my fortune"—and march past him toward the entryway.

As I reach it, a last bellow: "I'll disinherit you!"

I burst out laughing. Did the old fool think I ever wanted his money, or that I could be tied by it? "Too late, Pop: I disinherited you, years ago." He stands there gaping, astounded that anybody could ignore his Great God Money. Old fool. Leave him and walk on.

Oh, and here comes Georgie, whining about what an ingrate I am, and I'll be sorry, and how much I'm going to need my family, yatta yatta… Heft the suitcase and say only: "Get out of my way."

Does he have the sense to do it, or will he stand there until I'm close enough to slam him with the suitcase, then throw a punch, then repay him for all those kicks in my ankle years ago…

No, he's a coward too. Ducks aside, yapping like a small dog and just about as dangerous. Pass him without a glance, through the entryway and out the door to where my battered old car is waiting…

And there's Ronnie, of all people, at the foot of the front stairs. That old sweet charming smile, and the expected words: want to come back to you, understood what I'd lost, my one true love, it'll all be different this time— Damn, why did I never realize before that every sweet word he ever said to me was taken out of soap operas?! What a fool he must have thought I was!

I'm nobody's fool today, and he's standing in just the right position…

Kick high and hard, and oh the lovely impact. He doesn't make a sound as his face turns green and he crumples like wet tissue-paper. Walk right over him. Ah, that's perfect!

Now, into the car, throw in the suitcase, get in and start the engine. One last look back at that hated house and that collection of pigs that I once wasted my love on.

Goodbye, and good riddance! I'm away, back to Tucson and my new life, feeling the freedom grow with every yard I put behind me… They're all behind me, falling away like leaves of last year's calendar, crumpling like old paper, ashes blown away by the wind.

They're gone, and I'm free.

I'm free!

Her laughter sounded strange to her ears, muffled by banks of flowers, and Lorraine remembered where she was. But the vision was too good to release. She replayed it in her mind, adding details: another cutting remark here, another punch there, gleaming facets of the grim joy of revenge. *Yes, revenge is sweet!*

Lorraine wasn't surprised to note that she felt no guilt at all for it. Wasn't it Mama who preached that revenge was Evil? She'd learned in Chicago that revenge was often the only justice the poor and powerless could get. There was no shame in enjoying it, either.

She was still contemplating that lovely little gem of vengeance when she felt Treemark's aura approaching. In fact, she felt a twinge of regret when his touch pulled her back to full awareness of the here and now.

As always, his touch was sure and gentle and implacable; now it reawakened the hunger she'd been feeling all morning. Lorraine managed to keep still until he began brushing her, but as his hands worked downward over her skin she couldn't hold back a groan and a heavy trembling. Too much, too long… She wailed sharply as the brushes passed over one nipple, then the other, raising them to stiff coral towers, and she thrashed helplessly in the cuffs as he stroked down her buttocks and thighs. No, she couldn't endure another day like this—or even tonight—desperately needing release. When he asked his ritual question, yes, she would consent, even though it meant taking him…

But her empathic sense told her that he felt nothing of desire, not now, no more than yesterday or the day before. Why, then…?

In a sudden flash of insight, she realized that he hadn't been offering himself. He had only asked her to consent to taking a lover, whoever that might be. He'd told her, from the beginning, that she needed to seek love again, needed to actively hunt for it.

And hadn't she decided the same herself, just today?

Yes, yes… She no longer had to stand here, forced to face undeniable feelings and cruel memories; they couldn't hurt her anymore. Being swept away helplessly by desire—by any feeling—wouldn't automatically make her a victim; her nasty family and ex-lover had lost all hold on her. Love might have its dangers, but she was ready for them. *Nobody's chump, never again.* She was free to choose, and need only give the sign to be free completely.

As his hands came back up to her shoulders Lorraine sagged in the cuffs and laughed wildly, not caring how she sounded. Treemark rested his hands on her shoulders she could feel his intense concern through the contact—and asked his ritual question.

"Do you consent…?"

Lorraine drew a deep breath and nodded decisively: once,

twice, then a third time.

Through the empathic contact, his vast relief swept over her like a warm blanket.

He bent forward and gently kissed the back of her neck.

"Be free, then," he whispered.

He stepped back from her, paused a moment to reach for something, and then she felt his hands unfastening the snap-links. He pulled them away and let them fall to the floor with a soft clanging of metal rings. Lorraine felt her hands drift away from the columns and sagged, abruptly dizzy.

Treemark caught her, kept her from falling, and settled her carefully on her knees.

Lorraine managed to catch herself with her arms so she didn't go down completely. She heard a rustling of cloth, and was startled when he tucked the robe back over her head and pulled its folds down around her. Her skin felt so sensitized that even the touch of the cloth felt like a caress. She couldn't hold her head up anymore, but let it sag onto her chest, panting for air, wondering if she would faint. Something thick and soft wrapped around her, and she dimly recognized it as a quilt.

"Wait here," she distantly heard Treemark say. "I'll send someone to help; I can't carry you this time."

Lorraine scarcely noticed as his footsteps and aura faded, barely noted the growing strain in her arms and shoulders as they held up her weight. The aimless swirling desire was still there, and the sweeping euphoria of release; she wasn't sure if, should she try to stand, she would drop like a rock or float like a feather. Anything was possible now.

Another Elven aura impinged on her wavering consciousness, someone familiar, probably Daniel, approaching quietly. Only when his arm pressed around her waist to support her did she realize who her rescuer was.

Benjamin. Of course. Who better to understand…?

She couldn't keep from sagging like a rag-doll in his arms. She let herself be caught, lifted and carried, dimly surprised at the strength in that lean body. Her flickering vision crossed his face, and she saw that he was wearing that cat/owl mask again.

Lorraine wanted to laugh, but couldn't summon the strength. Her eyes drifted closed.

There came a steady and slightly jolting rhythm of walking, the sound of a door opening, then the footsteps softened as they passed over carpet. Lorraine accepted it without question, without thought. Eventually the rhythm changed, stopped, and the pressure of arms shifted, lowering her to another flat surface, much softer: more softness under her head, and more swept up around her. A brief glimpse showed that she was back in her own room, and then her eyes fell shut again.

Finally there came a rustling, a shifting of weight, and then the feel of a warm body pressing against her back, curling to match her from head to foot. A gentle arm draped around her, and soft breath warmed the back of her neck. Lorraine recognized the position, and the feeling; she'd done the same for him last night, and now it was her turn.

The formless desire shifted, transmuted into peace as vast as the sea, leaving her certain that she was safe, and free.

That was all she needed to ask of the universe. Utterly still, drained, profoundly quieted, Lorraine let herself sink into the soft and welcome darkness.

13.

STEVEN LISTENED to the voice on his cell-phone, chewing his lip, nodding occasionally. Finally he muttered: "Don't worry. I'll take care of it" and clicked the phone silent. He glanced around the monitor screens, making note of where everyone was, and slowly shook his head. Treemark must hear of this, but it wasn't so urgent that he need be interrupted now. It could wait for later: much later. Steven shoved the phone into its recharger, cast a brief apologetic glance at Helen, and strolled out.

Helen, raptly watching the screens, didn't even look to see him go.

***

Awareness returned slowly, lazily as summer dawn. Lorraine grew drowsily aware of the soft quilt wrapping her, the solid body behind her and the warm arm draped across her waist. Thought by slow thought, she remembered everything.

"Psychodrama"…? She couldn't have acted out that revenge fantasy without actively harming someone. *Good thing I was bound to the columns…* And if it hadn't been for those long sessions of forced meditation, and arousal, she might never have come to that point—faced down her memories and the miseries therein, defied them, and freed herself from their power.

So this was what Ben had known, what Treemark had tried to explain: the ecstatic relief of letting go, relinquishing control, releasing the spring. It was something she hadn't done in years, decades, as long as she could remember; she'd been ever-watchful, controlled, on guard for that long.

Her emotional armor had rusted shut. No wonder it had taken treatment as intense as this to break through.

How much worse, she wondered, was it for Benjamin?

Poor Ben… Though her limbs felt heavy and boneless as loaded grain-sacks, she burrowed one hand out from under the quilt and slid it down to grasp Benjamin's arm.

He twitched in surprise, and then lay still.

It was easy, in this drowsy mood, to slip into meditative state: harder to focus, extend her empathic sense toward the contact, toward Ben. She picked up impressions slowly.

Benjamin too lay quiet and relaxed in the aftermath of fierce tension; he too had thought he was alone in his need, and ached with sympathy for the—unknown—woman in his arms. Beneath all that lay a thread of keening sorrow that extremes like these were needed—for others as well as him. He thought of the need as a wound, or a weakness.

He was only sympathetic and curious for her, but ashamed for himself; that was his dark secret.

Oh Ben, don't be ashamed of this! Lorraine yearned to comfort him. *It's no worse than...going to the dentist every year to get your teeth deep-cleaned.*

But then, she remembered, Benjamin was several centuries old. He might have forgotten what it was like to live as a mortal, needing visits to the local doctor every year or so. He could have forgotten—as she had—what it was like to receive anyone's help.

He might think he was alone in his need, despite what he must have known about Treemark's weekend parties.

Her voice felt rusty, but she made it work. "It's all right, Ben," she said, patting his arm. "I understand it."

Benjamin flinched, and tensed all over. Too late, Lorraine remembered that she wasn't supposed to know who he was.

"Lorraine?" he gasped, pulling himself upright. "Lorraine?!"

She rolled on her back to look at him. He was still wearing his black owl/cat mask—and nothing else but bikini-briefs—but despite it, he looked utterly shocked.

Lorraine remembered her own mask, reached up and pulled it off with clumsy fingers.

Her bared face felt wet.

"God—" Benjamin tore off his own mask, exposing rumpled hair and a frantic expression. "He did that—he made me—my own student?!"

"Technically, I'm his student." Lorraine wondered why this was so important. "He was short-handed for assistants. We weren't supposed to know."

"Oh hell..." Benjamin pulled up his knees and rested his face on them, and shuddered.

Don't leave him like that. Lorraine stretched out a clumsy arm, and managed to touch his foot. "Ben, I did need that. I needed to understand..." *He doesn't know I saw him—* "I've been a warrior so long, I'd forgotten how to unbend." She was annoyed at how clumsy her lips felt.

Benjamin shivered again, but his breathing steadied. "Yes," he muttered. "I see it."

Lorraine could think of nothing to do but pet his foot.

Eventually he raised his head enough to look at her, and noticed the cuff on her wrist. He stared at it, then lifted her arm and peered closer, realizing that the cuff was sealed, and didn't come off. "How long have you been wearing those?" he asked.

"Since my third day here. I've had...counseling sessions, and other things, every day since."

Benjamin gave her a long thoughtful look. "I never guessed," he said. "I knew you were...guarded, but I didn't realize... You're so young, I didn't think—" He caught himself, then smiled ruefully. "I'd forgotten: you don't have to be very old to collect dents in your soul."

"Just live in interesting times," Lorraine smiled back, wishing she weren't so exhausted, wanting to sit up and wrap an arm around his shoulders. "Damn. Why am I so tired?"

Benjamin blinked, as if shifting mental gears. "Ah, it's the intensity: takes so much out of you." He reached toward her and pulled back the covers. "What you need now is something to drink, a long hot bath, then a proper massaging, and food."

Lorraine only nodded: all that sounded very good, but how did Benjamin know—

Ah, this wasn't his first experience, then. She wondered how often he needed that release…but knew she'd never ask him.

He reached toward the nightstand and came back with a tall glass of what appeared to be orange juice, then carefully lifted her head and held the glass to her lips.

Lorraine gulped it gratefully, surprised at how thirsty she felt. Yes, it was orange juice, fresh-squeezed and delicious, probably delivered personally by Daniel. She licked her lips dry as Benjamin put the glass away.

Then he pulled off the quilt, letting the air touch her, and Lorraine suddenly remembered that except for the cuffs she was naked. Treemark had said she was free…

Ironically, the last thing she could feel right now was desire. Ben's strong lean body felt very good against hers as he half-carried her into the bathroom, but that was a comforting feeling rather than anything erotic. He maneuvered her carefully into the tub, tossed in some bath-salts and turned on the water. Lorraine sighed in exquisite relief, and let herself go limp. She promptly slid all the way down into the enormous tub.

"What happened to my bones?" she mumbled, trying to pull herself up.

Benjamin shook his head, pulled off his bikini-briefs and stepped into the tub with her. "It's not your bones; it's your muscles," he said as he slid down behind her. "You've exhausted them."

He maneuvered them both until he was sitting with his back against the end of the tub, Lorraine half-lying against him, his legs stretched out on either side of her. Both of them ignored the fact that her buttocks were pressed against his genitals; it was irrelevant at the moment. He reached for the soap and the sponge. Lorraine couldn't keep from purring as the scented water rose, then sighing as Benjamin worked the sponge, with exquisite care, over her face and throat.

"Are you all right?" he asked, rubbing gently.

"Yes," Lorraine whispered. "Feels good."

"Yes," he echoed. "Aside from aches, which I'll deal with, you'll be euphoric with relief for awhile. Probably hypersensitive too, and of course tired, hungry and thirsty."

"Mmmm," Lorraine agreed, feeling his touch, and the lovely hot water, relax tensions she hadn't known she had. *Everything but horny.* She laughed softly.

"Joke?" Benjamin asked.

"I'm just thinking: here I am, stark naked in a bathtub with a handsome naked man, and I can't feel desire at all."

"Not surprising," Ben smiled, rubbing the sponge gently across her breasts. "The nerves are exhausted too. Just let them rest, and they'll recharge. When you wake up in the morning, trust me, you'll be randy as a cat."

"Ah." Lorraine glanced down at her bare body. *And I'll be able to do something about it,* she considered. Somehow, the thought of relying on her hands wasn't appealing. "But I'll be alone."

"No..." Benjamin sighed into her hair. "Not alone."

Lorraine didn't say anything, realizing that this was a tentative offer, not daring to break the mood.

But her silence made Benjamin uneasy. "I'm...not promising anything," he mumbled, "Only that I'll...stay with you, as long as you need me to..."

Lorraine raised a hand and briefly gripped his arm. "Thank you," she breathed. "I honestly don't know what I'll want...tomorrow or ten minutes from now. Just...I'm so tired of soldiering on alone... I don't want to anymore. Not now."

"I understand," he whispered. Saying nothing more, he rubbed the sponge lower, down her sides and belly, chastely as a bath-servant. He paused only once to turn off the water.

Lorraine leaned against him and let the gentle heat take her.

She could almost sleep like this, the comfort was so complete. She could trust Ben to take care of her...

The T-word again. Lorraine considered that, and twitched a smile at herself. For all of Dr. Treemark's harping on trust, the one person she'd found here that she could thoroughly trust wasn't her doctor but her fellow-sufferer.

After a time she noticed that the water was cooling, and a glance showed that her fingertips were wrinkling. "Time to get out and dry," Benjamin said, pulling his legs close and levering her upright. "Can you stand by yourself?"

The tub was furnished with sturdy towel-racks—or support-bars—and Lorraine managed to get to her feet, with Ben's help, without dumping both of them back into the water. He held her upright on the bathmat and simply wrapped a large fluffy towel around her. She also managed to walk, leaning most of her weight on him, back to the rumpled bed that she simply fell into.

Benjamin was just sitting down beside her when the intercom-phone rang.

Annoyed, he grabbed it and listened for a moment.

"It's Daniel," he almost whispered, "Asking if you want dinner in your room again."

"Here!" she snapped back. "...And you?" What if Benjamin needed more or different treatment, and had to leave? She felt astonishingly frightened at the prospect.

Ben shoved the speaker back against his face. "Here," he said. "Enough for two. I...won't be attending, either."

Lorraine sagged on the pillow, amazed by her own relief.

Ben quietly hung up the phone, pulled open the drawer of the nightstand and rummaged about in it. "He always has massage-oil in these... Ah, here it is," he explained, coming up with a small bottle. "As soon as you're reasonably dry, I'll work the last of the cramps out."

Lorraine nodded, and tried rubbing herself dry, through the towel, with boneless-feeling fingers. Her elbow nudged some-thing, and she turned to look. It was Benjamin's mask, one of its points aiming jauntily toward the ceiling like a cat's ear.

Like my cats... Abruptly the memory came, and with it a fierce ache of loss.

Lorraine felt tears sting her eyes, and her breath catch, even as she marveled that her emotions were so close to the surface, so easily roused.

"What is it?" Ben asked quietly. "Was it something I said?"

Lorraine shook her head, unable to stop the tears. "I miss my little cats!" she burst out. "Sable-Foot and Crimp-Tail. Sweet little Siameses, with big blue eyes and barbed-wire voices... I had to leave them with friends when I left Chicago."

"...Cats?" Ben wondered, glancing at the mask and tracing her line of thought.

"I know it sounds stupid, but they were all I had to love—and the only creatures on Earth that really loved me. I'm alone now, and I miss them."

"Not completely alone," Ben murmured. He hitched up the bed to sit beside Lorraine, and wrapped an arm around her shoulders. "And if you truly need a cat..."

"I need... Oh hell, I need a friend!" Lorraine sobbed. "Just someone I can..." *Trust. Trust with my heart!* There it was, and not even Treemark could help with it.

"I can be that," Ben said, very quietly. "I've been your trainer. I can be...at least as much as a cat." He tightened his grip and held her.

Lorraine leaned on him and let the sobs wear out by themselves. Her hands felt less clumsy as they wiped the tears away.

A discreet knock sounded at the door.

"That's dinner," said Ben. He suddenly noticed that they were both naked, and looked around quickly for something to throw over himself. He finally settled for pulling the towel off Lorraine, wrapping it around himself like a toga, and tugging the quilt over her. Lorraine suppressed a giggle as she watched him stride to the door, looking like a classic statue of a proper Roman gentleman. She wondered if he actually had been one.

Madge was at the door, carrying a loaded tray. Benjamin took it from her, and she thoughtfully closed the door as he turned away. He brought the tray back to the bed and cautiously set it down there, keeping a close watch on the teetering wine-carafe.

"I have no idea what this is," he said, pulling the covers off the plates, "But knowing Daniel, I'll bet it's delicious."

Lorraine sat up carefully, noting the rose-colored wine and the elegant glasses.

The plates contained a fluffy salad with cashews and red onions and strawberries, thick discs of white-meat chicken wrapped around slices of broccoli in a thick golden sauce, steamed corn-kernels in a matrix of melted yellow cheese, and delicate slices of pastry that looked like baklava. Lorraine heard Ben's stomach rumble, and her own echoed it.

They laughed, cautiously poured wine into their glasses, and attacked the food. It was exquisite, as always.

Only when the food was gone did Lorraine venture close to the unspoken subject.

"He told me it was…a hard and fast cure for repressed emotions, for being overcontrolled: forced meditation, and… conditioning to raise feelings."

"'Acting out', Brian calls it." Ben set the tray on the floor, setting only the carafe on the nightstand. "And 'psychodrama'. I can't argue with his results."

"It worked for me," Lorraine whispered, shivering. She couldn't believe how raw and immediate her feelings were, both physical and emotional. Yes, Treemark's treatment had indeed pulled away an invisible armor that she hadn't known she was wearing. "My jousting-helm, as you put it, is gone."

Benjamin said nothing further, but resumed his place beside her and put his arm back across her shoulders.

Lorraine leaned into the comforting touch for long moments, then found herself sagging. "I have to lie down," she murmured, sliding down onto the pillow.

"This way," Ben said quietly, pulling her around to lie on her belly. He reached for the bottle on the nightstand, and poured oil into his hand. "It will help."

Lorraine nodded once, and let herself drift. Ben's hands descended gently to her shoulders, then began spreading the oil. His touch was different from Treemark's: sure, but more cautious, lighter and more subtle. It felt very good, pressing away even the last memory of aches and tension, luring her toward sleep.

After a time she felt Benjamin pull up the blankets around them and nestle against her side, one arm resting softly across her back. There was no hint whatever of seduction in the gesture, only kindness and a quiet concern. Lorraine wondered if she'd ever slept beside someone who felt like that, or felt that for her; again, the only examples she could think of were her cats. *Big kitty,* she thought drowsily, as sleep swept up on her.

It was, in truth, very good to sleep like this.

***

It was well past midnight when Treemark returned to the clinic office, and he was wearily grateful to see that it was empty. Sighing in relief, he dropped into his chair behind the desk, pulled the laptop computer out of its drawer, punched in the security-codes and began adding to his case-notes. A discreet tap on the door made him frown.

"Come in," he called, quickly blanking the computer's screen.

Steven padded in, and shut the door behind him. "We have a problem," he announced quietly. "No, nothing to do with the guests. Someone broke into my apartment in town, and tripped the silent alarms. He didn't take anything, and my security people said he didn't leave anything, either. Are you thinking what I'm thinking?"

Treemark sighed and leaned back in his chair. "Either Lorraine's stalker is still active, or that contact in town was a hunter."

"Lorraine did give that address to her…Aunt Dianne, whom I'm beginning to wonder about. She said the woman was careless, but…it could be something else."

"A stalker, a false identity, and an aunt she can't avoid. It all fits." Treemark cracked his knuckles as he pondered his options. "Let's hope the hunter—or stalker—won't get any closer for another day. As soon as the last guests leave, we go on Yellow Alert."

"You have the lawyers lined up?"

"I'll call Victor at home, in the morning." Treemark tapped his fingertips on the desk. "Are you certain the hunter isn't after you, in particular?"

Steven shook his head. "I can't think of any tracks I've left uncovered."

Treemark shrugged. "Then we'll just assume for now that it's either Lorraine's stalker or a random hunter who struck pay-dirt by accident. Sleep well, Steven; you've earned it."

"So have you, boss," said Steven, heading for the door. "Don't stay up too late."

"Don't call me boss," Treemark tossed after him, as the door shut.

***

The dream came, fast and vivid.

She was Roxanne again, back in the union office, watching the hit-man pace past the door—but this time he turned and came into the storeroom, gun drawn, knowing she was there. Lorraine shoved the loaded shelves over on top of him, then ran to where his gun-hand stuck out from under the pile and stamped on it until she heard bones break.

She kicked the fallen books away from the hit-man's head,

pulled out her own revolver and shot him right in the middle of his bloodied face. Then she turned and ran out the door.

Beyond the doorway lay the open desert where Leila stood waiting for her, saddled and bridled and pawing the ground eagerly. Lorraine gathered the reins and lunged into the saddle, then steered the mare out into the desert and kicked her into a fast gallop. The tumbled rocks of the sacred spring stood ahead, beckoning, and she raced toward it until she felt the edge of its aura touch her. As she passed the border-stones she pulled Leila to a stop and slid to the ground, then tied the mare to a Palo-Verde near the spring.

Her aura-sense told her that another mutant was approaching, a stranger, and she knew he would be no friend of hers. She drew her pistol and crouched in the brush, watching and waiting. She saw him come stalking up to the border of stones and halt there, frustrated, spinning his gun on his trigger-finger like an old-time movie cowboy. It was the hit-man, right enough. She could shoot him from here...

But she didn't dare fight on sacred ground; the power from the node would burn her to death—permanent death.

She didn't dare step outside the node's aura, either; the man had to be a much more practiced shot—and probably swordsman—than she was.

How do I fight him? How? She pounded her fists silently on the ground.

The power of the spring seemed to swell at her back, and she knew—with no explanation at all—that the answer lay there.

Show me! she cried soundlessly. *I have to know!*

***

—and woke, lying on her side, Benjamin at her back, feeling his hand shaking her shoulder. "You're dreaming," he was saying. "Wake up, Lorraine."

"Yes," she panted, opening her eyes. "...What happened?"

"You were tossing and muttering and punching the bed." Benjamin shifted smoothly to massaging her neck. "You didn't seem to like it, wherever you were."

"In a quandary." Lorraine leaned into his touch, feeling the tension of the dream fade away. "I'm nowhere near competent yet."

"Competent?" His hand moved back to her shoulder, rubbing deeply.

"With weapons." Lorraine drew a deep breath, and then let it out in a heavy sigh. "I could probably fight off an ordinary mortal, but not a professional—or another Elf. And someone's after me."

Benjamin slid his arm around her and drew her close against him. "Don't be alone, then," he said quietly. "There's no shame in needing allies, needing protection."

Lorraine gripped his arm, feeling tears spring to her eyes. *Yes, I need someone!* she admitted. *A protector, a lover, a friend...* And she knew it was wrong, it was an imposition, to throw that need at Benjamin who had offered her nothing but kindness. *But I can't help it!*

"Will you help me, Ben?" she whispered, not daring to say more.

"I will," he whispered back, pulling her closer.

Lorraine could feel the subtle hills and valleys of his body pressed warmly against her back, his breath soft on her neck, even the faint but steady beating of his pulse through the skin. Her empathic sense extended, unbidden, revealing the truth behind his simple words; yes, he did care about her, truly did want to protect her—and had, incredibly, the confidence in his long-practiced skill that he could do it well. A vast relief swept her, knowing that she was truly safe here, as safe as anywhere on Earth.

"Thank you," was all she could think to say.

Ben said nothing further, but went back to quietly massaging her shoulder, then arm, softly pledging his intention with his hands. Lorraine relaxed into that welcome touch, dimly surprised at how deeply she could feel it.

She waited for sleep, but it glided away from her. Her awareness was snagged on the feel of Ben's hands, chaste and comforting though the pressure was meant to be. She sighed and stretched, and he obligingly changed position to rub softly at her back and ribs. It felt very good, echoing deeply through her flesh, striking subtle sparks where she hadn't expected them. Lorraine remembered Treemark's nerve-chart, and wondered if Ben was pressing some of those points without realizing it. She extended a cautious empathic probe, only a little, and found...

He was enjoying this. He liked the feel of her body under his hands: soft skin, then springy muscle, then solid bones. Like Treemark, he compared her to a fine horse—but there was more. He, too, saw her as a warrior who had been obliged to fight for too long, and too long alone. He recognized that sorrow, and grieved to see it.

Strangest of all, he did not see her—or any woman—as most modern men did: not as frail, soft, self-absorbed, hysteria-prone weaklings, easily deluded with flattery and gushy promises. He saw their minds as he saw men's, and their bodies as little different.

He could remember ancient tribes where women were competent hunters, farmers, herders, land-managers, artisans, merchants, judges, priests—and warriors. He could remember the Amazons.

Lorraine twitched as she realized that he had to be more than 2000 years old.

Helen, she recalled, was nearly 4000, and remembered an age when all of society was different. Benjamin too remembered a very different world.

As his hands worked down her back, and he wondered whether it would be permissible to proceed to her hips and buttocks, Lorraine sensed that he felt a deep-buried and well controlled desire for her: but it was the same desire—no different—that he had felt in the past for certain equally beautiful and strong-souled men. He could want, and love, either way—not steered by the quaint superstitions of any society which assumed, as so many of them did, that its own customs were the righteous standard for all human cultures, past and present, the world over. He had seen kings and countries, gods and their worshippers, come and go and pass out of memory—and he knew better.

He admired her for her courage, honesty and dedication. He understood and sympathized with her need.

And he wanted her.

And I, Lorraine realized, *Want him.*

Yes: those patient touches had reached deep, wakened an itching heat deep inside her and another between her nether lips. Yes: she wanted to be touched, strongly, smoothly, there and there. Yes: she wanted to feel his hands, mouth, whole body stroking and pressing and sliding on her, and up her...

Yes! She rolled to face Benjamin, and resolutely wrapped her arms around him.

He froze for an instant, startled—and struck with a twinge of surprised desire—then remembered himself and closed his arms gently around Lorraine's shoulders. "You don't have to do this," he whispered. "You don't have to thank me, buy my protection…"

"I want to." Lorraine pulled tighter against him, reveling in the feel of her breasts flattening against his lean chest, nipples colliding with startled twitches of pleasure. "You were right; I'm randy as a cat."

"You don't have to," Benjamin repeated, even as his hands unconsciously circled on her back. "Just because I'm here..."

"Who else should I give it to?" Lorraine asked, wrapping her upper thigh around his. "Who else can I trust?" *That word!* "I don't want just anonymous sex anymore, I want..." She bit back the rest, the imposition, and the implied demand for too much.

"A friend," he finished for her. "A friend in your bed. I know." And he pressed a long thoughtful kiss to her forehead.

Then there were no more words. His body slid against hers, sweet and strong and heated, his shaft lifting and rubbing against her thigh as his hands and mouth explored her. Lorraine wrapped herself around him, wanting to feel him with every inch of her skin, and soft reckless laughter bubbled up from her throat as she felt the itching, demanding heat flare and spread through all her flesh in a blazing rush. He licked fiercely at her throat and collarbones and breasts as his long fingers spread and clamped on her writhing hips, and then he pulled her over on top of him and maneuvered her body as if setting a sheath to a sword's point. She groaned in abandon as she felt the velvety tip of his pulsing shaft probe between her slicked labia, rubbing and nuzzling to find its pathway. "There! There!" she panted, wriggling to match him, then gasped as she felt the point slide home. She poised, quivering, for a long moment as his hands clenched and relaxed, clenched and relaxed on her buttocks, then slowly pressed herself down.

There! Her inner lips stretched wide, wider, as the pulsing column slowly climbed upward, deeper, up the center of her body, inflaming every nerve as it passed, reaching for hidden nerve-center that waited, yearning to be touched. Up and up—ah, so slowly!—while his hands held her still and his body arched, shaking with the effort to keep the steady implacable pace, taking her in a long smooth stroke. Lorraine groaned softly, repeatedly, trembling as she tried to keep still—as still as she had between the columns—and let him finish as he'd begun. Higher, and deeper, and— *There!* —the hot tip pressed into the secret nerve-center, driving invisible lightning-bolts up her spine, and she could hold still no longer. She thrust herself down onto the invading shaft, impaling herself to the hilt, felt his pubic curls press against her spread lips and swollen clitoris, and heard him groan deeply as his control fragmented and he bucked up into her, driving so deep she thought he would reach her thundering heart.

Then the universe closed down into a madly grinding mill of flesh that pounded out waves of all-engulfing flame and need, in a blind welter of clutching limbs and incoherent cries. Time vanished, and they hammered together endlessly, ever faster, harder, galloping to a finish neither could foresee until it was upon them, sweeping them up and over the edge to soar ecstatically on twinned breathless screams, never knowing the moment when they sank together into oblivion.

***

On Sunday morning the household woke in stages, Madge first, then Daniel, who checked the security-system before preparing food. Steven and Wally rose later and went to tend the animals, making no comment about Lorraine's absence. By common consent, the staff allowed Treemark to sleep as late as he could; the private counseling sessions wouldn't begin until 10 AM at the earliest, and the house ran smoothly enough that he wouldn't be needed before then. Most of the guests wouldn't rise until noon, and then only to share the elaborate luncheon Daniel laid out for them before packing to go home.

There were no psychodramas on Sunday, only counseling and rest and recovery, and the household moved at a leisurely pace.

There was no summons to breakfast or lunch from the intercom, and Lorraine drifted out of sleep with no sense of time.

For long moments she lay still, wrapped up in Benjamin's sleeping body, thinking of nothing but the quiet pleasure of contact. Eventually a perfectly ordinary itch on her thigh made her move, and scratch. The motion woke Benjamin, who purred and nuzzled at her cheek. She slid her arm over his waist and stroked his back softly. Neither of them, she knew, had the strength for anything more. They lay cuddling for a quiet stretch of time, until a twinge of different feeling made Ben grimace, smile ruefully, and reluctantly pull away.

"Bathroom," he explained. "I'll just be a moment."

Lorraine sat up, and felt her own bladder tickle warning. "I'll be in after you," she warned.

"Shall I start the bath, then?" he asked, sliding out of bed. "I daresay I could use another."

"Oh yes," Lorraine smiled. "Let's save water, and share this one too."

Benjamin laughed and trotted off to the bathroom. A moment later she heard the tub's faucet running. It was nice to know that Ben was also as clean as a cat.

This time they bathed with a little more energy, scrubbing each other's backs and playing with the soap. Despite their easy intimacy, Benjamin still seemed a little reticent, a little shy. They took turns drying each other, and he gave Lorraine the bathrobe and wrapped himself in a used towel.

"I should do something about clothes," he considered as they came back into the bedroom. "All I wore here were my briefs and mask."

Lorraine guessed that he didn't want to stroll through the house wearing those, not with the guests still present and the peculiar gathering still going on. A glance at the chair showed her sandals, caftan and belt, but none of Ben's clothing.

"I suppose we could use the intercom, call Daniel and have some clothes delivered," she tried. "Oh, but where did you leave your room key?"

"With Brian," Benjamin frowned. "He's probably busy right now."

"Helen told me there's a master-key kept in the security office," Lorraine remembered. "I suppose Daniel could get it."

"And I think I can trust Daniel to be discreet." Benjamin reached for the intercom-phone, then paused. "Hmmm, I really don't know what clothes to ask for. Did you have any plans for today?"

"I'd like to get away from the house and go riding," said Lorraine. "Possibly ride back to the node and do some more experiments."

"I wouldn't mind the company of horses myself," Ben smiled.

"Oh, wait," Lorraine remembered. "We'll have to wear clothes with no metal in them. No buckles, zippers, eyelets..."

"I think I can manage that." Ben thought a moment, then frowned. "But we really will have to carry our weapons."

"On belts then, so we can take them off."

"That's workable. Shall we send for breakfast along with the clothes?"

"Definitely."

14.

THIS TIME they chose to ride the two bay mares. The creatures trotted out willingly enough, but Lorraine decided that Leila was her favorite. The sun was still low enough that the weather was no more than comfortably warm.

Ben, she noticed, was increasingly silent and thoughtful as the ride progressed.

Remembering his shyness, she waited for him to settle his thoughts and speak—which at last he did.

"Lorraine, last night..." He paused to chew his lip. "It doesn't have to mean anything. You have no obligation to me."

"No," she smiled, remembering. "But don't tell me you didn't enjoy it too."

"Oh, I did." He twitched a brief grin. "And yes, I'd enjoy doing it again. What I mean is... It doesn't have to change our relationship. We can go right on being trainer and student, just as we were."

"With a bit of sex on the side?" No, she wouldn't obligate him by saying she wanted more.

"If you like." Benjamin didn't look at her.

"And...friends?" She didn't want to lose that.

"Definitely friends." He paused again. "And...I did promise to be your protector."

Lorraine felt her heart pounding, and sternly ordered it to be still. "For as long as we're both here, you mean?"

Benjamin sighed, almost guiltily. "Yes. I'd planned to leave soon, but there's no fixed date."

Lorraine remembered that he had a life outside this place, and wondered if she still did herself. "I don't suppose I'll be able to leave here very soon..." Then she recalled the troubles back in Chicago. "At least, not permanently."

Benjamin only nodded, accepting that. Lorraine considered another possibility.

"I take it," she said carefully, "That you have a serious relationship somewhere else."

Ben gave a sigh that seemed to empty him. "More than one, actually. One in Seattle, another..." Abruptly, he ground his teeth and straightened in the saddle. "You have to understand that exclusive relationships are difficult for our kind. We can have a stable life in one place for ten years, perhaps twenty; then we have to move on before the neighbors notice that we're not aging. Couples are more noticeable, more easily tracked, than single travelers. And we have to keep coming up with new identities, covering our tracks..."

"I wouldn't mind spending ten years with you," Lorraine said before she could catch herself.

Benjamin shot her a surprised, almost frightened look. "It's possible—" he said, then stopped short. He pulled another deep breath and went on, back in lecturing mode. "We have to be careful, to hide not only from mortals but from...Unseelie hunters. Mobility is our best defense, having several identities and bolt-holes, diving in and out of them. That makes relationships difficult."

"But not impossible?"

"No." He looked toward the horizon as if seeing far beyond it. "I know one clever couple who have stayed together for centuries, another who've darted in and out of each other's lives for nearly as long, and I... In past centuries, when populations were smaller and news took years to travel, I've...been married to mortal women, stayed with them until they died, then moved on."

"Ah. Not so easy now." Lorraine thought of empty and backward places in the world, where populations were still thin and news still traveled slowly—but then considered that Elven-kind would have to stay aware of events in the larger world, if only to avoid them. "You couldn't just hide out in a remote corner somewhere."

Benjamin shook his head. "Not for long. Remote corners tend to be 'discovered' with alarming speed. You have to keep in contact... I have to maintain my contacts." He drew another deep breath. "You've probably guessed Brian's dream—of reuniting those of us who don't like the game, want to live in peace..."

"The 'Seelie Court'?" Lorraine ventured.

"Elfland." Benjamin smiled bitterly. "I wish him luck. I've been trying something similar myself for the past several centuries, and all I've managed to assemble is a handful of loyal friends."

"And lovers?" Lorraine guessed.

Ben nodded, not meeting her eyes.

Lorraine remembered what Helen had hinted about Ben's past and present life, and saw a pattern fall together. "I think I see!" she marveled. "You've been cautiously hunting up other Elves. If they were the Unseelie sort you'd take care to avoid them, but if they were the right kind you'd...collect them? Seduce them into your...scattered harem?"

"Please!" Benjamin flinched. "I do care about...the good ones."

"So..." Lorraine glanced ahead at the approaching spring, seeing more details in the pattern. "Do any of them know about the others?"

"Some few," he admitted. "I'm the only one who knows them all."

"Do you ever intend to draw them together, make a family, a tribe?"

"Oh, if only—" Ben ground his teeth again. "If only I could convince them it was safe. If only I could be sure there'd be no jealousy. If only I could find a secure place, and persuade them all to come live in it, make it our base of operations, as Brian does here... But I can't. Not until that damned prophecy is discredited, or all the hunters are dead. Not until the mortal world changes, and we aren't bound by the beliefs of the societies we grew up in. Not until there truly is a safe place—and I've never found one."

Nowhere? Lorraine found that hard to believe. Surely there were forgotten corners of the world where odd cultures had survived for centuries: the New Guinea Islanders, the Amish, the Peruvian Indians. Was Benjamin taking an incredibly long view, or was he paranoid even for their kind, or did he have patient enemies after him—as she did?

Lorraine glanced back toward the ranch. "How long has Brian kept this place?" she asked.

"It's been 'in the family', as he's convinced the local law, for 80 years now." Benjamin shrugged. "That's a good run, I'll admit, but I don't know how much longer he can keep it up. Besides, it's taken him this long to collect the small number that he has. Others have come, stayed awhile, grown restless and left. I don't imagine I'd have any better luck."

Lorraine made another intuitive leap. "And do any of your...allies live here?"

Benjamin bowed his head. "Just one. Helen."

"I see." Lorraine remembered what Helen had told her about her own life, and customs. *"Consorts...for a season, a year, a lifetime"...*

"Don't distrust her on my account," Ben added hastily. "We've been allies, friends, occasional lovers, for centuries. We've never been exclusive with each other, nor expected it."

"But you have to leave, even though she's—" Lorraine stopped fast, suspicion dawning. *They're both old enough...*

"Yes." Ben gave her an infinitely sad look. "I'm the father of her child."

Lorraine thought that over, recalling again all that Helen had told her. Over age-long lifetimes had the Elven-kind outgrown jealousy, possessiveness, even mortal definitions of 'family'? Yet something must replace it; Elves were social beings too.

"And you don't dare stay?"

He shook his head, said nothing further, and fixed his gaze on the path. The border-stones were near.

"Add me to the scattered harem, then," Lorraine decided. "Whether I stay here or become a wanderer like you, make me another link between Brian's household and yours."

Benjamin jerked his head around to stare at her, his jaw hanging. She suppressed a giggle at how very young that made him look.

"You know which side I'm on, in this age-old war," she continued recklessly. "I'll do my part in weaving the Seelie Court back together, and you know it. But beyond that, I need...more than just friends, Ben. We've started something that I don't want to break, don't want to take back to square one. And no, you didn't seduce me; it was the other way around, if anything."

"L—Lorraine," he gulped. "Gods, we've known each other for scarcely a week!"

"In that time, I saw enough of you to care about." Lorraine took a deep breath. "Did you see anything like that in me?"

Benjamin opened and shut his mouth twice, with no sound coming out, before he finally managed to whisper: "Yes."

Lorraine felt as if the sun was rising inside her, and knew it wasn't just the feel of the sacred spring as they crossed the border of its range. A wild laugh bubbled up inside her. "You did tell me to follow my impulses!"

"So I did," he admitted, then laughed too. "I've been known to fall in love at first sight, and not so long ago. This is...well, a little more thought out."

They rode up to the edge of the pool and dismounted, letting the mares go ahead to the water. Benjamin, a sudden roguish look on his face, strode to Lorraine and swiftly hugged her. She leaned into the embrace, wrapping her arms around him and clasping her hands behind his back.

Right then, Lorraine felt that embrace from the other side: Ben feeling her arms around him and enjoying it thoroughly. She realized that she hadn't tried to *reach* for him; the contact had come as naturally as breathing. *So easy to feel him…* Was this another effect of pulling away her emotional armor? Had it expanded her psychic talent too?

If so, then she had no talent for broadcasting; Benjamin gave no impression of feeling her mind in return. He was only delighted, for this moment, to hold Lorraine close to him.

And it's enough, thought Lorraine, holding him tight.

They stood like that for long minutes while the horses drank, saying nothing, seizing the moment without thought to the future.

Only when the mares lifted their heads and began looking about for grass did they finally, slowly, let go.

***

"Wallistair," called the voice from near the door of the barn, making Wally jump so badly that he almost dropped the bucket of oats. He hadn't been called that in centuries. And yes, he felt the unmistakable aura of an Old One, a very Old One. Wally guessed who it must be. Sighing, he set down the bucket and turned toward the door.

There stood Helen, in one of her close-draped white gowns. The light from the doorway made her dress and pale hair seem to glow of themselves. He remembered that she had considerable psychic ability, and could readily guess why she'd been worshipped as a goddess in ancient days; she looked like a goddess now, and that made him nervous.

"Here," he said, trying to sound eager. "What're you doing here, in that get-up? You'll ruin your dress..."

"Wally," Helen snapped, not put off, "Do you know where Benjamin is?"

"Out riding," Wally gulped. "He took one of the red mares. I don't know where he went. He goes out into the desert a lot."

Helen pursed her lips. "And did anyone go with him?"

Wally squirmed. "Uh, he took his student, on the other mare."

"I see." Helen went still for a moment, and then sighed. "Brian..." she murmured, then seemed to remember where she was. "Ah, thank you, Wally. That's all I wanted to know."

She turned in a graceful swirl of skirts and swept back out the doorway. The sunlight falling on her made her blaze almost blindingly as she strolled away. Wally shook himself, wondering what all that was about, feeling as if he'd just avoided being struck with a thunderbolt.

***

Helen paced back toward the security office, her steps slowing as she made her way deeper into the house, golden eyebrows knitting in thought. "Brian," she muttered again, shaking her head. He'd used Lorraine to keep Benjamin here, and now his little plot had backfired on him. She didn't know whether to feel sorry for Lorraine, Brian or Ben. "Ah well," she sighed as she strode into the empty office, "It's not as if Ben was ever really mine..."

And Lorraine, she thought with a smile, had never really been Brian's, either.

***

"We have to take off everything metal," Lorraine explained, peeling off her belt—and then, after a moment's thought, her boots. "I'm not sure I can contain the flow tightly enough to keep it from heating any metal I'm wearing. I'll need more practice before I can do that."

"I'll take your word for it," said Benjamin, setting his belt aside.

It carried, Lorraine noticed, a pistol-holster and a sheathed sword: a considerable amount of metal. She stepped carefully away from the clothing, and away from the spring. "I don't want to risk drawing too much," she explained. "Even near the border, the power was... Well, I showed you."

"Let's try it with my blood," said Benjamin, turning back to pick up Lorraine's knife. "I suppose I'll have to cut fast..."

He moved to within reach of the border-stones, then pulled the blade quickly across his forearm. The cut must have been deep, for it spurted enough to make Lorraine gasp. He dropped the blood neatly onto the ground—not much of it, for the cut was already sizzling shut—wiped the knife on the ground also and replaced it in its sheath, and moved away. Lorraine stared at the blood-spot, trying to fix it in her mind.

"All right," Benjamin called, from a little way behind her. "Let fly."

Lorraine stretched out her hand until it spread directly over the blood-spot, nearly a yard above it, then closed her eyes and dropped into meditative state. Cautiously, she called up the image of her body as a network of energy-flows.

"Am I glowing?" she asked.

"No," Ben's voice replied, "But I can feel...something, a change in your field."

Very carefully, Lorraine felt for the spring's power and tugged at it. It came, hot and vast, and she hastily directed it through her body and outward, toward the spot. The power seemed unwilling to flow, backing up, heating her. She thought hard about the feel of sending power to Helen, and the energy sluggishly moved. *Flow, flow,* she thought at it, forcing the power out of her, toward the target. The power flowed a little faster, but the resistance made the heat in her body rise. *I can't do this for long,* she thought, shutting off the pull. The heat dropped slowly, leaving her sweating. She opened her eyes and looked.

The blood-spot was steaming, bubbling, blackened like over-cooked meat.

"Deus inferni," Benjamin whispered, "It worked."

"Not well," Lorraine admitted. "The current didn't want to flow: not my blood, not my healing. I had to really push it, and a lot of the heat went into me. I couldn't have kept on any longer."

"Even so," Ben murmured, studying the burned blood, "You transmitted some of it."

"Did you clean that knife thoroughly?" Lorraine asked. "I want to try with plain metal."

"Just a moment." Benjamin picked up the dagger, took it to the spring and washed it carefully, and then dried it on his shirt. "Here," he said, handing it to her, grip first. "See if you can transmit easier by fixing your sight on it."

"I have to close my eyes to concentrate," Lorraine considered, jabbing the knife's point firmly into the ground just between two of the stones. "But once I have the pattern..." She sat down, held her hand above the knife, closed her eyes and reached for meditative state again. *Focus, visualize–* ah, she was aware of Benjamin watching, taking notes—*draw, transmit...* Again, there came the heat of blockage. Dismayed, Lorraine opened her eyes and looked at the knife, trying to aim the power there. *Flow, dammit! Flow!*

And the power did flow; she could see the heated air rippling under her hand even as she visualized the violet energy pouring down toward the metal. A thin column of smoke rose from the knife as the handle began to char.

Enough. She cut off the energy-stream, let the power in her body drain out, took a deep breath and stared at the still-smoking knife.

"Incredible," Benjamin breathed, coming up to her. "Yes, it makes sense. I've seen the power strike randomly at nearby metal objects during—" He stopped fast.

"During what, Ben?" Lorraine prodded. "This is important."

"When..." He looked away. "When I observed one of us taking another's power."

"At a killing, you mean?"

"Yes." He hitched his shoulders higher. "I've been obliged to, more than once. It's not something I enjoy."

"Understood." Lorraine wondered how many Unseelie elves he'd encountered in his centuries of life, then shoved the thought aside. "Is there noticeable heat?" she asked. "Any sense of resistance?"

"No." He shuddered. "It's just incredibly painful for me, rather like being electrocuted." Then he stopped, struck by another thought, and looked back at her. "There's a random discharge of energy, besides what comes to me, that does amazing damage to the immediate environment. Yes, it does seem drawn to electro-conductive metals. I don't know how much of that happens because I do try to resist, and clench myself against the pain. Do you think the power flows more readily in nerve-tissue than in other cells?"

"I think so," said Lorraine, considering the image of herself as a network, "But I can't be sure. Certainly my nervous-system is controlling the flow."

"Fascinating." Benjamin stared at his hands. "Does it hurt so much just because I resist? I've wanted... There have been times when I wanted the power, the knowledge and skills, but... Not the memories, not the personality. Never. That's what I always resisted. ...And always will."

Lorraine shivered. "It's selective, then? The taking... You can choose? How?"

"I can't describe it." He sat down beside her and clenched his hands together. "It's so very subjective... I just feel it as an assault, and I hold onto myself and clamp down, as if I were being beaten with clubs and had to endure. It passes quickly, a minute or less."

Lorraine wondered how many times he truly had been beaten with clubs. She wrapped an arm around him and pulled him close.

"It's all right," he said, patting her knee. "Holding so hard to myself may create the resistance, the pain, but the gods know what I'd be without it. I've seen people taken over, losing their personalities... No, better that it hurts. That also keeps me from ever wanting to be a hunter. I'm quite happy the way I am, thank you."

"Yes," said Lorraine, infinitely relieved. "I hope I never have to... I'll just shoot, or stab, and run away."

"Pray so," Benjamin whispered. "Pray you always have that chance."

Lorraine shook off the mood, remembering something else that had nagged in her memory. "Do you know exactly what happens when elves fight near a node? Have you ever seen it?"

Ben looked at the ground. "I heard of one case, perhaps twenty years ago, where one of us attacked another in a Buddhist shrine. It must have been near a node, because the power discharged when their swords met. The force was enough to break one of the swords and knock both of them back several feet. They both got out of there quickly, in different directions."

"Hmmm. Any other cases?"

"None so well observed, or well documented." He shrugged. "Long ago—and from a considerable distance—I saw two of us fighting on ground that neither of them knew was sacred, and I suppose neither of them could sense the power. All I can tell you is that when the one stabbed the other there was an intense flash of light, and afterwards, when I went to look closer, I found two...extremely burnt bodies. That's all the detail I can give you."

"Was the stabbing done with metal?" Lorraine pondered.

"Yes. Copper, short-swords."

"Copper?"

"Hammered copper. This was very long ago, in a place where tin wasn't readily available to make bronze."

How long...? Lorraine shook her head. Despite Helen's assurance, she didn't feel it was entirely polite to ask an Elf his age; it hinted at a dangerous greed. "That would explain it," she said. "Copper is more conductive than iron, or steel. Metal and blood, metal and blood... Either alone will do, but both together..."

"Like salt and water with electricity," Benjamin noted.

"Fast healing, and burning," Lorraine considered. "There must be some other use for it. If only I can learn..."

"You've discovered that the power can be tapped and directed," Benjamin smiled, "And that's quite an innovation in itself, my young Einstein. Don't be impatient, my love; you have a lot of time for study."

Lorraine's gaze fell on the thick growth of plants within the ring of stones, and she wondered if the fertility of the ground was due only to the presence of water. "Do you think," she wondered,

"The power makes plants grow better?"

"I don't know." Ben considered that seriously. "Certainly, in ancient times people believed that magic would ensure their crops. I don't know how much of that was wishful thinking, how much was actual application of the power, and how much was due to...hmm, the discovery that blood makes good fertilizer."

Blood again. Lorraine sobered. *Elven blood, drawing the node-power.* "There must be a better way."

"There always is. In time, I'm certain you'll find it," Ben promised, his hunger for knowledge noticeable in his voice. "Shall we experiment on these plants first, or start with some outside the node?"

"Outside, first," Lorraine decided. "The ones in the house garden: no problem measuring their growth exactly. But later, please. I'm hot and tired." She really was tired, she realized; the power of the node energized her, but she felt a different sort of weariness from struggling to control the flows. "Nervous exhaustion, I think."

"Not surprising," Ben agreed, getting to his feet and reaching a hand to Lorraine. "Let's head back to the ranch and talk to Daniel about proper nutrition for that. He's made quite a study of the subject, you know."

"I believe it," Lorraine agreed, making use of Ben's proffered hand to pull herself upright. "A master of the art and science of food."

Benjamin laughed, and went to fetch the horses. Lorraine picked up the knife and collected her boots and the weapons-belts. The weight of Ben's sword surprised her, and pulled her thoughts back to her other problem.

Hit-man or Unseelie elf: who's after me, and what can I do about it?

The only solution she could think of was to stay close to the ranch, and to Ben's protection, and that made her uneasy. For all its weirdness she loved the ranch, and—yes she loved Benjamin, but she knew that other people couldn't protect her forever.

Sooner or later, she'd have to deal with the Mafia hit-man, or an Elven hunter of unknown capabilities. What on Earth would she do then?

15.

BY THE TIME Lorraine and Benjamin reached the ranch, the sun was on the horizon.

They had time to care for the horses, retreat to their separate rooms and wash for dinner, and still managed to run into each other on the way to the livingroom for the pre-dinner ritual of drinks and light conversation. They only smiled at each other, and Ben led the way into the room. All the guests had departed, and only the household members were present.

Ben, Lorraine noted, flinched only slightly on seeing Helen there before them, chatting with Treemark. Ben nodded generally to everyone, then headed for the liquor cabinet, where he turned his back on the crowd and seemed to disappear from everyone's attention.

So, he wanted to be discreet about their changed relationship. Was that because he didn't want to upset Helen—and could that mean that Elven relationships weren't quite as jealousy-free as he'd said? Or did he want to conceal the change from Treemark, or even the others?

Well, she could play that game and watch for further information.

Lorraine, back in her blue medieval dress, sandals and knife-belt, simply dropped onto the nearest couch, smiled vaguely at everybody and turned her eyes toward the diningroom as if she couldn't wait for dinner—which was very nearly true.

Treemark glanced briefly at both of them, but went on talking to Helen. They seemed to be arguing over the merits of contacting someone named Grace.

Benjamin strolled to the nearest couch, drink in hand, and politely asked Lorraine if she'd care for anything. Just out a perverse wish to do something different, she asked for "A Black Russian, if you can find the fixings."

"Easily done," Ben replied, setting down his drink. He trotted back to the liquor cabinet, and took his time mixing the cocktail.

Lorraine noted that Wally and Steven exchanged grins when they thought no one was looking.

Ben's timing was perfect; he returned with Lorraine's drink just as Daniel came in and announced dinner.

The meal—lamb chops with mint sauce, and buttered acorn squash—was relaxed and generally subdued. Lorraine, sitting in her usual place and glancing only rarely at Benjamin, concluded that this was the usual result of the end of the weekend ceremonies.

It was, she happily admitted, very nice to have the crowd gone. The place seemed utterly peaceful now, and she was unspeakably grateful for that.

Dessert was a luscious little homemade coconut-cream pie, and it complemented the last of her drink perfectly. Benjamin disappeared as soon as his plate was clean, so smoothly that Lorraine wondered if anyone else had noticed. The man seemed capable of fading into the woodwork when he wanted to.

Treemark departed next, and Helen shortly afterward. Lorraine waited for a minute more before getting up and strolling away to the clinic office.

She found Treemark sitting at his usual place, smiling thoughtfully at—of all things—a large pair of scissors lying on the desk. His smile widened as he looked up at her, and he waved her closer.

"Put out your arm," he said, taking up the scissors, "And roll up your sleeve."

Mystified, Lorraine did so.

Treemark took hold of the cuff, worked the lower jaw of the scissors under it, and began cutting. Lorraine stared at the procedure in amazement, wondering what he meant by this. The severed cuff finally fell off, revealing pale skin at her wrist, and the brass D-ring hit the desk with a small but resonant clang.

"Now the other arm," said Treemark.

"What does this mean?" Lorraine couldn't help asking as she held out her wrist.

"It means," he said, working the scissors around the second cuff, "That you no longer need these. "You've freed yourself, Lorraine. You've learned to release your control at will. I believe you'll find your frigidity problem solved now. Feet next."

Lorraine felt blood heat her cheeks, even as she duly lifted a foot, and was amazed; she had trouble remembering the last time she'd blushed. To cover her confusion, she laughed. "Then what do I do tomorrow, after exercises?" she asked.

"Proceed to the solarium as usual. Other foot, please. I think you can make your way there alone, and that you'll know what to do with what you find there."

"Why the mystery?" she asked, wondering what he was up to.

"Simply because I think you'll like the surprise," he grinned.

"Hold still… There."

The last cuff parted and Lorraine pulled away, feeling an odd mix of elation and regret. "So what's on the menu for tonight?" she couldn't help asking.

"Follow-up," said Treemark. "Sit down, relax… Shall I get you another drink?"

"No, I'll manage." Lorraine sank gratefully into her usual chair. "Follow-up to what, precisely?"

Treemark raised an eyebrow. "Your voyage of exploration yesterday," he said. "Haven't you noticed changes in yourself since then?"

Lorraine felt that treacherous blush threaten her cheeks again. "My…feelings are closer to the surface," she admitted. "I'm surprised by how raw they are."

"As tender as skin when the armor's removed," Treemark smiled. "Don't fear your regained passions, Lorraine; explore and enjoy them."

Lorraine remembered making love with Benjamin last night—or was it this morning?—and couldn't help smiling back at the memory. "Yes, I think I can enjoy them," she murmured. "Now, how do I keep them from clouding my judgment, making me do stupid things?" *Like throwing myself at a man with another lover under the same roof?*

"I don't think that will be a problem," said Treemark. "You've spent most of your life tightly controlled, thinking ahead, not letting your emotions rule you; that's your habitual pattern, and you're most likely to fall back on it. It's taking your armor off, and keeping it off, that's the problem for you."

Lorraine nodded slowly, thinking that over. "But I seem to be…learning to be impulsive. I never thought that was a virtue."

"By itself, it's neither a virtue nor a fault. You can always control your impulses if you must, when you know that they're inappropriate, but it's important to recognize them. Give them their due."

She nodded again, accepting that. There was another question that she badly wanted to ask, but she'd have to word it—even approach it—very carefully. "If you must know, I do feel like…hunting again," she ventured.

"Good sign," Treemark smiled.

"But that brings me a whole new set of problems." Lorraine interlaced her fingers, worried that they might tremble. "I'm part of a very different society now, and I know almost nothing about its customs—including courtship customs."

"Much like those of everyone else," he shrugged.

"What about relationships? Most of us aren't fertile… Do we have any standards of permanence? Do we marry, or anything like it?" *What Ben said… Is it true for all of us?*

"It varies with individuals, just like with mortals." Treemark steepled his fingers. "There are obvious dangers in any long-term affair with a mortal. Among ourselves, well… Again, there are obvious dangers. Make allowance for those, and a relationship can last as long as love does."

"Forever…" Lorraine marveled. "'Til the end of time, and all the other clichés. Has anyone done it?"

"There are a few—too few, for my tastes—who have stayed together for centuries. There have been others who loved until they died."

Lorraine remembered the end of the legend of Siegfried—Brunnhilda riding into his funeral pyre—and grimly wrenched her mind away from the thought before tears could sting her eyes. "Other problems: love under pressure, always fearing the hunters—what does that tend to do?"

"In general, it tends to draw lovers closer together: 'we two against the world', that sort of thing." Treemark spread his hands. "Again, it varies with the individual."

"And I suppose people can be lovers for awhile, break up, become just friends or eternal enemies," Lorraine ventured closer to her question. "Or does enough time really heal all wounds?"

"There are exceptions," Treemark frowned, "But time usually does smooth old grievances away. We have enough time to think things over, gain perspective, and always learn."

"I suppose that includes living in a lot of different societies, cultures, learning other attitudes."

"Oh yes."

"Acceptance of things like…bisexuality…"

"Plenty of cultures have accepted that."

"Polygamy…"

"And polyandry too."

"Or absence of possessiveness and jealousy…?"

"Live for a time among the Tahitians, or the Eskimos, and you gain a sensible perspective on that."

How can I be sure about Helen? "So the general attitude among us is…easy-going tolerance?"

"Usually yes, where we have any society at all." Treemark

sighed. "You must understand that contact between us is rare, tenuous. We're spread thin across the world. Choose your location well, and you could go for centuries without encountering another of our kind. Some of us choose to do that, simply for safety. Others stay on sacred sites, for the same reason—but such places aren't exactly conducive to love-affairs."

"You mean, communities like yours are rare?" Lorraine realized. "Even so few as seven of us?"

Treemark nodded once, a profound sorrow in his eyes. "We're usually solitary wanderers, a race of nomads, staying in one place for a year, or ten, or twenty, then moving on—alone."

"Damn," Lorraine whispered, seeing the immense loneliness of Elven-kind. Tears burned her eyes, and this time she didn't try to stop them. "This has to end!"

"You understand," said Treemark, watching her. "That when your training is done, I'll ask an oath of you: that you strive to draw our kind together in peace, that you kill none but the killers—and even of those, only the ones so taken with greed and bloodlust that they refuse to change."

"You needn't make me swear to that," Lorraine murmured. "I've already decided."

Treemark's only answer was a vast sigh of relief.

It occurred to Lorraine that she still didn't have the answer to her immediate question, but at least the answer was much closer. She would have to ask Helen for the rest, and ask very carefully.

But Treemark was still talking: "Among other things, your lessons will expand to include means of creating identities, making investments under different names, techniques of covering your tracks, and so on. Tricks of the trade, so to speak." He gave her a penetrating look. "I daresay you know some of those already, but this will be an advanced course."

Lorraine snapped her head up, wrenched back into awareness of her original problem. "Why do you say that?" she asked.

"You mentioned that a stalker was after you," Treemark continued calmly. "You're a practical enough creature that I assume you made some effort to hide where you were going, if not your identity when you got there."

"Yes…" Lorraine shifted uncomfortably. "But it doesn't seem to have worked."

Treemark took a deep breath. "How much can you tell me?"

Lorraine paused, remembering the searched apartment, Berringer, what Weber had said. How much could she tell, indeed?

"The police haven't been much help," she admitted. "I think some of them may be in on it. I came from Chicago, after all."

"Why would the police help a stalker?"

"Because he might be one of them." *Common enough in Chicago…* She thought of immortal Mafiosi, and shuddered. "I may have to go back to Chicago soon, for a police line-up if not a trial. Now I'm wondering how safe I'll be on the trip."

Treemark drummed his fingers together for a moment. "One of us will go with you, then—disguised as a lawyer, perhaps. In fact, I'll ask you not to go anywhere outside of this haven without a…an Elven bodyguard. You're at a very vulnerable stage, aside from your legal problems."

"I know." Lorraine frowned. "Obvious prey, and untrained." *And tomorrow I should call Weber again. And Berringer. Back to the salt-mines.*

"Which is why you should return here as soon as possible," he went on. "You should get at least a year's training before striking out on your own."

Lorraine was amazed at the relief she felt at those words. No, she didn't want to leave here, and not only because of Benjamin.

"Besides, if you can avoid spending your pay for a year, you'll have something to start investing," Treemark smiled. "Even at minimum wage, after taxes you should have a good ten thousand dollars. Put that into the right fund, and…"

"After a year here, I don't know how I'll face the outside world again," Lorraine admitted. "I'll be changed, and all that will be changed."

"You won't have to decide right away," he shrugged. "One thing you have is time. Think about what you want to do with your life."

Paint, Lorraine thought. *As a painter, I could travel anywhere in the world.*

Eventually she'd have to fake her age, fake her death, change identities—but she could always change styles and become another painter. "I'll have to take that Tools and Techniques course," she murmured aloud.

Treemark caught her meaning perfectly. "As for that, I have a present for you," he smiled, and pulled open a drawer of his desk, pulled out a large book and handed it to her.

Lorraine took the volume and stared at its cover. The title was *Techniques of the Old Masters.* Her eyes blurred as she realized what this was. "It's one of the course-books for that class I couldn't take."

"I'm not surprised; it's a standard text at many art schools. Make good use of it, Lorraine."

"I will."

***

All the way back to her room, Lorraine clutched the book tightly. She could barely wait to open it, study the illustrations, and unlock the door to the knowledge she'd lacked for so long. She'd never been able to afford it on her own, back in Chicago, nor any art classes either. Her life had changed in many more ways than one.

Once back in her room, she set the book lovingly on the bed, peeled out of her clothes and slipped on her nightgown, and settled down for some serious reading. The illustrations were so splendid that she peered through them first, leaving the text for later.

Ah, so that was how Rembrandt had done it, and Raphael: start with the medium background color, and then work toward shadow and light in the detailing. *But what about glazes?* To let the light shine through the semitransparent paint, one had to start with the lightest possible background color, then work toward dark…

The feel of an approaching Elven aura caught her attention, then the sound of a discreet knock on the door.

Benjamin, she realized guiltily. *I forgot all about him!*

She got up hastily and let him in. He entered smiling, and displayed a wine bottle and two glasses. She was struck by how pale his hand seemed against the dark bottle.

"I thought we could do with a nightcap," he said. "This is a much-underrated California sweet blackberry wine."

"I love blackberries," Lorraine smiled back, setting the book on the nightstand.

Benjamin noticed the gesture, and then did a subtle double-take as he saw that her wrists were bare. "The cuffs?" he couldn't help asking.

"Dr. Treemark took them off. He said I don't need them anymore." Lorraine wondered why she felt a blush creeping up her cheeks.

Benjamin thought about that, but said nothing further. He poured both glasses full, clinked Lorraine's glass lightly with his own, and turned to set the bottle on the nightstand.

"What have we here?" he asked, nodding toward the book. "Something interesting from the library?"

"A gift from the doctor," Lorraine admitted, wondering how Ben would take that. "I've always wanted to paint, and I've been lusting after that book for years. Sometimes I think he can read minds."

"Oh no," Ben chuckled. "He's just an astute guesser." He opened the book and thumbed carefully through the pages. "Hmmm, actually they're wrong about Raphael. He tended to work from light to dark, not medium outward."

"I was wondering about that. …But how do you know?"

"I saw him at work," said Ben, peering closer at the illustrations. "Once he picked up a brush, he was oblivious to the rest of the world. He needed that dragon of a butler to keep anyone and their cousins from just walking in off the street and strolling around the studio as they pleased. It practically took gunfire to get his attention. I watched for hours, and he never noticed that I was there. Ah, and he always used a brighter yellow than that."

"Wonderful," Lorraine whispered, and took a sip from her glass. "I've got to practice. I've got to paint again. I could never sell my art, and I suspect it was because I never developed my technique far enough. This will be a real help. I'll just have to assemble another painting-kit, get some canvases or hard fiberboards, an easel…"

"And a camera, I expect," Benjamin added. "If you're going to paint horses, you'll need to take pictures. The lovely beasts simply won't stand still and model."

Horses…and their riders… She remembered Ben riding Overcast. "Would you model for me?"

Ben's smile turned a little strained. "Only if you use photographs, and burn them afterward, and change my face slightly. One has to be careful about showing one's features too publicly, you know."

"I'll add a handlebar moustache, if you like." *Is this his normal paranoia, or…* "Ben, is someone after you, too?"

He took a sip from his glass and stared up at the ceiling. "More than a few hunters are after the legend of me," he said. "I'm taking great pains to keep myself a legend. In time, I hope, even that will fade out of memory."

"What legend, Ben?"

"Simply that I'm one of the older ones. Most of our kind are dismayingly young, only a few centuries old. Young and careless, and not too adept at covering their tracks, or not too smart at choosing their prey. The attrition-rate is worst for the newly Initiated, especially those who haven't yet found a teacher or haven't finished their apprenticeship. It's not quite as high for new graduates, out on their own for the first time, but still, most of us tend to be killed in their first century. The rate goes down steadily after that, as we gain more survival-skills."

"Then I should think anyone over a thousand would be safe."

Ben took another, larger, mouthful of wine. "Anyone over a thousand is a real prize. All that survival-knowledge, accumulated psychic ability—oh, that's catnip for a lot of the younger ones: a quick way to gain advantage over their competition. I've survived this long by being very, very discreet."

"I see." Lorraine draped an arm around him, remembering that brief chase with the unknown mutant in the city, and wishing she could think of some realistic assurance. "I can understand living with a practical-paranoid mindset, but doesn't it get tiring?" *Is that why you needed…*

"Yes, it does," Ben sighed, and set down his wineglass. "Which is why I come here—or go to other refuges—a few times a year."

Lorraine remembered him sagging between the columns, and shivered at the thought of what other refuges he might need. "What kinds of refuges are there? I know about sacred sites, but what else?"

"Sacred ground anywhere—unless it's not on a node and some hunter decides he's not superstitious. Or until the managers run out of money, and the monks or nuns have to move out and make room for a real-estate development. Or until some Lord High Glorious Leader decides to raid the place for the good of the Revolution and his own purse. Land of your own is good, especially if contains a node—so long as you have enough money and lawyers to keep it safe from the authorities, and no war comes rolling through. Land nobody wants is good too, until somebody decides he wants it after all—and of course it's hard to maintain the amenities there." Ben tried to smile archly, but his look was bitter.

"Hmm…" Lorraine drummed her fingers on his sharp-muscled chest and thought fast. "So the best place would be a long worked-out mine or oil-field, with a node nearby and enough money for lawyers, bribes, and a small private army. Run a business on it that nobody can complain about—say, a nut-tree orchard—and put it in the name of some religious group. Add a chapel to make it legally sacred land. That should cover all the bases."

Benjamin gave a genuine laugh. "Yes, that should work for a few centuries," he chuckled. "Then you'd only have to make it pay well enough to keep up with the bribes. Hmm, and at the same time make it look poor enough that nobody would want to steal it. Nice balancing act, but I suppose it can be done. There are vineyards in Italy and Greece that have kept working, turning out the same wine, for over two thousand years."

"Pay off the local politicians with wine—or hazelnuts," Lorraine giggled. "If they think you have good crops but no money…"

"Hazelnut cakes," Ben amended. "Wine or cakes, made from a secret recipe that's likely to die with the owners, so there's no point killing them to get it."

Lorraine considered the union's knowledge, contacts and resources. "I think I could find land like that," she murmured.

"I already own a few such places," Ben replied. "I admit, I hadn't taken the idea as far as you have." He slid an arm around her and rubbed idly at her shoulder. "I wonder if the Universal Life Church is still around…"

"I think so."

"I'll have to see what it takes to set up a chapter, and donate land to it."

"And get your other identities to donate money. Make it a religious retreat, and plant that orchard."

"I like it," Ben marveled. "I like the way your mind works."

"I may be young, but I'm cynical," Lorraine grinned, and tickled him.

"Yipe!" Ben yelped, and caught her hand.

She nipped at him instead.

That led to a playful wrestling-match that ended with both of them tangled up in pillows, clothes and bedcovers, giggling against each other's necks. From there to kissing was an easy step.

Ben pulled back enough to struggle out of his shirt, and Lorraine obligingly helped him with the rest. Her own nightgown slipped off easily. Finally Ben drew away the hair-tie and combed out her hair with his fingers.

"Damn," he marveled, stroking through her hair. "You're *fun*, Lorraine."

"Funny girl," she murmured, and ran her lips along his collarbone.

"I like you," he whispered, as if amazed at himself. He wouldn't say more, as if afraid to take another step, but his hands slid over her with a will of their own. Almost desperately, he kissed her again.

Lorraine wrapped herself around him slowly, feeling that this much of his shyness was very real. She might have repressed her impulses in the past, but he was afraid of his own. She must be patient with him.

Benjamin took a deep breath, as though making a decision, then kissed her again.

The kiss deepened abruptly, then his hand slid down to clutch fiercely at her hip, and then there was no more need for patience as the same invisible fire swept down on both of them and touch became everything.

16.

LORRAINE WOKE TO the disgustingly merry sound of the intercom buzzer, grabbed the phone and mumbled an inarticulate greeting into it. On the other end, Daniel cheerfully announced that breakfast would be available in ten minutes. Lorraine mumbled again and hung up. A bleary glance at the clock showed that it was indeed nearly six in the morning—and this was Monday. Ben stirred and yawned beside her, mumbled something about "damn Monday", and began crawling out of bed.

Only Daniel was in the kitchen when they arrived, and he made no mention of the fact that they showed up together but merely set out coffee, fruit and soft-boiled eggs. A glance at the kitchen clock showed that yes, they were late. They finished quickly, remembering to compliment Daniel on the simple but nonetheless delicious fare, and headed out to the stables.

After the weekend's minimal care, all the stalls needed cleaning and all the horses wanted currying. Lorraine was grateful for Ben's help, though the work gave them almost no chance to speak to each other. He could, she noted, rake out a stall or curry a horse as efficiently as he taught or used a sword. It was almost as comfortable to work beside him, even doing mucky labor, as it was training with him. Lorraine wondered if there was anything they could do together that she wouldn't enjoy.

Eleven o'clock, and the next duty on her schedule, came before they had any chance to exercise the horses. Lorraine left reluctantly, promising to see Ben in the *salle d'armes* if not sooner, and trudged off to the gym for her own exercise hour. It felt strange to perform the sit-ups without the presence of the cuffs. The exercises themselves seemed easier, and Lorraine wondered if she should ask Treemark for some wrist and ankle weights.

Noon brought a quick shower, a quick re-dressing, and lunch. Benjamin was in the kitchen waiting for her, and so was a marvelous tuna salad on kale-leaves, with spiced milk, berries and cream—and everyone else but Treemark. Helen questioned Madge and Daniel about planting an herb-garden, Steven and Wally talked about the horses, and Benjamin limited his comments to brief praises of the food. Lorraine, guessing that this unusual reticence would look suspicious, asked Benjamin about different sword-techniques.

"Actually, you're covering quite a lot of them with that Bastarde of yours," he brightened. "It does combine one-handed and two-handed technique, you know."

"So does katana," Wally tossed in.

"Ah, but katanas really aren't made for direct blocking," Ben countered. "I know they're terribly fashionable these days, but they're really more toward the scalpel rather than the axe end of the spectrum. The old European broadsword sits solidly in the middle of the scale, and can handle just about anything."

"Rapier is much more maneuverable," Helen noted, "And most sword-swingers these days don't expect it."

"Terrible for blocking, though," Steven considered. "All it can do is deflect, and only at a slight angle."

"I rather prefer saber, myself," Daniel put in.

"Leaf-blade," said Madge.

And that, of course, started off a lively discussion on which blade was best for what—that lasted until Ben noted the time and took Lorraine off "to practice for real".

His step was light and his expression cheerful as he led her away. She wondered if he'd noticed that she'd steered the conversation into something that made him look sociable, but he said nothing about it, and she didn't ask.

The first hour was spent at rifle-practice, with light loads and silhouette targets, and Benjamin noted that her pattern was "tightening nicely". The second hour they spent with the blunt swords, running through the forms he'd already shown her, slowly, then faster; he ended by teaching her a new attack-block-riposte combination that took all her concentration to manage. Lorraine was almost grateful when Helen came to take her out to the garden. A quick glance back showed Ben looking relieved as he carried the swords off to their rack.

In the garden, they settled on the familiar cushions and ran through the meditative practice-drills. Helen produced a handful of small jewelry, explaining that she wanted to test for 'psychometry'—reading psychic impressions off objects—but Lorraine could get no clear images. Next, Helen lit a small candle in a glass jar and asked Lorraine to try to move the flame with mental force alone—'psychokinesis', she called it. Lorraine called up the power-flows in herself and aimed them at the candle, and saw the flame flicker, but couldn't be certain that the motion wasn't due to random air currents.

"It's frustrating," Lorraine admitted, rubbing a small ache in her temples. "All I did was tire myself out."

"Actually, I'm not surprised. Psychometry usually takes a lot of time to develop, and psychokinesis is the rarest of the psychic gifts. I'm just covering all the bases here."

Lorraine sighed, trying to think of a polite way to put this. "Ah, can I ask you something about…social dynamics?"

Helen looked surprised. "Certainly. What would you like to know?"

Bite the bullet. "Relationships within the household. I think Madge and Daniel are an item…"

"Oh yes, for several years."

"And I've seen that Wally and Steven are something more than friends."

"Ah, I thought so," Helen smiled.

"But that still leaves three unaccounted for." Lorraine chewed her lip for a moment. "Brian, Benjamin, and you. What's the relationship there?"

Helen gave her a thoughtful look, and then smiled again. "Ben and I are old, old friends, but we've never really been more than that. I've been cautiously approaching Brian for the last century or so; I distrust people with missions, but Brian is very levelheaded about his particular passion, and I admit that it's one I share. I'm not sure how long Brian and Ben have known each other, but I know they have some history. I'm not setting my cap for either of them, if that's what you mean."

Lorraine nodded slowly, thinking that over. "Then you wouldn't mind if I…took up with one of them?"

Helen pursed her lips. "I confess I'd be worried if you became infatuated with Brian," she said. "He's a very controlling sort—and besides, you're his student."

"That leaves Benjamin," Lorraine said, finally.

"A much better choice," Helen purred. "His problem is that he's too secretive, too standoffish for his own good. I wish you luck getting through to him."

Lorraine raised an eyebrow. "No objection, then?"

"None whatever. Now, are you still tired?"

"…A little."

"Then best we don't overdo. Go on off to the pool, and relax as much as possible."

"Yes… Thank you." Lorraine pulled herself to her feet and plodded away toward the pool, feeling Helen's eyes on her back. *Well, now I know,* she told herself. *Ben was right… But then, why was he so cautious at dinner? ...And how much does Helen know?*

She could think of no way to find answers to those questions, nothing to do but put them off and concentrate on the moment.

Then she remembered that this was Monday, and she needed to call Weber, at least. Lorraine paused in mid-stride, wondering if it was safe to phone from inside the house. Certainly not through the house's own line; that could be tapped by anyone local.

The cell-phone? Berringer had admitted that it was safe for a long-distance call…

She stepped out into the empty space of the pool-area, pulled out the cell-phone and punched in Weber's number.

"Ms. Defarge!" his voice sounded delighted. "The suspect arrived this morning. We've got him safely locked up downtown. How soon can you get here for the lineup?"

So soon?! Lorraine felt strangely off-balance. *Why didn't Berringer tell me first?* "I— I don't know. I'll have to arrange it with my… Uh, how long can you hold him?"

"Technically? A couple weeks. Really? Three, four days. Please get here fast, ma'am."

"I will. Which jail, exactly? Where should I come to?"

"The big lockup on Madison. You know the address?"

"Oh yes," Lorraine grinned. Everybody in the union office knew that one. "And ask the desk-sergeant for the 'viewing room'?"

Weber laughed. "So they taught you the procedure," he guessed. "See you in a day or two, I hope."

"You will. 'Bye."

Lorraine clicked off the connection, thoughts whirling. She had to go back to Chicago, at once. How? Plane, train or car? One phonecall to Berringer, and the FBI would arrange it. But then, why hadn't the FBI office notified her? Something was wrong here.

And there was nothing for it but to proceed to the pool.

Lorraine was halfway through pulling off her clothes and stuffing them in the locker when she remembered that she had no bathing suit, and was no longer wearing even the cuffs. *Why the hell should it matter?* She thought crossly, remembering Treemark's casual nudity. She finished undressing and strode defiantly into the Jacuzzi.

The hot-water jets were wonderfully relaxing, as always. Lorraine settled in front of a jet, leaned back and let her mind drift, forgetting her other problem for the comfort of the moment.

Treemark's arrival, a few minutes later, barely roused her. He settled into the water, glanced at her, and smiled. "How are lessons coming along?" he asked.

Lorraine grinned impishly. "I thought you didn't want me to concentrate on intellectual matters while I'm here."

"True," Treemark laughed. "I just want to be sure Helen isn't pushing you too hard."

That made Lorraine raise an eyebrow. "She voiced similar concerns about you."

"We both want you to learn as much as possible, as soon as possible," Treemark admitted, "And neither of us wants you run ragged."

"Mmm," Lorraine drowsily agreed, more interested in the lovely feel of the water, dimly marveling at how aware of her body she'd become. Silence was no longer a burden, nor time a cause for worry.

Damn! Forgot! She jerked her head up. "I have to go back to Chicago, right away," she said. "They've caught a suspect, and need me to identify him."

Treemark looked at her, his eyebrows rising. "When did you learn this?" he asked.

Damn! "Just a little while ago. Cell-phone, long-distance: should be safe."

"True," Treemark considered, "Unless… Just whom did you talk to?"

"The detective assigned to my case."

"Hmmm…" He leaned back in the water, clearly running through ideas. "I'll have someone drive you there, and back, posing as your lawyer. No, two drivers; you can make it in twelve hours, driving straight through."

"I don't want to put you out…"

"Don't worry about it," he said sternly. "In fact, stop worrying at all. Lie back in the water and relax; there's nothing else to do before the trip starts."

Lorraine sighed and did as she was told. He was right; there was no point fretting herself to pieces before she had to leave. Best to enjoy the peace and quiet while she could. The water was still infinitely soothing…

Eventually Treemark called her out of the pool and off to the massage-table. She wondered, as she stretched out on the familiar towel-robe, if this time was a rest for Treemark too. Between counseling his patients, managing the ranch and training the horses, he must have been busy most of the day.

This time the massage-work was simple and straightforward, relaxing muscles and pressing the occasional joint into place. Lorraine let herself go with the flow, and was almost sorry when it ended.

"To the solarium, now," said Treemark. "I think you'll know what to do with what you find there."

Intrigued, Lorraine pulled the robe around her and retraced the familiar steps—this time alone, wondering what new exercise he had in mind.

Three steps into the solarium, she understood.

Just short of the columns stood an easel, and on it sat a blank canvas-board.

Beside that lay a thick sketchpad and box of pencils, and beside that a wooden valise, open, displaying an array of paints, brushes, and a palette. Next to that waited a standard cheap Polaroid camera.

Lorraine almost ran to them. She picked up the brushes and flicked her fingers lovingly over the bristles: wide nylon, narrow squirrel-hair, pointed sable—all new and perfect, waiting to be used.

A subject! All I need is a model! Laughing, blinking away tears, Lorraine grabbed the camera and ran out toward the stables—not caring that the robe was flapping open at her sides, showing that she was naked under it—out to the paddock where the horses grazed.

Overcast stood nearest the fence, and he turned a thoughtful eye at Lorraine as she steadied the camera on the top rail. Lorraine whistled to him, and he raised his head to look. *Click* went the camera. Overcast flicked his ears, realized that no carrots or other treats were offered, and shook his head in annoyance. *Click* again. He tossed his mane and stamped once. *Click.* Tired of the silly business, the stallion went back to grazing and ignored the fool human.

Lorraine smiled beatifically at him, then turned and trotted back to the solarium.

Out of those three pictures, she knew, she could sketch an effective pose. First the drawings, until she was satisfied. Then the transfer to the canvas. Then the background colors… *Light to dark, or mid-tone outward?* she wondered as she settled on the tile floor to look over her photographs.

She was still transferring the sketch to the canvas when Daniel's voice through the intercom politely notified her that there was only a quarter-hour until dinner, if she wished to dress for it. Lorraine was indignant at being interrupted, until a grumble from her stomach reminded her that eating was necessary. She sighed, packed up the valise, sketchbook, pencils, photos and camera, and hurried off to her room. The easel and canvas she left where they were; she couldn't think of a better place for them, or with such ideal lighting.

She was peeling off the towel-robe, wondering what she could throw on quickly, when she noticed something odd: a small green light blinking, on the chair where Madge had placed her work-clothes. A closer inspection showed that it was the cell-phone; someone had called while she was busy in the solarium. The number displayed on the small screen was all too familiar.

Berringer. Finally... But the displayed time of the call remarkably late; nearly half an hour past office-hours. *Strange...*

Apparently the message was urgent, probably about catching the suspect. But did Berringer expect her to get to a pay phone at this hour? There was no way she could do it. And tomorrow she would be on the road; whatever Berringer wanted her to do, it would be too late then. Was this safe? Was there a choice?

Lorraine punched the callback button and put the phone to her ear.

Berringer picked up on the first ring. "Roxanne dear," her voice crooned. "I've been trying to reach you all afternoon. They've got a suspect, and you'll be needed for identification. When should I come pick you up?"

She called me Roxanne?! "Not now," Lorraine snapped. "I'm...out at dinner. I'll get back to you right after."

With that she punched the Off button and slapped the phone shut. Well past office-hours, yet Berringer had answered at her office number: did that mean she was keeping late hours, or just had the calls transferred to her home-phone? And what had she meant about trying 'all afternoon'? *And why did she let slip my real name? Was she that confident that the danger was past? Or careless? Or what?* Lorraine poked more buttons and read off the list of unanswered calls. Yes, there were several of them and Berringer's number appeared every time—but the earliest of those calls had come over an hour after Lorraine had talked to Weber. Was it likely that the FBI would get news of the case later than the state police? Or was it just that Berringer's superiors took their own sweet time passing the word to her?

Am I just being Chicago-union paranoid, or is something wrong here? she wondered. *Could Treemark tell me?*

Perhaps she should tell him a good bit more than she had.

***

For dinner Lorraine threw on only her maroon dress, belt and sandals, and she arrived just as the others were heading into the dining room. Again she took her usual place, and again Benjamin was careful not to pay her much attention. She smiled to herself and concentrated on the food—a sweet-and-sour salad, beef bouillon with onion croutons, Beef Stroganov with red cabbage, and a dry red wine—which was excellent, as always. Dessert was blueberry cheesecake, and everyone lingered long over it—except Benjamin, who disappeared early and quietly.

As soon as her plate was empty, Lorraine made her way to the clinic office.

Treemark sat behind the desk as usual, jotting some notes on a pad. His smile, when he looked up, was a little fainter than usual. "I've been planning your trip," he said without preamble. "If you leave right after breakfast, you can reach Chicago by early evening. The drivers will have funds to check you all into a modest motel, and you can go to the police station in the morning. If you leave immediately thereafter, you should make it back here in time for a late dinner. Is that suitable?"

"Very," said Lorraine. "I'll need to pack for only two days…" Then she remembered her cats. "But I think we can do better than a motel. I have some friends in Chicago who could put us up for the night, if your people wouldn't mind sleeping on a sofa-bed." *Bob and Meredith. With Carl away at college, they can put me in his room. I can see Sable-Foot and Crimp-Tail again…*

"All right." Treemark jotted some more notes. "Can you pack tonight?"

"For a two-day trip? Certainly." She could do that in ten minutes, and had before. Then again, maybe she should ask Helen, or even Madge, which of her clothes would be best for the purpose. "Who'll be driving?"

"Wally. He knows every speed-trap from here to Canada, and makes a very efficient bodyguard." Treemark twitched a sardonic grin. "He was a bootlegger in the 1950s, and can outdrive just about anything on the road."

Lorraine thought about that, and laughed. "A man of many talents."

"Yes." Treemark set down his pen, folded his hands and gave her a serious look. "Lorraine, I won't ask for particulars, but I need you to think about this. Two days ago, someone broke into Steven's apartment in town. Nothing was taken, or left. I don't know if it was your stalker or the mutant whose field you brushed in town the other day."

"Oh, hell!" Lorraine whispered. "I gave that address to—to Aunt Dianne!"

"Could she have passed it on to your stalker?"

"Anything's possible…" *The FBI and the Mafia?! …Or maybe…* "Could it be someone after Steven? Is he in trouble?"

"No. It's only a bolt-hole apartment, and he can drop it easily. At worst, he can simply change identities and move somewhere else for awhile."

Lorraine sighed, thinking of Treemark's tiny household being reduced by even one.

"The question is," Treemark went on, "Which of you is he after? Could this stalker of yours have connected you with Steven?"

"Yes! If he was near the restaurant, if he saw us leave in Steven's truck…"

She'd have to tell Treemark more than that. "The thug who's after me has Mafia connections. They could have worms in anything from the Chicago police on up. It could very well have been me that the hunter was after."

"Then it's just as well that you start for Chicago in the morning." Treemark leaned back in his chair. "And now, as Monty Python said, for something completely different; how did you like your surprise present?"

It took Lorraine a moment to realize that he meant the painter's kit. She felt a wide smile spread across her face. "It's wonderful," she breathed. "I took pictures of Overcast, and made the preliminary sketches. I'll have the sketch transferred tomorrow, and then—" She remembered that she wouldn't be there tomorrow. "Damn! I'll have to wait until I get back. Two days… That's not so bad."

"So you'll have something to look forward to." Treemark's smile matched her own.

"More than that," said Lorraine, thinking of Benjamin.

***

When she strode back to her own room Lorraine was calmer,

resolute and resigned. Tonight she'd pack, tomorrow she'd drive to Chicago with Wally; they'd spend the night at Bob and Meredith's, then swoop down on the cop-shop without warning, make the identification and make their getaway. The faster they moved, the better their chances were. Wally probably had centuries of practice at this, and she'd played such games before.

...The time we hid that Reform organizer when both the cops and the Teamster goons were looking for him, house to house up and down the North Side...

She opened the door and stopped short.

Benjamin half-lay across her bed, studying her book on the Old Masters. He looked up and smiled as she came in.

Lorraine could feel her heartbeat picking up as she looked at him, and hoped she wasn't blushing. She also kicked herself mentally for being so self-absorbed that she hadn't noticed his aura.

"You left the door unlocked," he said apologetically, "And I just had to see more of this book."

"I understand completely," Lorraine grinned, shutting the door behind her—and taking care to lock it. "It's fascinating...and I've started on a painting."

"Of Overcast?" Ben asked, holding up the photos. "He's a lovely subject, I'll agree."

Lorraine was strolling toward the bed when her cell-phone rang.

"It's done that once already," said Ben. "I have no idea who'd be calling at this hour."

"I do." Lorraine strode around the bed and grabbed the phone, inwardly seething.

"Hello?" she asked, knowing perfectly well who it was.

"Roxanne," Berringer's voice sounded irritated. "Where are you, and when will you be ready for the pickup?"

"Does Macy's tell Gimbel's, Dianne?" Lorraine asked between her teeth. "I just learned that the address I gave you was wrong—but that one was also broken into, just a few days ago. You wouldn't know anything about that, would you?"

Berringer's gasp of surprise sounded genuine. "No, I don't. Roxanne, I can assure you that our office knew nothing about it!"

"Begging your pardon, Dianne, but this is the second time—within a week—that somebody has broken into a place where I've supposedly been staying—addresses that no one but you was supposed to know about—so I'm feeling just a wee bit paranoid. If it's all the same to you, I'll get myself to Chicago on my own. Goodbye."

Lorraine stabbed the Disconnect button, and then turned off the power completely. When she turned back she saw Ben favoring her with a raised eyebrow. She sighed, and dropped beside him on the bed.

"It's the stalker case," she explained. "I'm leaving tomorrow morning for Chicago, to identify the suspect. With any luck, I'll be back the night after."

"I know," Ben smiled. He reached into a pocket and pulled out something small, brown and fuzzy, and held it up to his face. A closer look showed that it was a fake moustache, just the color of his hair. "I meant to tell you: I'm going with you."

"What?!"

"I'm the second driver. I'm also going to be your lawyer."

17.

BY NINE IN THE MORNING, Lorraine and Ben and Wally were barreling up the highway in a Jeep Wagoneer with Tucson far behind. Wally was at the wheel, Ben in the shotgun seat and Lorraine lying on a small air mattress in the back, her head pillowed on her suitcase and Ben's duffel bag. She held *Techniques of the Old Masters* in her hands, but had given up trying to read it. She also didn't bother looking out the windows, knowing what she'd see: scenery racing by at nerve-wracking speed. Wally seemed to be impatient with anything less than 90 miles an hour, but he also had a reliable sixth sense about where speed traps, police hideouts and radar-placements were. The police-band radio and radar-detector under the dashboard also helped; Lorraine could hear the radio yattering meaninglessly above the sound of their wheels and the passing wind.

Hidden under the seats, she knew, was an impressive cache of shotguns, pistols, swords, and a hunting rifle with a telescopic sight. Her unofficial bodyguards were taking no chances with her safety.

"Get some sleep if you can," Ben said kindly. "We won't be stopping for another hour."

"All right." Lorraine dutifully lay back down and pulled the car blanket up around her, unconsciously clutching the book as if it were a talisman against evil. Yes, she'd do her part: win vengeance for Jack Palumbo.

She noted, without surprise, that her old, cold rage was back. She wasn't dismayed at it, didn't fear that it meant any kind of relapse. No, it was perfectly fitting, now that she was going into battle.

But where did that other mutant come into this? And what if he followed her from Tucson?

***

The drive up to Chicago went like a stealthy military operation. They stopped every two to three hours to eat, refuel, use bathrooms, change drivers—and, at one stop, buy a second-hand but respectable-looking briefcase. Always, one of the men remained in the car while the other accompanied Lorraine; they would bring back food and drink for the man left in the car, then change positions and move on. Always they chose truck stops, where the food tasted like cardboard but they could park right outside the diners' windows and watch for trouble. Always they listened to the police-band radio for any hint that they might face a roadblock. Always they drove as fast as they dared.

After crossing the Arizona border they hid all the weapons in various easily reached caches in the car, except for pistols artfully hidden under jackets. They kept to the freeways and tried to stay between trucks whenever possible. All of them managed to sleep in turn, in short catnaps on the air mattress, and kept thoroughly alert while driving.

At the outskirts of Chicago, Lorraine pulled out her cell-phone and called Bob's and Meredith's number. Meredith picked up on the second ring, and was gushingly delighted to hear who it was. Lorraine found it difficult to think of herself as Roxanne again, but managed to keep to necessities.

"Merry, have there been any more problems with the Teamster goons?" she asked. "Or the local cops?"

"Just minor things," Meredith assured her. "Tires slashed, rocks through windows, bullying phonecalls—kid-stuff, really. The local cops are walking around on tiptoe, being almost desperately helpful, as if somebody higher up was leaning on them."

Higher up? The state troopers or the FBI? Lorraine wondered. "Anything else I should know about?"

"Just that Bill's now the chief. He goes around with a body-guard of out-of-work members or retirees, and he got a new security-system for the office."

He's safe then. But is Merry's phone secure? "Merry, did you have this phone gone over for wiretaps after I left?"

"Damn right I did," Meredith answered proudly. "I had the state troopers do it, and they actually found a bug—but it was an old one, local-police type, half corroded away. It probably hadn't worked for years."

Probably safe, then. "All right, I need to ask a big favor of you. Can you put up three friends for the night? All reliable and gone in the morning, I swear."

"Three…?" Meredith hesitated for only a few seconds. "Can do. We can fit two on the sofa-bed and one in Carl's old room. Sure you'll vouch for them, now?"

"Positively. They'll be showing up at your door in…" She glanced at her watch. "Within the hour. They'll know where to come, and they'll have an identifying sign you can't miss. Okay?"

"Okay. Wow, this is like when we hosted those Teamster re-formers, isn't it?"

Lorraine winced at the memory, and the implicit question. "Sort of, but a little different," she admitted. "Not much danger — and if there is any, they can take care of it." *I hope.* "Will you be ready in an hour, then?"

"You know we will," Meredith promised. "And afterwards, you'll have to tell me what it's all about."

"No problem," Lorraine grinned. "'Bye, then." She shut off the phone before Meredith could keep her any longer, and thought of further possibilities. "I'll navigate you to the house," she said, "But we'll have to do a bit of recon before we go in."

"No problem," Wally echoed.

"Free-standing house, or apartment building?" Ben asked.

"Old apartment complex, parking in the back, driveways on both sides. We can go in the back way." Lorraine recalled something else. "Old-fashioned fire-escapes, sides and back: swing-down type, last length some 15 feet above the ground."

"Good," Ben approved. "We can do the sweep quickly."

"Piece of cake," Wally agreed, glancing automatically at the rearview mirrors.

***

Wally's adroit driving, and the information from the reliable radio, got them safely into the city and up to the right street. Lorraine pointed out the building, which Wally noted and then drove past. They circled the block, watching for signs of anything unusual, came back toward the apartment complex, saw that there were no other cars in the first driveway, and turned into it.

There was no one visible on the fire-escapes, or in the parking lot. Several cars were parked there, with no one inside, but there was an available space close to the back door. They parked, pulled out the weaponry, hid what they could under their clothes and wrapped the rest in the car-blanket. Finally they made their way to the back door. It was locked, but Lorraine took out her cellphone and called the apartment number again. This time it was Bob who answered.

Lorraine cut off his enthusiastic greetings as quickly as she politely could. "Bob," she said, "My friends are at your back door right now, and their names are Wally, Ben and Lorraine. Please go down and let them in. Okay?"

"Right," said Bob, and promptly hung up.

A minute later they heard a key turn in the lock, and the back door swung open.

There stood Bob, beefy and balding and wearing a T-shirt and bluejeans, as always. His eyes and mouth opened wide when he saw Lorraine, but she quickly stuck out a hand and said: "Hi. I'm *Lorraine,* and this is Ben, and that's Wally."

Bob recovered fast, shook her hand briefly and ushered the three of them inside, then firmly shut the door behind them. "Gawwwd, what are you doing back in the city?" he half-whispered as he led them through the shadowed basement.

"Going to a lineup tomorrow morning," Lorraine answered, just as quietly. "They've got a suspect. I'll ID him or I won't, but I'll be gone again right afterward. These guys are my…drivers."

"I get the picture," Bob nodded solemnly. "Merry'll be happy to see you again, and so will the cats."

Lorraine felt a pang of grief. "How are they getting along?" she asked.

That made Bob laugh. "Like bandits! You wouldn't believe the places they can get into, or how they just about mug you for petting, and we've got to feed them at the same time we serve dinner or they'll be right in our plates."

That made Lorraine laugh too: it was so familiar, and proof that Sable-Foot and Crimp-Tail were happy. "It's good to know they've settled in," she said.

Bob led them up the stairs, paused at the back door of the apartment to knock shave-and-a-haircut, and then waited for the sounds of a chain rattling away and a bolt being drawn.

"Ah, an old hand at this game," Ben noted with approval.

"You guys aren't the only practical paranoids I know," Lorraine couldn't help saying.

Meredith, her long brunette hair falling out of its bun, half-swooned and half-screamed when she saw Lorraine, then burbled happily all over her and her bodyguards, leaving Bob to close and lock the door behind them. She continued to bubble delighted greetings as she gave them the grand tour of the apartment—which, Lorraine noted, gave Ben and Wally opportunity to look out the windows and study possible exits and approaches. Wally smiled at the heavy pierced-metal screens on the windows overlooking the fire-escape, and their sturdy spring-catch releases. Ben made a point of opening one of those screens and looking down into the driveway below, then firmly closing the screen again. Lorraine tried to smile at Meredith's nonstop stream of welcoming gossip, and wearily dumped her gear on the bed in the absent Carl's room.

In the middle of the proceedings, the cats came out. They yowled imperiously as they spotted Lorraine, and nothing would stop them from climbing up her legs to demand petting. She was obliged to drop into the nearest chair so she could hold both of them on her lap and pet them both at once. No, they hadn't forgotten her; in fact, they insisted that she make up for her long absence with closer to a month's worth of petting. It was hard to keep tears out of her eyes as she stroked their sleek backs, rubbed behind their velvet ears and tickled their fuzzy chins.

"Beautiful creatures," she heard Benjamin murmur, and looked up to see him watching the animals with genuine fondness in his eyes.

"Well, enough of this," Meredith finished. "What's been happening at your end of the world? –That you can tell me about, anyway?"

"I've managed to get a good job," Lorraine volunteered, "And I'm signed up for some classes I've needed for awhile, so it may be some time before I get back here again. Maybe a year…" She thought of not seeing the cats again for that long, and bit her lip.

"Well, you'll be back for the trial, certainly," said Meredith. "You make that bastard hang."

"I think it's the chair in this state," said Bob, unhelpfully, "Unless they've gone and banned the death-penalty again, which is what you can expect when the cops, judges and politicians *are* the crooks. They're not gonna let themselves get fried."

"That's providing they've caught the right guy," Wally put in. "I'd really hate it if this was a wasted trip."

"I don't think it is," Lorraine murmured. But she had to consider the possibility, unlikely or not, that the Tucson stalker just might have nothing to do with the hit-man in Chicago. There might be some other game going on, and the suspect the New York police had caught just might be the wrong man.

"Anyway," Meredith announced, clapping her hands, "Dinner's almost ready. It's Pasta al Carabinieri, with bits of chicken and sausage added."

Lorraine winced, recognizing the dish: end-of-paycheck, use-up-the-leftovers food, quick and desperately cheap. They'd caught Bob and Meredith at a bad time, not that the good-hearted couple would ever admit it.

"With black olives?" Benjamin asked eagerly, raising his head like a bird-dog.

"And olive oil," Meredith laughed delightedly. "And a good Chianti with."

Only someone who knew him well would have guessed that Ben's smile had turned a trifle pained.

I'll have to talk to him, thought Lorraine. She knew that Treemark had sent them off with considerable traveling-money, and a hundred-dollar bill shoved into an envelope — along with a quiet phrase, something like "For protection, just in case"—would be the least Bob and Meredith deserved.

Sable-Foot caught her hand in his paws to notify her that the petting had stopped prematurely.

***

Dinner was excellent, despite the painfully cheap wine. Afterward they drew straws to determine the order in which everybody used the bathtub, and Wally won the shortest straw. While he trotted off to the bathroom the others sprawled in the living room, finishing off the wine, talking about union history, griping about politics, and petting the cats. Meredith lit a stick of jasmine incense, put an old Enya recording on the CD player, and served a plate of slightly stale but still tasty macaroons.

Lorraine snuggled Crimp-Tail in her lap, fighting back a surge of grief as she realized that an invisible gulf had opened between herself and these good, solid friends.

Yes, she might come back to Chicago and resume her old life, but it would never be the same. Less than two weeks ago, she'd been able to talk to them about anything in the world; now there was a vast hoard of secrets she must keep from them for all their lives.

She would lead a double life, at best: going on with her union work and her painting, but always giving first priority to the unseen war of Elven-kind. Her world had changed, and Bob and Meredith—and the cats—would inevitably be left behind.

Crimp-Tail nipped her hand, insisting that this silly human be sensible and live for the moment. Lorraine grinned apologetically, and rubbed the cat's belly. Crimp-Tail responded with an ecstatic purr.

Wally came traipsing out into the livingroom, holding his dirty clothes in his arms, wearing a tightly wrapped bath-towel and bemused grin, and nothing else. Bob gave a bellow of laughter. Meredith promised "Bathrobes we got!" and trotted off to fetch one.

"I'm next," said Benjamin, getting to his feet. He used the moment to slip something into Bob's hand, saying quietly: "For repairs, just in case."

Bob pursed his lips, nodded understandingly, and shoved the item quickly into his pants-pocket. Lorraine hid her smile by playing with the cat.

When Meredith came back with an armload of old but serviceable bathrobes, promising to wash and dry everybody's laundry before bedtime, Lorraine passed off the cat to Wally and went to the bedroom to unpack. She caught Meredith in the hallway and pulled her aside.

"If it's okay with you," she half-whispered, "I'd like to have Ben in here with me, just in case."

Merry grinned knowingly. "Fine with me," she said. "Besides, he's a handsome hunk. If I weren't a happily living-in-sin woman…"

"I'll keep him busy," Lorraine leered back. "Now hand me one of those robes, and I'll get out of these clothes."

Meredith obliged, and then trotted away, giggling to herself.

Lorraine waited outside the bathroom until Benjamin came out, looking surprisingly elegant in the aged bathrobe, and quietly informed him about the sleeping arrangements. He smiled brief acknowledgement, warned her that the hot water was running low, then strolled back to the livingroom to hold up his end of the party.

Lorraine could hear Wally describing the joys and hardships of working on a farm, and guessed that Ben would offer a background story of his life as a schoolteacher. She suddenly felt exhausted, as if this day had lasted 48 hours already, and hastened into the bathroom. The water was no better than lukewarm, and she hurried through the washing.

Once out of the water, Lorraine went straight back to the bedroom, closed the door and poked through the suitcase for the clothes Madge had picked out for her. There was a simple knit-polyester long-sleeved white blouse, an equally simple dark-blue long skirt, dark pantyhose, a plain white sports-brassiere, and a pair of socks that would provide warmth and padding inside her boots. With the jacket, these would look forgettable and nondescript; quite suitable for viewing a police lineup. In her own way, Madge too was totally professional.

Survival skills… Lorraine thought, as she laid out the clothes on a chair. *I have so much to learn.*

She pulled the robe tighter around her, turned off all the lights but the small table-lamp, and climbed into bed. The mattress was harder than she was used to, but the blankets were heavy and soft. She lay still and waited for sleep to come creeping up on her, but it approached slowly.

Some little time later, the door opened and Benjamin came in. He was, Lorraine drowsily noted, carrying his coat—which he laid carefully on the floor beside the bed, right next to the still-wrapped bundle of weapons. He sat down on the bed and turned to her, hands pausing undecidedly at the knotted belt of his bathrobe. "Would you like another glass of that dreadful Chianti?" he asked softly.

Lorraine smiled and shook her head. "I'm not up for anything right now," she admitted. "It's been a very long day, and I'm still in combat-mode."

"I sympathize," Ben grinned ruefully, and slid under the covers beside her.

She reached for him, wanting only the reassurance of feeling his solid presence, and encountered the soft-worn terrycloth. "You feel like a racing-model teddy-bear in that thing," she murmured.

Ben snuggled closer and wrapped an arm around her. "Did you know that teddy-bears were named after the bear that Teddy Roosevelt refused to shoot on his first big-game hunt?" he said. "As I recall, it was a grizzly: nothing cuddly about it. I suppose there's something hopeful in humanity's tendency to soften old threats and hardships into toys. The girdle was originally a piece of body-armor. Halloween was once a feast of the dead—"

"Shhh." Lorraine laid a gentle finger across his lips. "Just hold me. Tomorrow's going to be rougher than today, and we need our sleep."

Without another word, Ben kissed her chastely and pressed against her.

A soft thump of weight quivered through the bed, then a second, followed by a wiry meow. Lorraine raised her head and saw the cats come picking their way across the blankets, looking for a comfortable place to settle. She smiled fondly, remembering this.

Sure enough, Crimp-Tail picked a spot just behind her knees to circle and lie down.

Sable-Foot proceeded up to the pillows and folded into a furry lump behind Benjamin's head.

"*Menage a trois*—or *quatre*—with cats," he muttered, but didn't move.

"Fearless bodyguards," Lorraine whispered back, immensely comforted. Short-lived or not, ignorant or not, mortals and even animals were friends too good to lose.

18.

EARLY NEXT MORNING, the war party moved out. After studying the terrain from the windows, they hurried down the back stairs and into the parking lot—with Bob locking the door behind them— and, after a quick inspection, into the jeep. They pulled out of the driveway, circled the block watchfully, and then moved into traffic toward Madison Street. At that point Lorraine took out her cell-phone and called Detective Weber.

"Yes, it's me," she answered his greeting. "I'm on my way to the Madison Street station, and should be there in half an hour. How soon can you get there?"

"I'll beat you to it," he promised. "See you at the front desk."

"I don't think so," Lorraine muttered as she hung up. "I suggest we circle the building, see where we can get in, and how close to that we can park."

"Can do," Wally chuckled approvingly. "You two go in, I'll stay with the car and cover you as long as I can."

But the police station was a massive featureless oblong build-ing, with the parking lot in the back and the only unlocked en-trance in the front—and of course there was no parking allowed in the front. After a few moments' thought, Wally pulled into a space near a featureless door in the rear. "Try to come out that way," he said. "I can at least cover you there."

Seeing no better choice available, Benjamin and Lorraine got out and walked, as fast as they could without drawing attention, around to the front door. Behind them, Wally picked up a city street map and pretended to concentrate on it.

The walk seemed intolerably long, and even this early there were too many people about, most of them police. At least there was no feel of Elven aura; none of them were other mutants.

The cavernous entrance seemed to swallow them like a stone monster, and the subtle stink and constant noise inside reinforced the impression. They had to go through a metal-detector at the door, but they were ready for it; they'd left their keys and metal pens in the car, and the door-guard passed them through without comment. Benjamin nervously shifted the briefcase to his other hand and patted his false moustache while Lorraine strode up to the mammoth desk at the end of the entry-hall.

"I'm here to view a lineup," Lorraine announced to the rumpled clerk. "Where do I go?"

The clerk picked up a pen and squinted over a mammoth ledger-book. "Name?" he asked.

"Roxanne Defarge," she said. "And this is my lawyer…ah…"

"Adam Benjamin," Ben said. "How soon can you accommodate my client?"

The clerk sneered, and wrote slowly. "Case number?" he asked.

"I have no idea," Lorraine snorted.

The clerk gave her a lofty look. "Then who's the officer in charge of the case?"

"Detective Weber, Illinois state police, CID."

That earned her a double-take. The clerk looked at his book, looked at her, finally shrugged and pointed. "Through that door. Turn right, go down to the end of the corridor, then right again."

With a bare "thank you", Ben and Lorraine headed that way. A glance backward showed the clerk picking up his desk-phone.

"I didn't think Weber would be here, whatever he said," murmured Lorraine as they picked their way down the crowded hallway.

"Oh? Why not?" Ben asked neatly avoiding a beefy uniformed cop who came barreling up the corridor past them.

"The usual rivalry. The city-cops will try to keep him tied up with something for as long as they can…" But there were another possibilities she could think of. *What if Weber's been taken out by the Mafia? Or what if he's the Mafia contact?! It's not impossible…* "If we get lost, we'll just have to ask someone here."

But no, the clerk's description had been accurate; the hallway ended in a T-junction, with a handwritten sign saying "lineup" pointing to the right.

Just before they reached the end of the corridor, Lorraine felt the shocking surge of an Elven aura. Ben stiffened and grabbed her arm. "One of us," he whispered. "Close. Be careful."

"What can he do here?" Lorraine asked. "Too many eyes and ears for an attack."

"If he's a cop, he can find some excuse to lock us up—and of course we don't have any weapons."

"If Weber's here, we have a chance," Lorraine considered. *Unless he's the Mafia's man…*

They drew themselves up and stepped around the corner. Beyond lay another hallway, lined with doors, more thinly populated with perambulating police. Halfway down the hallway stood three men, arguing, and as Lorraine approached she could feel that one of them—she couldn't tell which one—was radiating the characteristic field.

They were Oshansky, Weber and Harding, and they seemed to be squabbling about jurisdiction. They caught sight of Lorraine approaching, and stopped arguing to look at her.

One of them. Lorraine felt a large piece of the puzzle slide into place. The aura was faintly familiar; she'd felt it once, just once before—in Tucson, the day she'd met with Berringer. *No coincidence!* They'd all met her, the day of Jack's murder or the day after, and any of them could have recognized her for a pre-Initiate. That was reason enough for continuing interest, even without Mafia motives. Any one of them could have followed her to Tucson, and all of them had to know she'd be coming back today.

Did the mutant want to protect her, or take her power? Did he want to silence her or use her as a witness? Those incidents in Tucson implied that his intentions weren't friendly—and he had to know by now that she was Initiated, fully powered, a prize worth taking.

All three of them watched her come toward them, Weber smiling, Oshansky scowling, Harding expressionless. They were standing close enough that she couldn't begin to pick out which one was the source of the aura.

Lorraine plastered a smile on her face, walked up to them, stuck out her hand and grimly extended her empathic sense. "Hello again," she said, offering her hand to Oshansky first.

He took it briefly, squeezed rudely hard, and pulled away. Lorraine caught a sullen anger, fueled by an almost knee-jerk resentment, and under that an unmistakable greed. She couldn't tell just what he was greedy for—money, local power, or something more exotic—nor whether he was the mutant or not.

She turned to Harding, who gave her a perfunctory grip and no more. His hand was cold, and so was he: coldly calculating, analyzing, shuffling files in his head—and under that lay the patient hunger of a hunting beast: not the stereotypical J. Edgar Hoover bulldog nor the trademark bloodhound, but a coolly practical wolf tracking its prey.

There wasn't enough contact to tell her if he was Elven-kind.

Weber came last, taking her hand eagerly. He was warmly delighted to see her, to close a trap, finish a hunt; he was as hungry after his prey as Harding was—but again, she couldn't tell precisely what prey he meant, or if he was a mutant or not.

It could be any of them.

"And you are?" Harding asked, peering at Ben.

"Adam Benjamin," Ben replied in practiced lawyerish tones. "I'm Ms… Defarge's attorney."

"What do you need one for?" Oshansky demanded. "This is just a lineup."

"Maybe not a bad idea," Weber shrugged.

"Irrelevant. Ms. Defarge," Harding intoned, "You must realize you violated the terms of the Witness Protection Program by refusing to accept the Bureau's transportation."

So he knows that already, Lorraine considered. *But then, the Tucson office would have reported that I was coming.* "I found the Tucson office to be too careless for my tastes," she said frostily. "Frankly, it was safer to make my own way here anonymously. And as you see, I arrived in one piece."

The other two looked at Harding, Weber amused, Oshansky sneering. Harding ignored them both. "Let's get on with the procedure then," he said coldly, and turned toward the nearest door. "This way."

All three of them followed Lorraine and Ben into the small dim-lit room with the glass window along the wall. A dialless telephone hung on the wall, and Harding made a point of taking possession of it. "Bring them in," he said tonelessly into the speaker.

Lorraine moved to the window and peered through to the room beyond, which was featureless except for the overhead neon lighting, the numbers one through five painted on the floor and wall, and a door at the far end. As she watched, two uniformed police entered, both wearing headphones; they flanked a line of five men—all dressed in casual pants and shirts and jackets, all roughly the same height and build and coloring—and herded them to stand behind the painted numbers.

None of them was dark-blond, like the man she'd seen that day. They all had dark hair, and two of them showed paler patches of skin on their lips and cheeks, as if they'd recently shaved off beards and moustaches. All of them had slight tans.

Lorraine bit back a complaint about none of them matching her description, and looked closer. Certainly an experienced hitman, either going out to a job or returning from one, would do everything easily available to change his looks; grow a moustache or shave one off, dye his hair, use different clothes, possibly put in colored contact-lenses.

What could a man not change, given a few days? She studied

the anonymous men one by one, conjuring up the memory of that brief glimpse in the union office.

"Take your time," she heard Weber say, as if he'd read her thought.

Number One, she decided, was out; his chin was too pointed, and the angle of his eyebrows was wrong. Number Two was possible, but she couldn't say just yet. Number Three was likewise out; forehead too high, face too short from eyes to jaw. Number Four… No, the cheeks and ears were wrong; those cheeks were wide with fat, not the width of facial bones. Number Five…he was possible too, very similar. Maybe…

"Tell Number Two to step forward and turn sideways," she said. "Then have him turn his head and look at the window."

Harding relayed the request through the phone. Number Two hesitated a moment, then stepped forward and moved as he was bid.

No, there was something wrong with his walk—too rolling, steps too short—and the curve of forehead, eye and cheekbone was subtly different.

It wasn't him. That left only one. But then, perhaps none of them was the right man…

"Now Number Five, the same," she said.

Number Five also hesitated, but for half a second longer. He shuffled into place and looked, almost coyly, over his shoulder. His expression was almost childishly bewildered, as if trying to say: "You don't mean me, do you?"

And it was faked.

That line of eye and cheek fell into place with her memory, like a gear engaging, and Lorraine only wondered that she hadn't seen it before.

"That's him," she said, looking the three officers up and down. "That's definitely the man I saw in the office that day."

"You're sure?" Weber and Oshansky said together.

"Positive. He could dye his hair, stain his skin, even put in colored contact lenses — but he couldn't hide the shape of his eyes. That's the man I saw walk out of Jack Palumbo's office, just a few seconds after the shot broke the window. That's him."

Weber sighed in satisfaction. "Then that's it," he said. "Bind him over for trial."

Oshansky nodded once, frowning.

Harding only turned back to the phone and ordered: "Take the prisoner back to his cell, and dismiss the rest."

"Now," said Benjamin, stepping forward, "Since you'll have no further need of my client until the trial, please show us immediately to the exit nearest the parking-lot."

Weber looked surprised. Harding raised an eyebrow. "We should have her sign a statement," Oshansky rumbled.

"That is quite unnecessary, under Illinois law and procedure," snapped Ben, tapping his briefcase. "Any further papers can, I'm sure, be delivered by Ms. Defarge's contact at the FBI. Now, unless you *want* that man's business associates to eliminate Ms. Defarge as a witness, I *strongly* suggest that you show us to that rear exit. Right now."

It was Oshansky who moved toward the door, muttering "this way", beating out the other two. Lorraine and Ben hurriedly fell into place behind him, with Weber and Harding following. Out in the hallway again, Weber fell back a few paces. Oshansky plodded ahead, and Harding made effort to move closer to Lorraine.

"Ms. Defarge," Harding insisted, "You have seriously imperiled your standing in the program. If you wish to continue your status, you must remain in closer contact with your assigned agent and give her accurate and timely information."

"No problem," Lorraine lied cheerfully. "I'll call her as soon as I get back to Tucson."

Ahead of them, Oshansky pushed open a door. Gray Chicago sunlight fell though it, and the parking lot appeared beyond.

"Thank you," said Ben, taking Lorraine's arm and steering her toward the doorway, almost trampling Oshansky, who lurched sideways to avoid him. A fast glance showed where the jeep waited. Wally spotted them, and promptly started the engine.

Ben didn't precisely run, but he walked fast enough that Lorraine had to trot to keep up with him She was acutely aware of the suspect three at the door behind her.

"Three of them," Lorraine whispered fiercely. "Two against one. He doesn't dare try anything…"

"Get in fast," was all Benjamin said, as he pushed her around the front of the jeep to the passenger side.

Wally already had the doors open, and they scrambled in quickly.

"Back out," Ben snapped, slamming his door. "Don't let them see the license plate if you can help it."

Back at the doorway, all three cops were still watching.

"Can do," muttered Wally, shifting the jeep into reverse. He glanced around the lot, saw a police car pulling in, and smiled. He pressed the pedal, and pulled the jeep backward across the lot, clear out of the path of the oncoming cruiser. He reached out the window and waved 'go on' to the police car, then shifted to forward gear, and turned. He pulled past the slow-moving cruiser just as it approached the empty space, letting the car block his rear plate from the watchers' view, then drew close behind the line of parked cars and accelerated. "Done," he announced. "They never got a clear sight."

"Straight to the highway," said Ben, peering in the rearview mirror. "And not the way we came."

"West, then south," Wally promised. "The long way, but there's no rush now."

***

They went west as far as Nebraska before turning south again, and this time there was no question about spending the night in a motel. Ben, now lacking the moustache, got them two rooms in a rundown inn at the edge of a truck-stop, and moved Lorraine and all the gear into one of them. Wally trotted off to the attached restaurant, and returned shortly with forgettable sandwiches and a six-pack of good beer. The three of them piled into the first room, leaving the television on in the second. Wally took one of the beds and the TV remote, Lorraine and Ben curled up on the other, and the three of them wordlessly ate and drank and watched the ten o'clock news.

Lorraine scarcely noticed her surroundings, turning the known facts over and over in her mind. *The Tucson stalker got the address of Steven's bolt-hole…from his truck license-plate number, or from my telling Berringer.* All three of her suspects were police, and any of them could have done it.

The FBI agent was the obvious choice—he'd simply have Berringer report to him — but perhaps too obvious. All three suspects lived and worked in Chicago, but any of them could have taken time off, followed her by car to Tucson, found the safehouse and waited for her there—and just missed her because she'd gone job-hunting on a Saturday, which no Chicagoan would have imagined. He would have seen Berringer, if he hadn't known already that she was Lorraine's contact, and followed her to pick up the trail again. He hadn't expected Lorraine to be Initiated already, and had come too close—letting her pick up his aura—in Tucson…

Or, seeing her with Benjamin, had he thought it was Ben's energy-field he felt?

He might have thought Ben was Steven, the owner of the truck; he need only have caught the license-number as they pulled away, and then traced the truck to the apartment's address.

If the break-in at Steven's apartment had anything at all to do with this.

In any case, he had to have been in Tucson that one day. If only she had access to their work records, could see which one hadn't been at work then…but she might as well ask for the moon. Any one of them could afford to take a day off work, or pay for a round-trip plane ticket, or for transportation in the city— especially with a little help from the Mob.

Which one? Which one?

Harding was FBI, and needn't have followed Berringer to know where Lorraine was going. Come to think of it, why had Berringer been in Chicago the week before, if she was attached to the Tucson office? Why had Berringer slipped and called her by her right name? Just carelessness? Who did she report to? No one got to be regional director in the FBI without having their past investigated to a fare-thee-well, which should have turned up any hint of Mafia connections—let alone a faked childhood and an unusually long lifespan—but Harding was still a good possibility.

If Harding was the mutant, and had recognized Lorraine for a pre-Initiate, he would certainly have wanted to keep an eye on her. But was he the Mafia's man, too?

Would he want to Initiate her himself, then kill her for her power, thus satisfying the Mafia and himself? If he had nothing to do with the Mafia, would he want to Initiate her, make her his student, and swear her in on the side of Law And Order? Or would he simply want her power?

She didn't want to suspect Weber; he was the only one of the lot who'd been decent to her. Then again, a few centuries' practice could make a good enough actor out of anyone. He surely must have been trained in the classic Good Cop/Bad Cop game, the Mutt'n'Jeff Routine, the Sweet and Sour Pork Act. If he were the mutant, recognizing what she was, what better way to keep close to her than to play the sympathetic Good Cop? And hadn't it worked? Hadn't she gone out of her way to contact him?

He could have followed her to Tucson; it wasn't impossible for a state-cop to take a day or two off work to go to another state. As for catching up to her in Tucson, once she'd slipped the trap at the apartment, he would have seen Berringer on the trip and could easily have followed her to the meeting at the restaurant. He could have flown home to Chicago the next day, and continued his planning long-distance, or could have stayed to check Steven's apartment. He too might be Mafia-connected, or have nothing to do with them. Either way he could have motive for killing her. If Weber was Mafia-connected, it would explain why he knew facts about the hit-man's case before Berringer did. He'd said that it was his department that had put out the multi-state bulletin on the hit-man's description, but that could have been a lie. To what purpose? To make her distrust her FBI contact, for one: the Sweet and Sour Pork Act, played with greater subtlety.

But then, why had he wanted her to come to Chicago so quickly—even before Berringer told her about the suspect? Was it, again, to make her do just as she'd done—distrust Berringer, refuse FBI transport and make her own way to Chicago? What would have happened if she'd trusted him enough to tell him her exact plans for getting there, say, asked him to meet her at the airport, train or bus station? If he was on the Mafia's payroll, that would have been the end of her.

It would be a similar case with Oshansky, and he was more likely to have Mafia contacts. He was also unlikely to know his way around Tucson, and would have had to follow Berringer closely. It might have been harder for him to take a day off—let alone several—but not impossible. Whether he was Mafia connected or not, she didn't think—from the impression she'd gotten through the handshake—that he wanted her for a student, or a witness.

As for how all three of them had managed to appear at the police station at the same time, Weber would have had to inform the local police to arrange the lineup, and that meant informing Oshansky. If Harding had been keeping a close eye on the suspect, he would have been notified of the lineup too. No mystery there.

And there was always the chance that none of them were on the Mafia's payroll, that it was a Mafia goon who had followed her to Tucson and waited for her in the 'safe' apartment, and who got into Steven's place. She might have two enemies, rather than one. They might be working together, or at cross-purposes, or in total ignorance of each other.

Lorraine sighed, pulled a pen out of her purse and looked around for some paper; she'd have to write all this down just to keep track of the possible patterns. She noticed, to her surprise, that Wally had left without her noticing.

"What are you looking for?" Ben asked, setting down his beer.

"Paper. To outline suspects."

"Try my briefcase. It really does contain a legal pad."

Lorraine did as he'd suggested, came back with the pad and began sketching a graph of possibilities for each suspect. Ben turned off the distantly-yattering television and pulled up beside her to watch.

"…'Berringer'?" he asked. "Who's that?"

"My 'Aunt Dianne'," Lorraine growled. "She's either reporting to a Mafia-connected cop, or incompetent. Yes, she's my FBI contact in the Witness Protection Program."

"'Never attribute to malice what can be adequately explained by stupidity'," Ben quoted. "You're certain that one of those three was our mysterious man in Tucson?"

"Positive. I can tell by feel…" She raised her head, struck by an odd thought. "You mean, you can't?"

Ben leaned back on the bed, looking distant. "A few," he said, "People I know well, not strangers who happened to brush by. I don't have your sensitivity, Lorraine. My only real talent is surviving."

"And learning, and teaching," Lorraine added firmly, surprised that he could think so little of himself.

"That's part of survival." He smiled. "So your name really is Roxanne Defarge?"

"Not anymore," Lorraine heard herself say, and then realized that it was true.

"Just as well," said Ben, resting an understanding hand on her knee. "I like Lorraine Farrier better. Roxanne was the name of the wife of Alexander the Great, and she was a nasty little piece of goods. Defarge was the name of one of the villains in *A Tale of Two Cities*."

"And DeFargo was the name of the victim in the legend of the Wendigo," Lorraine added.

"You, Lorraine, are nobody's victim." Ben's grip tightened reassuringly.

"But one of these three is trying to make me one," Lorraine snarled, tapping the outline with her pen. "You know they won't stop. There's still the trial to get through, and even after that the Mafia thugs might try to make an example of me. If they fail, there's still our Elf-in-blue. Even if he's not on the Mafia payroll, he's more likely to be a hunter than a friend."

"Forewarned is forearmed…" Ben rattled his fingers on her knee. "As a student, you have experienced protectors; one of us will take care of him. When he either disappears, or his body is found in more than one piece, I think even the Mafia will cut their losses and give up."

Lorraine shoved the pen and pad aside and lay down beside him. "The hell of it is, he can use the law and the cops to come after us. What better job for an Unseelie hunter than among the bullies-in-blue? What better way to hunt than under color of authority?"

"Even kings aren't omnipotent." Ben slid his arm around her shoulders. "Simply to protect himself, a headhunter must get you alone. Our kind must kill each other in secrecy, and that's your persecutor's weakness. There are ways to fight him, and between the lot of us we have considerable resources for combat."

"I can't wait to get home," Lorraine sighed, "But I'm afraid of bringing this after me."

"We'll manage," Benjamin insisted. "Now go wash up and get ready for bed. We want an early start, which means getting to sleep early, which means gearing yourself down out of combat-mode. Make it a long, hot, leisurely bath. And if that isn't enough, I brought some whiskey in a hip-flask."

Lorraine couldn't help laughing at that. "The perfect lawyer-disguise! You were wonderfully convincing. Hmmm, it was Oshansky who wanted to hold us there…"

"Bath, Lorraine," Ben ordered sternly. "You shift gears; I'll do the worrying for a change."

"I'm going, I'm going," Lorraine promised, sliding off the bed. "I'll bet this place doesn't provide bathrobes, or large towels…"

Benjamin waited until she closed the bathroom door and turned on the water, then picked up her forgotten cell-phone and dialed Brian's number. He had a lot to report.

***

Lorraine lay in the water until her fingertips wrinkled, but the hot bath didn't have the desired effect. She was no longer tense and wary, no, but neither was she relaxed or sleepy. A deep, sullen irritability flared through her, and now she understood what it was; her rage had returned, with a vengeance. She wanted to rip out the hit-man's throat, but that was the least of it. She wanted to catch all three of her suspects—Harding, Weber and

Oshansky—in her rifle-sights, one after the other. She kept think-ing of ingenious ways to kill them, using their own greed to bait them.

I want to kill someone, she thought, unsurprised. She felt no guilt at the thought. A hit-man, a Mafia spy, a headhunter: they were threats to herself and her adoptive family, and deserved little else.

Have I lost all sense of ethics? Lorraine wondered as she climbed out of the tub and reached for a towel. After a moment's thought she decided that no, she hadn't; she badly wanted to know which of the Big Three was truly the headhunter. Yes, she would leave the innocent alone. It was only the guilty that she itched to destroy.

Lorraine wrapped herself in the towel, gathered up her rum-pled clothes and strode out into the bedroom.

The next day's clean clothes were laid out on a chair and on the small bureau, and the duffel bag sat nearby. The bed had been peeled open and Ben lay in it, half-sitting against the head-board, obviously naked under the sheet. He had turned the TV back on, and to judge from the sound effects, he was watching some sort of horror-movie.

Her pistol lay on the nightstand, and his sword beside the bed.

Lorraine shoved her laundry into her suitcase, a little more roughly than necessary, and climbed onto the bed. Benjamin turned a watchful gaze on her.

"Not relaxed?" he asked casually.

"Not tense, but I want to kill someone," she said, settling down beside him.

"I understand completely." His smile was tight and bitter. "There's an almost ecstatic relief in permanently getting rid of a bastard who's trying to kill you."

"Yes." Lorraine shuddered and felt her teeth rattle briefly, not in fear but in acceptance of a grim truth. "Unseelie hunter, or Mafia, or both—I want him gone. I keep thinking of ways to get him, once I know exactly who…"

Ben sighed, and rolled out of bed. "My turn for the bathtub," he said. "Try watching the monster-movie—and cheering for the bad guy."

He strolled, unselfconsciously naked, off to the bathroom. Lor-raine watched him go, admiring the play of muscles in his small firm buttocks, then turned her gaze to the television screen.

Ah yes, the usual teen-exploitation film: there were the typical wisecracking but otherwise brainless teens running around screaming, and there was the unseen monster picking them off in gory but ingenious ways. *Why,* she wondered, *Does it always take them so long to realize they're being hunted? Why do they never pick up a gun, or a bow, or an axe, get everybody into a good defensive position and stay there?* Yes, the supposed good guys in these movies were so irritatingly stupid that she really did feel like cheering for the bad guy. *Go, monster, go! Whack that squally bimbo! Chop that macho idiot! ...Oh, that was imaginative...*

By the time that Benjamin came out of the bathroom, the victims were down to the standard core group: the token Black, the token Latino, the token Oriental, the hero and the heroine. That meant there was probably half an hour of mayhem to go.

"Which one do you think will get whacked next?" Ben asked, sliding under the covers. "I'll bet on the cute Chinese girl."

"Why her?" asked Lorraine. "I would have guessed the Latino boy."

"Smallest percentage in the general population," said Ben, reaching for the flask on the nightstand. "Therefore smallest percentage of voters, taxpayers and buyers: smallest losses if they get annoyed because their Identification Character loses out." He took a hearty swig, and then handed the flask to Lorraine. "Why would you bet on the Latino?"

Lorraine took a solid mouthful before replying. The taste was sharp, but there was no bite as it went down. "Character," she said, returning the flask. "He's mouthy, pushy and arrogant: the kind of bully you'd love to smack."

"I'd bet on him next." Benjamin took another gulp from the flask. "Ah, here comes a kill-scene."

They watched, passing the whiskey back and forth, while the screaming teens ran aimlessly through the Abandoned Mansion until the Token Oriental wound up artfully impaled on a meat hook.

"You win this round," said Lorraine, squeezing his thigh.

Ben laughed, showing teeth—and for an instant Lorraine could truly imagine him as a barbarian warlord. "But your Latino kid's next," he grinned wolfishly, and took another gulp.

"I hope it's gory," said Lorraine, and took the flask from his hand. The whiskey might as well have been water for all the effect it had. She wiped her mouth and handed it back. "Now they're going to scream and dither and emote for awhile, instead of planning something intelligent."

"Why do they never think to leave the house?" Ben wondered. "They could simply run down the road and keep going, but no, they stay right there with the deranged killer. Brilliant."

"And they never think of fighting intelligently." Lorraine sipped thoughtfully, pulled off her towel and snuggled closer. "Maybe it's a class thing: the middle-class attitude of never dirtying your hands with vi-o-lence, so you never learn how to do it well."

"How very modern," said Ben, taking the flask. "In earlier ages, the richer you were the more fighting-skills you learned—the better to keep the peasants in line. Oh, here we go again."

More running, more screams, more senseless struggles, and—sure enough—the Latino boy fell three stories onto an open piano, and was cut to pieces by the piano-wires.

Ben and Lorraine burst out laughing.

"Egg-slicer!" Lorraine howled. "For a hard-boiled egg!"

"An ad for Steinway," Ben nearly choked. "Built to take anything!" His hand slid heavily up and down her thigh.

The surviving three teens shrieked and dithered and ran some more.

"Down to three," said Ben, handing over the whiskey. "Black guy, white guy, white girl. Forty years ago, there'd be no question; the black kid would die next, the white kid would defeat the villain in personal combat and win the girl. But the formula's changed since then, and it's anyone's guess who'll survive. How do you bet?"

"I've seen a few films where the black guy is the last man standing, but usually the girl survives too. I'll bet on the girl surviving alone."

"In any case, I'll bet the white boy dies next."

"Damn, the flask's empty." Lorraine set it regretfully on the nightstand. "Oh, what are they doing now, stopping to argue in the middle of combat?! Idiots! Come on, monster: kill them both! They deserve it!"

"Kill!" Ben agreed, pounding his fist on her hip. "Kill! Kill!"

Lorraine couldn't have told why she did it, but she grabbed Benjamin and bit his shoulder.

He gasped, seized her buttocks and pulled her hard against him.

Lorraine scrambled on top of him, feeling his erection jab into her belly, and clawed at his flanks. He growled and yanked her forward, trying to fit into her.

Enflamed, she spread her thighs wide and pinned his hips still while she maneuvered her vulva into place—up the shaft, over the tip, there! He lunged under her, thrusting furiously upward, fingers digging into her buttocks. Lorraine snarled and pressed down on him as hard as he drove up into her, wanting to take it all, right now, all the way in. A nameless hot ravenous pressure was surging inside her, and she thought it would burst her open if she didn't hammer it down to there, there. Benjamin howled and thrust and clawed at her back. They slammed and pounded together, losing track of time in the sound of flesh slapping fiercely on flesh and their own animal growls against a background of crashing and screams.

On the screen, blood spattered and flames roared as the hapless teens finally met the axe-wielding Maniac of the Mansion, casting a leaping red light over the madly wrestling bodies on the bed. Screams and roaring blended with hoarse shouts of savage victory, of rage and need satisfied.

***

Some measureless time later, Lorraine summoned the strength to turn her head a little, rest her cheek on Benjamin's slowly heaving chest, and roll her eyes to the flickering screen. Yes, against the background of the burning Monster Mansion, the girl—alone—stumbled blindly across the lawn, sobbing hysterically.

Silly twit, Lorraine thought drowsily. The girl should be facing the flames, dancing and laughing with joy that her enemy was dead. *Won my bet, anyway…*

Her eye caught on something red that stayed, didn't flicker. It was a streak of blood across Benjamin's ribs. A parallel streak lay a little lower, and another below that.

Claw-marks, she realized: surely healed by now, but the blood was still there. *Did I do that?!*

Fragments of memory told her that indeed she had. A glance further showed similar thin lines of blood on her visible thigh. She didn't remember getting them.

Beneath her, Benjamin pulled a long deep breath and let it out in a sigh that was closer to a groan of exhaustion. "*Pardeo,*" he whispered. "…haven't…done that…decades…"

"…not alone…" Lorraine panted.

Ben slid a slow and strengthless hand down, searching for the blankets.

Understanding, Lorraine made the prodigious effort of slipping off him, finding the edge of the sheet and tugging it upward, over both of them. The blanket dragged along with it, and so did the television-remote. Lorraine took it, managed to find the power-button, and turned off the set. Silence descended peacefully. Lorraine dropped the remote on the floor and helped Ben pull the blankets up to their chins. He dropped a weary arm around her, turned his head to yawn cavernously, then fell into stillness and sleep within seconds.

Lorraine followed his lead, but slower. Too stunned and exhausted to think, she was nonetheless quietly amazed at herself: first for what she'd just done, and second that she felt no guilt whatever over it.

It seemed a perfectly fitting end to a day that had begun in a war-zone.

19.

EVER AFTERWARD, Lorraine looked back on the next two weeks as a time of peace between storms. She and Wally and Ben returned to Tucson the next morning, and slipped smoothly back into the house's comforting routines. Lorraine gladly resumed her schedule and worked meticulously on the painting of Overcast—warmed by the addition of Benjamin's presence and her continuing tasks.

On the next Monday morning Helen, riding the gray mare, packed their saddlebags full of small potted plants and accompanied Lorraine and Ben out to the node.

There they spent the next hour charging some of the plants with the node's energy, leaving an equal number to absorb it passively, taking careful pictures and measurements and notes, and then carrying certain samples back to the ranch. Helen and Benjamin swapped stories of ancient fertility goddesses and sacred trees with a familiarity that suggested they'd seen such things themselves, and Lorraine pestered them for details. In the afternoon session Lorraine tried charging certain plants at the ranch with only the energy she could draw from herself, or from other plants, while Helen and Benjamin watched and took more notes.

By Friday there were noticeable differences in the growth of the plants, with the ones Lorraine actively charged at the node outstripping all the rest.

The plants she'd drawn from, at the ranch, withered and died within two days.

After that, Lorraine firmly refused to blight any more plants—and absolutely rejected Helen's suggestion of experimenting with mice.

On Tuesday Benjamin took her out into the desert, along with a device for tossing clay target-discs, and had her practice with the shotgun. By the end of the hour she could hit two targets out of three at 100 yards, and Benjamin promised she would stay at that distance until she could hit every target. He also noted that her sword-practice was improving by leaps and bounds. Lorraine had always warmed at Benjamin's honest praise of her skills, but now she found that the warmth went much deeper—and warned herself sternly not to fall into the trap of wanting nothing but to please her man; that way lay disaster, she knew.

In the late afternoons, she painted. Cautiously at first, then with more confidence, she filled in the basic drawing on the canvas board, starting with dark background color and working toward light. The towel-robe she generally wore grew steadily more paint-stained, but Madge didn't grumble.

The after-dinner counseling sessions turned into classes on investment strategies, establishment of front-companies, creation of false ID documents and similar tactics for living a hidden life. Lorraine listened carefully, and took thorough notes.

And in the nights, there was Benjamin.

Even at love, he enjoyed teaching. He showed her caresses and games that surprised as much as delighted her; she would never have thought that her toes were erogenous zones, or that having her hair brushed could be exciting, and it was astonishing what could be done with scarves. She found Treemark's booklet on nerve-points wonderfully helpful, and Benjamin was more than willing to experiment with the information. The wide bed became a world of its own where they explored and played to sweet exhaustion.

On Friday evening they retired to her room early and had dinner delivered; neither of them wanted to join the weekend's formal play-acting. Lorraine dared to ask what sort of theatrics went on there, and Ben only looked thoughtful as he answered.

"Emotionally intense little scenes." He spread his hands expressively. "Some very private, done in the guest-rooms, some acted out before the whole company, varying from very simple to quite elaborate. One that I saw, once, taken from the headlines— about a woman who killed her children to please a would-be lover—rapidly turned into a re-enactment of the legend of La Llorona. As it happened, I knew that the woman acting the central role was having problems with her own children at the time. She became much more patient with them afterwards, but eventually wound up divorcing her husband."

"Because she acted out killing them—and regretting it!" Lorraine shivered. "Yes, I suppose that would work."

"Brian's methods are a bit extreme," he explained, "But I must admit that they're very effective. He's had a lot of practice, after all."

"If only more of us were healers," Lorraine murmured, pillowing her head on his chest. "There's so much we could do…"

"To make the world a better place?" He smiled sadly. "Some of us try. We do make a bit of progress here and there… And then along comes some disaster or war or dictator, and knocks everything to ruins. Germany in 1933 was one of the most progressive and enlightened countries in the world, and just five years later…" He looked away. "Constantinople in 1340 was the world's center of trade, knowledge, wealth—and then the Black Plague came. I look out at our busy little modern world, and find myself wondering when the axe will fall…and from what direction."

"Pessimist," Lorraine smiled, circling his navel with a light finger. "Remember that in all those disasters there were plenty of people who survived, and progress went right on progressing. I suspect that our people had a hand in that."

"Hands on both sides," Benjamin murmured, sliding his fingers down her back, "Some of us have been vicious conquerors, and tyrants, and everything else."

"Organize, as the old union says." Lorraine paused to plant a kiss on his near nipple, making him twitch. "Build the Seelie Court, become a unified force for good in the world."

"Define good," Benjamin frowned, his gaze growing distracted and distant. "Define evil."

"Easily done," Lorraine smiled, "From a practical working-class viewpoint. 'Good' is whatever makes people healthy, wealthy, wise, happy, creative, free—and alive. 'Evil' is whatever makes people sickly, poor, stupid, miserable, dull, enslaved—and dead."

Benjamin raised an eyebrow and thought long about that. "Damn, but that works!" he marveled. Then he laughed, and rolled over and kissed Lorraine between the eyes. "Woman, you give me hope," he whispered, "And that in itself is a miracle too big for words."

Then he kissed her firmly on the mouth, and after that there were no more words for a long time.

They spent the rest of the weekend in the stable, out riding in the desert, or in bed.

The only annoyance was a pestering phonecall from Berringer, nervously asking Lorraine if she was well, if she had any letters to send, and pleading again for her to "keep in touch".

"Speaking of that," said Lorraine, unconsciously baring her teeth, "Tell me, Aunt Dianne: why were you in Chicago in the first place?"

"…Chicago?" Berringer sounded slightly poleaxed. "I was there last…why, when I picked you up, to bring you here."

"Yes, but why were you so conveniently there that day?" Lorraine couldn't help adding: "With all that's happened, you must admit that looks suspicious."

"Nothing of the sort!" Berringer huffed. "I'd just delivered another witness—on a tax-evasion case—and I was filling out the papers when the local director asked me to take you back with me. There's nothing suspicious about it, Lorraine! Really."

"Mhm…" *Probably true. "Never attribute to malice…"* Lorraine promised to call again soon, and hung up as quickly as she could.

***

Two days later, while riding back from the node, Lorraine and Benjamin and Helen simultaneously felt the edge of another mutant's field.

"It's him!" snapped Lorraine, recognizing that aura. She reined in Leila and tried to pinpoint the intruder's direction and distance.

Helen and Ben exchanged looks, but kept riding. "Keep up with us, Lorraine," Helen said, just loud enough to be heard at the distance. "The less he knows about who can sense him and who can't, the better for all of us."

Lorraine saw the sense of that, and heeled Leila forward. The hunter's aura promptly faded; he had backed out of range, somewhere in the direction of the road.

"How in hell did he find me?" she snarled. "Did he trace Steven?" She couldn't imagine how that could have happened; Steven had been careful not to use the same truck, the few times he left the ranch.

"Good question," Ben considered. "We'd best discuss it with Brian." He gave no signal that Lorraine could see, but Overcast picked up his pace.

As they rode into the stableyard another thought occurred to Lorraine. *Berringer. All those warnings about cell-phones…* Oshansky, Harding or Weber: any of them could have gotten their hands on the sophisticated equipment needed to track a call from, or to, a cell-phone — especially with the help of a little Mafia money. Any of them could have obtained Berringer's office-phone number. After that, all the hunter had to do was wait until Aunt Dianne called Lorraine again.

The hunter had narrowed down his search to the ranch.

That thought kept Lorraine distracted and brooding for the rest of the day, and Treemark noticed. At the after-dinner counseling session, his very first question was: "Do you want the hunter driven away?"

"No," Lorraine smiled humorlessly. "Lure the bastard here. I want him dead."

"How badly?" Treemark asked, leaning forward. "And why?"

"A lot. He's a threat to me and mine, and if I let him just walk away, God knows when he'll come back at me—or any of you—and try again." Lorraine took a leisurely sip of the scotch. "I strongly suspect he's connected to the Mafia hoods who killed Jack Palumbo and took shots at Bill and Wendy, but in any case, he's after me—and possibly Steven, and maybe the rest of us too. I want him dead, plain and simple."

Treemark smiled understandingly. "Did you ever believe in the idea that vengeance is wrong?"

"Hell, no." Lorraine set her glass down. "I saw, at an early age, that people who preach against revenge are the front-men for—or are themselves—people who abuse others and get away with it. Mama Dear used to mouth that platitude: 'revenge isn't justice'. Well, I've seen for myself that law isn't justice either. At best, law is only the public means of trying to get justice; revenge is the private means. When the public means fail, the private means are all that's left."

"Mhm." Treemark tapped his fingers on the desk. "And you don't think much of…the public means?"

"Not even before Chicago," Lorraine laughed. "I once read through the Bible from cover to cover, and I came across a line that said there was no king in Judea for awhile, and 'every man did what seemed right in his own eyes'. I asked myself: what was so bad about that? It couldn't be worse than every man doing what seemed right in the eyes of the nearest king, preacher, or other politician."

"So you don't think some people are more fit to rule than others?"

"Nobody's fit to rule!" Lorraine reached for her glass again. "If anything, people who actually get power are less fit than others."

"Why do you say that?"

"Because power corrupts." Lorraine took a long leisurely drink, noting how intently Treemark watched her. "Power corrupts," she repeated. "I've seen that myself. And anybody who wants power enough to chase after it is already corrupt."

"If every man does what seems right in his own eyes," said Treemark, otherwise not moving a muscle, "Then how do we get any social agreements, any society at all?"

Lorraine smiled, remembering how the union had done it. "Everybody concerned sits down and talks it over until we get a consensus—every time, every argument. Hell, I've seen better justice—and better politics—delivered that way at a union New Year's party than in your average election."

"And if you can't get consensus? Then what?"

"Then you fall back on majority rule. If the minority can't put up with it, let them quit and go found another society elsewhere. Maybe they'll succeed. Who knows? They might be right after all." She took another sip, which emptied the glass.

"And what if…what the minority decides to do is dangerous to the majority? Or vice-versa?"

Lorraine remembered the time the union had damn near split itself in the argument over whether or not to help the Teamster reformers. "You wait to see if it really is dangerous, and if it is, then I don't see that you have any choice but to fight." She shrugged, remembering. "It usually won't come to that, though. Most people have too much respect for the integrity of their own hides to risk it."

Treemark drew a deep breath and leaned back in his chair. Lorraine wondered why he looked so relieved, or why he muttered to himself something that sounded like "queen of Elfland"

"I may as well tell you the rest of it now," he spoke up. "You must understand that, technically, all of us are criminals by mortal law."

Lorraine raised an eyebrow. "How do you mean?" she asked.

"First, we have to hide what we are from mortals—"

"Obviously."

"—and plenty of governments would consider that a crime in itself."

"Oh, of course!" Lorraine guessed. "How dare we hide hard-to-kill soldiers from El Supremo's army recruiters? Heh! …Besides, governments always want to know everything about everybody, and they call it a crime if you don't tell them. And that's not to mention creating fortunes for ourselves, under several different names, so no government can tax it all."

"Precisely." Treemark shrugged. "It's impossible for us to be 100% law-abiding, even if we want to."

"Besides," Lorraine considered, "If you live long enough, you'll see laws and governments and whole societies come and go. That would tend to make you…not think much of mortal law."

"And we don't have a cohesive enough society to make any

law for ourselves," Treemark finished the thought. "All we have are a few legends and a few customs, and nothing really to enforce them. Each of us does, in fact, do what seems good in our own eyes. Do you see the problem?"

Lorraine saw it, but she could also see the answer. "Consensus," she repeated. "We have to be able to talk to each other. In ancient times we could have used messengers, or letters. Nowadays we can use everything from couriers to the Internet. We can talk from a safe distance. Talk is safe, and God knows we have the time to discuss and argue until we get consensus."

"Or at least a majority decision." Treemark smiled widely, showing most of his teeth. "Helen has been trying something like that."

Lorraine laughed as a sudden vision blossomed. "Elf-band Ham radio, CB frequencies, computer forums and chat-rooms! I don't think any place in the world is out of reach of the phone system, and Ham radio can reach anywhere."

Treemark caught the vision, and laughed too. "Even the most paranoid of us can accept that, I think. Oh, the wonders of modern technology! Gods, yes, it's possible."

"I'll do my share," Lorraine promised. That reminded her of something else. "By the way, I've finished the painting. Would you like to see it?"

"Certainly. …Now, you mean?"

"Yes. Besides, I'd best get my painting gear out of the solarium again, what with the weekend coming."

"Let's go, then." Treemark pushed back his chair.

The walk to the solarium was brief, allowing Lorraine no time for second thoughts. Not that she had any, she decided. Let Treemark say what he liked about her painting; she had to begin somewhere. Treemark followed her, saying nothing, pausing only to turn on the overhead lights before stepping into the solarium.

The revealed painting showed Overcast, standing in the pasture, tossing his head.

It was, Lorraine admitted happily, as realistic as a photograph.

"Excellent," Treemark beamed, studying it. "Your technique is flawless. I hope the book I gave you was a help."

"It was, at that," Lorraine agreed.

"Would you like me to broker it for you?"

"…What?"

"I have fairly extensive contacts in and around the city," Treemark smiled, "Including some in the art business. I can take this around to certain amenable galleries, if you like."

Lorraine gulped and thought fast. "Standard commission: ten percent," she rattled off. *He likes it? He can sell it for me?!* This opened a whole new realm of possibilities; if he could market her paintings, if she could become an established professional artist…

"I can do that," Treemark agreed, studying the painting. "First I'll want to take this and photograph it, and make at least one full-size print for myself."

"Good to know," said Lorraine, relieved. She tapped a cautious finger at the paint, found it acceptably dry, picked up the painting and handed it to him. "I'll get the rest of the gear," she promised, reaching for the easel.

By the time she'd folded the easel and picked up the paint-kit, Treemark had left.

She wondered if he had any framing material in his crafts workshop, and had gone to see if it would fit. In any case, she guessed, the evening's counseling session was over. She carried the painting gear back to her room.

Benjamin was there, waiting for her, with two cut-crystal glasses and a half-carafe of that lovely blackberry wine. He noted the load she carried, and helped set the folded easel in a safe corner. "The painting's finished?" he guessed.

"Yes, and Treemark liked it." Lorraine dropped onto the bed and bounced happily. "In fact, he offered to market it for me."

"Really?" Ben raised an appreciative eyebrow. "I'll have to go get a look at the finished product before he trots off to the galleries with it. That's quite high praise, you realize; Brian knows his art, and the art-market. He wouldn't have made the offer if he didn't think your work was good."

"Yes." Lorraine grinned from ear to ear. Yes, she knew her technique had improved greatly, thanks to that book; she knew her work was good enough for sale, somewhere on the commercial spectrum. She just hadn't known how good, how others would value it. "You know, the one thing I never lost faith in— despite Mama-Dear's best efforts—was my painting. I knew I could be good at it, if I just got the right training. …I suppose I have Treemark to thank for that, too."

"You couldn't have learned so much from one book unless you already had the talent," Ben agreed, pouring the glasses full. "Here's to your first sale. Cheers."

They clinked glasses and drank, and Lorraine wondered if this was a different wine or if the taste of success made it sweeter. Already she was thinking of the next painting: Leila, against a desert background. She'd have to take photos in the mid-morning to get the lighting just right…

"But how many portraits of horses can I sell?" she pondered. "That's a fairly limited market."

"Quite enough to keep you in pocket-change," Ben smiled. "Besides, if you can paint horses, you can paint other things."

"Horses in desert landscapes…" That would be the next logical step, with Leila's portrait. "Or horses with people: horse and rider portraits."

"Horses and riders and deserts?" Ben offered.

"Deserts—" Lorraine stopped, remembering. "The stalker's still out there."

Benjamin set his glass down, and ran a comforting hand up and down her arm. "Brian didn't ignore the warning, you know," he said. "He's sent for a contingent of security-guards, with dogs. They should be here Monday."

"Dogs, and guards, can be gotten around." Lorraine frowned, remembering old tales from Chicago. "What about house defenses?"

"I assure you, Brian has a superb detection system." Benjamin slid his hand up to her shoulder. "If the stalker comes anywhere near the house, we'll know it—and we'll deal with him. We've played this game before."

"I have too." Lorraine felt her eyes narrowing. "The union always had enemies."

"Ah, this will be a bit different." Ben sat up and pulled her close. "Remember, he's one of us, and we don't know how old, or how long he's been hunting."

"And he's a cop of some sort," Lorraine added. "He'll have firepower, and legal backing, and maybe Mafia help."

"We can handle that," Benjamin murmured into her hair. "During the Middle Ages, we survived small armies and bandit-gangs; cops and Mafia aren't much of a change. We can keep you safe, Lorraine."

Safe… She knew he meant it. She didn't have to be afraid… *But I'm not afraid. I'm angry. I don't want to run or hide; I want to fight.* "Just how helpless am I?" Lorraine asked, idly running a hand up and down his near thigh. "How useless would I be in a fight?"

"Not very," he said, kissing the top of her head, "Especially with the shotgun, but pistol will do. If you see him at all, I'd prefer that you drop him at a distance."

"And then what?"

"Let any of the rest of us deal with him." Ben looked away, his expression turning hard. "As your teachers, it's our right to take up challenges offered to you. Besides, I really don't think you want to take…that kind of power-surge, not yet."

"I'm not really interested in that experience." Lorraine considered another problem. "But I'd have to be present, to cover for the rest of you. Right now, I'm the only mutant he knows about; let him keep on thinking I'm the only one here—at least until you can get him where you want him."

"He'll know that you have a teacher."

"Hmmm, all right: let him know there's one other, but no more than that."

"And someone will have to stay near you at all times." Benjamin kissed her hair again. "I'm willing to volunteer for the duty."

Lorraine purred and rolled against him, marveling as always at how good he felt.

A twinge of tension pulled at her shoulders, but she knew that a word from her would have his wise hands massaging it away. It never ceased to amaze her how strong he was, and how well he concealed that under his lean build and constant gentleness. There were times when it took effort to get past that gentleness…

That thought made her wonder about her own ferocity, her reliable fury, and how far it would rise before this long campaign was over.

His hands pressed, ever so slightly, at her back. "Are you afraid?" he whispered.

That question again. "No, I'm furious," she considered, "My reliable rage is waiting—and I don't know how long it will wait. My feelings are so much stronger, now that I've…taken my armor off."

Ben's fingers circled thoughtfully on her shoulderblades as he pondered that. "Wait and see where it goes," he decided. "Your emotions aren't hidden anymore; they'll tell you readily enough what they want, when they want it."

Lorraine gave a long sigh of relief, and snuggled closer. "I'm just not used to trusting—" *That word again!* "—my feelings this much. My sense of perspective is skewed. It's like… When I was little, I broke my ankle…" *The one Georgie kept kicking. I walked on it without support while it was still weak.* "Papa put it in a walking cast to make certain it would heal straight, but the cast was godawfully heavy. I got used to walking almost normally, hauling that weight around for weeks. Then, when the cast came off, I couldn't walk properly for days. The muscles were so used to dragging the weight that when it was gone… At every step, my knee came up much too high. I pranced like a pony." *And never mind how Mama Dear laughed at that.* "Is this making any sense?"

"Oh yes," said Ben, rubbing his cheek against hers. "It should settle within a year, at most, probably much sooner. In any case, the problem isn't acknowledging your feelings but letting them run away with you—and I don't think that's your style."

"There's one emotion that does tend to carry me off," Lorraine admitted, wrapping her arms around his smooth waist, "But only when I'm with you."

"In that case…" Ben nipped her earlobe, making her yelp. "You have someone to help you chase after it."

"Yes," Lorraine sighed, tickled and relieved at once. She sat up and pulled off her robe, and tossed it into the nearby chair. "Let it run," she said. "For now, let it run."

Ben laughed, and pulled her down, and licked her neck.

***

Again, they spent the weekend with the horses, or at the node, or in bed. Sunday evening, when the ceremonies were over and the guests had departed, dinner was wonderfully quiet and relaxed. There was little conversation, except for Helen happily informing Treemark that she'd made progress contacting various other mutants; Benjamin recognized some of the names, and gave her an appreciative smile. That set Lorraine to wondering how Elven-kind approached each other, when they first met as strangers, if they wanted peace. Did they take care to meet in crowds, or on sacred ground? Was there any formal tradition to it?

That was the first question she asked Treemark when they got to the clinic office.

"Nothing but cautious practicality," he sighed. "Yes, stay in a crowd, then offer to arrange a meeting in a church or something like it. Helen has made quite an art of it; you could learn tactics from her."

"I will," Lorraine promised, and took a sip of her drink.

"Concerning your easily-summoned anger," Treemark

dropped the question on her, "Just how did that influence your decision to join your union and take up social-reform causes?"

Oh, of course Ben and Wally told him about Chicago… "Well…" Lorraine floundered for an answer. "I suppose I just don't like seeing people miserable. The sorrows and injustices of the world have always ticked me off, which is the main reason why I joined the union. Other people's misery isn't something I can ignore." *As Mama Dear so carefully did!* "It's like…like air pollution, poisoning the whole environment that I happen to live in. …I'm not explaining this very well."

"Actually, you are: 'No man is an island'."

"Peninsula is the farthest you can get," Lorraine grinned.

"I have to remember that one," Treemark laughed, then sobered. "Ah, by the way, I placed your painting in one of the local galleries."

"You did?" Lorraine marveled. "So quickly? …Er, was it well received?"

"Quite." Treemark interlaced his fingers. "It sold, for $450, within the day."

Lorraine felt her jaw drop, and hastily pulled it back up.

"I took the liberty of buying more canvas-boards," Treemark added dryly. "I hope you'll produce more paintings."

Lorraine only nodded dumbly, suspecting that there were social forces at work here that she didn't see. How many of Treemark's clients worked for art galleries, or art museums for that matter? How many of them had that kind of money to spend on a whim, or on a portrait of a horse? Had Treemark done a bit of advertising—or arm- twisting—to get that painting sold?

If so, then such artificial success wouldn't last. She could use it to establish a reputation for herself, but she'd have to expand that on her own merits. She'd have to paint something more than horses…

"Moving right along," said Treemark, pulling a paper out of the desk's top drawer, "This is an outline of the security-systems and the traps we've set in the house and grounds. The others have already seen it; memorize it thoroughly, stay close to at least one of us at all times, and I think we can catch our stalker without exposing you to any significant risk."

"Yes," said Lorraine, taking the paper. Yes, she'd study it, and with Ben's help. She wasn't sure whether or not she liked the idea of staying within the farm's defensive borders for an indefinite time, but the chance of finally catching the stalker made her feel a grim and raging eagerness. She had Helen's and Treemark's and Benjamin's assurance that she wasn't turning bloodthirsty, but still, this hunger for revenge amazed her.

I don't like ordering people around or dominating them, she considered, *But revenge is something else again.*

Given all she knew of Elven society, she could see no problem with an honest desire for vengeance.

When you have no government-made laws or church-made morals, she realized, *What's left to hold your society together? Nothing but custom, manners, common sense and…revenge.*

The hell of it was, she could see how to make a strong and viable society out of no more than that.

The whole problem of rulers turning into despots, legal structures inevitably being corrupted by power—it was all unnecessary. Rules and rulers never had been needed, not by Elvenkind—and not by mortals, either. Not needed: parasites at best…

An idea for another painting sprouted in her mind—a mood, an image: very personal, probably much too personal to appeal to the local art market—she shouldn't waste a whole canvasboard on it—but still something she needed to express. And there was a way…

A board has two sides. It's been done before…

She'd probably need Ben's help pulling pictures off the Internet to use for models, but the rest she could provide for herself; there was plenty of film left in the camera.

***

Helen was waiting, draped in an elegantly simple nightgown, when Treemark came to bed. He smiled at her as he pulled off his shirt, but the expression was fleeting and Helen wasn't fooled.

"So, what's the latest problem with Lorraine?" she asked, turning down the covers for him.

Treemark gave her a pained look as he toed off his shoes. "Not a problem so much as…well, a remarkable feature. I confess it's set me back on my heels."

"Her fury?" Helen guessed. "That's not at all irrational, with the hunter about."

"No, something else." He sat down and tugged at his socks. "I've learned that Lorraine is absolutely lacking in what Nietzsche called 'the will to power'. She has no interest whatever in enforcing her will on others, but lives—or wants to live—in a universe of equals, settling disputes by consensus whenever possible, and she resents whoever threatens that."

"So?" Helen smiled. "You'll have a warrior that will never become a tyrant. I should think you'd be pleased."

"Not just that." Treemark stretched out beside her and stared up at the ceiling. "Think, Helen: if we can ever collect our scattered sympathizers, create a coherent society, rebuild the Seelie Court, who better to rule it than someone who can never be corrupted by the temptations of power?"

Helen sat up and stared at him. "You're not just grooming her for a champion—" she whispered.

"Not just a champion," he concurred, "But a queen."

***

On Monday the guards arrived, with their dogs: tightly-trained Dobermans, so sleek they looked like machines more than animals. The men introduced the dogs to all the humans and animals on the property, set up the portable kennels and started patrolling the borders of the grounds. Lorraine ignored them, taking pictures of Leila.

By Tuesday, with a little help from Benjamin, she had all the photos she needed and had started on the final sketch. Wednesday she started the new painting.

20.

THERE WAS A DREAM of riding a pale-gray horse across rolling plains…

…*Not desert…* Lorraine noted sluggishly.

…and laughing with a fierce joy of freedom, ohhh, freedom! No one stood on the empty plain ahead, and no one was riding behind him…

…*Him?* The discrepancy was enough to pull Lorraine up to waking—up to awareness of Benjamin's arm draped across her and the *feel* of his dreaming mind.

I picked up his dream, she marveled. It was almost as clear as the waking image she'd caught that day, reaching for him, out at the node…

But I wasn't trying, wasn't even awake! she realized with a jolt of surprise. *And I'm not drawing on the node-power now.* That link of empathy had come without effort, without thought. Did this mean that her psychic sense was expanding without her realizing it? *…Or is it because we've been so close? Are we…attuned, because of love?*

That was something she'd never considered in her experiments and exercises, but it made such excellent sense. Her psychic sense was a product of both her body and mind; certainly it had to work through her emotions as well. Of course there would be a natural tendency to reach out toward anything, anyone, she liked…or loved.

And could it also mean that Benjamin might sense her feelings too? Could they be linked in a true two-way communion? Could she know? *Reach further…*

No, at the moment Benjamin was slipping into another dream-image, of riding Overcast alone in the desert. Only one corner of his mind was thinking of her—but that one little corner reached for her as naturally as he breathed, as if her presence and his concern for her were as much a part of him, as automatic a response, as his heartbeat.

Lorraine relaxed her psychic probe, content to wait and ask later, more than content to know that she held a constant place in his heart. Whether the psychic link worked both ways or not, she could be certain of his love. That was happiness enough that the rest of the world didn't matter, at least for now.

And then the clock-alarm sounded.

Benjamin grumbled incoherently, then hauled himself upright and pried his eyes open. He glanced first at Lorraine, and noticed her expression. "What are you smiling about this early in the morning?" he yawned.

"Just thinking about my psychic experiments," she grinned. "When do you think we can go out to the node again?"

"Maybe later this morning," he mumbled, rubbing his eyes. "Let the guards widen the perimeter a bit. Mm, did you see where my socks got off to?"

"On the chair." Lorraine smiled wider. "If you're going to spend every night in here, don't you think you should bring some clothes?"

Benjamin aimed a playful swat at her rump, and muttered something about moving his whole wardrobe just to save commuting-time. Lorraine laughed and rolled out of bed, wondering what Daniel would have for their breakfast.

***

They finished the stable-work early, and led out Overcast and Leila again.

Benjamin finished saddling the stallion, then paused to check the sheathed sword hanging from the cantle, the pistol on his hip and the cell-phone in his pocket. "Best turn on your phone too," he suggested, "Just in case something happens to mine."

"Good point." Lorraine clicked her phone to receive, and then shoved it back in its holster. She had to admit she'd been leaving it turned off quite a bit lately, frankly trying to avoid another call from—

The phone rang.

She sighed as she flipped it open, already guessing who the caller was.

"Lorraine!" At least this time Berringer got her new name right. "I've been trying to reach you for days. Where *are* you?" She sounded rattled enough to be sincere. "I checked on Johnson Hauling, and nobody has lived or worked at that address for weeks. Lorraine, what's going on?"

There was no point in putting this off. Lorraine took a deep breath. "I switched jobs and location again, after somebody broke into my last employer's place. I'd worked only a few days at this ranch when someone came poking around here, too—shortly after your last call to me. That's three times now, Dianne. I don't believe it's a coincidence."

Berringer paused for a long moment. "You must realize," she finally went on, "That your security is now compromised. I'm afraid this changes your status in the program, and—"

"And I'm afraid that the program didn't do very much for me." Lorraine tried to keep her voice gentle, but couldn't keep from adding: "At least this place has full-time security guards. I really think I'm safer here than I ever was under the Bureau's care."

Berringer heaved an audible sigh. "I'm afraid you're right," she admitted. "I still think it was just bad luck—certainly no one inside the Bureau is behind the break-ins, and nobody passed on the information. I haven't found any evidence… I've been looking…"

Her voice trailed off.

Lorraine was seriously tempted to pity the poor woman, who was probably honest anyway. "No harm done," she said. "I'm protected, I've identified the killer, and I think I can keep safe until I testify at his trial. You don't have to worry about me anymore."

"I'll still worry," said Berringer. "All right, I won't call you again until we have a trial date—but please, leave your phone active, if only for that. And…you can still call me, anytime you want to."

"I'll bear it in mind." Lorraine felt moved to add: "Thank you, Dianne. None of this is your fault."

"All right," the woman sighed. "Well, good luck. And…just nail that Mafia bastard, and everything will be all right."

"Will do," Lorraine promised. "Goodbye, Dianne."

"Goodbye." The connection clicked off.

Poor woman, thought Lorraine, closing the phone. She shoved it fiercely into its holster, and finished saddling Leila. As she mounted, Lorraine caught Benjamin watching her with a thoughtful look, but he didn't say anything until they were halfway out to the node.

"Is 'Aunt Dianne' causing problems?" he asked quietly.

"On the contrary." Lorraine peered at the land ahead. "She's doing her best, but her bosses don't tell her even as little as they know. I actually feel sorry for her."

"Understandable." Benjamin patted idly at his gun-holster again, wearing a thoughtful look. "It's really miserable being a good servant to a bad master."

Lorraine studied the countryside around her, seeing nothing unusual. "You must tell me, sometime, about your adventures in that department."

"I wouldn't know where to begin," he muttered. "That's a very ancient misery."

***

Lorraine spent half an hour channeling energy at the tagged plants while Benjamin took notes; it was obvious by now that the more heavily charged plants grew taller and thicker than those left alone, and Lorraine seriously reconsidered Helen's suggestion of working on mice. She also wondered if she could use the power for healing non-mutants, and toyed with the thought of setting up a clinic directly on a node.

"You'd do better to make it a religious sanctuary," Benjamin suggested. "That way you can always explain the healings as miracles rather than your own doing. You don't want to draw too much attention to yourself, you know."

"I know," Lorraine sighed, setting that daydream aside. Another idea nibbled. She took Benjamin's hand and *reached* for him.

Yes, there was his presence, strong and clear—and his happy eagerness for learning, and his solid feeling for her, and the slight cramping in his thighs from crouching on the hard ground, and the steady pull of his breathing…

"Lorraine?" he asked hesitantly, "What are you doing now?"

"Can you feel me?" she almost whispered. "Not just my presence: anything else?"

"Something," he murmured. "I can't describe it."

"The node's power…" It was difficult to talk and concentrate together. "I think…it increases the psychic sense too. Communication…"

"It's possible."

For a moment Lorraine considered making love with him here at the node, seeing if that would increase the psychic contact too, but a glance at the rough ground discouraged that idea. She sighed, released his hand, got up and walked back to the border of the power-zone. Benjamin rose and followed. Lorraine drew her knife, bit her lip and cut her forearm again, taking care to get as much blood as possible on the blade before the cut closed.

"Watch where the knife goes," she said, and then threw it as hard as she could.

Lorraine had never been expert at knife throwing, and the dagger hit the ground handle-first some 20 yards away.

"Go observe it," she said. "I'm going to try again."

She closed her eyes, heard Benjamin move away, and set herself for the right state of mind. *Trance, ground, visualize… There.* It was growing easier with practice; the power flowed more easily this time, though the concentration took more effort.

Lorraine closed her eyes and *pushed* the flow through her body to the distant knife. It moved sluggishly, but it moved. Yes, she could project the power as much as 20 yards past the border, given a piece of conductive metal with her blood on it...

"Lorraine, enough!" Benjamin shouted.

She released the circuit and opened her eyes, and saw Benjamin staring at her in astonishment. At his feet, all around the dagger, the ground was steaming. In his hand he held a branch of mesquite, and it was burning.

"Where did that come from?" was all she could think to ask.

"That bush," he gulped. "I picked it up and held it between the knife and you, where I saw the air rippling, and..."

They both looked at the branch, which now only smoldered and smoked, and then at the ground near the knife, which was no longer steaming.

"I think we can call this experiment conclusive," Benjamin said, a little shakily.

"Only 20 yards," Lorraine muttered, "And only heat."

"Which means, at least, that you've expanded the node's protection that far."

Benjamin dropped the branch and stamped out the last of its sparks, then bent and picked up the dagger. The wood of the grip was charred black, all over its surface if not deeper.

Lorraine went to him, feeling weariness take her the moment she stepped outside the node's border. "So I have a psychic sword and shield, but only here," she said.

"And you can't spend your life on sacred ground," he finished the thought.

"Damn," Lorraine sighed. "Well, let's go home. I need to paint again."

Back within the node's reach, Lorraine felt its energy fill her again. Her fatigue dropped away, but the itch to paint grew stronger. She went to where they'd tied the horses, heard Leila nicker a greeting, and was distracted by another thought. She patted the mare's satiny neck, rested her forehead against Leila's, and *reached* for the mare.

Yes, the contact was stronger here. She could *feel* the mare's pleasure in the stroking, the wordless intelligence, and the odd sensations of standing on four legs in that big powerful body. *Now, send...* Lorraine concentrated on projecting a single sensation: right front hoof raising, pawing, and scraping the ground.

Leila hesitated, then raised her right forehoof and pawed the earth: once, twice.

Enough. Good girl! Lorraine tried to transmit her satisfaction while she petted Leila's neck. The mare stopped pawing, and nudged Lorraine with her velvet nose.

"I can send thoughts here," she whispered ecstatically. "To you, to a horse…"

"I felt your…personality," Benjamin smiled, "But no great urge to dance."

Just then they both felt, faint but distinct, the field of another mutant.

Benjamin stiffened, his smile vanished as if it had never existed, and glanced quickly around them. Lorraine drew her revolver. She recognized that aura.

"It's him," she said, very quietly. "He's somewhere near."

Benjamin crouched low, pulling Lorraine down with him, and reached for his gun. "He might not come onto sacred ground," he whispered, "And there are two of us."

The feel of presence faded away as swiftly as it had come.

"Moving off," Lorraine whispered, "But where?"

Instead of his gun, Benjamin pulled out his cell-phone and punched its buttons.

"Helen," he said into the microphone, "Our unwanted visitor is somewhere out here in the desert with us. Alert the guards." A moment's pause. "Out by the node, yes."

Another pause. "I don't know if he's heading toward the house or away from it." A short pause. "All right, we'll wait right here." He clicked the phone closed, and shoved it in his pocket. "We stay here," he said to Lorraine. "She's sending some guards out to accompany us back to the house. I don't think our visitor wants to take on that many."

"Not armed and alert," Lorraine agreed. She rose slowly to her feet, stretching her psychic sense, hoping the node's power would add to her range. She could *feel* the node, Benjamin, the horses, the general mindless life of the plants around the spring, the tiny creatures who lived among them—and further: a passing bird overhead, a ground-squirrel sleeping in his nest, a plodding tarantula…

There! Out there, at the limit of her expanded range, a hint of that particular aura again.

"He's out there," Lorraine reported. "Somewhere to our left. I can't tell how far: at least 50 yards, maybe 100. He's moving…not toward the ranch, not away either. Sideways, around the perimeter, I think…" Then the tenuous contact faded as the unknown mutant moved out of range. "Gone. I've lost him."

"Say, 100 yards. Out of pistol-range, but still dangerous." Ben calculated. "I daresay he has binoculars, possibly a 'scoped rifle. He's watching. Stay down, Lorraine; don't give him a clear shot." He pulled out the cell-phone again, called Helen, and then patched through to the security guards heading toward them. "The intruder is approximately 100 yards south of us," he relayed. "May be moving, probably watching, almost certainly armed."

Lorraine closed her eyes and tried to stretch her psychic sense further, but found nothing.

A few moments later, they heard the sound of an approaching jeep.

"Stay low," Benjamin cautioned, still holding the phone to his ear. "They haven't found him."

"I doubt they will," Lorraine considered. "I get the impression he's good at this game."

"An experienced hunter," Ben agreed. "And here's our escort."

***

The guards stayed with them until they reached the stables, then drove off quickly. Ben and Lorraine unsaddled and curried the horses, turned them loose in the pasture, and reluctantly went their separate ways on their separate schedules.

They didn't meet again until it was time for weapons practice. This time Ben took two rifles, plus three boxes of ammunition, and led Lorraine outside, into the desert at the edge of the pasture.

"Aim at that mesquite branch," he pointed out for her, "The one just above the ground."

"That's…about two hundred yards away," Lorraine guessed, lining up the sights.

"Anyone can become competent with a rifle at two hundred yards. Shoot."

Lorraine fired, and the dry branch broke neatly in two. The baritone bark of the rifle echoed off the distant hillsides for several seconds thereafter.

"Very good." Ben's smile was wider than a simple good shot should have justified. "Now try…that Prickly Pear pad, over there."

After firing half a dozen sufficiently good shots, and hearing the cascade of echoes every time, Lorraine guessed that Ben was warning off the stalker. In the still air of the desert, the sound must have carried for miles—and an experienced shooter could tell from the sound that it came from a large-caliber rifle.

"I don't know whether to be annoyed with you or relieved," she said as they trudged back to the house. "I want the stalker dead, not just driven off, but I don't want to put any of us at risk." *...Or burden you with my protection...an imposition...*

"I didn't realize I was being so obvious." Ben gave her a rueful smile. "But as a general rule, it's best to avoid fights if possible. I'm giving our friend a chance to change his mind and back off."

Lorraine remembered that she was pledged to end a war, not encourage one. "What if he doesn't back off?" *If he's the Mafia's man, he probably won't.*

Benjamin shrugged. "We'll be ready for him. In any case, we've given him an honorable chance."

A code of honor, Lorraine considered, was also a way of keeping a society together in the absence of any supreme authority. That made it something to encourage, if only by punishing—or removing—those who didn't have it.

***

Psychic practice began with studying a chart that Helen had made: "Your individual strengths and limitations, Lorraine; you're high on projective and receptive empathy, medium-low on receptive telepathy, very high on channeling the energy-flows and low on everything else."

"Good grades, but in only a few subjects," Lorraine grinned.

"With years of practice, I think you can improve your low-score abilities," Helen smiled back, "But during your basic training you should concentrate on your strengths."

Lorraine looked down at her hands. "Would you say that if we didn't have the problem with the stalker?" she asked.

"Yes," Helen answered firmly. "All fledglings are at risk. You have to learn adequate survival skills as fast as you can. Later, after you've won your first duel, you can afford the leisure to...expand your education."

Why didn't I see it before? Lorraine mentally kicked herself. "You've trained other fledglings before, haven't you?"

"Oh yes," Helen sighed, her gaze wandering away into some far distance. "Many times. Many, many times..."

She was silent for a long moment, and Lorraine wondered how many of Helen's students had survived to the present day.

And how many fell in this age-long war?

Helen gave a little shake, and resumed her confident smile. "Now, seeing your success with the plants…" She reached behind her and pulled a scarf off what Lorraine had thought was a large oblong cushion. It was two small cages, with half a dozen white mice in each. "I think you're ready to work properly with animals. Reach into this cage and pet the mice — don't worry, they're tame—and try to put the healing/growing force into them, just as you did with the plants. The other cage we'll simply leave alone."

Lorraine dutifully reached into the cage and picked up a mouse. As the tiny creature cautiously explored her hand, she marveled at how small its life-force/presence felt. She'd have to be very careful not to pour too much energy into it, or… She winced as she thought of burning, exploding mice.

***

After the usual relaxation session by the pool, Lorraine hurried off to the solarium and her current painting. The portrait of Leila was almost completed, needing only a few more details of background and highlighting. Once those were done, she turned the painting around and peered at the white-coated back of the board.

Yes, the transferred master-sketch was quite good, at second look. It was time to put in the basic colors: blue for the clear sky, gold for the field of wheat, earth-browns for the farmers harvesting the grain, and ugly gray for the rat-like creatures stealing half the crop behind the farmers' backs. Start with the darkest tone; succeeding layers would work toward light.

As she spread the color, Lorraine chewed over ideas for a title. 'Infestation' was too long, and a bit obvious. 'Blight' and 'Plague' didn't exactly fit the imagery.

"Parasites", she decided, considering what the rat-things represented. And no, it wouldn't do to put caricatures of various politicians on the rat-creatures' faces; that would turn this into nothing but a political cartoon. Besides, it wasn't individuals she meant but a whole system, a concept, a type. That would be harder to express. Perhaps she could add suggestive details to the rat-things: a battered crown here, bits of uniforms there…

Daniel had to phone to remind her of dinnertime.

***

The nightly counseling session consisted mostly of going over maps of the guards' patrols and the house defenses. Lorraine was surprised to discover that the entrance to the house security office was behind the hallway bookcase; she'd passed it dozens of times, and never noticed. *The old door-hidden-behind-the-swinging-bookcase trick, straight out of 1930s mystery-movies. But it works!* Also, there was an escape tunnel leading out of the basement, accessible through the hidden door in the supply-closet or by a stairwell concealed under the altar in the house's chapel. Its far end was off the map.

"Where does this exit?" she asked, noting the tunnel's direction.

"All the way out at the node," Treemark smiled. "I had it dug during the Great Depression, supposedly as a mineshaft. No, I didn't file any paperwork with the city about it; nobody knew but the workmen, who were glad enough to get jobs in those days. I doubt if anyone alive remembers the tunnel now."

"Or the basement?" Lorraine guessed.

"Precisely. The few renovations since then, I did myself. No outsider knows."

"Like a medieval castle, with its keep and hidden escape-passage," Lorraine murmured, suspecting that Treemark had lived, and fought, in more than one of those.

"And how are you dealing with your anger at the stalker?" he tossed at her, another of his out-of-left-field questions. "How much time today have you spent gnawing over the problem of his presence?"

Lorraine blinked. "…Not much," she considered. "I think I'm distracting myself with the painting." *Particularly the other side…*

"Art is always a good use for any passion," Treemark agreed. "I'm eager to see your new work."

"Not yet." Lorraine had never cared for critics watching over her shoulder while she worked. "A lot of the detailing may change before I finish, giving different impressions. It's still in progress…"

It occurred to her that if she didn't want anyone walking in on her while she painted, she'd best move the easel and kit elsewhere.

But the only private place she could think of was her own room. *Not the bedroom,* she decided. Madge would give her hell about dripping paint on the carpet.

The bathroom was a better bet; large enough that the easel wouldn't block the facilities, and there'd be no problem getting oil paint off tile. The overhead lighting was also good, and steadier than sunlight.

"I'm quite sure I can sell your next painting for as much as the first," his voice broke in on her thoughts, "If not more. The gallery-owner was quite impressed by your technique, and you know how quickly the last one sold."

Sell it… Yes, Lorraine realized, she intended to sell this painting too. That meant that, sooner or later, someone would see the second painting on the back. *It doesn't matter,* she decided, feeling strangely defiant, *Let them look. Maybe someone will understand—and think about it.*

***

Benjamin wasn't there when Lorraine returned to her room. She dropped her house-defense maps on the bed, went to the bathroom and turned on the tub-faucet. As she pulled off her clothes she studied the bathroom's layout, and finally decided to set the easel beside the stretch of cabinet-top between the sink and the toilet; that would give her plenty of space to lay out rags and brushes and her paint-tray.

She was just turning off the water when she felt Ben's approaching aura.

Lorraine wrapped herself in a towel and went to let him in, noting that his expression was thoughtful and a little grim.

He kissed her quickly, shed his clothes without comment, and only when they were both in the tub did he speak again. "I'd suggest," he said quietly, "Not going beyond the guards' perimeter for a few days."

So, he'd been studying the stalker problem too. Lorraine was surprised at the rush of gratitude she felt.

"How long will it take the hunter to scout the grounds from a distance?" she asked, scrubbing his back. "Assuming he hasn't done it already, that is. He could have found a good hunting-stand days ago."

"We wait three days, maybe four," he said. "Ah, that's enough. Turn around, and I'll get your back. After that, seeing no one come out of the…fort, he'll either give up or grow impatient and start moving closer. He'll meet the dogs and the sonar alarms, which will alert the guards. With luck, they'll take him—and then Brian will deal with him."

"And if they don't?" Lorraine, restless, rinsed off and pulled herself out of the tub. "He's invested so much time and effort in this hunt…"

Benjamin ducked his head under the water, came up quickly, opened the drain and climbed out of the tub after her. "Then he'll try to find another way into the house. I don't think he'll try to bluff his way in under cover of law, cop or no."

"No? Does Treemark have some local legal clout?"

"Just a couple of good lawyers," Benjamin smiled grimly, reaching for a towel. "He hasn't told me what he's done in that department, but he seems confident about it."

Lorraine toweled off quickly, and slipped into her robe. "Will the stalker try to shoot his way in, past the guards, do you think?"

"Too risky." Ben rubbed his hair semi-dry. "Yes, Brian prepared for that, too. No, I suspect he'll try something more subtle, and I'm trying to guess what that will be."

"I take it there's someone in the security office all the time," said Lorraine, heading into the bedroom.

Benjamin wrapped himself in towels and followed her out. "Yes, for the past couple weeks. In fact, we're the only two that haven't taken a turn watching the screens — probably because we're simply the least informed about the system."

"Then we can trap him in the house." Lorraine looked around the bedroom, saw the book, and remembered her earlier intention. "Can you help me get my painting gear out of the solarium?" she asked.

"At this hour?" Ben raised an eyebrow. "Won't it keep?"

"Not really. I want to get an early start tomorrow."

Benjamin shrugged, and followed her out into the corridor. They encountered no one on the way to the solarium, and Lorraine suspected that nobody in the household would have commented on the two of them traipsing around in bathrobes anyway.

The painting was just as Lorraine had left it. She picked it up and folded the easel, and Ben reached for her paint-kit. She led the way back into the bathroom, and set the easel against the cabinet, under the overhead light. Ben studied the painting while she laid out her paint-kit and arranged the brushes on the edge of the sink.

"This isn't the oddest condition I've ever seen for creating art," he said, placing the painting neatly on the easel. "During World War Two, I saw one stalwart artist working in subway bunker in the midst of a bombing-raid. Just watching the man work was enough to keep the others from panic. It wasn't that fine a painting, really—just a still life with drapery and dried flowers—and he wasn't that good an artist, but everyone admired the man's sheer dedication. He eventually sold that painting to one of the people who'd shared the bunker with him, and for a far better price than it really deserved."

"Artistic dedication," Lorraine chuckled, already thinking of the next brushstrokes. She paced back to the bedroom, with Ben close behind. He helped her pull off her robe, and slid under the covers beside her. They snuggled together, too tired for anything else, and sank swiftly into shared sleep.

***

The next day was much the same, save for everyone staying close to the house, concerned with the same tasks.

Lorraine, nagged by her muse, went straight from the pool to the painting.

Benjamin appeared soon after she did, and sat watching, fascinated, as she painted for the rest of the afternoon. Nothing broke their concentration until Daniel called them for dinner. Ben hurried off to his room for fresh clothes, Lorraine hastily cleaned her brushes and palette and threw on her simple black caftandress, and they met in the livingroom just before the summons to the table.

Dinner was Chicken Divan with a wonderfully rich sauce, fresh croissants and a salad of mixed fruit and sweet onions, with an excellent white California wine that Daniel pronounced "a steal, far too modestly priced for its quality". The enrapturing taste of the food finally seduced Lorraine away from her concentration on the painting, and she glanced around the table at the others. Steven asked Benjamin about the condition of the horses, Treemark and Helen exchanged a few quiet words about the security systems, Madge and Daniel argued amiably about the economics of buying a whole cut-up beef carcass, and Wally questioned Lorraine briefly about Leila's behavior as a trail-horse.

Afterward, she followed Treemark out to the livingroom, where he paused to collect two drinks, and then into the clinic office.

"How is your rage holding?" was the first thing he asked as he sat down.

"Manageable." Lorraine took a sip of her Scotch. "There's the stable-work, and the painting, and—" She caught herself before she could mention Benjamin. "I'm still wondering about my last experiment with the node. I managed to project power, heat anyway, for almost 20 yards. I also found I could establish two-way psychic communications there."

"With whom?" If Treemark's ears had been mobile, they would have pricked up like a cat's.

"A little with Ben, more with Leila. I got her to paw her hoof, but he got only an impression of my awareness."

"He's a little more complicated than a horse," Treemark smiled. "But you can do this only at the node?"

"Only where I can draw on that power," Lorraine admitted. "On my own, I can only receive impressions, not send them. Also, outside the node I can draw power only from myself or other living things."

"But you can transmit power; I've seen Helen's notes on the plant and mouse experiments."

"I can transmit to—or draw from—only what I'm touching. At the node, I can send across distance. …I had an idea about building a clinic, of sorts, at a node. If I can encourage plants and animals to grow, I could possibly heal them—if I can learn enough about medicine and anatomy."

"That's an interesting idea," Treemark murmured, his gaze taking on distance.

"Ben said…" *Careful. Don't seem too familiar.* "It would be better to set up a religious shrine at a node, and claim it had healing powers. That way, I'd draw less notice to myself."

"And also less official investigation," Treemark smiled. "I've done that myself a few times. The worst that any king's soldiers are likely to do is chase off the 'worshippers' and 'priests', take over the shrine for themselves, then abandon it in disgust when it won't work healing miracles for them. Meanwhile, you and your True Believers set up shop somewhere else. In time, you can come back to the old shrine and start business as before."

"I take it you've done that a few times, too!" Lorraine laughed.

"Oh yes," Treemark smiled. "If you're serious about this idea, you could study medicine as a quiet sideline while pursuing your art career."

"It's a thought…" Lorraine took another mouthful of scotch while considering that. Yes, so much was possible now that she had time, decades and centuries of time, to study and plan. *And invest. Think.* "The painting I'm working on… I can't tell for myself if it's going to be as good as the last one, but I'd like you to broker it for me when it's finished. Hmmm, and can you recommend a discreet bank?"

"Easily done," he smiled back. "Are you learning to think

ahead, in Elven terms?"

"A little." She'd toyed with the idea of setting up new identities, a couple of birth certificates to begin with, before the stalker had appeared. "My concern with our stalker has kept my attention stuck in the here-and-now. Once all that's finished…"

Then she remembered that Benjamin had another life somewhere, and he'd go back to it as soon as the current crisis was over. She couldn't expect him to stay here for a year or more while she finished her training.

She would have to let him go, and endure until he came back. And trust that he *would* come back.

"Lorraine," Treemark's voice gently broke in on her thoughts. "Once a battle is over, it's over. Write up the account in your memory, put it on a shelf in your mental library, take only the lessons it's taught you, and move on. Go on with your life, with your long-term plans. Don't let yourself be chained to any one incident, or time or place—"

Or person? Lorraine thought.

"—but move on. For us, life is very long; very much comes and goes. Not letting go of the past can hobble you. Remember that. Remember everything, but be bound by nothing."

"Nothing?" Lorraine shivered. "Just let everything flow past and away?" *Ben?*

"Not necessarily away," said Treemark. "We have each other, and our mortal friends and lovers for as long as they last, and there's always the chance of return."

"How do you mean?"

"For example: I've held this land and house for over 80 years, but I could abandon it tomorrow if I had to—and then come back 20 years later, posing as my own son or nephew, demanding my rights to the old family homestead. There's a small castle in Portugal where I've done just that. Nothing has to stay lost."

"Except lives," Lorraine considered, thinking of the old crowd back in Chicago. "Mortals die."

"Except for whatever is destroyed, yes. But then we can preserve the memories, better than mortals can. Many of us are historians, for just that reason. But what I'm saying is, don't become fixated on any incident, or time or place, so that it endangers your chances for survival." He smiled. "Once the present problem is done with, we'll go on with your training and setting up your future. Don't let anything keep you from that."

Lorraine nodded, and sipped her drink. Yes, life could be very long. If Benjamin left, she'd meet him again in time. She could afford to wait.

It just wouldn't be easy.

***

As Lorraine left the clinic office, she saw Benjamin sitting alone on one of the couches in the livingroom, absorbed with a conversation on his cell-phone.

"Tell him to be patient, Joe," he was saying. "I'll be back in a few weeks. You know I don't stick to rigid schedules." He paused, listening for a long moment, then laughed. "Well, at least I stay in one place longer than she does. Tell him not to worry; if I don't see him there, I'll catch him in Paris. Stay loose, and keep taking notes. 'Bye."

He clicked off the phone, looked up and saw Lorraine. He smiled, pulled himself up from the couch, and stepped toward her. "Shall we?" he asked, holding out a hand.

"We shall," she answered, taking it.

They strolled down the empty hallway holding hands, aware of their daring, even if there was no one to see.

This time the lovemaking was slow and lazy, with no urgency, savoring every gesture from the pulling away of clothes to the long sleepy caresses afterward. Only long moments later did Lorraine bring up her question.

"Do you plan to leave soon?" She kept her voice as neutral as possible.

Benjamin sighed, and gently drew a lock of hair away from her cheek. "I'd planned to leave weeks ago, but…so much came up."

"Including this?" Lorraine couldn't help saying, arching her body to rub against his groin.

Benjamin laughed. "That too," he admitted. "Look, I have to take off for awhile, once we've dealt with the hunter, but I'll be back soon." He frowned slightly. "I always come back here, sooner or later."

Lorraine abruptly remembered that scene in the solarium, and the weekend theatre. How often did he need that?

For that matter, did he need her?

"You know I'll miss you." *How will I stand it?* "I'll manage, but it won't be easy."

"It's never easy." He pressed his face against her neck. "We'll have a commuting affair until you…graduate. After that, who knows? Have you ever been to Paris?"

"No," Lorraine smiled. "The closest I got was studying French in school."

"You'll love it," he promised, pulling her close.

She hugged back, even knowing that he wouldn't be going to Paris just for her sake. "Nomadic lifestyle," she murmured, "With your scattered gypsy tribe."

"Exactly," he whispered. "My tribe."

"I'd like to meet them." *Love him, love his tribe. I'll manage.*

"You will." Benjamin sighed. "And I hope…"

"I know. I'll try," Lorraine vowed, remembering all that was at stake here. *Tribe. Society. Family…* Yes, she would be patient for the sake of that.

She would also be resolute. She might have to share his time, his attention, heaven knew what else, with the rest of his tribe—but she would not give him up.

21.

THE NEXT DAY'S SCHEDULE was much the same, except that it was Brian Treemark who came to the *salle d'armes* as Lorraine was finishing her sword-training session.

"Sorry to interrupt," he smiled sheepishly, "But seriously, Ben, I'm going to need your help with Gold Eagle. The fool beast needs to be ridden on a lunge-line, and Steven and Wally are busy with lead-training the foals. Can you help me out here?"

Ben threw Lorraine an apologetic look. "If I'm not really needed…"

"Go on," Lorraine smiled, putting her practice-sword back in its rack. "It's almost time for my next class, anyway."

Ben sighed, put up his sword and went off with Treemark. Lorraine followed, slower, and met Helen on the way.

"Lorraine, there's noticeable progress with the mice," she beamed. "Come see; I think you'll be surprised."

Out in the garden sat the two mouse-cages. In the unmarked cage, the untreated mice wandered about, nibbled food, bumped noses with each other or slept. In the marked cage there was a very different scene; two mice faced off against each other, glaring fiercely in each other's eyes and then pouncing and wrestling furiously with loud squeaks before breaking off to glare at each other again, while the other mice raced around them in excitement.

"Is this normal mouse behavior?" Lorraine asked, wondering how on Earth her simple energy-charging could have caused this.

"It is, among mice that are lively, energetic, and bored. I'd like you to transfer them to a more interesting cage—and charge them during the transfer."

Helen pointed to an odd contraption under a nearby rosebush, and Lorraine saw that it was a much bigger cage—containing a treadmill-wheel, a ladder and slide, and a simple maze of connected small plastic boxes.

"A…playground?" Lorraine guessed. "Toys to keep them from being bored?"

"Precisely," Helen grinned. "Once they have new territory to explore, I think we'll see the fighting stop. I've noticed the same phenomenon among small children."

That wouldn't surprise me. Lorraine smiled back as she

reached for the first mouse. The mice stopped squabbling as they saw her hand draw near, and one of them actually leaped toward her fingers. She noticed that the wee creature held still as she fed the small charge of energy into him, and guessed that he enjoyed the feeling.

As Helen had predicted, once charged and released into the playground-cage, the mice set about happily exploring their new environment. She and Lorraine watched for long moments as the little animals sniffed and poked and began playing with the new toys, and saw no further fighting at all.

"I think we can assume," said Helen, "That you've made the mice lively and energetic, blooming with health, and eager to exercise their little furry minds as well as bodies. I also think this strongly indicates that you can heal animals."

"Don't go injuring a mouse just so I can practice on it," Lorraine cautioned.

"Would you mind if I injured a plant, then?"

"Well…not seriously injured."

"No." Helen produced a small pruning-knife, pulled down a branch of the rosebush and cut a small gash in it. "Here," she said, pushing the branch toward Lorraine. "Try to close the gap."

Feeling a little out of her depth, Lorraine clasped the slender branch on either side of the oozing cut, closed her eyes and settled back into meditative state. Once there, she summoned the image of energy-flows in her own body, then tried extending the flow into the branch between her hands. She could see—no, *feel*—the gash in the stem, and led the flow deliberately across it to form a bridge of violet-blue light. It wasn't enough, she realized; the plant's own cells had to grow, fill in the gap—and how was she supposed to make them do that? She tried visualizing the cells dividing, creating copies of themselves, using her energy-flow as a power source. The image felt slightly unreal, incomplete…

Water, Lorraine guessed. Those cells needed water, and food, to copy themselves, and they'd lost water with the sap flowing out of the cut. *Fluid…*

Impulsively, she bent her head close and—carefully avoiding the thorns—licked the cut. She thought of cats licking their wounds, and remembered that saliva contained a host of chemicals; hopefully, some of those would be of use to a plant. She licked again.

Drink, eat, grow… Lorraine visualized the plant cells taking up the offered water and chemicals, and dividing; this time the image seemed more solid, more real. She concentrated on guiding the growing crowd of new cells along the path of the energy-flow until the gap filled. There her imagination gave out, and she could think of nothing more to do.

Lorraine sighed and opened her eyes, surprised to find that she felt tired and dizzy, saw Helen watching her intently, and looked down at the branch.

The cut was still visible, as an indentation in the thin bark, but it was closed. Sap no longer ran from it, but formed a thin glaze over the surface. "…Healed?" she mumbled, lips clumsy with sudden fatigue.

"I'd say so," Helen agreed. "And I think I should get you a book on cell anatomy."

"…Cell…?"

"That's the level where healing takes place. I find it intriguing that you could make the plant-tissue heal when you seem to have so little psychokinetic ability."

"Maybe I'm just communicating with the cells." Lorraine let the branch go, and it sprang back to its usual place. Watching it, she felt herself sway dangerously.

"Dizzy…"

"Tired," Helen pronounced. "That's enough for today; it's time to go to the pool and get some rest."

"Right." The idea of the pool seemed wonderfully inviting right then.

Nonetheless, it took some help from Helen for her to get to her feet and walk the distance to the Jacuzzi. For once Treemark wasn't there, though a cup and carafe of fruit-juice awaited her. Not knowing whether to be disappointed or relieved, Lorraine lounged in the bubbling water and drank the juice until she felt rested enough to get up, get out of the water and return to her room.

Once the door shut behind her, she remembered the painting. All other thought took second place, and she went to the bath-room where the easel waited. The picture, she had to admit, was shaping up nicely; it was time to add the detailing on the wheat. With luck, she could also finish detailing the rat-creatures by to-night. Concentrating on the next step, she picked up her palette and reached for the paint-tubes.

***

This time it was Helen who came to fetch her. Lorraine recognized her aura as it approached, and paused in surprise, brush halfway to the canvas. Helen, now wearing a soft dress that resembled a caftan, studied the new painting and nodded in appreciation.

"I can't wait to see it finished," she murmured. "But enough for now. It's ten minutes to dinnertime."

"I'll barely have time to change!" Lorraine wiped off the brushes and dunked them in the turpentine, then cleaned off the palette with hurried strokes.

"It doesn't matter. Dinner tonight, Daniel assures me, will be *al-fresco* in the garden. That means exceedingly casual; your painting-robe won't be out of place."

"I must tell Daniel I'm grateful." Lorraine squeezed out the brushes with the paint-rag, guessing that she'd need a new one soon, and dried them as best she could. "You know, I never thought much about clothes before I came here."

"You should," Helen smiled. "Dress is another weapon in your arsenal."

"Cooking too, I imagine," Lorraine considered as she packed the brushes and palette away in the case. "I suppose I should ask Daniel for some basic lessons."

"He'll be delighted to teach you." Helen smiled, then sobered. "Meanwhile, there's something I'd like to ask about your experiments with absorbing and transmitting the power. Lorraine, except for that one time you accidentally drew from me, have you ever tried drawing from another person?"

"No!" Lorraine flinched back. "You saw what happened with the plants!"

Helen nodded slowly, fixing Lorraine with a keen look. "The power to bless or blight crops…"

"I can't see any good reason for blighting crops, let alone…" Now that she thought of it, there was one good reason for drawing the Elven life-force out of another person. She shuddered at the idea.

Helen sat down, gracefully—as she did everything—on the edge of the tub.

"When I was a goddess in Mycenae," she said, "One of my duties was to make a Progress around the neighborhood and bless the newly-planted fields. The first few times I did it—actually transmitted power, not just going through the motions—I drained myself nearly to exhaustion on the first field, and simply faked the blessing with all the others. Of course that proved unsatisfactory. Next, I tried spending only a little energy on each field. That too was unsatisfactory. I could charge myself with the node-power from the temple, but there was—as you've seen—a limit to what I could carry away."

Lorraine only nodded, not wanting to guess what came next.

Helen's face tightened, just a fraction. "Then I discovered that I could draw from mortals around me, particularly when they were in a worshipful mood—psychically open, so to speak."

"From mortals?" Lorraine stopped quickly. Whatever the Elven power was, she realized, mortals would necessarily have less of it—probably much less.

"My first few experiments were…disasters," Helen admitted. "I soon learned to draw only a little, just enough to leave the subject feeling slightly weak and dizzy, from each of my worshippers. After that, I made certain that I was always surrounded by a large crowd when I made my Progress. I would drain myself to bless the plants, then draw power from my worshippers to replace it. By the end of the holy day, we would all come home exhausted—but nothing worse—and the crops would thrive. Do you understand what this implies?"

Lorraine only shook her head, not really wanting to think further, knowing she must, but preferring to let Helen lead her through it.

Helen smiled knowingly, as if she understood. "Two things: first, that you've discovered in a few weeks what it took me years to learn. You're quiet talented—and inspired, Lorraine."

Lorraine only bowed her head, certain that she could feel a blush spreading across her cheeks.

"Second…" Helen's face grew mask-like again. "Consider that if you're ever forced into close combat with a mortal—or even one of us—and you have no other weapon, all you need do is touch your enemy and…draw from him, very fast, very strongly. You can drain a mortal to death, if you pull hard enough."

Lorraine bit her lip. "Vampires…" she whispered.

Helen nodded, not flinching away from her gaze. "We could be. For us, it's not the blood that is the life."

"No." Lorraine shivered and looked away.

"As for our own kind," Helen's voice went on inexorably, "it's possible to draw enough to weaken your enemy—weaken him to the point where you can defeat him in the usual manner. The power can be transmitted even through clashing weapons, if they're both made of conductive metal, though that takes considerable practice. I've done this myself a few times, to survive."

Lorraine didn't answer. The stark images Helen's words aroused made her think of drinking blood. This was vampirism, by any other name.

"Lorraine, this is a weapon—like any other weapon. The question of how, when, where and whether to use it is entirely at your discretion. Be aware that very few of us know of the existence of this trick, and fewer still have the psychic ability to perform it. You're one of them." Helen rose smoothly to her feet. "You need not think about this today; only file away the information for consideration later, and don't lose it. For now, come to dinner."

She turned and slipped away as softly as a wandering ghost, leaving Lorraine alone with her thoughts.

***

Dinner was very casual and relaxed, consisting entirely of 'finger foods': elaborate variations on a theme of shish-kabob and fondue, accompanied by an all-purpose white zinfandel. Wally and Steven looked smug, Benjamin and Treemark tired but satisfied, and Lorraine guessed that they'd been successful with the day's horse training. Helen chatted happily with Daniel and Madge about having the gardeners plant an herb-garden within the week. Lorraine, surrendering her earlier discretion, sat close to Benjamin; she was shaken to realize how much she needed the comfort of his presence.

For his part, Benjamin noticed her distraction but said nothing. He only played silly games with the food, such as using two impaled fried shrimp as stick-puppets for a short comedy routine that had everyone chuckling. He also managed to do it without spilling so much as a crumb.

The technique worked, for Lorraine was in a better mood when she went to Treemark's office. He glanced briefly at her sadly stained robe, but made no comment on it except to ask how the painting was coming along.

"Quite well," Lorraine admitted. "I'm getting faster, more…fluent with the new techniques. I'm fairly sure I'll have this one finished by the weekend."

Treemark kept his eyes on hers. "Are you uncomfortable discussing your relationship with Benjamin?"

He knows. They all know. It was almost a relief to realize it.

"No, I'm just… infected with his discretion, I think. He's rather secretive, and I can see the sense of it."

"Hmmm. And do you understand that he also survives by being elusive? Staying too long in one place makes him anxious, and he'll be leaving the ranch soon. What will you do then?"

"Wait for him." Lorraine had given this considerable thought. "He'll be back, soon enough. If he can't stay long, he also can't stay away very long."

"True." Treemark smiled in appreciation. "But you are happy with him?"

"Very," Lorraine grinned back. "Happy enough that I can wait patiently for more of the same."

Treemark chuckled and raised his own glass in salute, then changed the subject. "The guards have been patrolling rather visibly all day, and they've seen nobody. The dogs didn't notice anyone either."

"So the stalker has the sense to back off," Lorraine considered. "He's seen we have serious protection."

"That in itself may be enough to make him give up and go home. He might not be comfortable playing a lone hand against such odds."

Lorraine remembered the old union's experiences, and the persistence of thugs and police. "I'm not too sure of that. He's put a lot of time and effort in trying to take me down, and he may be getting some pressure from the Mafia too. It's more likely he'll keep at it."

"In that case…" Treemark thoughtfully rubbed his chin. "He'll probably make a move in the next few days. He can't stay away from his job in Chicago much longer if he wants to keep that cover, and it's clear that he's invested considerable time and effort into that, too. The next week should tell the tale. Stay close to the house, Lorraine."

"I don't have anywhere in particular to go." Lorraine recalled her earlier disturbing thought. "Helen told me something, about psychic technique. Did you know that I can draw power from other people? Elven-kind, certainly—possibly mortals. It's possible that I could…drain someone dry that way, drain them even to death. It sounds like being a…psychic vampire. Did the vampire legend start with us?"

"No," Treemark said firmly. "That comes from the ancient belief that blood is the life-force, which isn't the case with us. As for psychically draining people…" He drew a deep breath. "Yes, it's possible—just not very probable. Helen tells me that it takes years, decades, of practice. Frankly, I don't know of anyone besides her who's ever done it, let alone in combat. You'd do better to concentrate on ordinary martial-arts practice until you're thoroughly proficient with physical weapons."

"That in any case." Lorraine heaved a sigh of relief and took another sip of her scotch, feeling as if she'd been reprieved. "Does Ben know all the house defenses? Can he keep me up to date on them?"

"Yes." Oddly enough, Treemark looked as relieved as she felt. "You might discuss with him the various contingency plans on what to do if the stalker tries to get onto the grounds, let alone into the house."

"I will," Lorraine promised, imagining how lively that discussion could become, and how it would end. She could almost feel Ben's elegant hands on her, already.

***

Helen was awake and waiting when Treemark came into the master bedroom. He didn't slam the door, but shut it decisively. "You told Lorraine about the Lamia trick," he accused. "What on Earth were you thinking of?!"

"Nothing that she wouldn't have guessed for herself, very soon." Helen met his eyes unflinchingly. "The very first time she experimented with energy-drawing, she accidentally drained me. I thought it best to explain the facts, rather than leave her to draw her own conclusions—which might have been dangerous."

Treemark rocked back and forth on his feet, still angry, but seeing the sense of that. "And did you tell her that it requires physical contact? I don't want her within shooting distance of an experienced headhunter!"

"I told her, and she didn't like it. In fact, she seemed upset about the whole business." Helen pushed down the covers, revealing an enticing space of empty bed-sheet. "Did she mention the word 'vampire'?"

"Yes," Treemark admitted. He sat down on the edge of the bed and pulled off his shoes. "Dammit, I don't want her frightened of her powers, either."

"Tomorrow I'll start teaching her about using the node to heal animals," Helen promised. "And no, I won't go out and deliberately break some creature's leg just so she can repair it; we'll start with anatomy textbooks."

Treemark sighed, lay back on the bed and stared up at the ceiling. 'Now it's my turn," he said, "to wonder if she's learning too much, too fast."

22.

OUT OF THE DEPTHS of blank sleep came a stirring, like a change of current in the ocean. It nudged Lorraine's consciousness up from darkness to recognition, then to a sudden peak of apprehension. She snapped to full wakefulness, lunging out of the covers, an unconscious snarl baring her teeth.

Intruder! Close!

The hunter, the feel of him familiar and hated, was within her range.

Is he in the house?!

She grabbed Benjamin's shoulder and shook it roughly, eliciting a grunt of surprise.

"Wake up!" she whispered fiercely. "He's here."

Benjamin said nothing, but promptly rolled to the side of the bed and reached for his sword.

Lorraine scrambled out the other side of the bed and grabbed for her gun-belt.

Her hand encountered the terrycloth of her robe, and she snarled again as she realized she had no clothing ready to hand—nothing fit to fight in, anyway. Holding the gun-belt in one hand, she darted for the bureau and yanked open the drawers. Damn, how many minutes would it take her to wrestle her way into underwear, bluejeans and sturdy shoes?

Behind her, Benjamin whispered hurriedly into the intercom-phone.

An eternity of frustrating seconds later, they darted out into the hallway—Ben leading, his sword in one hand and pistol in the other. Ahead, Lorraine saw Daniel hurrying toward the main room, similarly armed.

"Let me go ahead," she snapped. "I have to cover for everyone. He still thinks I'm the only one."

"He's probably guessed you have a teacher here," Ben insisted. "He'll know you're not alone."

"But he doesn't know about all the rest of you! I have to be the first or second one he sees, no more."

Ben muttered something that might have been a curse in some ancient language, and let her dart ahead of him. Lorraine ran after Daniel.

They met in the living room, joined within seconds by Madge, Treemark, Helen, Steven and Wally—all armed, all watchful and wary. Treemark held a cell-phone to his ear, muttered into it briefly, and then looked up with a frown.

"Our northeast sentry isn't responding," he said. "I think we can assume the dogs are also taken out."

"Where is he?" Helen snapped. "How close?"

Benjamin turned to Lorraine and gave her a questioning look.

Lorraine ground her teeth, then deliberately dropped into trance-state and *felt* for the intruder, narrowing in on his sense of presence. There, that way…amid a distinct scent of flowers…

"There!" she whispered, pointing. "The garden, the patio. Coming for the door."

She started in that direction, and within two steps the others were flanking her, spreading out in combat-formation, guns and swords at the ready. Treemark got ahead of her, snapping orders into the cell-phone as he ran. Lorraine hurried after him, shaking hotly with impatient fury; she'd wanted to be first, to see the intruder, finally learn who he was—and shoot first.

Treemark reached the door to the veranda overlooking the garden, and crouched low to unlock it. As his hand turned the doorknob, from outside came the sounds of barking and running dogs. Lorraine *felt* the intruder's jolt of alarm and frustration.

"He's turning—he's getting away!" she almost shouted.

Treemark threw the door wide open and darted out into the shadowed veranda, Lorraine one step behind.

At the far end of the garden sounded running footsteps. Lorraine jerked her head toward them just in time to see a dark silhouette dash through the open gateway. The dogs bayed louder, closer.

"There!" she shouted, pointing. "Set the dogs after him!" She started to run across the veranda, but Benjamin's hand caught her elbow.

"The dogs are outside the wall," he explained quickly. "They'll reach him before you can."

Then they heard a soft popping noise, closely followed by a dog's yelp of pain, and then a short burst of unmuffled gunshots.

Treemark swore and ran into the garden. Lorraine lunged after him, and Benjamin let her go but followed close behind. It took forever to reach the gate and peer out into the darkness beyond.

Nothing was visible out there, and nothing more could be heard except the angry yelping of the dogs. Lorraine could *feel* the intruder's presence receding, hurrying away, and swore bitterly. Treemark paused to use the cell-phone again, snapped a few fast questions, listened, then sighed.

"No," he said into the phone, "Pull back. You can't find him in the dark, and he'll only shoot more of the dogs. You track him in the morning, as soon as there's enough light."

Lorraine kicked the nearest shrub in frustration. "We almost had him," she growled. "Almost had him!"

"I think he knows that," said Benjamin, taking her arm again. "He won't be back tonight—and probably not tomorrow, either. He'll have to spend time spoiling his trail, to lose the dogs."

Lorraine heaved a vast sigh, feeling her rage-powered strength drain out of her.

"The excitement's over for the night," Ben insisted. "Come back to bed."

Lorraine had no answer for that. She let Benjamin lead her back to the veranda—past the others who muttered theories about how the intruder had gotten this far past their defenses—through the darkened living room and down the hallway, back to her own room and waiting bed. She sat down and dragged off her clothes with weary hands, hearing the soft clank and thud of Benjamin arranging his weapons near the nightstand.

"We almost had him," she repeated. "It was almost over."

"He knows that," Ben considered. "Perhaps now he'll have the sense to cut his losses and run."

Lorraine shook her head and stretched out on the waiting sheets. "No, he won't."

She wasn't sure how she knew, but she was certain of this. "He's too determined. He won't leave until he kills someone—or gets killed. We have to go out and hunt him ourselves. He knows I can't stay locked up in here forever, and he's waiting for me to come out. If we can use that to hunt him…"

Benjamin's arms tightened around her. "I will not use you as bait!" he whispered.

Lorraine hugged back, almost desperately. "What other choice do we have?"

"There are better ways," he insisted, in a voice that brooked no argument.

Lorraine lay still, thinking about that—and was jolted by a sudden revelation. *Distance! I felt his presence at more than 50 yards, his mind at more than 20… Not touching, and here—not at the node.*

Her psychic ability was expanding rapidly. This would make her an even greater prize for a hunter, but it also gave her an advantage at her own hunting.

***

Lorraine woke late to find Benjamin gone, and his weapons with him, but a note perched on her intercom-phone. "Breakfast," it said, in his neat spare handwriting, and: "Strategy meeting."

Why did he let me sleep so late, then? Lorraine wondered, as she dressed in the clothes she'd put on the night before. *It's nearly nine…* She took care to belt on her revolver and dagger, added the holstered cell-phone, and pulled on her riding boots.

The breakfast table was unexpectedly crowded, for everyone was there. A coffee service sat in the middle of the table, but all the other dishes had been cleared away to make room for maps, which everyone was studying. Daniel, seeing Lorraine approach, hastily got up and pulled a plate, holding a small mushroom-stuffed omelet, out of the microwave oven. He set it at Lorraine's place with a subtle flourish, and then filled her cup before settling into his own place. The others glanced up and smiled, except for Benjamin, who bit his lip and looked away. Helen pushed the cream and sugar toward Lorraine's place, grinning knowingly.

"Enjoy Daniel's delightful omelet while we fill you in," she said. "First, the dog that was shot is at the nearest veterinary clinic, and is likely to survive."

Lorraine nodded briefly before taking another mouthful of the admittedly excellent omelet.

"Second, the other dogs—and their handler—were shot with tranquilizer darts, and are recovering well. The guards are extremely annoyed at their failure last night, and are, as they put it, just itching to get this guy in their sights."

Lorraine chewed thoughtfully, considering that. Police of any jurisdiction had easy access to tranquilizer darts; no help there. Yes, the guards could help hunt; they might not know how to kill the Elven stalker, but if they shot him they would put him out of action long enough for someone else to finish him.

"We've been discussing search-patterns and possible ambush-sites," Helen went on, "And we've come up with a tentative battle-plan."

While I was asleep, out of the way… Lorraine frowned. Of course she had almost no experience at this sort of thing, but they might have asked her where and how she wanted to be deployed. "If it involves any of us going outside the walls," she said, "You'll have to take me along for cover."

Benjamin frowned and took a quick mouthful of coffee.

"Three groups," said Treemark, tapping his finger on the map. "The guards and the dogs will spiral outward from the house. I'll lead the second party—on horses, taking two of the dogs—with Helen, Madge and Daniel; we'll search to the west, on a square grid-pattern. You, Benjamin, Wally and Steven will ride eastward, in the same fashion. We'll communicate by cell-phone. Does everyone have their batteries fully charged?"

Lorraine couldn't let that go by without comment. "Why two groups of us? If he senses any of you, and I'm not there…"

"He'll expect you'll have a teacher, and—as the ranch owner—I'm the likeliest candidate." Treemark smiled, showing teeth. "Most of our kind can't pick out separate auras in a group; the hunter will think the other three are mortals."

Lorraine privately wondered how probable that was, but said nothing. She noted that the eastward search-area would bring her close to the node while the hunter's tracks had led away to the west. Since she had to be included in the search, the others were taking what steps they could to assure her safety. Lorraine suppressed a twinge of annoyance, and studied the map further.

"You said his tracks went off to the west," she murmured. "Why not use the dogs to follow them?"

"We tried that, as soon as the sky was light," Steven volunteered. "He was smart enough to get into rocks as fast as he could, and used some chemical to break his scent-trail. We have no idea where he is now."

"He's an old hand at this," Madge admitted, "And good at it."

"So we'll be riding around in the blazing sun for hours," Lorraine gloomed, "And he might slip past us anyway."

"We'll pack plenty of water," Daniel smiled. "And if we miss him today, there's always tomorrow."

Lorraine abruptly remembered Jack Palumbo's long-ago tales of deer hunting, and realized that, yes, this was an efficient way to flush the game—especially game that was unlikely to flee, much more likely to hunt them in turn.

"But will he approach if he sees four of us together?" she couldn't help asking. "There's only the one of him."

Dead silence answered, and the others exchanged quick and guilty looks.

Right then Lorraine realized that the real purpose of this hunting-party was not to find the stalker but to scare him away. She clutched her fork in a sudden surge of irrational anger.

"No," Benjamin replied coolly, "We expect him to run. He'll be on foot, and we'll be mounted. We'll ride him down, and we'll shoot him."

Lorraine almost missed the furtive glance that Treemark shot at Benjamin; it was partly gratitude, yes, but partly something else. She remembered that shooting wouldn't permanently kill a mutant. What did Treemark plan to do with the man once they'd caught him?

Treemark, she remembered, was dedicated to preserving their species; he wouldn't kill a potential breeder if it weren't necessary. Surely he would try, first, to change the man's mind—make him give up the Unseelie blood-sport, renounce power-lust…possibly even alter his personality. If anyone could alter a personality, it was Treemark; he had the skills, and with an Elven subject he would have time—decades, or centuries of it.

Lorraine shivered, remembering an old argument back at the union hall, about the death penalty and Behavior Modification. Was it crueler to execute a man or lock him up in prison and effectively torture him for the rest of his life? Was it kinder to kill or to deform the mind? Was it more ethical to destroy the body or the soul? She remembered what she'd argued then.

"If there are no more questions," said Treemark, rolling up the maps, "Then let's set the house defenses, saddle up and ride."

***

Half an hour later, riding through the desert on the first leg of her assigned grid, Lorraine was still chewing over her questions. Leila plodded dutifully under her, as if understanding that this would be a long ride and one shouldn't waste energy in this heat.

Benjamin rode some twenty yards ahead on Overcast, his face closed and thoughtful.

Wally and Steven, on the two bay mares, rode another twenty yards or so to either side.

It was no accident, she knew, that they'd formed this defensive triangle-pattern with herself in the center; no doubt Treemark had warned them—if Ben hadn't—to protect her above all else. She should have been flattered.

Instead, she kicked Leila forward to come up beside Benjamin, so she could speak to him without being overheard.

"If we find him," she said quietly, "We kill him. Permanently. Right there. We don't take him captive and bring him home; we just kill him and have done with it."

Ben gave her an unreadable look. "Are you eager to learn what a power-transfer feels like?" he asked, his voice expressionless.

"Hell, no," Lorraine snapped. "You take his power if you want it, or give it to Wally, or Steven. I just want him dead. It's the quickest and surest way to be rid of him, shed of him forever, and that's what I want."

Benjamin said nothing, but only nodded, his expression thoughtful and distant.

His silence made Lorraine shiver in the heat. "Do you think I'm a bloodthirsty bitch?" she asked bluntly.

Benjamin raised his eyebrows in surprise. "Oh no," he laughed, "Just practical. That's exactly what I would do, you know."

"I think Brian wants to capture him alive, and convert him," Lorraine admitted. "He's so concerned with us being an endangered species, I don't think he'd want any of us killed."

"Brian has great faith in his own powers of…conversion," Benjamin frowned. "I suppose he could do it, but I'd rather not take that risk."

Lorraine realized, without reaching to *feel* for him, that Benjamin had some of the same doubts that she had—and didn't want to mention them, no more than she did. *Give him another reason.* "'Convert a man against his will, He's of the same opinion still'," she quoted. "This stalker has made it clear that he's very devoted to this blood-sport, and I don't want to take any risks with him."

Benjamin nodded again, his expression lightened. "Pull back into central position," he said, trying to sound stern. "You're too easy a target where you are."

Lorraine dutifully reined Leila back until she was placed between the other three riders again, and realized that there was another advantage to her position. Her mare was unlikely to run away with her, surrounded like this, so she could forget about guiding Leila and concentrate on using her psychic sense to search for the hunter. Treemark's party needed dogs to increase their hunting-range, but she didn't. She clasped her hands on the saddle-horn, closed her eyes and *felt* the countryside around her.

The first consciousness she felt, of course, was the mare under her. After that came impressions of Benjamin ahead, Steven and Wally behind, and their horses.

Beyond them stretched the mindless vitality of desert plants, the quick sparks of assorted small animals, the distant wordless intensity of a solitary hawk—and nothing more, nothing human anywhere within her reach. Pace by pace the search party moved forward, and nowhere did Lorraine feel any threat.

Long minutes passed, the climbing sun beat down, and the quiet of the desert stretched long. Lorraine found herself tiring of the fruitless search, and her mind began to wander. Just as an experiment, she tried pulling energy off one plant to transmit to another, and found that she couldn't do it at a distance. She tried influencing a scorpion to crawl into the hunting-territory of a near-by cactus owl, and couldn't do that either.

Whatever she might be able to do within the range of a node, there were still limits to what she could do outside of it. That thought was oddly reassuring.

They reached the northern end of the search-route, not coincidentally at the foot of a steep-sided mountain ridge, where Lorraine stretched her psychic sense to the limit, trying to blanket the entire mountain slope, and found nothing but small animal life.

Benjamin consulted the map, then led them eastward along the edge of the ridge. After about 50 yards he glanced at Lorraine, who shook her head, and then turned south.

Again the hunting-party paced through the desert, searching with eyes and psychic sense, finding nothing. The sun rose higher, and the heat lay on them like a heavy blanket. They paused briefly at the bend of a narrow stream to let the horses drink, and then moved on.

Lorraine, her psychic sense stretched wide, began to lose her awareness of just where she was. She seemed to be part of this patch of desert through which they rode, connected to every living thing within it, conscious of the animals hiding from the sun in any patch of shade or in their burrows, aware of the plants digging their roots into the cooler ground, everything moved by the universal need to find and hoard water and avoid the fierce heat…

There! The sudden difference shocked her back to herself. *There*— Just at the edge of her range, to the southeast, a human presence, all too familiar.

"There!" she shouted, pointing. "It's him! Behind that clump of brush! Less than seventy yards—"

Benjamin snapped a fast curse, drew his pistol and spurred Overcast into a gallop toward the brush-pile. Lorraine did likewise. Wally and Steven followed, Steven pulling out his cell-phone to rattle the information into it.

Lorraine could *feel* the intruder's sudden alarm at seeing them charge toward them, and knew he planned to run. He'd turned around, was scrambling with something, some means of escape. She had to hurry. *Faster!* She dug her heels into Leila, urging the mare into a flat-out run. The target was only forty yards away now, thirty…

From the mound of brush came the cough, then roar, of a motorcycle engine.

Lorraine swore as she understood how the stalker meant to flee, then stood up in her stirrups and fired at where she knew the man must be.

Benjamin fired a second after she did.

An instant later, the cycle came bursting out of the brush with the stalker crouched low on top of it, heading due south. Its license plate, Lorraine noted, was obscured with mud.

"He's going for the road!" Benjamin shouted, and reined Overcast to the right.

Lorraine did likewise, understanding that she had only this brief chance to cut off the stalker's retreat. The gap between them was closing; on the rough ground of the desert the cycle couldn't safely make full speed, as the horses could, but once on the road it could pull away from them.

Damn him! Lorraine thought, firing again. The shot had no effect that she could see. All she saw of the stalker was his camouflage-clad back and side, the loose cloth shrouding his shape. *Weber? Harding? Oshansky?* He could have been any of them.

All she could *feel* of him was his intense determination. There was no fear in his flight; he'd done something like this before.

Benjamin stuffed his reins in his teeth, stood in his stirrups, aimed carefully as he could, and fired again.

The stalker flinched visibly, a sudden red patch showing on his right shoulder, and the cycle wobbled and slowed.

We have a chance. Lorraine measured the narrowing gap between her and the cycle, stood in her stirrups and aimed—trying to see the pattern of the unavoidable motion of her arms—and fired.

Metallic sparks flashed briefly off the frame of the cycle, but it rolled on.

To either side of Lorraine, Wally and Steven fired too. Another flash blazed near the handlebars and a fountain of dirt shot up near the front wheel, but the cycle kept moving. Lorraine saw the brief sizzle of violet sparks on the rider's shoulder, and knew that he was whole again. The cycle ducked expertly behind a saguaro cactus, and Lorraine cursed as the gap between them no longer closed. If only there were more brush, more rocks, to slow him down—

She grew aware of Leila's noisy breathing, and knew that the animals couldn't keep up this pace for long. She remembered Steven saying that a horse had only a quarter-mile of all-out speed; how much of that had they used already?

The others were firing again. Once more, Lorraine rose in her stirrups and did likewise. The only effect was another flash, low down on the engine. The cycle stuttered, but kept running. Now the gap slowly widened.

"We're losing him!" Lorraine howled in frustration. "He's getting away!"

And she had maybe three shots left in her revolver, and no hope of reloading at a dead gallop. The cycle was maybe fifty yards ahead now, and pulling further away. She bitterly wished she'd thought to bring the rifle—even though firing that would have taken both hands. She stood and aimed and shot again.

This time the rider flinched, and scraps of leather flew from the top of his boot.

He bent lower on the cycle, but didn't slow it. His hands tightened on the grips, and the cycle picked up speed.

The vegetation, Lorraine realized, was thinning out. They were approaching the road. The others saw that too, for they fired off another flurry of shots.

"Gas tank!" Wally was shouting. "Aim for the gas tank!"

They tried, but the angle was too shallow. Someone's shot blew rubber off the rear tire, but didn't penetrate. The horses were breathing noisily now, and the cycle was still pulling ahead. They fired their last shots as the cycle reached the road, turned left, and roared away at full speed down the tarmac.

They reined to a halt, let the animals put their heads down and pant deeply, while they watched their quarry escape. Lorraine used up every filthy word she could think of, and unconsciously bared her teeth at the highway.

"A cycle, with off-road tires," Wally was saying. "We didn't think of that."

"Makes good sense, though," Steven admitted. "He could have walked it in, hidden it at his hideout, scouted the land quietly on foot…"

"Let's hope," Benjamin murmured, patting Overcast's bowed

neck, "That this little contretemps has scared him off."

A cell-phone beeped, and Steven picked his up. "No," he growled into the speaker, "The bastard had a bike, and got away. We only shot him a couple of times."

He listened awhile, muttered "Okay," and clicked the phone closed. "Boss says to head on home," he announced. "The bastard's not likely to come back today."

"As soon as the horses are rested," Benjamin promised, un-slinging his canteen. "And we should give them some water."

23.

LUNCH WAS SIMPLE, subdued, and light: a frothy salad laced with shreds of crabmeat and an iced wine-punch. Everyone, Treemark included, was relaxed and cheerful from their temporary triumph.

"We should keep the guards, and the dogs, for another week anyway," Helen said as she forked up a sliver of radish. "There's still a chance he might try to sneak up and set some building afire to bring us out. As I recall, that was Mouzakian's favorite stunt."

"Mouzakian," Wally noted, "Has been dead for a century and a half."

"The trick still works, though," Steven added quietly.

"We'll keep the guards," Treemark agreed, "Though I expect our visitor has realized by now that he's bitten off more than he can chew."

"That depends on how dedicated he is." Benjamin turned to look at Lorraine. "Can you give us any insights on his personality?"

"All I know is that he wasn't afraid when he started to run, but that may have changed when our bullets reached him." Lorraine paused to think. "He's put a lot of effort into this hunt, but he's also gotten hurt with every move."

"We've shot him, we've set dogs on him, and we've stopped him at every turn," Daniel elaborated. "He also has a nice job in Chicago, which he might not want to jeopardize by prolonged absence."

"Nonetheless," Madge narrowed her eyes, "He might try one more stunt. He still has his official standing in Chicago, and he could use that in some way."

"But whether he's a local, state, or even federal cop," Treemark added, "He's based in Chicago. What could he call on there to attack us here, several states away?"

"Nothing official," Steven considered. "Any equipment he wanted, he'd have to sneak out. That limits his options."

"Planning and executing that," Daniel smiled, reaching for his wineglass, "Will take several days, at least. I think we'll have peace for awhile, if not permanently."

Lorraine toyed with her fork, pondering the possibilities. The enemy mutant might not be limited to what he could draw upon from his job; they had no idea how old he was, what secret fortune he might have amassed, what private sources he could call up — including the Mafia. For all they knew he might have a cache of pirate gold, or a storehouse of weapons from World War Two, or some third-hand Vietnam-era fighter jet at his disposal.

She didn't think he would give up and go away. Then again, that might just be her own Chicago paranoia speaking.

She finished her salad, and said nothing more.

After lunch, she went straight back to her easel and finished off the last details on "Parasites". Once the final stroke was in place she paused only to pick up her photos and sketch of Leila, then turned the canvas around and studied the portrait of the black mare.

She found a few details left that she could fill in, and picked up the fine-point brush to add them. A touch of pale orange here, green there…

"Very nice," said Benjamin from behind her.

Lorraine spun around, startled. "I didn't hear you come in," she accused. *Or feel you, dammit.*

"You were too absorbed to notice me," Benjamin smiled. "Tell me, why haven't you moved your easel back to the solarium? Or the crafts room, for that matter?"

"It just seemed like too much trouble…" She turned back to the painting, studying the curve of Leila's tail.

"There are more comfortable places to paint than your bathroom," he nudged.

"Maybe tomorrow, the crafts room…" she said, applying a brushstroke of yellow-green to the background.

Benjamin stood, came up behind her, and rested his hands gently on her shoulders. "Or are you hiding in here?" he asked quietly. "Hiding from the hunter, or from everyone else?"

Lorraine stabbed her brush into the jar of turpentine, feeling irritated. "Neither," she snapped. "I'm just taking out my feelings on painting, since there's nothing else I can do with them. That takes concentration. So?"

"So, what feelings?" Benjamin's hands began kneading her shoulders, making her notice how tired they really were. "Name them."

Lorraine sighed, and set down her palette on the sink. "Impatience, or anger," she guessed. "I have no evidence to convince the others, but it's not over; the stalker isn't going away. And you are."

"Ah." He worked his hands slowly down her arms. "I promise, I won't leave until this business is settled, one way or the other. You don't need to start armoring your heart against sorrow. Not yet."

Lorraine was astonished at how deeply those words struck her. Saying nothing, she turned again and hugged Benjamin—hard—then reached up and kissed him.

His arms slipped around her as if they had always belonged there.

She didn't know how long they stood like that, or where she would have gone from there, for Ben pulled reluctantly back from her and held her at arm's length. "No time for more, dear heart," he said. "I came to tell you that it's almost dinnertime. …Ah, and you've got a paint-smear on your jeans."

Lorraine didn't know whether to laugh or cry, but she settled on cleaning her brush and palette—and pants—and then following Benjamin out to the dining room.

***

Dinner was excellent as always—an authentic southwestern-Indian cornmeal-and-chili pie with genuine venison, chicken soup with sage, a cactus-fruit salad and a chilled fruit wine. Lorraine addressed herself to the food and let the conversation roll past her.

Her mind kept wandering between the finished painting, the feel of Benjamin's kiss and the question of what the Unseelie stalker would do next. Only over dessert—a delicious cherry tart—did she remember that she had a session with Treemark after dinner.

Neither of them said anything as they walked to the clinic office, closed the door and sat down.

Treemark took a good mouthful of his drink, then set it aside. "All right," he said, "Are you still angry about missing your shot at the stalker?"

Did Benjamin talk to him? "Yes!" she snapped. "You know he isn't going away, and all that hopeful talk at lunch was only wishful thinking. He'll be back, and we don't know when or how."

"Are you afraid, then?"

"No, furious. I want him dead, as fast as possible, before he thinks up some other harm to do."

Now Treemark did raise an eyebrow at her. "You've lived under threat before. Why is this particular stress so especially bad?"

"It's not the threat, it's the helplessness." Lorraine slugged down a quarter of her drink. "We have to wait for him to come at us, at his own time, on his own terms—and we can't even guess what those will be."

"We can guess at his limits."

"What if we can't? He could be Mafia-connected, and those bastards can cover a lot of ground."

"They want to silence a witness against one of their hit-men," Treemark agreed. "So your best choice is to stay hidden inside our fortress until the trial. Once you've testified, the mob will have less reason to give the stalker extensive help. We can still make some guesses about his limits."

Lorraine took a slower sip, and thought that over. She had to admit that staying in the house had its appeal; she could go out riding later, and her studies at the node could wait. One thing she had on her side was time. And, just possibly, Benjamin might stay a little longer…

No, laying obligations on him could be a good way to lose him.

"That would still leave me hiding in the house for an unspecified length of time," she said. "How long will he wait before giving up? For that matter, he might choose to come after my teacher instead—one power-drain being as good as another. None of us would be safe, unless we all stayed in the fortress. What kind of life is that?"

"We've done it before." Treemark smiled grimly. "At one point, during the Thirty Years' War, I and my household stayed in a castle under siege for nearly a year. After that, being snowbound in a cabin for three months, during the Alaskan gold-rush, was no great strain."

Lorraine stared at him, struck anew by the weight of years behind this man. No, she still wasn't used to thinking in Elven terms.

"The hardest part, then," Treemark went on, "Was keeping amused. Our castle bard ran out of songs, and had to invent new ones. Nowadays that's much less of a problem; we have television, and the Internet, and recordings of nearly everything. Now, how long do you think you'll have to wait until the trial in Chicago?"

"I don't know…" *I could call Weber. If he doesn't answer, that will prove he's the hunter…unless he has a call-forwarding system. Oshansky wouldn't give me the time of day, even if I knew his number. The FBI…* "Dianne," Lorraine remembered. "She's not part of the stalker's army, and she owes me."

"So call her."

"Yes…" *Anytime, day or night, she once said.* Lorraine reached for her belt, found the holstered cell-phone, and slowly pulled it out. Her mind felt blank, but her fingers remembered the number.

Berringer picked up on the second ring. "Lorraine?" she asked, sounding amazed.

"Yes, it's me. Do you have any idea when I'll be called on to testify?" *There. Short and sweet.*

"How did you find out?!" Berringer squawked in the phone. "We only heard about it this evening; I was going to call you in the morning… Trial begins this Thursday, Superior Court, room three, 8 AM…er, I have the address here…"

"Pen! Pad!" Lorraine snapped, coming out of her daze. How, she wondered, had the Chicago DA pushed the case forward so fast? These things usually took months…

The media must be all over this one, she concluded. *Or maybe the governor's leaning on the courts…*

Treemark reached into a drawer, brought out the requested items, and set them in front of Lorraine. She grabbed the pen just as Berringer's voice came back on the line, and duly scribbled down the day, time and address. "Got it," she muttered. "Got it!"

"Lorraine…" Berringer sounded half desperate. "Will you accept our help getting there?"

"No," Lorraine answered firmly. "I think I can make safer arrangements privately." A twinge of conscience prompted her to add: "Thank you anyway, Dianne—for everything."

She clicked the phone off quickly, and looked up at Treemark. "Thursday morning," she said, tapping the pad. "This address, Chicago."

"I'll arrange transport," said Treemark. "A bullet-proof limousine will take you—and Wally and Benjamin—to a small commercial airport, where you'll board a private plane and fly to a similar airport just outside Chicago. Another armored car, and guards, will take you to the courthouse. Yes, I've been thinking about this since your last trip."

Lorraine remembered that trip, and Benjamin's role in it. This would be shorter, possibly without an overnight stay, but Ben would be with her through all of it. She was almost embarrassed by her relief, her gratitude at being protected; was it a weakness to want to lean on someone else for a change? She'd never really had that in her life…

Then something else Treemark had said finally registered.

"Then everyone else will stay here?"

"Oh, yes." His grim smile was back. "If the stalker learns that you're no longer in the house, but feels an aura anyway, he'll assume it's your teacher—me—but only if I'm visible."

Brian will take my place as bait? Lorraine felt the hair prickle on the back of her neck. "And…what if he tries for you?"

"He'll have to come into the house, and I'll catch him this time." Treemark's smile was less grim, almost merry, and somehow terrifying. "I've made a few improvements to our in-house defenses."

"If you take him alive…" Lorraine knew she wouldn't like the answer, but had to ask. "What will you do with him?"

Treemark shrugged. "Make him renounce the ways of the Unseelie Court."

Lorraine had a sudden vision of the unknown mutant stretched between the columns in the solarium, and shuddered. "And just how do you plan to do that?" Her voice sounded hoarse in her own ears. "Brainwashing? Or does lobotomy work on our kind?"

"No!" Treemark snapped back, looking honestly offended. "Neither do drug-treatments, or…" He caught himself, and gave Lorraine a thoughtful look. "I plan to tell him as much of the truth as is safe, then cure his addiction to the power-transfer."

"Whether he wants to be cured or not?"

"I expect he won't want to be cured." Treemark smiled sadly. "Yes, I've done this sort of thing before. The way to cure a junkie is: first take away his junk, then give him something better to obsess about. Obsession is what really makes junkies; the physical side of addiction is the least of it."

That was a tempting subject, but Lorraine refused to be sidetracked. "Just how do you cure obsession?" she demanded, remembering her college Psychology 101 course. "Some people simply have obsessive personalities. What can you do about that?" *Break down the personality, and rebuild it along lines you like?*

Treemark sighed, almost in defeat. "It's possible to alter an obsessive personality, but it's difficult, and takes a long time, and usually requires the willing cooperation of the patient." He shrugged again. "Without that cooperation…" He shrugged. "Well, there are other ways."

Yes. Lorraine unconsciously leaned forward. "Just how far would you go to… change someone's mind?"

Treemark looked puzzled for a moment, then gave her a double-take. "Helen told you to ask that, didn't she?" he frowned.

Helen?! "Please just answer the question."

"All right." Treemark dropped his hands into his lap and met her gaze. "Yes, I'd do anything I could to make our kind give up genocide. I might not be successful, but yes, I'd try."

"Anything?" Lorraine insisted. "Even if you wound up with a mindless hulk, just so long as the body could live to breed?"

Treemark's shoulders tensed, as if he were clenching his fists in his lap. "In time, the mind would re-grow…"

"It just wouldn't be the same mind, the same person, would it?"

"Dammit, Hel— Lorraine, there are so few of us!" He sounded desperate. "You know what happens to a species with too little genetic variety, and there can't be more than a thousand of us in the whole world! Every loss diminishes us… Yes, yes, I *would* break down and rebuild the man's mind just to keep from killing him. Yes. Can't you understand why?"

And here's where we part company. "Aren't you forgetting something?"

"What?"

"Convergents—like me." The image spread out clearly in Lorraine's mind, and she found the words to fit it. "God knows how long the gene passed down on both sides, through how many generations—enough to pick up a host of different chromosomes, enough to guarantee all the genetic variety you could want. You don't have to price seed above the mind. If we really do have souls, then they're worth a little more than that."

Treemark only looked at her, saying nothing.

"That's why you sent me off to the east today," Lorraine went on, "When the stalker's tracks led west. Were you trying to keep me safe from him, or him from me?"

Treemark managed a bleak smile. "You're worth a dozen of him, easily. I didn't want you to face each other, period. It's a lose-lose situation."

"I'm not particularly eager to face him myself," Lorraine admitted. "I just want him gone, permanently—and not chained up in the basement, thank you. If you catch him first, promise me that you'll either kill him outright or… send him off to be a lab-rat somewhere else."

"All right." Treemark raised his hands in surrender. "I know a place where I could send him. It won't be easy, but…" He shrugged.

Lorraine didn't know whether to feel guilty that she'd forced him into difficulty, or flattered that he valued his promise to her that much. Then she wondered if he weren't trying to manipulate her with either emotion. "Do it, then," she said curtly. "I won't promise to spare him if I catch him first."

"Just promise to survive, at all cost."

"That in any case." *Wait: not at all cost. I wouldn't sacrifice Ben to save myself...* Right there, Lorraine realized just how much she loved Benjamin. The knowledge was dizzying.

"So," Treemark smiled, "How is the painting coming along?"

Lorraine almost wilted with relief at the change of subject. "I've finished it," she said. "If you'd like to see it now..." She suddenly hoped that Benjamin wouldn't be waiting in the bedroom.

"Certainly," said Treemark, pulling out of his chair.

***

The bedroom was empty, thank whatever gods there were. Lorraine led Treemark into the bathroom and simply pointed toward the easel.

"Painting in the bathroom?" he puzzled, glancing about.

"More privacy, fewer distractions."

"You could always paint in the crafts-room," said Treemark, studying the portrait of Leila. "Nobody else is using it at present, and the lighting is very good. ...That's a truly excellent rendering, by the way; you've caught her quirky personality perfectly."

"Let's hope it sells for the same amount."

"Or better," Treemark considered. "You've greatly improved your detailing."

Lorraine chewed her lip. "The problem," she admitted, "Would be what to do about the other side."

"Other side?"

Lorraine resolutely took hold of the board and turned it over, revealing the brooding allegory on the other side. "It's called 'Parasites'," she added. "I suppose it could be covered up during the framing process."

Treemark shook his head slowly, staring. "I don't think that will be necessary," he murmured. "In fact, it may add to the price."

Lorraine let out a breath she hadn't realized she was holding. "Take it, then," she said. "Same commission as before."

Without another word, Treemark carefully picked up the painting by its edges and carried it away. She couldn't translate his expression as he left, save that it was thoughtful.

So, now there was nothing to do but take her bath and wait for

Benjamin. There was no need to move the easel and kit tonight; it could all wait until she came back from Chicago.

She was just about ready to step into the bathtub when she felt the familiar aura, and Benjamin came in.

***

Helen was awake and waiting when Treemark came into the master bedroom, and she noted instantly his sullen look. "Hard session?" she asked. "You're later than usual."

Treemark dropped to the bed and began pulling off his boots. "Congratulations," he muttered. "You've won another ally."

"I beg your pardon?"

"Lorraine. She won a promise from me that I wouldn't do all-out personality modification on our stalker, if I caught him. She has the same attitude toward souls that you do. Did you put her up to that?"

"No." Helen sat up, amazed. "We never discussed it. In fact, outside of meals, I haven't seen her all day. Benjamin said she was throwing herself into her painting…"

"So she thought that up by herself?" Treemark turned to look at Helen. "Wonderful. I'm surrounded by pious, bloodthirsty women."

"Brian, don't start this argument again."

"Then forgive me for believing that our survival is more important than any one man's personality—particularly if it's a vicious mind to begin with."

"That's not what worries me." Helen draped an arm across his shoulders. "I'm more concerned with what your belief can do to you."

"Me?"

"The ends don't justify the means, and the road to hell is paved with good intentions—

"Spare me the old quotes, please."

"And technique is morally neutral," she finished. "If you can destroy a soul for a good cause, you can just as easily destroy it for a bad one. What sort of monster would that make of you?"

Treemark opened his mouth, then shut it again.

"I don't need to be a psychiatrist to see that there's more than a touch of the obsessive about you, Brian." Helen reached down to tug his shirt free of his waistband. "In fact, you're right on the edge of becoming a fanatic."

"Because I believe in our survival?"

"Because you think you can save all of us—every last one—when you know it can't be done."

Treemark winced, then gave a sigh that seemed to empty him. He pulled off his shirt and lay down beside Helen. "'If a clod is washed away, Europe is the less'," he murmured. "'Ask not for whom the bell tolls…'"

"You can't save them all." Helen slid her arms around him and rested her head on his shoulder. "Yes, there are times when you have to judge who will get into the lifeboat. Which of us would you risk to save this unknown headhunter?"

"None of us, and you know it." Treemark closed his eyes. "I've killed, before this, to preserve my household. I didn't like it then, and I don't like it now."

"I'd be worried if you did like it." Helen massaged his shoulders gently. "So what will you do if you manage to catch him alive?"

Treemark twitched a half-smile. "Knife him through the heart, bundle him into a crate, and send him to Vassily."

"Vassily?!" Helen gave him an outraged look, which of course he didn't see. "But you know what he'll do!"

"Oh, yes." Treemark grinned, not opening his eyes. "His methods may be ancient and crude, but they can be quite effective—up to a point."

"Fasting and prayer, flogging and isolation—"

"And a nice safe cell in the monastery basement. A few decades of that—maybe half a century—should make our stalker reconsider his ways."

Helen snorted, but not in disbelief. "Well, it will keep him away from Lorraine long enough, anyway."

"Yes. …And by the way, she'll be going back to Chicago tomorrow. The trial starts Thursday morning."

If he was expecting an explosion, he was disappointed. Helen only sighed and turned away. "Who besides Benjamin is going with her?" was all she said.

***

Lorraine lay quiet in Ben's arms, trying to settle the whirl of her feelings, wondering how to break the news. There was, she finally decided, no easy way.

"The Chicago trial starts Thursday morning," she said. "I have to be there. Treemark's making the arrangements."

Benjamin tightened his grip a fraction of an inch. "I'll be going with you, of course, and we should take Wally again."

Lorraine gripped his arm and fought off a sudden urge to cry. "I'm so tired," she admitted, amazed that her voice was shaky. "This is the big step. Once I testify, it's over; the Mafia won't bother me again, and the stalker will run out of support. He'll have to give up. Just this one trip, and it's finished. I should be delighted, but I'm just… so tired."

"It's reaction." Ben kissed her neck. "This has been a rather stressful day, after all. Right now you have time to rest, and your body is telling you to take advantage of that. Sleep, Lorraine. Rest and gather your strength."

"Yes…" *But I'll have to pack tomorrow…*

She knew there was more; Chicago meant going into the enemy's lair, where he might have left ambushes for her. It also meant a chance to see her friends, and the cats, again—if that didn't put them in more danger. It meant trusting to Treemark's 'arrangements', whatever those were, and she had found reason—on one small point at least—not to trust him completely. Chicago—and its approach and exit—was dangerous.

Her old city wasn't home anymore.

The ranch was.

24.

THE CAR PARKED outside was a suspiciously heavy limousine, plainly bulletproof. Wally was waiting in the car as Lorraine and Benjamin tossed their bags in the trunk and then climbed in.

"The driver's armed," Wally announced cheerfully, then pointed under the seats. "Of course, we are too. And note that there's a guard sitting with the driver."

"Damn!" Lorraine snapped, remembering. "I left my gun and sword in my bag."

"No problem," said Benjamin, patting the underside of the seat. "We're quite adequately supplied."

The limousine rolled out, and Lorraine took a long look at the passing scenery.

There was Gold Eagle out in the paddock, looking subdued and chewing busily on the grass; Treemark or Steven must have given him a lot of work this morning. She couldn't see Leila anywhere, or Overcast, and that too gave her a pang of loss. Tears stung her eyes, and she rubbed them away quickly. "What if the stalker shows up while I'm gone?" she couldn't help asking.

"He'll walk into a bear-trap," Wally grinned. "Don't worry, Lorraine; you won't come back to a pile of smoking rubble."

Lorraine managed two syllables of a nervous laugh; that was, in fact, close to what she'd been thinking. Stupid, of course: Treemark had centuries of combat experience to draw upon, and knew how to manage a siege. "And if the stalker's following us," she added, "He's staying out of range."

"And your range is considerable," Ben murmured.

Right there Lorraine felt a sudden savage hope that the Unseelie hunter really would follow her, come to Chicago to try for her again. He might have resources there, but so did she; the union would surely rally to protect her, to make certain that the killers of their General Secretary had no chance to silence the witness. A single phone-call could do it. She tapped her fingers on the holster of her cell-phone, and turned to Wally.

"What's planned for Chicago?" she asked. "He probably can't stop us between here and there, but what do we do in the city?"

"Guards will meet us at the field," Wally grinned, "In another limo like this one, and we all go off to a very discreet hotel."

"To the penthouse, to be precise," Benjamin added. "Nobody will get onto that floor without our express permission."

"Penthouse!" Lorraine marveled, considering how much even a single night in such a place would cost. Treemark was sparing no expense to guarantee her safety. "And from there to the courtroom too, I suppose?"

"Not quite to the courtroom," Wally frowned. "We can go armed only as far as the courthouse door. They won't let even the most respectable armed guards through the front doors—or the back. The guards will be unarmed body-blockers, and nothing else."

"Still," Benjamin cut in smoothly, "I really doubt that our friend will try anything in a crowded courthouse."

"He might, being a cop himself." Lorraine frowned, calculating. "That's our window of vulnerability…" But perhaps there was a way she could close that. "Can we get some disguises?" she asked. "I have a few ideas…"

Wally and Benjamin exchanged looks. "I'll call Brian. He can have the goodies sent to the penthouse," said Ben, pulling out his phone. He paused to glance at Lorraine. "Do you have something specific in mind?"

"I'm thinking," Lorraine smiled grimly, "That I could arrange for friends of mine to line the hallway, straight from the front door to the courtroom—and inside it. We'd just have to blend in with them… Have you got that legal-pad handy?"

Ben did, and Lorraine spent a few minutes making notes and sketches. He laughed when she showed him the result. "Yes, dammit! That would work beautifully. Who would suspect?"

"For that matter…" Wally thoughtfully scratched his chin. "We could call up the DA, explain that somebody's trying to stop you from getting there—somebody who could well be a cop, and have his office provide the extra protection."

"Be sure to mention that the stalker might be a state trooper, or a federal," Lorraine added. "If we can make him believe it…" —*then I won't have to put my union buddies at any more risk than necessary.*

"I'll pass that on to Brian," Benjamin promised, then bent over his phone and jabbed buttons. "Brian? Good. Look, we've come up with some last-minute ideas; tell me what you think of them…"

Lorraine leaned back in her seat, feeling suddenly drained by relief. She didn't have to organize the defenses herself; someone else could handle the details from here, and quite competently—and that was a marvel too great for words. She let Ben's words stream past her, feeling so relaxed that she thought she could sleep. She hadn't slept well the night before.

Don't lose your edge, she reminded herself. Protection like this was not something she could count on forever: only for today, and tomorrow, and perhaps a little time beyond that. It was a rare jewel, not something to be taken for granted.

"Right. …All right." Benjamin closed the phone. "They'll call back in an hour or so," he said. "They've been thinking along similar lines, and he'll see what can be done."

Protection, official and unofficial… Right there Lorraine was struck with another inspiration. She sat up fast and reached for her cell-phone. "I just thought of the perfect touch for the disguises," she said. "Something that will alert our friends, but our enemies won't notice. You'll have to give me the name and address of that hotel…" She punched buttons, hoping that Meredith was at home.

***

Treemark set down the phone, sighed and stretched until his joints crackled. Yes, it was good to know that Lorraine was thinking in broader and deeper survival terms—even if that meant he'd had to make some hurried phonecalls and detailed arrangements. Helen's input had been very useful, and that idea about disguises wonderfully simple and clever—and of course she'd known everyone's clothing sizes. Yes, his protégé would be amply protected in Chicago.

As for the rest of his household, the improved security arrangements would guarantee their safety as much as anything could in this world. *The traps, especially…*

He found himself wishing that the stalker would come today, tonight, tomorrow at the latest. He could take the man alive if he came while Lorraine was away; the odds would be worse once she returned. Not that he would hesitate for a moment to sacrifice the unknown Unseelie for Lorraine—that was beyond question—but he badly wanted to save the fool's life if it were at all possible.

There are so few of us!

Lorraine's accusing look, Helen's worry, came back to haunt him. Gods, was it truly worse to break a man's mind than to kill him outright? Was the mind that much more valuable than the life, or the genes, when the species was endangered? Was he becoming obsessed himself? He didn't have any answers.

Well, it might not be so extreme a choice as that; the stalker might be amenable enough that Vassily's methods would work quickly and easily. The ancient monk, former priest, knew more about the artful uses of pleasure and pain and isolation than Treemark himself did—had been his teacher, more than once—and knew enough about psychological manipulation that he'd made the Russian government leave his hospital alone, even during the worst of Stalin's temper-tantrums. If the stalker were a youngster— less than 1000 years old, knowing only what the modern Unseelies knew—Vassily could change his mind readily, without having to radically alter the personality. Millions of common mortals changed the course of their lives for nothing more than a good reason, or a good opportunity; Vassily could provide that, and more.

And if the stalker truly was a power-junkie, addicted to the surge of the power-transfer, rejoicing in the deaths of his own kind… Well, Vassily had methods for dealing with that, too. Simply altering the man's choice of addiction wouldn't be much of a change. Lorraine couldn't complain about that, if she learned of it, if she asked.

Treemark sighed again. Yes, it was true; the student affected the teacher as much as the teacher taught the student. He would never have agonized over what to do with the stalker before he'd met Lorraine. The woman's fierce ethics were infecting him.

He was awed, and a little dismayed, at what he was setting loose on the world.

***

The airfield was small but well tended, and the two burly men in mechanics' jumpsuits would have seemed part of the scenery if Lorraine hadn't been watching for them. They sauntered closer as the limousine drew up beside the sleek little plane, and nodded almost imperceptibly as the driver leaned casually out the window.

Professionally wordless signals passed; the driver turned off the engine and got out, and opened the limousine door nearest to the plane. Benjamin and Wally flanked Lorraine for the few short paces to the steps. Behind them, Lorraine noted, the driver's assistant opened the limousine's trunk and the two 'mechanics' pulled out the duffel bags.

The plane's interior was luxurious for its small size, with the pilot and navigator seated just ahead of the door, six passenger seats behind that, a tiny refrigerator and bar in the back. Benjamin and Lorraine took the first two seats, Wally settled into the seat behind Lorraine, and a moment later the two men came in with the duffels, set them on the seat beside Wally, and took their own places in the next row behind them. The door closed, the plane's engine started promptly, and in another minute the little plane leaped neatly into the air.

Lorraine, who'd never ridden in anything but commercial airliners, was intrigued by the feel of the smaller craft; it was rather like riding a horse, feeling the subtle motion of the wind against the plane's metal skin, the eager thrust of the engines, the pull of the air above the wings. The craft flew closer to the ground than the big airliners did, so she could see the details of the land below her as they soared over it. Fascinating as the scenery was, she knew it wouldn't hold her attention completely for the length of the trip.

Maybe she'd nap after all.

As if he'd read her mind, Benjamin pulled something out of his coat pocket and leaned across the aisle to hand it to Lorraine. It was a paperback book—a collection of British legends about elves—and thick enough that it should keep her occupied for every spare moment of the next two days. As she took it, Lorraine smiled at Ben. Bless him, he thought of everything.

Ben raised a quizzical eyebrow and murmured, just loud enough for her to hear: "Union buttons?"

"Of course," she grinned. "The whole local will be turning out for the trial. It's not only a recognition signal but also a warning. Nobody with a lick of sense assaults a union member in front of other union members—not in Chicago."

Lorraine leaned back in her seat and imagined the look on the stalker's face—and his Mafia buddies'—when the whole local showed up at the courtroom, and her among them. Even if the stalker recognized her through the disguise, he wouldn't dare come after her there. Not even the cops would try to break through one of the union's defense-lines; they'd tried it many times before, and failed. And while the courthouse's metal-detectors might not let knives or guns get through, the union's people were wonderfully adept at smuggling in wooden pick-handles and baseball bats; they'd done that a few times before, too.

***

Helen leaned back on the couch, glanced at the untouched drink on the table before her, tapped her fingers on the closed cell-phone in her hand, then returned her gaze to the land beyond the window. The guard patrols had found nothing, as expected, and no one in the house had felt any touch of a stranger's aura. The stalker was keeping a safe distance, possibly studying the pattern of the patrols. He might try his luck after dark again—and be picked up by the long-range sonic detectors, whereupon everyone in the house would be ready and waiting for him. Hopefully, they could catch him in the garden this time: take him down with a silenced gunshot or two… *And then drag him into the basement, prepare him for the trip and send him to Vassily. Out of our lives and off our consciences…and far away from Lorraine.*

Even more than Treemark, she emphatically did not want Lorraine to meet with the stalker. Never mind the physical risk to her protégé—that was as well deflected as the household could manage—but because she didn't like the thought of Lorraine in combat. There was a deep ferocity in the girl that Helen didn't want to see aroused, much less encouraged. If Lorraine killed the stalker…

…if she takes his power, and finds that she likes it…

No, that was too terrible a possibility to contemplate.

Helen felt a sudden savage wish that the stalker would come tonight, and she'd find him first. Brian's 'shipping preparations' might take too long, and the man must not be in the house when Lorraine returned. No.

If Brian couldn't find it in himself to kill the meddling bastard, she could.

***

Everybody entered the hotel in formation, the assistant limo-driver in the lead, the two 'mechanics'—now wearing unremarkable suits—next, only the driver staying behind. Lorraine guessed that he was staying with the car, just in case of sabotage attempts. Benjamin reached the desk, said a few quiet words and was given a small envelope full of key-cards, and a moment they were all riding up the elevator to the penthouse.

The last of the sunset was gleaming blue and gold over Lake Michigan, a glorious view through the wide windows of the sumptuous apartment, but Lorraine scarcely noticed; she kept her eyes on the bodyguards, and noted how they promptly deployed through the various rooms. Ben and Wally waited, flanking Lorraine, until the guards came back from their search to report with no more than a nod that all was clear. Ben picked up his bag and

Lorraine's, and led her to the nearest bedroom off to the left. A quick glance back through the door showed Wally and one guard taking the bedroom next door and the other heading for the room beyond that. Lorraine closed the door and carefully bolted all the locks.

Benjamin set down the bags, went to the nightstand phone where a small red light was blinking, picked up the phone and punched the button. He muttered into the speaker for a moment, and then set it down.

"There's a package waiting for us," he announced. "I'll send one of the guards down to get it. Would that be from Brian or your friend?"

It turned out to be both—a large new suitcase and a small envelope, brought by the assistant driver. Ben set the suitcase on the bed and opened it.

"Perfect," he laughed, pawing through the contents. "Everything you asked for, and more. What have you got there?"

Lorraine poured the contents of the envelope into her hand, and held it out for him to see. "The union buttons," she smiled. "Now we have everything."

"Excellent." Benjamin kicked off his shoes and lay down on the bed. "We'll have to send for room service," he grinned. "It won't be anything like Daniel's cooking, but it should be edible at least."

"Daniel spoils us for anyone else's cuisine," said Lorraine, settling beside him.

"I sometimes wonder," Ben purred, "If he isn't Brian's best recruiting tactic. Well, if you'll fetch the room-service menu, I'll make the call."

"And we can lay out the disguises while we wait," said Lorraine, picking through the suitcase's contents.

Benjamin eyed her thoughtfully. "After dinner," he said quietly, "Shall I turn on the TV and look for another stupid monster-movie?"

Lorraine froze, remembering. "Do I look that bad?" she couldn't help asking.

"Fierce as an army poised for battle," he answered, "Which is, I suppose, exactly what we are."

I am that, Lorraine admitted, tapping her fingers on the suitcase. "No," she decided. "Let's just watch something lightweight, eat a leisurely dinner, enjoy the nice bathtub I'm sure this place has, and then trade long, slow backrubs."

"I'd like that," Benjamin smiled, looking ever so faintly relieved.

Lorraine caught the meaning behind that look. "I'm not made of spun glass, you know," she snapped. "You don't have to analyze my every word and move for signs that I'm going to fall apart. Just get me into that courtroom so I can testify; once I've said my piece and put that bastard behind bars, the pressure's off."

"A good part of it, anyway," Ben considered. "Please don't be annoyed by our concern, Lorraine. You're a fledgling—the most vulnerable stage, for us: not only because you have a signal that can attract hunters, and don't yet have the skills to fight them off, but also because of the sheer stress of discovering what you are—and all that means. It's like being a child again; what you learn and decide now can set the course of the rest of your life. Can't you forgive us for acting like anxious parents?"

Lorraine had to stop and think before answering that. Her experience with hovering parents hadn't been happy. Then again, if this was a second childhood, could she get it right this time? Could she mature now in a family, of sorts, that truly did love her? Was that really how Treemark and Helen and the rest thought of her?

"Who are the parents here?" she murmured. "Are Wally and Steven my older brothers, then? And are you my childhood sweetheart?"

"I suppose we do fit those roles rather easily, don't we?"

"Would that make Daniel and Madge the kindly old retainers or the dependent aunt and uncle?"

"Possibly something in between." Benjamin picked up the suitcase and set it on the floor, clearing bed-space for Lorraine to lie down if she wished. "Family itself is a rare and treasured thing among our kind."

"Yes," Lorraine remembered. Now that she thought of it, she'd been incredibly lucky to find Treemark—or that he found her. She'd been luckier still in finding Benjamin. And yet…and yet she couldn't entirely trust this new family of hers. Was it only because she'd known them for so little time, or because she'd learned early to be wary of anyone promising love? Was it reasonable or neurotic to be so cautious?

Benjamin rolled toward the nightstand, picked up the room-service menu and opened it. "So," he said calmly, "What shall we order for dinner?"

***

Dinner, eaten in the dining area of the main room and including both the guards, was a quite decent roast beef with a not-bad wine, but Lorraine thought it a poor imitation of the usual dinners back at Treemark Farms. She was surprised at how homesick she felt, and how alien Chicago had become.

Wally and Benjamin plotted intently with the guards, going over the disguises and the timing.

"It might," Benjamin considered, glancing briefly at Lorraine, "Be a good idea if we showed up an hour before the doors open, just in case there's a long line."

Lorraine nodded agreement, imagining the whole local lined up at the courthouse door, possibly with axe-handles hidden down their pants, probably ready to show their union cards if anybody questioned them…

"My card!" she suddenly remembered. Much to the others' surprise, she hopped out of her chair and ran back into the bedroom, grabbed her purse and searched it until she found her wallet. *Strange how I haven't used that in so many weeks…* Yes, there it was, and yes—tucked into its usual place in the flap—her union card. She chuckled as she realized that she hadn't paid this month's dues. *Maybe I'll find a secretary-delegate while waiting in line…* She flinched as she remembered that the local delegate was Bob now. How would he react, seeing her again—in disguise, in mysterious company? For that matter, would Bill Carminski be there? And how would he react?

Best to see if Meredith was there first. In fact, a phonecall would guarantee it.

Lorraine picked up her cell-phone, then paused to think, then tucked the wallet back into her purse and thoughtfully carried the phone back out to the dining room.

"Is it safe to make a local call on the cell-phone?" she asked, "Or should I use the land-line from this room?"

"Cell-phone," one of the guards promptly retorted. "If your friend's phone is bugged, you don't want anyone knowing just where you're calling from."

"Good point." *Merry said the state troopers swept for bugs, but they might have missed one.* Lorraine opened the phone and poked the familiar sequence of numbers.

***

After dinner, Wally and the others deployed—it was too well planned to call 'scattered'—to various ends of the penthouse. Benjamin, with a smile, produced a bottle of blackberry brandy and a container of ice, and invited Lorraine back to their bed-room.

Once there, he casually locked and bolted the door. Then he filled a waiting glass with ice-cubes, poured the brandy over it and handed it to Lorraine. While she sipped appreciatively, he set their weapons neatly on either side of the bed and went to the entertainment cabinet. The television there had a respectably large screen; he turned it on and went hunting through the chan-nels until he found a station that featured music videos, then pulled off his shoes and outer shirt and lay down on the bed.

After a moment, Lorraine kicked off her shoes and stretched out beside him.

"Why brandy for after dessert?" she asked, sipping further. "It's quite good, but I would have thought coffee was more appropri-ate."

"For one thing, we need to get to sleep early tonight," he smiled. "For another, you need to relax. One of life's harder les-sons is learning to rest completely before a battle. Overnight jit-ters sap your strength."

"I see." Lorraine toyed with her glass, remembering Wally and the guards. "I assume somebody will be awake, in shifts, all night?"

"Yes. It'll be fairly easy, with four of them taking turns."

Lorraine took another sip and tried to concentrate on the tele-vision. It was difficult; the music and accompanying videos seemed insipid. She felt restless and irritated.

Benjamin noticed. "Shall I change the channel?" he asked.

"Yes. Maybe you'd better find that monster-movie."

Ben raised an eyebrow, but dutifully took up the remote control and clicked through the other channels, looking for something that resembled a scary film. Nothing likely appeared. "There doesn't seem to be much," he apologized. "Are you sure you wouldn't prefer a nice hot soak in that scandalously large bath, then a long and leisurely back-rub, followed by equally leisurely love-making?"

"Yes," Lorraine laughed, "I suppose that's a better idea."

The tub was huge, and took a long time to fill. Meanwhile, Benjamin took Lorraine's glass and set it on the toiletries-shelf, and helped her out of her clothes—artfully sprinkling kisses on the flesh his hands exposed. Lorraine found herself caught be-tween annoyance and laughter at his subtle little seduction.

Lorraine stood up and deliberately peeled off the last of her clothing by herself—taking care to set her gun-belt beside the tub, within easy reach.

Benjamin wordlessly took off his own clothes, placing his gun and knife close to Lorraine's, then hung two bathrobes and large towels nearby. He also set Lorraine's drink close to the tub and, almost as an afterthought, reached for a cluster of switches on the wall nearby. The strains of classical music chimed softly in the tiled room.

They stepped into the large tub together, and settled almost awkwardly into the foam-covered water. Lorraine stretched out in the heat and consciously made herself relax. Deliberately, she picked up the iced brandy and took a sip. Its sweet chill made a delicious contrast to the invitingly hot water.

"How long has it been," Benjamin asked, "Since you let any-one baby you?"

Lorraine frowned in thought. "I don't think anyone ever did," she considered. "Not even when I really was a baby…"

A memory rose unbidden: herself, small and clumsy-handed, being wrapped in layer after layer of cloth—diaper, pajamas, sweater and cap, blanket and quilt—then stuffed into a stroller and covered with yet another quilt. The swaddling wasn't comfort-ing but constricting; she could barely move under it, and her hands—soft, shaped like little pink balls with ineffective fingers sticking out like thick noodles—couldn't push or pull the imprison-ing stuff away.

"Restraints!" she realized. "It wasn't to keep me warm or pro-tected, or make me feel safe; it was to keep me from moving around, so that Mama could put her attention on more important things." *Is that why the cuffs had such an effect on me?!*

Lorraine realized that what she'd said hadn't made much sense, except to herself. "No," she explained, "Nobody ever cod-dled or comforted me, except for their own purposes—to keep me out of their way, or get something from me. I could never trust it."

And there was that word again, which Treemark had tried so hard to teach her.

Benjamin muttered something in an unknown language, its meaning plain enough. He reached over to the bath-rack and came back with a large soft-bristled brush, rubbed soap onto it, then gently took hold of her nearer foot.

"Did you ever think," he asked rubbing the bristles carefully over her toes, "Did you ever imagine, that there might be another reason for…kindness?"

"I imagined it, but never found it…before," said Lorraine, watching him with a lazy fascination. His hands, she realized, were humbly making love to her foot. "What's your reason, Ben?"

"I like you," he said slowly. "I like your lovely body, and I very much like touching it. I also like the keen warrior spirit inside it. I don't like seeing either of them harmed, or even threatened. I like seeing both of them pleased. I find myself anticipating what might make you happy, as well as safe, and then doing it—just because that, by itself, pleases me. Can you understand this? Can you believe it?"

I know what I can believe. Without effort, Lorraine expanded her psychic sense and *felt* him through the touch.

Yes, he was concentrating on giving her pleasure, through the simple act of washing her foot, and he enjoyed it. Behind that was a touch of sorrow, of regret, and beneath all of it lay a warm affection—mixed with a tinge of…could that actually be admiration? He found something fascinating in her, and was absorbed by it.

"Yes," she breathed, "I can believe you."

Benjamin smiled, darted his head forward and lightly kissed her big toe.

Lorraine chuckled as he leaned back and began working the brush slowly around her ankle, feeling how his hands enjoyed the smoothness of her skin and the springy muscle beneath.

Slowly, almost imperceptibly, she felt the tight watchfulness inside her relax.

Turn it off, she understood. *Go with the flow. Turn it off... For now.*

As Benjamin's hands worked higher up her calf, Lorraine let herself sink deeper into the lovely hot water, blanked her mind and let the sensations own her.

She managed to maintain her determined trance until Benjamin flicked open the drain and tried to lift her bodily out of the tub.

"Enough," Lorraine grumbled. "Ben, this is getting ridiculous; I can stand up by myself, and there's no point in giving yourself a hernia."

She punctuated that by standing up and stepping out onto the bathmat, letting the water slosh in heavy waves behind her. Ben sighed and pulled himself out after her.

"What, won't you let me be a little bit romantic?" His attempted pout was spoiled by the twinkle in his eye, but he managed to snag the terrycloth bathrobe first and drape it around Lorraine's shoulders. "Besides, our breed doesn't have to worry about hernias."

"No?" Lorraine grinned as she wrapped the robe around her. "Maybe not, but I'll bet that slipping and falling back into the tub, splashing water all over the floor, whacking our heads on the tile and knocking ourselves out, and then drowning in the bath water would be…at least a minor inconvenience."

Benjamin whooped at that, and she noted that he had a good mellow laugh when he let himself go. She rubbed herself down thoroughly, and padded into the bedroom under her own power—half afraid that Ben would try to pick her up and carry her if she didn't forestall him.

…and would that be so bad? a treacherous corner of her mind whispered. An image flashed into her mind: Benjamin happily carrying her…over a threshold.

No, she quashed that idea firmly. *That's not for him. Or for me.* Benjamin's survival—and his hope—rested on having a harem of lovers, not a single commitment.

As for herself, she couldn't believe in the old romantic promise of white dress and wedding ring and happily-ever-after; she'd seen too many bad examples. *Not just Momma and Pop, but so many of my old friends from school…*

More disturbing memories flashed as she dropped onto the bed and rolled onto her belly: Veronica, her personality withering in her state-of-the-art upscale house in the suburbs; Barbara, who'd walked out on the same kind of home and thrown herself headlong into local politics to get her life back; Marianne, who'd bounced from marriage to marriage in a hopeless search for Mr. Right; Georgie and his succession of wives, none of them lasting more than two years. Come to think of it, she'd only once seen a happy marriage, and that was Jack Palumbo's. Aside from that, the happiest couples she'd seen were old lovers, cheerfully Living In Sin for decades, like Bob and Meredith.

Of course their children had complicated matters, but then, Lorraine wouldn't have to concern herself with that for another several centuries. No, it was better to have a reliable lover—with no promises, no binding contracts, and no burden of society's expectations.

She'd have no reason to need any binding contracts for another 1200 years, anyway. Until then, simple and honest love would be enough.

25.

THE ALARM WOKE THEM at 6 AM, and Lorraine came up remembering everything.

Combat-readiness jabbed her fully awake, hurried her into the shower and then out to her suitcase, even before the early room-service breakfast arrived. Benjamin followed, fast and efficient and quiet. Neither of them ate much.

Next came the disguises. Benjamin's was simple: a faded quality suit, such as a typical working man might keep for decades and take out of the closet for special occasions: weddings, funerals, and going to court. A union button on the lapel was all it needed to look authentic.

Lorraine's was more complicated, requiring elaborate makeup, a sports-brassiere and a rib-belt over it—and she was grateful she'd gotten used to that during her daily exercises of the past few weeks. On top of that went sturdy jeans, knit shirt and boots such as a factory-hand would wear, formalized by nothing more than a matching denim jacket, and a watch-cap under which she hid her coiled hair. The union button went on the lapel, her wallet went into a hip pocket, her purse and weaponry were tossed into the luggage.

Benjamin applied the final touch, grimacing at the smell of the medical adhesive, and finally stepped back to study the finished work.

"Perfect," he smiled. "You look like a factory-hand who took the day off to attend a notorious trial."

"Exactly the effect we want," Lorraine agreed, studying her reflection in the nearest mirror. "It'll be hard for even Meredith to recognize me."

Benjamin stepped beside her to examine himself in the same mirror. "And do I pass muster?" he asked.

"Oh yes," Lorraine grinned at him. "You look like an underpaid CPA, or law-clerk: the kind an honest union could afford."

"Excellent." Benjamin shouldered the duffel bag, which clanked embarrassingly.

"Let's go see how the others look."

"And give them their union buttons," Lorraine agreed, clutching the remaining pins. "What time is it?"

"A little before seven. With any luck, we'll be at the head of the line when the doors open." He picked up the key-cards and led the way out into the main room.

Wally and the guards stood waiting, likewise dressed as factory-hands on their day off.

"One advantage of these suit-jackets," Wally noted, patting the space below his armpit, "Is the way they hang loose from the shoulders. I could hide an Uzi under here."

The three bodyguards traded sheepish grins.

"Ah, but that's the point of the classic 'sack' suit," Benjamin smiled. "It was designed to make the flabby figures of managers look good, and to hang all wrong on a decently-muscled workingman's frame."

Lorraine laughed fiercely, then wondered if he'd been on either side of the great labor battles of the 20th century. She handed the others their union buttons, and watched while they pinned them on.

"Pity we'll have to leave the hardware in the car," Ben continued, leading them toward the main door. "And we'll have to park the limo somewhere unobtrusive."

They rode silently down in the elevator.

***

Even this early in the morning, there was a line in front of the courthouse door.

The waiting figures were dressed much as Lorraine's party was, and many of them visibly sported union buttons. Almost first in line, noticeable by her long peasant skirt and puffy jacket, was Meredith. Just ahead of her stood Bob, looking grim and purposeful. Seeing them, Lorraine grinned from ear to ear. This would be easier than she'd thought.

"Stop around the corner and let us out," she said, not caring who passed the word to the driver. "Park somewhere close, and we'll phone when we leave."

A few minutes later, Lorraine's squad came strolling back around the corner and up the sidewalk, looking calm and businesslike. The guards and Wally took places at the end of the line, but Lorraine and Benjamin plodded to the front where Meredith waited.

Lorraine grinned as she pulled out her union card and held it open. "Hey, Meredith," she called out in her best Chicago accent, keeping her voice pitched low, "Izzer a delegate around 'ere? I wanna pay my dues."

Meredith turned and stared, frowned in puzzlement at Lorraine, then looked at the open dues-book. She did a classic double-take, gave a whoop that drew Bob's startled attention, clapped a hand over her mouth and quivered like jello in an earthquake. Bob, worried, looked from her to Lorraine, to the dues-book to Benjamin, then back to Lorraine again. A huge smile split his face.

"Pretty good, Ro—Rocky," he chuckled. "Yeah, I've always got my traveling delegate-kit with me. How many months you wanna pay in advance?"

It took Lorraine a surprising effort to remember how much money she had with her; she hadn't had to pay for anything in weeks. "Uh, gimme six months," she said, fumbling with her wallet.

"Nice disguise," Meredith managed to whisper. "Really, really nice." Then she sailed off into a fit of giggles.

Bob pulled a pen, a folded form and a roll of dues-stamps out of his pocket. "The cats are doing fine," he added. "They trashed a lamp-shade just last night, and gave us hell about trimming their claws."

"Yeah, they'll do that." Lorraine blinked away sudden ridiculous tears. *It may be months, maybe a year, before I see those exasperating little fuzzies again...* She scarcely noticed when Bob pressed the stamps into her dues-book and jotted down the dates.

"Can we crowd in here?" Benjamin asked, "Or do we go to the end of the line?"

"Come on in." Meredith glared at the next man after her to see if he'd complain, which he didn't. He was wearing a union button too, and Lorraine recognized him for one of the local's regulars.

Benjamin waved a casual signal to Wally and the bodyguards, then slipped himself and Lorraine into line between Bob and Meredith and unobtrusively pushed Lorraine toward the courthouse wall so that his body blocked even the sight of her from the street. "Have you seen anyone around that you don't recognize?" he asked quietly.

"Nobody yet," Bob replied, handing the dues-book back to Lorraine. "Not even any slow-moving cars."

"Is anybody packing, do you know?"

"Don't ask, don't tell," Bob grinned toothily. "I told our guys not to bring anything that can be picked up by the metal-detector, anyway."

"So, no range-weapons? What if the goons try for a drive-by?"

For answer, Bob patted his jacket-pocket and grinned wider. "Y'know, wooden slingshots and glass marbles don't get picked up by the metal-detectors."

Benjamin laughed heartily.

Meredith stepped sideways, took a look down the growing line, and moved back.

"Looks like the whole local's showing up," she confided to Lorraine, "And it's another half-hour, already, before the doors open."

"If the goombas are planning anything," Lorraine considered, "They won't try it out here."

"Nor inside." Meredith huddled closer. "Once we're in the courtroom, you and your buddy take the first-row seats right behind the DA's table. We'll pass him a note that you're here and ready, and you'll be surrounded by the local, back and sides."

Lorraine nodded, understanding. If the entire local showed up, there wouldn't be room for anyone else in the courtroom. She couldn't ask for a better shield. Until she stood up to testify, no one but Bob and Meredith would know who she was. Even then, neither stalker nor Mafia thugs could get at her.

Unless, of course, the thug or stalker was already inside—as one of the court officers, perhaps—and desperate enough to take a shot at her in a crowded courtroom.

That was remotely possible, but unlikely.

***

At 8 AM sharp, the doors opened and the crowd pushed through them. All four of the metal-detectors were manned and operating, and the police working the detectors looked nervous. The operators set the detectors' sensitivity so high that they picked up belt-buckles and tooth-fillings and the union buttons, but after seeing the sheer number of union buttons—and the grim, impatient expressions of the people wearing them—they took care to be quick as well.

Bob, Meredith, Benjamin and Lorraine were the first to get through, and they waited for the rest of the crowd to come and surround them. Lorraine noticed Bob passing furtive hand-signals and quick whispers with the other members—and one of them was a worried-looking Bill Carminski. Only when the crowd had filled the front hall did the local begin—slowly, taking time for the rest to catch up—moving down the corridor toward the designated courtroom. Lorraine saw that, under Bob's direction, they formed a tight flying wedge around herself and Benjamin, with Bill taking the point position. As the wedge marched down the corridor, filling it from side to side, the passing cops ducked into doorways to get out of the way.

"In union there is strength", she remembered, smiling.

The union local marched into the courtroom and deployed outward from the prosecution-table. Lorraine found herself just where Meredith had promised, flanked by Ben—with Bob on his other side—and Meredith, with Bill beyond her. She glanced at the next row back and saw Wendy Wexler nearby, surrounded by members from the printshop. Union buttons glittered under the diffused ceiling lights, a sullen sea of them.

The media-corps, coming in behind the crowd, had to scramble to get to the press box and looked a little dismayed at the prospect. Then two bailiffs entered from the rear doors, flanking some dark-suited men with briefcases who proceeded thoughtfully to the prosecution table. *The DA's team,* Lorraine guessed. Benjamin held out a small notepad and pen, as if she'd asked him aloud; she took them gratefully and jotted a quick note: "I'm here and ready. –Roxanne Defarge". She folded the note and handed that to Meredith, then gave back the pen and pad. Meredith handed the note to Bill, with an accompanying whisper. Bill looked puzzled, but leaned over the railing and waved the note at the prosecution team until one of them noticed and took it.

Lorraine didn't see the DA's reaction because, at that moment, a rear door opened again and more bailiffs came in, this time flanking not only two men with suits and briefcases but an all too familiar figure in handcuffs.

The hit-man—Lorraine realized that she'd never learned his name—looked as if he'd put on a bit of weight. He'd changed his haircut, but it still showed a pale line where the dye had grown out. He'd grown a moustache too, but it didn't disguise the line of his cheek and jaw. She recognized him easily.

There was no Elven aura about him. In fact, there was no Elven energy-field detectable anywhere in the courtroom.

Lorraine turned to study the crowd, but couldn't see any of her three suspects in the crush of bodies and faces. Any two of the three could be there, unseen, and only the mutant was absent— off her radar. *Which one?*

Harding had legitimate reason not to be here; it wasn't his case, his only connection with it was Lorraine's request for the Witness Protection Program, and she'd taken herself out of that. Weber was more questionable; he was one of the team of state troopers who'd responded to her phonecall. Wouldn't he expect to be called as a witness? And what about Oshansky? He'd been close enough, when the shots were fired at Bill and Wendy—*if he didn't fire them himself*—to have chased them all the way to the union office; wouldn't he be called to testify? Were they here? And if not, what were their excuses for being absent?

Lorraine was still pondering that when the bailiff announced: "All rise!" and the judge came in. She got to her feet a little slower than the rest of the crowd, and sat down faster—staying surrounded and hidden by bodies, just in case. The judge made the expected opening pronouncements, then the rear doors opened again to admit the jury-candidates, and the process of selection began.

The defense lawyer took his own sweet time—quite understandably, Lorraine thought—asking each prospective juror a host of largely irrelevant questions. Seeing that even the judge looked bored, she guessed that the lawyer's purpose—besides trying to find somebody, anybody, who would sympathize with the poor Mafia thug—was to bore everybody into a near stupor, make them miss details, lose their edge and their edginess.

If so, to judge by the grim-faced union members in the audience—and how many of them were quietly taking notes—the strategy wasn't working. The DA, by contrast, snapped out a few quick questions to each potential juror, and then moved on.

It was noon before the jurors were finally selected, and Lorraine barely had time to note how many of them looked distinctly middle-class and elderly before the judge announced a recess for lunch.

The judge, bailiffs, lawyers, defendant and press departed, but the audience stayed put. Lorraine noted that a lot of them pulled sandwiches and plastic bottles and paper napkins out of their pockets and began eating right there, proper courtroom procedure or no, and nobody made a move to stop them. The local membership wasn't going anywhere, and none of them intended to lose their seats.

There were, however, a few people who got up and formed a small line in the aisle.

"Potty break," Meredith explained before Lorraine could ask. "Even that, we do in a bunch. You need to go?"

"Not yet." Lorraine glanced at Benjamin, who shook his head. *Good thing we went light on the coffee,* she considered. *This costume might cause a problem.*

"Good thing we emptied out thoroughly before we came here," Ben chuckled. "I really like your union's sense of strategy and tactics."

"We got that in the old labor-wars," Bob commented, "Which really were shooting wars. So's this, in a way. It started when we supported the reformers inside the Teamsters…"

He gave Benjamin the whole back-story, in detail, until recess ended and the main participants in the trial returned.

And still there was no feel of another mutant, not anywhere in the court.

***

The first witness was one of the state troopers—not Weber— who had responded to Lorraine's phonecall. He read a transcript of the call, which was quite accurate as far as Lorraine remembered, then told—neatly, quickly and thoroughly—what he'd found when he arrived at the crime scene. The defense lawyers asked for details, and more details, trying to find some discrepancy among them. The trooper calmly replied with thoroughly corroborated details, none of them contradictory.

Finally the defense lawyer let fly with what he'd clearly hoped was a bombshell: "How could you be sure that the woman you found at the scene wasn't the murderer?"

The audience growled, but the trooper only smiled. "First," he said, ticking off fingers, "There was no gunpowder residue on her hands or clothes. Second, there was no gun found on the witness, nor on the premises, nor anywhere within a good walking-distance of the premises. Third, there was no blood on the witness nor on her clothes. Fourth, all evidence found on the premises was consistent with the witness' story. Fifth—"

"Defense won't get far with this line," Benjamin chuckled. "He's scrabbling around like a starfish trying to pry open a tightly-closed clam."

Lorraine smothered a giggle, tickled by the image.

Next came the parade of forensic experts, with charts and photos. They were well prepared, and the defense lawyer's questions dug far into quibbling details of procedure—so far that the jury began growing bored and restless—without finding any uncertainties he could play upon.

Lorraine, grimly remembering the fateful day, was struck by a sudden thought.

She half-turned and saw Wendy Wexler still sitting calmly behind her. Likewise, Bill Carminski sat unmoved and quiet at his place in the audience. None of the witnesses so far had yet mentioned their presence in the union hall before and after the shooting.

Weren't Wendy and Bill going to be called to testify? And if they weren't, then Oshansky wouldn't be called either; he had his excuse.

Then she felt Benjamin's elbow nudge her gently in the ribs, and turned to see the DA standing, looking a little nervously over the audience, holding her note in his hand.

"We call Roxanne Defarge to the stand," he said, a little louder than necessary.

Lorraine almost lunged to her feet, pushed her way down the row around quickly withdrawn knees and feet, and came through the gateway in the railing that separated the audience from the court proper. The DA looked at her and did a classic double-take.

A bailiff hurried to step in front of her. "Are *you* Roxanne Defarge?" he sneered, holding up a hand to stop her.

Lorraine laughed, remembering what she looked like: dressed as a factory-hand, hair covered by a watch cap, breasts bound flat, face hidden behind a short false moustache. Enjoying the momentary drama, she snapped back: "Yes, I am."

With that, she yanked off her watch cap with one hand—letting her hair fall free—and with the other she pulled off the moustache.

The audience reaction—laughter and cheers—was all she could have hoped for.

She cast a quick glance at the defense table, and saw a dismayed look flicker across the hit-man's face. Lorraine smiled coldly and marched past the apologetic bailiff to the witness' stand. The audience was still chuckling as she raised her hand and took the oath.

The DA smoothed away a grin as he came up to the stand and began the questions. Lorraine answered clearly, concisely, leaning into the microphone. Yes, she was Roxanne Defarge. Yes, she had lived in Chicago for eight years and worked in the union's office nearly that long. Her duties were mainly clerical and editorial, working on the union newspaper. Yes, on the day in question Jack Palumbo had called her and the rest of the staff into his private office to warn them about possible trouble from the Teamsters—

"Objection! Irrelevant!" defense council tried.

"Goes to motive," the DA replied, unperturbed.

"I'll allow it," said the judge.

Lorraine went on with her story, remembering Jack's words as best she could.

The defense lawyer tried objecting to the term 'Mafia', but the judge allowed that too.

After that Lorraine took care to be very precise: how soon afterward Bill and Wendy had departed, how long she'd spent clearing the editorial desks, how long it took her to go out in the alley and dump the trash, exactly where she'd been when the second shot came through the office window and exactly what she'd done afterward.

At that point the DA halted the narrative to bring in a floor plan of the office—which included outlines of the standing-shelves in the storeroom—and Lorraine dutifully pointed to just where she'd been, and just when.

"I crouched behind the shelves and peeped out," she went on, "I heard the office door open and heard footsteps, and then I saw a man come down the hallway past the open door to the storeroom. He had his head half turned to glance through the doorway, and he was shoving something with a black handle under his coat."

The audience growled softly.

The DA paused dramatically before asking the inevitable question. "And do you see that man in this courtroom now?"

"Yes," said Lorraine firmly, standing up, remembering to pull the microphone with her. She pointed to the hit-man sitting at the defense table. "That's the man. He's changed his hair-color, and tried to grow a beard, and put on a little weight, but he can't disguise the shape of his face. That's the man I saw, and no mistake."

The audience roared. The defense lawyer and the hit-man looked at each other without expression. The judge banged his gavel for order. Lorraine sat down and put the microphone back in its cradle.

The rest of the questions were anticlimactic, but Lorraine saw the necessity of them. She told, precisely as before, how she'd waited until she heard the front door close, had crawled out to look and be sure the hit-man was gone, had crawled into Jack's office and found him dead on the floor—complete with description of where the body lay, how it was posed, and how far the blood had spread. She told of tiptoeing around Jack's desk, worrying about fingerprints, remembering the hit-man's gloves and using the phone to call for help.

The DA glanced at the witness' table before asking the next question. "Why did you call the state troopers rather than the city police?"

Forestalling the defense's argument, Lorraine guessed. "Because I had reason to believe this was a Mafia hit," she snapped. "Because I've lived in Chicago for eight years, and I knew how bad the local cops are at catching Mafia hit-men."

A knowing chuckle went through the audience, and another through the assorted journalists in the press box. The defense lawyer looked pained.

A few more questions followed. What had she done until the troopers arrived? Crouched in the kneehole of the desk and waited. How long did they take to arrive? It seemed like hours, but was probably only twenty minutes. How many troopers responded? Half a dozen of them. Did they take evidence samples from her clothes? Yes, they'd stuck tape here and there, and had scraped her shoes. Did they perform a gunpowder-residue test? Yes, they put sticky stuff on her hands, and pulled it off again, and stuck it in evidence-bags. They'd also taken scrapings from under her fingernails. Did she observe the troopers taking other evidence? Yes, she'd seen them taking photos and scattering powder and going over the inner office inch by inch.

"No further questions," said the DA, glancing obliquely at the defense table. "Your witness."

The defense lawyer got up slowly, and Lorraine saw hesitancy in that. *He knows,* she guessed, *That his only chance is to discredit me, and that won't be easy.* She leaned forward and waited.

"So, you worked eight years in the union office, did you?" he began.

"Sure did," said Lorraine. "I know the place inside and out."

"And how many of those years was Jack Palumbo your boss?"

Where's he going with this? Divert him. "Don't say 'boss'," Lorraine corrected. "That's a dirty word around a union office."

The audience tittered.

"Answer the question." The lawyer tried to sound fierce.

"Almost four years," said Lorraine. "He was in his second term, and terms run two years. Before that, Bruce Reidel was Secretary, and before him it was Janet Creve. I think it was Walter

DiAngelo before that, but I wasn't there then."

The lawyer frowned. "And how would you describe Jack Palumbo as a— an employer?"

Divert. "He wasn't my employer; the union elected him and hired me."

"Yes, yes," the lawyer hurried, "But how did you get along with him?"

Get along? Right there, Lorraine saw a pattern shaping: the scenario the man was trying to weave together. She fought down a laugh at how ludicrous the concept was.

"Pretty well," she said. "He mostly stayed in his office and dealt with the regional delegates and national problems. The rest of us worked in the outer office, taking in the reports and the mail, getting out the newsletter and the paper, shipping out forms and pamphlets, and all that."

Mr. Defense frowned again. "So you didn't see him in the course of the day?"

"Just when he came in, or went out, or called us in for conferences." *Us. Plural.*

The lawyer slid closer. "And did he ever call you into his private office alone?"

Lorraine could have laughed out loud. "Hell, no," she grinned. "If he wanted to confer, he'd call us all in. If he had a message for just one of us, he'd stick his head out the door and yell."

The defense lawyer paused for a moment, face carefully blank. "Then you claim that you were never alone in the office with Jack Palumbo?" he asked, a little too casually.

Trick question. Lorraine thought for an instant, and realized where the trap was. "Do you mean *the* office in general, or *his* office in particular?" she shot back.

Another frown, and the man actually took a step backward. "The office in general," he clarified.

"Hmmm," Lorraine pondered. "Well, whenever we took the paper to the printer, whoever was left behind got to clean up the leftover mess—as I was doing that day. Sometimes it was me, sometimes one of the others, so I guess you could say that a couple times I was alone in the front office while Jack was alone in the back."

"But he never came out to the front office and spoke to you alone?" the lawyer tried again.

"No." Lorraine put on a puzzled look. "Why should he come all the way out? As I said, if he wanted anything he'd just stick his head out and yell."

"And you never went into his office alone?" The man's attempt was becoming obvious.

"No." Lorraine deepened her puzzled look. "Why on Earth should I?"

"Because you…wanted to?" the lawyer nudged.

And that was as far as she let it go. Lorraine leaned back and laughed, good and hard. "If you're trying to hint," she managed, "That I was having a red-hot love affair with Jack Palumbo, why don't you ask his widow? She was married to him for nearly thirty years, and believe me, she'd *know.*"

The audience rumbled indignantly. The defense lawyer didn't move, but seemed to shrink a little. "So you're saying," he tried, "That your relationship with the deceased was purely business?"

"Don't say 'business'," Lorraine chided. "This was a union office, after all."

"'Professional', then," the lawyer conceded, wincing at the snickers from the press box. "Your relationship was nothing but professional?"

"Damned right," Lorraine warmed to her topic. "Jack Palumbo was the most professional General Secretary the union's had in a long time. He was damned good at it, and that's why he got elected to a second term. He was a great organizer and administrator, and everybody in the union admired him."

"'Admired'…" the lawyer repeated, and Lorraine remembered Benjamin's lovely image of a frustrated starfish groping over a firmly-closed clam. "And did you 'admire' him too?"

Lorraine guessed where this was going; the fool was still going for the Jilted Lover scenario. "Sure, all I saw of him—which was mostly his speeches and position papers and strategy statements. Like I said, the man was a great organizer. We got more new shops under his administration than in the previous six years."

"So he was an object of…hero-worship?" the man tried.

"Your Honor, is there a point to this line of questioning?" the DA cut in.

"Goes to credibility," mumbled the defense lawyer.

"I'll allow it," said the judge. "Witness will answer the question."

Lorraine was ready for it. "Worship is for churches, and heroes are for the comic-books," Lorraine sneered. "Jack was a damned good General Secretary, and even people who didn't like him respected the hell out of him."

"Didn't like him?" the lawyer pounced on that crumb, perhaps grateful for a more promising lead. "Who didn't like him, Ms. Defarge?"

"Bosses!" Lorraine laughed. "He was a real hawk at contract negotiations, and if you'll look at the union's records you'll see that we got more Directive Bargaining Orders out of the NLRB than any other union in the country. Bosses sure didn't like him." She took care to add: "Including crooked union bosses, and their Mafia buddies. We helped out the reformers inside the Teamsters, and you can bet their bosses didn't like that."

The audience rumbled again, and the lawyer looked quickly at his notes. "So," he tried again, "Did you ever personally meet anybody who didn't like Mr. Palumbo?"

"Sure," Lorraine shrugged elaborately. "I took notes a couple of times at contract negotiations, so I sort-of met the bosses he was dealing with. And cops who sometimes tried to roust the office. And, of course, the hit-man—although we didn't exactly meet."

The lawyer played with his notes again, and Lorraine could almost see what he was thinking. He couldn't find a single anchor-point for his Thwarted Lover Did It scenario. Would he try to cobble up a Dirty Money story—as he would probably have done if she were a man?

As if her thought had suggested it, he said: "You've bragged that your union is wonderfully honest, Ms. Defarge. But just how would you know?"

Ah, that was a question she could—and did—answer in great detail. "First off, the dues-money comes in with the delegates' reports, and every member's payment and name and union-card number is in those reports. Then—" She got all the way to the description of the monthly audit before the lawyer caught up to her.

"That's enough, thank you," he snapped. "So you're absolutely certain that nobody can make secret or unauthorized use of the union's funds?"

"No way in hell," Lorraine grinned. "And nobody's even tried to, in more than 50 years."

The lawyer blinked at that, and the journalists in the press box looked at each other. Lorraine wondered if these Chicago professionals found it inconceivable that any organization could be that honest, for that long.

The defense lawyer plowed on anyway. "And what would you

do, then, if you found an official attempting to make unauthorized use of the money—to cheat the union, besmirch its honesty that you're so proud of?"

Is he really trying for this? Lorraine marveled. "Hell, I'd report the facts and figures to the General Executive Board, and they'd call in another accountant, and when the figures didn't tally up, well, the crooked bum would be out in the gutter so fast it'd make his head spin—and then we'd hold an emergency election to replace him."

"Ah, but that's a time-consuming process, isn't it? And if the danger was imminent—"

"No, not at all," Lorraine cut in. "Everybody in the office knows the names and phone numbers of the Board. It'd take maybe 20 minutes to call them all and report the news, maybe another hour for the Board members to call each other and send for the accountant, less than 24 hours for the accountant to get there and go over the books and come up with the verdict. And of course, nobody could get at the bank account while the accountant was working. No, the union can move fast when it wants to." She gave him a wry look. "Why? Are you trying to pretend that Jack stole money, so we all conspired to do him in—and blame some stranger—for the honor of the union? Get real."

An ugly laugh rippled up from the audience. The lawyer glanced briefly at the jury, then away. Lorraine could almost see the thought in his head: *Not a conspiracy, just you.* She also saw that the hope was frustrated by lack of even a ghost of evidence.

She almost missed the DA's complaint, and the judge summoning both lawyers up to the bench. They muttered together for a moment, and then stalked back to their original positions. The defense lawyer gave Lorraine a long unreadable look, and she gazed coolly back.

Finally he pointed to the hit-man. "Before the incident in question," the lawyer said, "Had you ever seen this man before?"

"No," said Lorraine. "I'm not even sure what his name is, though it's been mentioned here a few times."

"Lambrusco," snapped the lawyer. "Bart Lambrusco. And you're certain you'd never seen him before that date?"

"Never met him," Lorraine said firmly.

"Then how—" He pulled a paper out of his notes with a dramatic flourish. "How do you account for Mr. Lambrusco's statements that he visited the union office several times over the past six months, that you led him into an affair, and when he tried to break it off you made threats against his life?"

The audience roared in unmistakable fury. The DA looked hard at Lorraine, who only rolled her eyes in disgust. The judge rapped his gavel repeatedly.

"Simple," said Lorraine, as the noise quieted. "He's lying through his teeth."

"And it's only your word against his."

"Also the forensics evidence that the state troopers collected."

"He also claims that on several occasions he heard you arguing loudly with the deceased in his private office!" the lawyer almost shouted.

"More lies, easily disproved. Ask the rest of the union office staff."

"Your friends, who would back up your story!"

"Not if I'd killed Jack Palumbo, they wouldn't."

"How do you account for the fact that the accused knew your name, and included it in his statement?"

"Easily. He got it from the police reports, which are public records."

"Don't you think the police would withhold the name of a material witness?"

"Not if they were paid enough."

This time the audience roared with laughter. The judge banged his gavel again.

"Then how—" the lawyer shouted over the retreating sound, "—do you account for the accused knowing your description? How could he describe you exactly if he never met you?"

The answer to that was all too easy. "That only proves that he watched the office, and saw who came and went, before he made the hit. He saw who went out to the printer's that day, and when he heard there was a witness, he guessed who was left."

"Then you claim that you never had any kind of affair with the accused?"

"Never in hell." Lorraine took a deep breath, felt the rib-belt pull across her breasts, and was struck with a sudden idea. "And I can prove it!"

"Prove it?" the lawyer fumbled, fatally. "How?"

"Have him describe my breasts. If he had an affair with me, he would certainly have seen them." Lorraine grinned toothily at the hit-man, who kept his expression carefully blank. She remembered that for the weeks prior to the killing the weather had been cold; she'd always worn her bulky jacket to and from work. "Ask him what size and shape my breasts are."

There was a long moment's hush, and Lorraine could feel everyone in the courtroom staring fixedly at her chest. She smiled coolly back, knowing that the denim jacket she wore today hung almost straight from her shoulders, and remembering why.

As a slow muttering began to rumble through the audience, the judge called both lawyers up to the bench again. There was another quick, muttered conference, then an equally swift return to their respected tables. The defense lawyer was chattering quietly, fiercely, with the hit-man.

"The accused can answer from the defense table," the judge intoned. "Mr. Lambrusco, are you ready to respond?"

"Uh, yessir," said the hit-man, getting to his feet. His voice was amazingly small and squeaky for such a burly man, and his face was a little flushed. "Uh, well, her titties — uh, breasts I mean… They're…" He glanced at Lorraine again. "Sort of small and… shaped like, uh, little round pyramids, like…"

He drew shapes with his hands, which made the audience snicker.

"Conical?" the defense lawyer suggested.

"Yeah, like that. About, uh, B-cup size, I think." The hit-man smiled bashfully.

Lorraine wondered briefly if that was the closest he could come to an innocent look. A small sound from the front row drew her attention for a moment, and she saw Benjamin almost doubled over, hands pressed hard against his mouth, shaking like jelly with the effort not to laugh out loud. He could guess what she planned.

"Not true!" she shouted into the microphone. "Not true, and I can prove it!"

With that Lorraine stood up and stripped off her jacket. Fast, fast, before the judge or the bailiffs could think to stop her, she yanked her knit shirt up over her head, exposing the rib-belt that bound her breasts. She threw down the shirt and pulled off the rib-belt with a rip of parting Velcro-seals.

Her freed breasts jumped forward like rabbits, until halted by the jogging-brassiere. She grabbed the front of the brassiere and pulled it down almost to her nipples, revealing the cleavage that long-gone Ronnie had once compared to the Grand Canyon.

"Not true!" she shouted. "Not small and conical: big and round! Big, round and D-cup! 38-D, and he's lying through his teeth!"

The audience roared like the sea, but Lorraine was sure she

could hear the click and whir of concealed cameras from the press box. The DA looked poleaxed, but his assistant was bent over laughing. The judge banged his gavel repeatedly.

"Silence in the court!" he bellowed, "And the witness will put her shirt back on!"

Lorraine bowed her head and meekly obeyed, not replacing the rib-belt. As she pulled the shirt down she glanced at the hit-man and saw him glaring at her with hopeless and miserable hatred. She smiled back coldly.

Back in the front row, Benjamin had recovered enough to breathe normally. He couldn't keep from grinning like the prover-bial Cheshire Cat.

"Do you have any further questions for this witness?" the judge asked.

The defense lawyer only shook his head.

"Then court is adjourned until eight o'clock tomorrow morning." The gavel banged down one last time, and the judge got up and hurried toward the rear door, his robes flapping like wings behind him.

Lorraine grabbed up her jacket and dashed across the space to the front row, neatly dodging the bailiffs. Benjamin caught her in an embrace so fierce it almost pulled her over the railing. The union members nearest crowded close, trying to shout congratu-lations and pound joyful fists on her shoulders. The bailiffs hung back, really not wanting to interfere.

Lorraine finally clambered over the railing, kissed Benjamin briefly, and returned several of the proffered handshakes. Bill was shaking his head in wonder, Wendy was laughing like a hyena, Meredith was practically jumping up and down whooping in de-light, and Bob—smiling so wide it seemed to split his face—was trying to clear a space around Lorraine. He didn't have much luck until Wally and the bodyguards assisted the effort. Benjamin steered Lorraine into the gap they made, and bit by bit they worked their way through the cheering crowd, toward the doors.

"What now?" Lorraine panted, dizzy with the adulation—and relief. "Back to the hotel?"

"No," Ben whispered in her ear. "We get into the car and drive straight to the airport. When we get to Tucson, we check into the nearest motel; we'll go to the ranch in the morning."

"But the trial—"

"You've done your bit, and the DA won't need you again. We get out of town fast, before the stalker has time to guess where you've gone."

Lorraine noticed that one of the bodyguards was holding his cell-phone to his ear, and talking quickly into it: calling up the limo, no doubt.

Ahead of them the doors opened, and the crowd spilled out into the hallway.

Again, even while jubilant with victory, the union membership formed a flying wedge around Lorraine and her companions. Nobody got in their way, and they reached the front doors with remarkable speed. The limo waited there, idling by the curb.

As Lorraine tumbled into the back seat, Meredith pushed her way forward. "Rox, aren't you staying with us again?" she asked.

"Sorry, can't risk it." Lorraine felt tears sting her eyes as she reached to pull the door closed. "Pet the cats for me, and thank Bob for everything."

As the limo pulled away from the curb Lorraine saw the whole union local lined up along the sidewalk, fists raised in the old 'solidarity' salute.

She waved back until they were out of sight, and then suddenly collapsed as a wave of sobbing shook her. She clung to Benjamin, unable to stop the tears, amazed at the force of her own reaction. "My little cats," was all she could think to say. "I didn't…get to see the cats."

Ben said nothing, but only pulled her close. Wally reached for the neatly concealed mini-bar set into the back of the front seat, and pulled out a one-shot bottle of scotch. "Here," he said, handing it to Lorraine. "You deserve it, Secret Agent 38-D."

Whether he'd intended it or not, Lorraine felt her sobs change into whoops of laughter. Everyone else joined in, including the driver and guards in the front seat.

Lorraine managed to grab the bottle, but uncapping it took special effort, and it was a good two minutes before she could actually get the biting liquid down her throat.

"Better?" Ben asked, smiling. "If you like, we can phone ahead to the airport and make certain that the plane is well stocked. You can stay drunk all the way to Tucson."

"I don't think I'll need that much," Lorraine giggled, "But a few more shots wouldn't hurt."

Wally obligingly reached for the mini-bar again.

"Goddammit," Lorraine muttered, remembering her earlier problem, "None of them were in the courtroom. I still don't know which one it is, or where he is. He might not have come back to

Chicago at all. He might still be waiting in Tucson."

"We won't know until we get there," said Benjamin, rubbing comforting circles on her back. "In any case, he won't have much access to Mafia help now."

"Meanwhile," said Wally, holding out a bottle, "Have another scotch."

Lorraine took his advice.

The waiting plane was indeed well supplied when they reached it, and a few more drinks were enough to let Lorraine sleep all the way back to Tucson.

26.

LATE IN THE MORNING the limo pulled into the driveway at Treemark Arabian Farm, and Lorraine could hardly wait for the car to stop before heaving her duffel bag on her shoulder and lunging out the door. Wally and Benjamin, chuckling, took up the rest of the luggage and trotted after her. Daniel opened the door and welcomed them in with a beaming smile.

"There have been absolutely no problems since you left," he announced. "'All quiet on the western front', so to speak."

"Thank whatever gods there be," said Lorraine, heading for her room.

She paused there only long enough to drop her luggage, then hurried back to the entertainment room to turn on the television and search for news. The satellite-dish provided hundreds of channels, and she hunted for half an hour before finding one that originated in Chicago. That one, unfortunately, was currently showing an insipid movie.

Lorraine ground her teeth, and sat back to wait. She'd put up with hours of this drivel, if she had to, for one 30-second sound bite of news about the trial.

Somewhere during a cluster of commercials she grew aware of Madge's presence, and turned to see the Elven woman quietly placing a coffee-set on the table.

"Thanks," said Lorraine, gratefully pouring herself a cup. "So, there was no sign of the stalker while I was gone?"

"Not a peep," Madge smiled. "Did you notice anything in Chicago?"

"Nothing." Lorraine frowned at the TV screen. "He's keeping his distance. Maybe I'll learn something from the news coverage of the trial."

"Let's hope." Madge gave her a thoughtful look. "Just try not to fret yourself to pieces over it. If he comes, we're ready. If he doesn't, there's no point worrying."

Something in her certainty snagged Lorraine's attention. "Were you ever stalked by a hunter?" she asked.

"Oh yes," Madge chortled. "Nearly two hundred years ago, in Kentucky."

"How did you deal with it?"

"Stole away to Tennessee. Would you like something to eat?"

"No, thank you. This is fine."

Madge nodded acceptance and went back toward the kitchen. Lorraine returned her eyes to the screen, but her thoughts strayed to Madge's suggestion. If the stalker didn't return before Benjamin left, should she go somewhere else? Helen had mentioned other enclaves, other teachers... But going among strangers struck her as a bad idea.

Could she talk Benjamin into taking her with him?

She pondered that as the commercials slid into more of the stupid movie, wondering if there would be a safe enclave where Ben was going, or if she'd be a burden — possibly a danger—to him. Treemark had said she'd need at least a year of martial arts training before she could be considered minimally competent…

The movie dwindled off into more commercials, which gave way to—of all things — a cooking-show. Lorraine swore quietly, and poured herself another cup of coffee.

Another aura impinged on hers, and Lorraine recognized it as Treemark's. He said nothing, but sat down beside her on the couch and watched the show in patient silence.

How long will he wait? Lorraine wondered, a little irritably. Treemark was not, she knew, that interested in recipes for fondue. "It's a Chicago channel," she said, finally. "I'm waiting for the local news, to see if there's anything about the trial."

"There was a brief mention of it last night," Treemark replied evenly. "Just a quick statement that 'a witness positively identified the accused in the Palumbo murder trial', with no picture."

"Too bad," Lorraine smiled, remembering. "There were some lively photos taken, I daresay."

"No doubt. Benjamin told me about your dramatic entrance, and your 'that's the man' pose, and…" He chuckled. "…your positive proof that the thug's story was false."

"I just hope I impressed the jury," Lorraine grinned.

"I don't doubt it for a minute. Your hit-man will go off to prison for a good long stretch, and not even the Mafia can stop it. Since he failed to prevent your appearance in court, I doubt if the stalker swings much weight with them right now; in fact, they may give him some troubles of his own."

I hadn't thought of that! Lorraine sat up straighter, adding the new factor into her equations. Yes, the Mafia might spend some effort on punishing a witness who'd sent one of their own to the Graybar Hotel, but they were more likely to punish someone on their own team who'd failed an assignment. Maybe the stalker had stayed away from the Chicago courtroom for good reason.

Perhaps he'd grabbed his suitcase and gotten out of town the minute he heard that she'd appeared in court. Possibly he'd dropped his old identity and was running to another country right now. There was a good chance that he'd lost all interest in hunting her, or anyone else at the well-guarded ranch.

"I think we can assume he's no longer in Chicago," Treemark went on, "And I'd bet he's preoccupied with setting up a new identity somewhere else. We'll keep up security at the ranch for another month, but I believe the danger is minimal."

He set down his cup, reached to Lorraine's shoulders and began rubbing them.

She flinched, even though his touch was exactly as chaste and therapeutic as it had always been.

"Relax, Lorraine," he said quietly. "Take off the armor, and get back into your regularly scheduled life."

Not yet. "The news…" She pointed vaguely at the screen. "I have to know."

"You can relax while you watch the news." His hands didn't miss a stroke. "You can relax and still think, and plot, and calculate. You don't have to be emotionally or physically ready to jump up and fight for your life at an instant's notice. I assure you, you'll have at least five seconds' warning."

Lorraine smiled at that, and made herself lean back into the pressure of his hands.

Yes, there was no point in being coiled tight as a spring right this minute. She was, after all, safe inside a fortress—and her allies surrounded her, and she had the gun on her hip.

And her enemy was alone, stripped of allies, possibly being hunted himself. *But I have to be sure…*

So she sat and waited, and Treemark patiently sat beside her, until at last the news came on.

She'd expected the account to be third or fourth, if it was mentioned at all, but no: it was the lead story. The news-anchorman started straight out with: "New developments in the Palumbo murder case were revealed in court this morning, as two more witnesses testified to shots fired at the same time as the killing."

"Wendy and Bill!" Lorraine gasped, leaning forward.

So they'd testified after all. Had Oshansky? Or had he disappeared? Was there any way to find out? Was it only coincidence that he hadn't appeared in court, if he'd appeared at all, until Lorraine was safely out of range?

The picture—not a photo but an 'artist's rendering'—showed a wispy redheaded woman, scarcely recognizable as Wendy Wexler, gesturing as she explained how close the bullets had come. The anchorman's voice continued, noting that this "lends support to the theory that the murder was a gangland assassination, as an earlier witness testified".

The picture shifted to another colored drawing, this one showing Lorraine, in her factory-hand's suit, pointing dramatically toward the defense table.

"At least they didn't show the scene where you displayed your…talents," Treemark purred.

"No doubt it'll show up in the tabloids," said Lorraine, sinking back into the couch. "So, they really will take some lumbering steps after the Mafia, and the Teamster goons who hired them. That will…inconvenience the thugs, at least."

"Enough that they won't feel any gratitude toward the stalker," Treemark concluded. "At worst, he's on his own. At best, he's running away. I believe the danger is, if not past, then greatly reduced."

"Yes." Lorraine heaved a vast sigh, and felt an invisible weight slide off her. The drawing disappeared from the screen, replaced by video-footage of another story, but the photos seemed flat and unreal by comparison. Reality, she realized, was sloppy: full of irrelevant details. It took the eye of an artist to focus on what was important. *That's what art is for!* "Paint…" she murmured. "I have to paint again." Another visual concept was taking form, something about dishonor among thieves...

"Your equipment is in the crafts-room," said Treemark. "You have to get back on your regular schedule, but remember, this is Friday."

"Yes!" Lorraine pulled herself off the couch and headed for the crafts-room, absorbed by her vision. The image clarified as she made her way down the corridor, past the laundry-room and through the plain doors. The crafts-room was well lighted, by a wall of south-facing windows as well as overhead lamps, but Lorraine had eyes only for the table where her equipment waited. She seized the sketchpad, scrabbled a charcoal pencil out of the pen-box, and sat down to draw.

Unnoticed time and several thrown-away sheets later, she had it. This picture would be a tall upright, rather than a horizontal, oblong. At the bottom toiled peasants and workmen of every age, wearing primarily white clothing. Above and behind them rose gray walls, the architecture suggesting first the façade of a courthouse but then rising to crenellated out-thrust battlements that leaned over the laboring crowd. On those battlements stood, and peered, and silently shouted, assorted soldiers and police and overseers—again, from every historical period recognizable: the first line of defense, the side of law and government and social order that the peasants below would usually see.

Behind and above that rose a bloated castle with wide windows, through which the activities inside the castle were displayed—and all of them were scenes of command, conspiracy and betrayal. Everywhere in the castle, higher-ups abused and commanded their underlings—and conspired with, and betrayed, each other. In the top central window sat a king, plainly giving orders to a host of ministers and officers—while others drew daggers behind his back and poured poison in his cup. Above and behind him rose the pointed towers of the castle, dark against the background/sky, framed by wispy clouds.

All the details contributed to the main shape of the image, which was a man wearing a crown. The toiling peasants made up his shirt-covered shoulders, the castle walls formed his collar, the castle-keep was his head, the clouds were his hair and the towers formed his crown. The windows, and the scenes behind them, shaped his features; the totality formed a face that was haggard, ugly, greedy and depraved—but the viewer had to step back and see the whole picture from a distance to recognize it.

Lorraine chewed the end of her pencil for a moment, then scribbled in the title: "Lawful Order".

She looked at those words for long seconds, and then knew what she would paint on the other side of the board. It would not be a horse this time.

...And too much to start on right now, Lorraine considered, setting down her pencil. She sighed, stretched her sore shoulders—and suddenly noticed that she wasn't alone in the room. The aura was well known, but still, she mentally kicked herself for ignoring it so thoroughly—and not for the first time.

"I didn't want to disturb you," said Benjamin, stepping close behind her. "This is incredible work."

"I didn't even notice when you came in," Lorraine admitted guiltily. "That's inexcusably careless."

"Not inexcusable when you know you're safe." He ran his fingers lightly through her hair, making her shiver. "And since you've come to a natural stopping-point, how about sneaking back to the staff wing with me, and ordering dinner?"

"Is it that late?!" *I missed lunch. And my physical-therapy session. And everything else. ...And it's Friday night! The weekend gathering...*

"So much like Raphael," Ben smiled. "Carried away on his vision, concentrating for hours, he'd often forget to eat. 'Artistic passion', he called it. You have that."

"But I don't know if I have anything near his talent, or technique." Lorraine leaned into his hands, noticing for the first time how tired she was. Yes, it would be very good to take a break now.

"You have those too, in my humble opinion." His hands slid down to her neck, and began rubbing out the kinks there. "Also in the not-so-humble opinion of Brian's contacts. Did he tell you that he sold your second painting for $1200?"

"What?!" Lorraine gulped. "Where? When? It's been only two days…"

"At a gallery owned by one of his clients. He let friends know where to find it, and it was sold by yesterday afternoon. The gallery is eager for more of your work."

"Damn…" Lorraine recalled "Parasites" and wondered if it were really that good, or if this was only a display of loyalty by Treemark's clients, or if two-sided paintings carrying political/philosophical statements were such a novelty. She wouldn't know until she'd sold more of her work, exhausted any personal-loyalty market and worn the novelty away. Only then could she tell how good a painter she truly was.

"Come along now," Ben insisted gently, "We'll have to go outside and come back in by the staff-wing door."

"Yes…" Lorraine remembered to take the sketchbook and the pencil before she got up to leave, her mind already drifting toward the idea for the reverse-side of the painting. She noticed that Ben had taken her hand and was leading her around the house like a blind man's guide, and laughed at herself. "Tell me again about Raphael's ferocious butler," she recalled. "I may need someone like that."

***

They took a long and leisurely bath, knowing that the rest of the staff was busy, draped themselves in robes and returned to the bedroom just in time for Madge's knock. Dinner was an exquisite goose in sweet lemon sauce, accompanied by the usual elaborate salad and a bittersweet chocolate torte for dessert. The wine was a mild white whose name Lorraine didn't catch. She ate slowly, feeling restless, her attention constantly drifting back to the sketchbook.

"Penny for your thoughts," said Benjamin, licking chocolate off his fingers.

"The painting…" Lorraine reached for the sketchbook and spread it open on the bed as Ben neatly set the dinner-tray on the floor. "Step back a few paces, look at this, and tell me what you see."

Benjamin obligingly stepped back and looked, then did a classic double-take.

"It's a face!" he marveled. "The people, the castle— That's incredible! Your technique is growing by quantum leaps. God, what a ghastly face; who is it supposed to be?"

"Father Sin," murmured Lorraine, startling herself.

"'Sin'?"

"The real Original Sin." Lorraine gestured vaguely as the idea took clearer form. "Power-lust, desire to rule over others, turning people into tools… If there really is a root of all evil, it's that."

Benjamin considered that for a long moment, and then went off on another tack. "Which horse will grace the reverse of the painting?" he asked, "Or do you mean to leave it blank this time?"

"No, and no horse," said Lorraine, turning to a blank sheet of paper. "The reverse is…the alternative. 'Natural Order', Mother Nature." She took up the charcoal pencil and began sketching in the outlines: ground, tree and sky. "An old woman's face…" *Her hair…tree branches…an Afro?* "A wise and kindly old woman."

"You must know," Ben murmured, "That there's a lot of cruelty in Nature—and competition, and scrambling for dominance too."

"I know." Lorraine paused as the idea took shape. "But that's all for the purpose of survival, not…not the dirty fun of reducing everything to a tool. And even that's mitigated by other natural forces."

She resumed sketching, using light streaks and dots to outline the face in the tree, the neck and collar. "I read a story once, about a troop of monkeys that some naturalists were studying. In that troop, the average top-dog male stayed leader for an average of six months—but this troop had lucked into a really good leader: wise and kindly, willing to groom all the females and play with the babies, very good at finding the best fruit and the safest trees. He remained leader for three years, which is a good piece of a monkey's lifetime."

"Ah, but didn't the other male monkeys get ambitious?" Benjamin smiled knowingly.

"Most of them liked the leader, and he had a lot of 'lieutenants' who copied his ways and were well-liked too. But there was one ambitious monkey who wanted the top slot. He challenged the old monkey. The old boy's lieutenants stood up to take the challenge for him, but the old monkey solemnly waved them aside and waded out to take the challenge himself."

"And he lost?" Benjamin guessed.

"Badly. The ambitious monkey wasn't content with defeating the old man, but beat him so hard that he died. For two days the other monkeys hung around, bringing the old monkey water and fruit, licking his wounds and covering him with leaves to keep the sun off, but he died anyway."

"Monkey nursing care?!"

"Elephants have been known to do the same. But as soon as the old monkey was dead, the new boss started throwing his weight around. He picked fights with everybody, beat the females, chased the babies, and generally terrorized the whole troop."

"Establishing his rule, no doubt. Machiavelli proposed something similar."

"It didn't work." Lorraine smiled grimly. "Within a week, the whole troop took up sticks and stones and chased the new king out of their lands—beating him hard enough on the way that he didn't try to come back. They chose the old monkey's oldest lieutenant to be their new leader, and he ruled as wisely and kindly as the old man had."

"In…credible," Ben said slowly, an odd look spreading over his face. Then he shook himself and visibly changed gears. "This looks to be quite an ambitious painting, and I don't doubt that the gallery could sell it handily. They'll charge ten percent commission on sales, but considering the prices your previous works have brought in, you'll still collect a very nice piece of change."

"And Treemark?" Lorraine duly followed the subject. "If he's acting as my agent, he should get a cut."

"He said he'd take nothing, since the gallery's doing the selling and all he'll do is the transportation," Ben smiled. He shifted position and rested his hand on Lorraine's neck, and began rubbing gently. "You're not in debt to us, you know," he said quietly.

"It's because of me that the stalker's here," she growled, finding it difficult to concentrate on the drawing. "If I hadn't gone to town that day—"

"Then the stalker would have picked up on my field, and come after us anyway.

When he approached the house, he could have felt any one of us. This isn't the first time we've attracted hunters, and it won't be the last." His hands worked slowly deeper, unkinking knots in the muscles. "He started after you in Chicago, before you were even Initiated, before you had any idea what you were, and he knew enough to follow you to Tucson. You threw him off your trail, but that didn't stop him from hunting. My guess is that he knew enough to follow Berringer around; you couldn't avoid her forever, and whenever you contacted her he would have tracked you. There's nothing you could have done to prevent that."

"He was so determined…" Lorraine worried about that as she set down her pencil and surrendered to those enticing hands. "He wouldn't give up easily."

"But every attack he's tried has backfired on him." Ben worked his hands down to her shoulders. "He's been shot, chased hard, and now he's incurred the resentment of the Mafia. I really think he has more to worry about than you, by now."

"If he has the sense of a goat, he's on a plane to Timbuktu by now," Lorraine agreed, flattening herself on the bed to give Benjamin room for massage. *But junkies aren't famous for common sense,* a thread of thought nagged. *And power-junkies are the worst of the lot. And we don't know what resources he has…*

"We'll keep the guards on, and stay alert, for another few weeks," Ben reminded her. "Still, I think the main danger has passed. I've thought about him, as you can imagine, and I can't think of any approach he can use that we haven't guarded against."

Yes, there was that, Lorraine had to admit. Ben, Treemark, Helen—to say nothing of Steven and Wally—had been at this game for centuries, and had to be far better tacticians than she was. If they thought she was safe, there really was no excuse for her own paranoia.

Ben paused to close the sketchbook, pick up the charcoal pencil and lay them both on the nightstand. Then his hands returned to Lorraine's shoulders, and rubbed deeper.

She purred and toed off her bath-slippers.

***

Saturday dawned cool and clear, with a faint hint of clouds low on the horizon. Lorraine and Benjamin woke slowly, traded soft kisses and poured themselves out of bed. They dressed in companionable silence, went out the staff-wing door and around the house to the kitchen. Madge and Daniel were nowhere in sight, but the remains of a buffet breakfast waited on the sideboard. Ben and Lorraine loaded their plates lightly, finished quickly, and headed out to the stables.

Wally and Steven were there before them, busily raking stalls while the horses waited in the paddock. Lorraine and Benjamin fell easily into their tasks, and time passed unnoticed.

At eleven o'clock Lorraine remembered to go to the gym for her exercises, and almost regretted having to return to her old schedule. Ben was nowhere in sight, but she guessed he'd know where to look for her if he had to. She suspected that Treemark would be too busy with his clients to give her the usual physical therapy session that afternoon, which meant all the more time to sketch out the painting.

She would, she remembered, need the photographs for models before seriously detailing the Tree of Life, and Treemark would also be too busy today to get them for her. Once the sketches were finished, she'd best begin on the Castle of Evil first.

She met nobody while fetching her pen-box and sketchbook, nor on the way to the crafts-room, either. All the life of the house had withdrawn to the clinic office, the livingroom, the guest-rooms…and, probably, the solarium.

Except, of course, for the guards and dogs on duty outside the house, perpetually circling and watching.

Protected, safe…and alone. Lorraine sighed in relief as she closed the crafts-room door behind her. She went to the table where her paint-kit waited, and paused suddenly as her eyes fell on a stack of photographs lying near the easel. No, she realized as she looked at them, not exactly photographs: they were computer-printed pictures of assorted plants, animals, and even microbes—exactly the models she needed. Who but Ben could have left them here?

Smiling, Lorraine sat down and opened the sketchbook, took up a pencil and spread out the pictures. Her vision of the Tree became clearer: two great branches for the plant and animal kingdoms, secondary limbs for the soft-stem and woody-stem plants and the vertebrate and invertebrate animals, plant and animal branches overlapping and intertwining to show their dependence on each other—and always that great ancient face showing through them. Her pencil fairly flew as the details took form.

Another aura impinged on hers, and she looked up, expecting to see Benjamin.

Her smile faltered as she saw that it was Daniel, bearing a plate and mug.

"I didn't want to disturb you," he said, being the impeccable butler once more, "But you did miss lunch, and dinner will be late again tonight."

He set down the mug—a dark beer, she noted—and the plate, and Lorraine laughed in disbelief as she saw what was on it.

"A cheeseburger?" she laughed. "A *cheeseburger?!*"

"A proper classic cheeseburger," Daniel corrected, his moustache twitching over a subdued smile. "Made with good lean beef, which I ground myself, and a suitably aged medium cheddar. In place of the usual fat and water—" He shuddered delicately. "—I added beef-marrow to the meat. Tell me if it's not superior to the commercial variety."

Lorraine couldn't help but take a bite, after that. She noticed that the bun was a round croissant, the lettuce was Romaine, the onion was an Italian Red, the pickle-relish was made of sweet gherkins and the tomato was a fine-sliced Romano. In the next second she forgot about the details and let the exquisite taste take her.

"Much, much better than the commercial variety," she agreed. "Daniel, you're a far better artist than I am."

Daniel glanced pointedly at the open sketchbook, and shook his head. "I wouldn't say that, Ms. Lorraine," he said quietly. "Will you want dinner served here or in your room?"

"Uhm…" Lorraine flicked her attention back and forth between the sketchbook and the magnificent cheeseburger, remembered Benjamin, and chose the sensible course.

"In my room, thank you. I expect I'll be done by then."

"Very good, Miss." Daniel turned and paced away, all butler again.

Lorraine took her time over the food, and the beer that complemented it perfectly, remembering that there were other passions besides art. When she finally set the plate aside and took up the charcoal pencil again, she seemed to see the image with a fresh eye.

The troublesome spaces between the main branches, she

saw now, could be filled in by foliage drooping from the other side of the tree: more of the same leaf-green, bark-brown and dark leaf-shadow blue-green. The old woman's eyes could be clear spaces between branches, their whites only glimpses of cloud, their irises rounded bunches of bright green leaves. Yes, it was all coming together.

She sipped the last of the beer, and suddenly remembered an old Celtic legend about the Cauldron of Inspiration. *Amber beer and cheeseburgers?* she smiled. But then, wouldn't Daniel qualify as a clever old wizard? Madge could certainly play the part of the Fairy Godmother, who magicked up the perfect clothes for Cinderella's ball. Helen had truly been an ancient goddess. And the others…

Legends… Just how much truth was there in legends, myths and fairy-tales?

Lorraine hurried to finish the details of the sketch, taken with a sharp desire to read that book of legends that Benjamin had given her. Would she find more hints of real Elven-mutants there? Was there more to the gift than what met the eye?

***

Benjamin found her in her bedroom, a good hour before dinnertime, absorbed in the book. "I take it the sketches are completed?" he smiled as he closed and locked the door.

"Yes," Lorraine murmured, holding the book open. "Tomorrow I'll transfer them to the canvas. With luck, I can start the underpainting Monday. …Ah, Ben, I've been reading this book you gave me…"

"Find anything interesting?" he asked, settling on the bed beside her.

"There's this one tale, from Welsh mythology…" She tapped her finger on the page. "It's about a small band of Elves, or minor gods, who travel disguised among mortals to search for their missing kinfolk. Everywhere they go, they try to make their living by honest trades—but they're so good at it that mortals grow jealous and try to kill them, so they have to move on. That story has a bitter taste of reality about it."

"I know. I've heard it before." Ben leaned back on the pillows, his expression thoughtful. "I wasn't there, so I can't tell if this particular tale is true, but I know a lot of similar stories that are."

"If Treemark's theories are right, then we once did have a society—a civilization—of our own," Lorraine prodded. "There once was an…Elfland." *And might be again.*

"Olympus, Valhalla…" Benjamin intertwined his hands behind his head, and looked up at the ceiling. "There were several, actually: enclaves like this…"

"You remember it?!" Lorraine gasped. "The time before—"

"I didn't live in Elfland, but like Helen—in a place, a time, when our kind were known and accepted among mortals. We didn't always fight among ourselves, and it wasn't just the greed for each other's power that destroyed our culture." He twitched, as if touched by an old memory.

"When mortals knew about us, some of them were greedy too. Ask Helen about how they started demanding more and more of us: magic we couldn't do, powers we didn't have, the secret of immortality that we couldn't give them…" He gave a short, harsh laugh. "There's a quaint old Irish legend that if you catch a leprechaun you can force him to tell you where he keeps his gold. Think about what that implies!"

"I think I can guess." Lorraine lay down beside him. "How did you escape?"

Ben shivered. "I told them that another mortal had already robbed my treasury—and I gave them the description of a local rich bastard who had more gold than he could have come by honestly. They believed. They let me go, and went after him instead. I took the opportunity to get far out of the country."

Lorraine wrapped an arm around him and squeezed gently. She had wanted the truth, but this was almost more than she'd bargained for. She didn't have to stretch her empathic sense to feel the ache of old pain radiating off him.

"They can never know about us, Lorraine," he almost whispered. "Their curiosity is bad enough. Their greed is worse, and their jealousy… It's a secret worth killing to keep, believe me."

"Do any mortals know?"

"A very few, and even they can't always be trusted." He slid an arm around her shoulders. "Next time I'm here, I'll give you an advanced course on keeping secrets."

Lorraine sighed, knowing that there was no avoiding this. "You'll be leaving soon, then?"

"A few days. I've been away too long already."

Lorraine didn't know what she would have said next, for just then a discreet knock sounded on the door. Benjamin sighed and sat up. "That will be dinner," he said.

Lorraine said nothing, knowing that no matter how delicious

Daniel's present creation was, it would taste of ashes and loss.

A few days… She'd have to make the most of them, give herself memories enough to carry her through the barren weeks—or even months—ahead. She would endure, she could wait for him, but the waiting would be a constant quiet pain.

She had discovered real love, and wouldn't have traded that learning for the world — but did the sorrows of love have to follow so quickly on the heels of its joys, and last so long?

27.

BY LUNCHTIME ON SUNDAY, most of the guests had gone and the stable-work was finished. Lorraine and Benjamin sat in the kitchen, quietly demolishing a superb egg salad and trading long looks. Their sentences were brief and disjointed.

"I don't have any deadline for the painting…"

"The horses need exercising."

"I'd like to visit the node again."

"You shouldn't go alone."

"Don't the guards work today?"

"Yes, out circling…"

They got up, almost shyly, and went back to the stables.

Steven saw them coming, and smiled, and called something to Wally. By the time Ben and Lorraine reached the barn door, Wally was already leading out Overcast and Steven was bringing the saddle. *They know,* Lorraine smiled to herself. *The whole household knows about us.*

Benjamin stopped to open the cabinet by the door and pull out, of all things, a cavalry saber. Lorraine noted a discreet host of other weapons inside that cabinet, and guessed his reasons for choosing that one when she saw how easily the sheath attached to his saddle. She felt for the holster and knife-sheath at her waist and decided against taking one of the swords for herself; she wasn't familiar with any but her own Bastard, and would probably do better with her pistol.

Steven led out Leila next, who danced with anticipation as Wally saddled her.

She nipped playfully at Overcast on the way out of the barn, and for once he made a show of nipping back. The horses settled down and lengthened their strides as they left the fences behind and moved out into the open desert.

The land lay hot and still, its silence broken only by the distant sound of an engine, probably the guards' jeep. A lone hawk circled overhead, then abruptly veered away to the south. The timelessness of the stark landscape suggested the vast reach of eternity—time that supposedly healed all wounds.

Lorraine tried to concentrate on her planned study of the node-power, but couldn't do it. All she could think of was spreading the saddle blankets on the ground and making love to Benjamin at the edge of the pool. Would the power burn them both if they did?

She wrenched her mind away from the idea, but that only dragged her attention back to Benjamin. Riding easily on the gray stallion, he looked like a king in disguise: lean and strong as a sheathed sword ready to be drawn. *God, but he's beautiful,* Lorraine thought, feeling her heart ache. *How will I last without him? How will I sleep alone?*

He must have felt her eyes on him, guessed her thought, for he half-turned to look at her, his expression thoughtful and sad.

"Lorraine," he said quietly, "I…appreciate the fact that you haven't begged me to stay, or to come with me."

"It would be dangerous, I know," she murmured.

"Yes." He shivered in the heat. "You're vulnerable because you're young, and you're a prize target even so. I'm a prize because I'm old. There are other stalkers in the world… And there's the constant danger from mortals. You're not used to disguising yourself from them, and it has to be second nature. You have so much yet to learn! It takes years, and I can't stay here that long."

"But you'll come back…?" She had to hear him say it.

Ben twitched a half-smile. "'Though hell should bar the way'," he quoted.

Lorraine almost smiled in return, but then remembered the rest of the poem that line had come from. *"The Highwayman". Both the lovers died…* "Stay alive!" she whispered fiercely.

"I should be saying that to you," he smiled wider. "It makes a good farewell: so much more realistic than 'goodbye'."

The sound of the engine returned, louder. "Damn," Lorraine muttered. The presence of the guards would mean more safety, but no more privacy.

The noise grew louder still. Too loud.

"That's not a car!" Benjamin snapped, standing in his stirrups to look about.

Right then, at the edge of her range but rushing nearer, Lorraine felt that familiar but unwanted aura.

"It's him!" she shouted. "The stalker!" *He never left! He waited here for me…* "Where?!"

His question was answered as the noise rose to a thundering racket above the near ridge. Something soared over it, something like a giant dragonfly. No, it was—

"Helicopter!" Ben shouted, furious. "We never thought of that!"

"Phone!" Lorraine gasped. "Call—" She fumbled at her belt, then remembered she hadn't brought her cell-phone. But Benjamin had his.

"Run for the node!" Ben shouted, slapping the ends of his reins on Leila's rump, making her leap forward. "I'll get help."

Lorraine leaned forward over the galloping mare's neck and steered the frightened animal toward the rock outcropping ahead. Yes, they'd be safe at the node. But what was Ben doing?

She looked back, and saw him bent low above Overcast's neck, galloping at top speed—in the opposite direction, reins in one hand and his phone in the other. Above them, the helicopter circled and returned. Its course carried it over them, between both their trails, as if wondering which one to follow.

Lorraine realized what Ben had done, saw with perfect clarity the brutal sense of it, and was outraged at him for risking himself like this. They were close enough to the node that he couldn't possibly reach the ranch ahead of the stalker. If the guards in the jeep were close enough, they might intercept—but what if they weren't? If the stalker decided to go after Benjamin—

She remembered that they were dressed much alike, in cowboy hats and gear.

From the air, the stalker couldn't tell them apart, didn't know which one to strike.

Which one would he attack, and how would he do it?

Then she heard the gunfire. It was loud, recognizable even over the roar of the helicopter's motor, like a string of firecrackers.

Sub-machinegun—

She turned to look back, just in time to see Overcast tumble like a broken wheel and Benjamin fall with him. Broad red dots stained both of them.

Overcast! she almost cried. Ben could recover from shooting, as she could, but…

But what if Ben were unconscious, and the stalker landed, and went after his helpless body with something that could kill an Elf?

It's me you want, you bastard!

Lorraine ripped off her hat and threw it away, letting her hair fly in the wind—let it identify her as clearly as a glimpse of her face.

The border of the node was just twenty yards ahead.

Above, the roar grew louder as the helicopter swung away from Benjamin, back toward her.

He'll shoot in another second.

Lorraine stretched out on Leila's back, tightening her grip, making sure that her body would shield the mare and stay on the animal's back even if her consciousness blanked out. If Leila only kept running in the same direction…

Gunfire rattled again, chewing the ground to the right and ahead of Leila's hooves.

Lorraine dug her heels into Leila's sides before the mare could shy away, and *felt* hard at her: *Go! Go on! Safety ahead!*

Leila plunged forward, faster than before. The helicopter roared closer, coming lower for another shot.

There! The line of rocks whipped past under Leila's galloping feet. Lorraine felt the node-power settle over her like a blanket.

But more shots whipped through the brush to her left.

Doesn't he know?! Lorraine couldn't believe this. Didn't the stalker realize that the node was sacred ground? Or did he think that shooting animals didn't count?

Cover— In any case, she had to hide Leila. She leaned back and tugged the reins, signaling Leila to turn and run into the shelter of a patch of Palo-Verdes near the pool.

As the mare bucked to a stop, snorting and rolling her eyes, Lorraine swung out of the saddle. She knotted the reins on Leila's neck so the mare could run away if she had to, then ducked into the screen of brush and ran for the pool.

The helicopter circled thunderously overhead, and Lorraine could *feel* the stalker's frustration as his sight—a telescopic gunsight, to be precise—failed to find her.

She scrambled into the tumble of boulders where they were still shaded by the brush, crouched and waited. Surely he'd realize, soon enough, that this was sacred ground.

The noise grew unbearably loud, and a sudden wind hammered down from above.

Lorraine realized the stalker was landing, and intended to come after her on foot. Now he'd have to feel the node's power, realize where he was, and retreat.

Would he then go back after Benjamin?

The engine whined to a stop, and in the sudden silence Lorraine heard a metal door open, then footsteps crunching across the sandy ground. She *felt* for the stalker again, saw a brief flash of vision through his eyes and realized he'd already passed the border of stones. He was within the node's power. Couldn't he feel it?

Remembering how sound carried out here, Lorraine stretched around one side of the nearest boulder, cupped her hand and shouted: "You're on sacred ground, you fool!"

The stalker's answer was a surge of glee, and a quick shot—which ricocheted harmlessly off the wrong boulder.

"That's all right," he laughed. "I'm not superstitious."

Lorraine yanked herself back under the boulder's shadow, mind reeling. That was not Weber's voice, but it was familiar. And the stalker didn't believe in the taboo. She stretched to the other side of the boulder and tried again.

"Superstition, nothing: the power is real! Can't you feel it?"

"All I feel is you, sweet thing." He fired again.

Lorraine winced as the bullet whined close overhead. A single shot; he wasn't using the sub-machinegun now. He didn't believe, and if he felt anything he believed it was only her aura. And there was no burst of power to show him otherwise; twice now he'd fired, and the node had done nothing.

Then again, the bullets hadn't touched her. There was no physical contact between the two of them. No blood spilled…

Metal and blood. No blood. Only metal.

Thinking as fast as she ever had in her life, Lorraine pulled off her gun-belt and set it aside. *No metal…* The boots had metal buckles; they went next. Her shirt: metal buttons, off. Bluejeans: copper rivets, brass zipper, off. There was no metal in her cotton briefs, socks or sports-bra, thank all the gods that ever were.

In the desert silence she could hear his footsteps crunching closer, still some distance away.

Lorraine took a deep breath, dropped into the meditative state and stretched her empathic talent until she could *feel* the stalker as surely as if she stood right beside him.

He was searching, looking for a place to aim…

And she could feel the power of the node like a rushing river, already drawn to the metal—the automatic pistol in his right hand—beginning to warm it slightly, needing only a slight push or pull to flow harder.

She gathered that power, aimed it, and then thought of the importance of timing.

"It's real," she called again, "And it follows intent—"

Sure enough, he fired again. The bullet pinged off rock to her left.

Now! Lorraine drove the power through herself, toward that assembly of metal, hard as she dared. It surged through the glowing net of her nerves like a lava flow.

Explosion: a sound like several firecrackers. The stalker screamed.

Shut it off! Lorraine cut off the flow and dropped to the ground, panting, needing to touch something solid, feeling like a deflated balloon. She'd never held a flow as strong as that, and the after-effect was amazing.

She could hear the stalker still howling, crawling, and then staggering away. He wasn't dead; how long before he healed?

Lorraine pulled herself to her feet, then thought a moment and picked up her dagger. She might need a piece of metal again soon. The sounds were fading, but she could follow them. She wouldn't need cover now, not for a few minutes at least, and she needed to see her enemy. She hurried to where she'd heard him last, saw blood, saw—

–a lump of fused metal smoking on the scorched ground. It was torn like ripped tinfoil, and droplets of melted lead lay sizzling nearby.

The heat set off the rounds, she realized. *Exploded in his hand...*

She wondered how he had survived that, and how badly he was hurt. Any sensible man would give up now, run away to heal his wounds in safety, but this one was somewhere beyond sense. She had to make sure of him.

There, ahead, she saw his camo-clad back as he stumbled away from her. He staggered to the border of stones, then over it, and stopped and turned.

Lorraine followed, stopped just inside the border, and looked.

He was cradling his ruined hand to his chest, bent over it. Even at this distance, Lorraine could see that fingers were miss-ing. The violet sparks played over the mangled flesh even as it still dripped blood on the ground.

"Bitch, bitch, bitch," he was groaning. "Blew my hand off..."

Lorraine thought of telling him that it would grow back in a cen-tury or two, that he could spend the time in safety on sacred ground, but caution held her tongue. Instead she said: "Now do you believe me? We can't fight here."

He glanced up, and at last she saw his face.

He was Harding. Wilson Harding, FBI Regional Director.

No wonder he knew where I was! It explained everything. He'd known what she was, and began his hunt, the day she'd walked into his office—or possibly before, when he'd gotten the word from the Mafia. He'd followed Berringer—poor dumb honest Di-anne—and caught up to her with Benjamin that day in Tucson. He'd come too close, let her feel his aura, because he hadn't realized she was Initiated. After that he'd hunted her from a safe distance, through underlings, using the power of his position:

casual questions to the Tucson regional office, a sudden vacation with no questions asked, finally the use of a helicopter.

"Bitch!" he snarled. "Damned bitch. I'll get you for that."

There was none of his usual icy calm now; that had burned away, leaving his true soul revealed. *Crazy as a junkie.*

"I'm not going anywhere," said Lorraine, feeling her reliable fury seethe. "I can wait here until my friends, or your Mafia buddies, come for you."

"'Mafia buddies'?" he said, genuinely startled. "Who?"

Lorraine's eyebrows climbed to her hairline. "Those 'Chicago businessmen' who hired you to get rid of me!" she almost shouted. "I survived, and testified anyway, and now their hit-man's going down. You didn't stop me, and they won't forgive that."

Harding stared at her as the sparks faded from his hand, leaving sealed stumps.

Finally he laughed, a harsh and nasty sound.

"Mafia? You thought I did it for the Mafia, you brainless bitch?! Hell, I hunt those mortal pigs for my living." He laughed again. "When I'm not hunting our kind, that is."

"So…" Lorraine marveled, "You didn't care one way or the other, until I walked into your office that day."

"I knew what you were." Harding glared at his healed but maimed hand. "I knew where you were going, took some vacation time and came hunting."

"I wasn't even Initiated then! Why bother with me?"

Harding looked puzzled for a moment, then shrugged. "It would be easy enough to give you your first death, then take off your head when you revived. Not much power, but a meal's a meal."

And a junkie is a junkie, whatever his drug of choice is. Lorraine looked him up and down. "You bit off more than you could chew. Why didn't you cut your losses and go home?"

"A better meal than I'd hoped for." His face twisted into something close to a leer, and he fumbled at his belt. Lorraine saw now that a sheathed sword, or perhaps machete, was strapped to his leg—but what he came up with was a cell-phone. "I don't have to wait until you come out of there," he said. "One phonecall, one whisper of 'drug nexus' or 'terrorist cell', and I can have a federal SWAT-team come and drag you out."

It would work, Lorraine knew. Yes, they'd come here if called, and they'd have no respect for sacred ground. "That will take time," she retorted, "And my friends will show up before then."

Benjamin started the emergency call. Someone must have heard, noticed the sound of the chopper. Ben must have revived by now... She tried to look past Harding, to see if there was a cloud of dust on the horizon.

"Friends?" Harding grinned knowingly. "You mean your teacher, and his rent-a-cops? My federals will roll right over them, and I'll get two heads for the price of one."

"That depends on who gets here first," Lorraine countered. "If you're dead and the body's hidden before your boys show up—"

Harding waved the cell-phone like a flag. "They can be here in ten minutes! I put the team on alert before I took off, and one push of the button will bring them!"

That just might be the truth. Lorraine chewed her lip, imagining what would happen if the household went head-on against a team of federal cops.

"And once you're alone in a cell, anything can happen," Harding went on. "You'll have no chance to fight, then. Now you do. Just step out here, and I'll face you one on one." He looked her up and down, smiling like a shark. "You've only got a knife, but then, I'll have to fight left-handed, won't I?"

That, Lorraine knew, still wouldn't be anything like a fair fight. She had no idea how old or experienced he was, and she was still a fledgling, just starting her training. Then, far behind him, she saw a line of dust rising along the ground. She stretched her empathic sense and felt the edge of a familiar aura.

Benjamin! And maybe others... Rescue? Or putting everyone she cared about in danger?

One push of the button. Ten minutes. Mortals must never know...

No. She had to stop him herself. Now.

Metal and blood...

Lorraine stretched her talent again, and felt several auras: Ben, and Treemark, and Helen—and Steven and Wally not far behind.

She was out of time.

Metal and blood. The burning branch...

"Very well," said Lorraine.

She tightened her grip on the knife and slashed it once, lightly, across her thigh—just enough to draw blood. *My blood on the blade...*

Harding looked puzzled, but he holstered his cell-phone and drew his own weapon: a broad-bladed sword, not a machete.

Lorraine knew she wouldn't stand a chance against that, not with just a dagger.

As the node-power sparked in the wound on her leg Lorraine took one small step back from the border stones, feeling the slight but noticeable rise in the node-power. She took the knife by the handle and threw it.

Harding jumped aside neatly, and the dagger clattered to the ground behind him.

"Missed!" he laughed. "And now you've got nothing! Come on out, you stupid bitch. At least you'll have a chance to run—in your socks."

Lorraine sidestepped, just a little.

Harding matched her, showing his teeth as he readied his sword. Now he stood directly between her and the bloodstained dagger.

Burning branch. Draw and send!

The hoofbeats were louder, the riders in sight—Ben riding double behind Treemark, on Gold Eagle. Helen was holding a gun, trying to aim while galloping, at too far a distance.

Lorraine opened her empathic sense wide, felt the node-power like a river behind her and drew on it. It came hard and fast, and she thrust it forward as hard as she could—

Toward the bloodied knife.

Harding took a step forward, sword flicking.

Lorraine closed her eyes and ignored everything else, concentrated, flinging one arm outward toward the target, reaching toward the node with the other – and *pushed* the power outward.

Sluggishly at first, then faster, the power flowed.

More! Harder! She drew at the node, feeling the power swell and rampage through her, like a flood raging down a storm-drain and threatening to burst free, more than she'd ever dared pull before. She could barely contain it, knew she was stretched to the limit and dared not draw more—nor risk anything less. *Flow…flow…*

Sounds outside the silent roar of the power snagged a corner of her attention: screams, shouts, a nameless crackling, horses whinnying in fright. She had to look, even at the risk of dividing her concentration. Lorraine set her mind to controlling the flow no matter what happened, and slowly opened her eyes.

There was a fire before her. Flames, gold-tipped blue, leaped higher than her head and generated a column—no, a spreading tree—of greasy black smoke.

In the flames, feeding them, lay a hump of something black: something that looked like a heap of tumbled sticks and bits of rag.

Beyond that stood three recognizable figures, holding the reins of rearing, frightened horses: Ben, Helen and Treemark, white-faced and staring. Ben had dried blood on his clothes. Helen was shouting something, and Lorraine managed to recognize the words.

"Lorraine, stop! Shut it off! Shut it off!!"

Yes… Lorraine remembered to close herself off from the node first, then let the last of the power run down her leading arm toward the knife. *The knife…?* Yes, there it was, a few feet beyond the fire, blackened and distorted and smoking.

And now the fire was sinking down, sizzling to little low blue flames, then winking out. Smoke still rose from the blackened heap, stinking of burned bacon.

Where's Harding? she wondered for an instant. *He was standing right there…*

Then she realized just what she was looking at, and began to shake.

Burned to ashes…almost to ashes… So fast?! How long did I stand there— It couldn't have been that long— How much power did I…

"Lorraine!" Ben almost screamed. "Get out of there! Come here, fast!"

Burned to ashes. The node—

Lorraine jumped forward, took two wild leaps—first over the border-stones, then over the smoking remains—and ran straight for Benjamin.

She didn't make it.

Just three steps short of him, something struck her in the back like an electrified hammer and knocked her to the ground. For a second she thought it was Harding, but it felt nothing like human hands, or even a police stunner. She pulled her twitching limbs under her and tried to crawl toward Benjamin, but the nameless force struck her again.

This time she could see it: flashes of violet lightning that ran down her outstretched arms and crackled from the ends of her hair. And it *hurt*—like burning, like electric shock, like being clubbed, and more—enough to make her howl.

A third time the force struck her—and stayed, racking her endlessly—and she screamed madly. Beyond the pain there was something worse: a creeping sense of presence, like an Elven aura rather than the blank feel of the node's power, and then a distinct impression of personality.

It was a familiar personality: a foreground of leashed hunger, cold eagerness, calmly shameless greed—a sharpened perception of the mind she'd touched back at the Chicago police station.

Behind that came lightning-lit flashes of memory and knowledge, intricate and ugly: a range of techniques—from crude torture to subtle terror—for making a mortal confess to anything, a host of skills for tracking a deer or a man through a forest, a set of memories on how to flatter a king's minister, glimpses of clever murders and clever concealments of them, how to create evidence against a man before the crime was even committed, images of firing a long-bow at fleeing farmers…

He hadn't always been called Harding; before that it was Hardy, and Handy before that. The chaotic range of memories went back to thatched huts heated with smoky wood-fires, plowing muddy fields with scrawny oxen, endless meals of bread and porridge and turnips with an occasional bit of mutton thrown in, drinking sour beer in a one-room tavern that stank nearly as much as the privy-hole out back, catching and raping a poor widow—not because she was pretty but because she was available—and dying in a drunken brawl beside a dirt road.

His teacher had been an armed guardsman who served a local baronet and wanted a loyal squire; he was illiterate, ignorant of everything but his trade, who knew dimly that their kind were descendants of the never-seen Faery Folk, and not terribly intelligent.

The student had surpassed his master early, and set out to seek his fortune—first in a mercenary company, then in a king's regiment, then as a royal guardsman, and onward.

Always, lacing through every memory and snippet of knowledge, threaded the self-absorption and greed and love of power for the pure joy of wielding it—like a taste of rotten meat in an elaborate stew. It stained abilities that might otherwise have been virtues: his patience, his cleverness, his skills and insight—all perverted by that basic sin.

Father Sin!

And now that greed was turned on her. Lorraine felt it creeping in with the memories and knowledge, trying to gain foothold in her mind and body, crawling over her in hopes of finding entry—like the hoping-groping hands of drunken frat-boys at college parties, like that fool defense lawyer trying to paint her as a murderously jealous slut just to save a killer, like dear Momma probing for a weakness by which she could manipulate Baby-Girl one more time, like a starfish trying to pry open a clam—

Like a goddamn rapist.

Lorraine roared in fury, and turned to fight.

It was not a physical battle, but she struggled as if it were: scrambling like a Chicago street-fighter, using any weapon that came to hand, clawing the electric slime off her, grabbing for the misty opponent's throat to strangle or crush or rip, hammering her fists on the formless thing to beat it against the ground, lunging out of its grasp and turning again to punch, claw, tear, throw—throw it out and off and away, away.

And it went away. The ravening tide of power receded, sinking back like an exhausted wave into the sea, taking the sharpness of the memories and the impression of the mind with it. Lorraine crouched, panting, watching to see if her enemy tried for her again—but he didn't; he was fading, even his memories fading, into nothingness.

Instead, slowly, she grew aware of aches all over her body, a sharp soreness in her fingertips, and the feel of hard ground grinding into her hands and scraped-raw knees. Lorraine pulled her eyes open, wondering just when she'd shut them, and looked down at her hands. Her fingertips were raw, clotted with dirt and blood, as if she'd been clawing the hardpan ground. As she rolled over and sat up, she saw that her elbows and knees were much the same, and there were bloodied claw-marks—the size and span of her own fingernails—all up and down her body. From the flickers of pain, she guessed that there were similar marks on her face. She knew she must have done that to herself, fighting off that…thing. The violet sparks began flashing through her wounds, easing the pain, but the blood-marks remained.

She could feel the presence of the others, close and tense but not touching her, and she raised her head to look for them.

Treemark, Helen and Benjamin stood poised, almost crouched, in a half-circle around her, wearing expressions that were variations on a theme of fear. Helen's hands were half raised, as if to ward something off. Unnoticed tears were tracking through the dust on Treemark's face. Ben had two parallel scratches on his cheek and a bruise on his jaw—visibly healing as she watched. All of them were staring at her.

"…How?" she asked, pointing shakily at the marks on Benjamin's face, afraid she could guess the answer.

"…never seen anyone struggle like that…" Helen muttered.

"You took it hard," Ben managed to say. "You went into what looked like convulsions. I tried to hold you, but…" He shrugged, and half-smiled apologetically.

"I was fighting that thing," Lorraine panted. "Fighting it off. Didn't see you, didn't know."

"Fighting it off?" Helen dared to step closer. "You didn't want the power?"

"Him?!" Lorraine gagged, remembering. "Thoughts, memories, his mind—all filthy! Perverse— He was a pig! No, a worm! Lower! I didn't want anything of him."

The blood and dirt on her skin suddenly felt unbearable. She remembered the pool, and yearned for it. "Water," she gasped, struggling to her feet. "I need to wash…"

Benjamin stepped forward, took her by the shoulders and steadied her, and led her toward the pool. She needed his help as she passed the blackened spot where Harding had last stood; what lay there now were charred and scattered fragments of a skeleton, draped with burned scraps of cloth and leather and melted plastic—and a soot-marked sword nearby—surrounded by black burn-marks and ashes on the ground.

I did that… Lorraine swayed and would have fallen if Ben hadn't held her up.

She fixed her eyes firmly on the ground ahead and walked, as fast as she could, toward the pool. She could hear the others following quietly.

"What in hell will we do about the body?" Helen worried.

"The helicopter," Treemark decided. "There's no one else in it. Move it here, right next to the body, then set it on fire. Later we'll call and report it."

"The police will come looking…"

"I'll use his own rifle to shoot through the fuel-lines, into the gas-tank: make it look as if he started the fire himself, by accident."

"Won't they learn who he was?"

"No. The bones are too badly burned even for dental records."

Lorraine shuddered, and found enough strength in her legs to run the last few yards to the pool and throw herself into it.

28.

THE SHOCK OF the cool water was heavenly. Lorraine burrowed as deeply as she could into the shallow pool, pulling her head up only when the need to breathe grew urgent. Slowly, with infinite relief, she began washing away the blood and dirt. The steady and featureless power of the node spread through her like a blessing.

But not necessarily forgiveness.

Benjamin leaned into the water beside her, not noticing as the water soaked his sleeves, and gently brushed the hair away from her face—helping to smooth away even the memory of the wounds. Almost as an afterthought, he cupped a handful of water and washed the blood off his face. She could *feel*, without effort, that he wasn't thinking of forgiveness nor condemnation, but was concerned only that she survive—and survive whole—right now. That in itself was wonderfully comforting.

Treemark came closer, and crouched warily at the edge of the pool. His tears had dried, but their tracks still showed on his cheeks. "It's supposed to be used for healing," he murmured, dipping one hand into the water. "What are you feeling, Lorraine?"

"Better," she admitted. "Clean."

Treemark chewed his lip. "Why did you burn him with the node-power?"

"No choice," Lorraine panted. "No other weapon. And no time. He was going to…call in a federal assault-team…on all of you. Cell-phone, one push of a button…"

Ben and Treemark traded sharp looks. "'Federal'?" Benjamin asked. "It was Harding?!"

"Yes." Lorraine realized that they hadn't had time to see the man's face before she had thrown the power at him. "Never was Mafia. Just after me. I guessed wrong."

Helen, behind her, muttered something about thieves in high places.

"Power-junkie," Lorraine tried to explain. "Ambition. Top-dog monkey. Father Sin…"

Helen and Treemark traded puzzled glances, but Benjamin understood. "Power-junkie," he repeated, as if that explained everything.

It seemed to recall Treemark to an earlier thought. "Lorraine," he asked, bending closer, "Did you enjoy it?"

"What?!" Lorraine sat up, spluttering. "Are you crazy?! God, no! It *hurt!* Hurt like hell, and he—he tried to crawl into me after he was dead! I fought him off—that's what I was fighting— Ben thought it was convulsions…"

Then she noticed the subtle but profound look of relief on Treemark's face. A quick glance showed the same from Helen, and even Benjamin.

Relief…? she wondered sluggishly. *Why?*

Slowly the picture came together: Treemark's bizarre questions, Harding's greed, and the goal of the Unseelie Court…

Power-junkies!

That was what they'd feared, all along—that if ever she took another Elf's power, she might enjoy it, grow addicted to it, and become one of the Unseelie herself. That was another reason, not just preservation of his endangered species, that Treemark hadn't wanted her to kill the stalker. That was another reason, not just the danger to herself, that Benjamin and Helen had wanted her to stay within the enclave, protected, away from the ancient Elven war.

And that was another reason, besides straightening out the kinks in her admittedly-battered psyche, for Treemark's intense counseling and bizarre treatment; he'd been searching for any sign that she might fall for the lure of Elven power, and no doubt he'd been prepared to condition her away from it if he found it. For a moment she was furious with him.

Then she remembered that this was the weakness that had destroyed a civilization, started an age-long war, and reduced her kind to a tattered remnant. Of course Treemark had reason to be afraid!

"It was hell," Lorraine said aloud. "How in hell could anyone enjoy that?"

"There's no accounting for tastes," Benjamin smiled bitterly. "Some people love heroin, too, which accounts for that sort of junkie. Where did you leave your clothes, Lorraine? And why did you take them off in the first place?"

"Over there, behind that rock." Lorraine pointed, and saw Helen hurry off in that direction. "Metal snaps, zippers… I had to get rid of all metal, except for the knife. I knew I'd have to use the node-power, couldn't fight him any other way. He didn't believe in it, came onto the site after me—"

"He chased you onto sacred ground?!" Treemark looked

shocked.

"At first he didn't know that it was. Then he said he wasn't superstitious…"

"Oh, gods!" Treemark groaned. "If that taboo is breaking down—"

"Then I burned his gun-hand, and he believed enough to get back over the border." Lorraine pulled herself to her feet, with a little help from Benjamin. "But he still wouldn't give up, even with his hand mangled. God, he was so crazed with greed!"

"Perhaps he thought that taking your power would help him grow it back," said Ben, combing her hair with his fingers.

"I don't think he knew it would grow back. He knew nothing about the node-power. That's how I knew I could defeat him with it."

Hoofbeats thudded close, and another aura brushed against hers. Lorraine turned and saw Steven come galloping up on the dun gelding. He reined the horse to a stop and sprang out of the saddle, and she saw that he was holding one of the collapsible buckets.

He hurried to the pool, and Lorraine hastily got out of his way.

"It's for Overcast," Steven said, by way of explanation.

"He's alive?!" Ben marveled.

"Yes, but he's bad." Steven dunked the entire bucket in the pool, trying to fill it fast. "One bullet just creased his shoulder, but the other got him through the lung. We can't move him."

"Overcast!" Lorraine suddenly remembered the stallion falling, almost somersaulting as he tumbled, from a full gallop. A sharp pang of fury jolted through her, the old outrage at the world's injustice. No, no it wasn't fair that even innocent animals should suffer from human greed, human wars, mortal or Elven. "Dammit, no!"

Scarcely thinking of what she did, Lorraine lunged toward the rock from which the spring bubbled, the center of the node's power, and pressed her hands to it. Not stopping to think of whether this was wise, so soon after what she'd just endured, she called the power into the network of her own energy-web— pulled until she reached that swollen-balloon feeling again, filled herself with as much of the power as her body could contain. She noticed flickers of the violet lightning darting off the ends of her wet hair.

"Lorraine!" Treemark shouted. "What are you doing?"

"Healing!" was all she said. Lorraine turned and ran out of the pool, past Benjamin's startled grasp at her, past Helen returning with her clothes and gun-belt, back to where she'd left Leila. No, she wouldn't let anybody's fears stop her now. And she had to hurry, before the power could bleed away or dissipate. *Hurry!*

Yes, thank whatever gods there were, Leila was still there, hidden under the Palo-Verde trees. She nickered greeting as Lorraine ran up to her, and turned obligingly to let the human mount. Lorraine scrambled into the saddle, seized the reins and guided the mare back the way they'd come, not caring that she was nearly naked and the stirrup leathers chafed at her bare legs. She kicked Leila into a trot, then a canter, and then a hand-gallop as they cleared the border-stones, back down the path to the ranch. She ignored the shouts and footsteps behind her. Let the others come if they would, or stay behind if they were afraid. Meanwhile, she had to hold onto the power, hold it until she reached the fallen stallion.

And there he was, ahead, lying on his side amid the sage-brush. Wally knelt beside him, stroking his neck and whispering useless promises. As Lorraine rode up and reined to a stop, she saw that Overcast's saddle had been pulled off, exposing the wounds. Blood painted his gray coat, and more lay puddled under his muzzle, and the stallion was groaning quietly on every breath.

Lung-shot… Lorraine dropped the reins and threw herself off Leila, who nickered worriedly after her. She ran to the fallen horse as fast as she dared, feeling as fragile as an overloaded wine-glass with the power she carried. Wally looked up, startled to see her, but she ignored him and rested her hands on the stallion's flank, searching for the sources of all that blood.

There they were: one deceptively small hole near Overcast's back and another, I larger, down near his belly. This close, Lorraine could *feel* the hidden wound-channel: long, hot, aching, and full of blood. She set her hands over the two holes, with the torn tunnel in between, and tried to imagine how to deal with this. She could simply feed the power into the wounded stallion, which would strengthen him, but how could she repair all that damage?

The cut in the branch…

Multiple hoofbeats and auras approached, all four of them coming after her: Treemark and Benjamin, Steven—still carrying the filled bucket, and—thank all the world's gods—Helen. Helen, ancient goddess in Mycenae, who had promised to teach her healing: surely she'd know.

"Helen!" Lorraine shouted, "Tell me what to do! He's torn inside—full of blood — I don't know how to mend it. Show me!"

"Yes!" Helen dropped neatly off her red-bay mare and came running, Steven close behind with the bucket of precious water. Ben and Treemark, riding double on Gold Eagle, reined up behind them. Ignoring the rest, Helen knelt behind Lorraine and pressed both hands to her temples. "See it," she whispered, as her aura tightened focus.

Lorraine felt first a sort of pressure, then a sharpened awareness of Helen's presence, and then an image: the lung as a vast sponge, threaded with an intricate branching of blood-vessels— vessels that even now were draining helplessly…

There. The first task: seal off those broken, leaking tubes. *The cells…* Make the cells grow together, snatch material from clotting blood, close the gaps. Close them firmly, tight against leakage. Stop the flow. Feel the power drain… There.

Overcast gave a windy sigh or relief, as if he'd felt the change. Steven bent close to his head and dripped handfuls of water onto the stallion's muzzle, into his panting mouth. Lorraine ignored them and concentrated further.

Next task: clear away all that blood in the channel. Where could it go? There had to be some way… *There!* An image of fine yellowish tubes, roughly parallel to the sealed veins and arteries—lymphatic tubes?—not closed, their ends open to the blood-filled gap: use them. Make them draw, pull like tiny vacuum pumps, drain out the fluid: yes, like that, swelling uncomfortably with the extraordinary load, but holding. Oh, there: blood-cells clumped together, clotted, forming lumps that couldn't be drained; that tactic was meant to prevent more blood-loss, but it was interference now—impeding the drainage, creating knots that would become scars later. They must go. Use the power to break them apart, scatter them as lone cells or broken pieces, small enough to fit through those draining-tubes. There, and there: nothing left in the channel now but clear serum, draining, and the gap itself collapsing until it was almost closed.

Last, and hardest: make the spongy cells of the air-tubes multiply, grow, fill in the gap. *Breed, divide, reach this way. Faster, faster…* And with them, re-grow the missing veins, arteries, lymph-tubes that serviced them. *Breed! Grow! Increase! In this pattern…* It was exhausting, difficult to hold the pattern and feed the power-flow and order the cells in their millions—like commanding a vast army, or building a dam with tiny bricks. Lorraine could see the pattern, see it working, *feel* the cells blindly obeying—natural action, fiercely accelerated by the power poured into them—but it was draining her to the bones. It was growing hard to concentrate, growing dim…

***

Lorraine came up out of darkness into twilight, feeling as limp as a rag and hideously thirsty. It took effort to realize that she was lying on her back, on smooth sheets, in a bed—and more effort to drag her eyes open. She saw that she was lying in her own room, with the lights dimmed, and that Benjamin lay beside her, in only a robe, on top of the covers. He sat up as he felt her move, peered anxiously into her face, then grinned widely in unabashed relief.

"Welcome back," he whispered. "Would you like some chicken soup?"

Lorraine managed to twitch a half-smile at the thought. *Chicken soup, indeed!* Elves didn't get sick… But then, why was she so weak?

Ben rolled away, and then came back with a large coffee-mug in one hand. With the other hand he lifted her head enough that her mouth could manage the cup. Lorraine was grateful for that; her own hands were too weak to hold up themselves. The soup, of course, was delicious. She wondered if Daniel had boiled a whole chicken, complete with the bones and liver, and never mind what spices. Her thirst slacked off, and her belly warmed—as if it had been uncomfortably empty before, but had been too polite to mention it. She felt a giggle working its way up her throat. Fortunately, Ben took the cup away in time.

"Better?" he asked.

This time Lorraine managed to nod her head. "What…?" she whispered.

Benjamin sighed, and set the cup down. "You drained yourself until you fainted," he said. "Helen thinks it's because you lost track of yourself. Brian thinks it was a form of atonement."

Lorraine ran her tongue around her teeth, feeling stronger already. "…Overcast?" she asked.

"Well enough that he could get to his feet and walk—slowly—back to the barn.

Helen took over after you passed out, and managed to finish rejoining the blood- vessels." Ben took on a perfect imitation of Helen's disapproving look. "She says you should have done that first, then used what strength you had left to start on the lung-tissue proper."

"First time," Lorraine apologized.

"Priorities," he smiled. "Helen, being pregnant, wasn't about to drain herself to exhaustion, as you did. The lung will heal, without scarring, but she says it will take a few weeks—and that you need more lessons."

"Back to the schedule," Lorraine agreed. There was something very comforting in the thought.

"Not right away," Ben admitted. "You'll need at least a day to recover, yourself. Of course, Daniel's cooking should help with that. Want more soup?"

"Not yet." A question dug its way to the surface. "Is Treemark…still afraid of me?"

Ben's expression slid from startled to respectful. "Not afraid, no, but a bit stunned, I think. What you did was…really unprece-dented. To the best of our collective knowledge, nobody has ever used the node-power like that before."

Lorraine remembered the tears on Treemark's face. "Maybe sacrilege," she whispered. "He said…it was supposed to be used…for healing."

Benjamin raised an eyebrow. "Is that why you filled yourself with as much as you could carry away—plus whatever you got from Harding—and ran off to heal Overcast?"

"…Balance…" Lorraine struggled to put the concept into words. "I wanted to… set things right. The damage was…because of me."

Ben's other eyebrow caught up to its twin. "You," he said sol-emnly, "Take too much responsibility on yourself. …Like some-one else I know." He lay back down beside her, and pulled her close. "I was lucky to find you," he murmured. "You give me rea-son to hope for the future. Treemark's dream doesn't seem so impossible anymore."

Lorraine sighed and snuggled against him, content to treasure the moment.

Benjamin would leave soon, possibly tomorrow, but now she had absolutely no doubt that he'd return. He truly did love her, and that knowledge would keep her warm while she waited for him.

She only hoped he'd stay long enough that they could make love one more time before he left.

Then his free hand began meandering idly up her arm, and

she knew that her wish would be granted.

***

In the master bedroom Brian Treemark lay propped up on the pillows, staring at the ceiling, his fingers tapping together, his attention lost to some far distance.

Helen could wait no longer. She rolled over and rapped a finger on his nose, making him blink. "I know that look," she growled. "What are you plotting now?"

"Not plotting," he frowned at her. "I'm trying to take it all in. The implications are incredible. She's a genuine sorceress! How many do you know of, in all the world?"

"Well, there's Sandra…"

"Does she have powers like this?"

"No," Helen admitted, "Different ones. So do I, for that matter. I confess, I never heard of anyone who could…do that. And it may be partly my fault; I showed her how to draw and transmit power, and told her about the Lamia Trick. I should have guessed that she'd think of its opposite—overloading, instead of draining."

"She's very good at thinking fast under pressure."

"And she thought she had no choice. Do you really believe he would have made good on his threat, could have called in an assault-team to drag her away?"

"No," Treemark smiled bitterly, "But she didn't know that."

Helen drew a resolute breath. "I know it's tradition that a student graduates with his or her first kill," she said, "But this is an exceptional case."

"I am *not* going to send her away," he snapped. "It's far too soon, and she needs — gods!—specialized training. I won't let her out of my sight, if I can help it, until I'm sure she's ready."

"Mhm." Helen rolled up on her elbows and stared down into his eyes. "Brian, she's willing to learn from you, but whatever else you hoped for you can give up. You've lost her. She's not yours."

Treemark winced, but met her gaze. "She never really was mine," he admitted. "She's a wild mare, consenting to be ridden for a good cause, but never truly tamed. I'll be her teacher, her friend, her therapist perhaps, but nothing more." He smiled, a trifle bitterly. "I knew I'd never have her, any more than you could ever hold Ben. That's why I…gave him to her."

"You—you arranged for them to fall in love?!" Helen gaped at him.

"They both desperately needed intimacy, but couldn't trust it. A perfect match, really." He shrugged. "I arranged for them to be fellow sufferers in the same cause, gave them reason to sympathize with each other, and then left them alone together."

"Matchmaker!" Helen rolled onto her side, and thought for a long moment. "And…if she becomes the queen you hope for?" she finally asked.

"Then let's hope that she has need of a loyal adviser."

Helen sighed and turned on her back, knowing that this was as close to a surrender as she was likely to get. "I think Lorraine will need a lot of teachers," she added, "More than we have here."

"All we can get," he acknowledged. "Whoever you can persuade to come. Whoever's safe."

Helen smiled and closed her eyes, and rubbed her near hand on his chest. She had plans in that department already, foundations laid for more contact between the enclaves. Brian would try to reunite their scattered kindred in his own way, and she in hers. Between the two of them—and Lorraine—the old dream had a hope of reality.

Treemark stroked Helen's arm, but his eyes wandered back to the ceiling—as if he could read the future there, if only he watched long enough.

He hadn't known hope, or fear, like this in over a thousand years.

ABOUT LESLIE FISH

BORN IN NEW JERSEY, 11 March 19-something, to a mundane dentist father and singer mother Leslie Fish is a filk musician, author, and anarchist political activist.

Her music can be found at www.random-factors.com. You can also find more about her by visiting lesliefish.com.

9 781944 322182